The Sentry

The
Sentry

Ross Kasminoff

CROWN PUBLISHERS, INC.
NEW YORK

Published by Crown Publisher, Inc., 201 East 50th Street, New York, New York 10022. Member of the Crown Publishing Group.

Random House, Inc., New York, Toronto, London, Sydney, Auckland

CROWN is a trademark of Crown Publishers, Inc.

Manufactured in U.S.A.

Design by Mercedes Everett

Library of Congress Cataloging-in-Publication Data
Kasminoff, Ross.
    The sentry / by Ross Kasminoff.
        p.   cm.
    I. Title.
    PS3561.A6995S46 1995
    813'.54—dc20   94-37352
                                                                     CIP

ISBN 0-517-59715-2

10 9 8 7 6 5 4 3 2 1

First Edition

Acknowledgments

To Ruth, my first editor, my best friend, my toughest critic, and love of my life. Without you, nothing is possible.

> *You are my true and honorable wife,*
> *As dear to me as are the ruddy drops*
> *That visit my sad heart.*
>
> William Shakespeare

■   ■   ■

To my fallen brothers of Company C, 1st Battalion, 9th Marines—
"The Walking Dead"—July '67–August '68

> *What peaceful hours I once enjoyed!*
> *How sweet their memory still!*
> *But they have left an aching void*
> *The world can never fill.*
>
> William Cowper

■   ■   ■

To the men and women of the New York City Fire Department, specifically the members of the Bureau of Fire Investigation. A special thanks goes to the members of Ladder Company 23 and Engine Company 80 in Harlem, for the privilege of learning my trade from the best firefighters on earth. You are truly "the Bravest." To John Masterson, a great partner, a loyal friend, and a helluva fire marshal.

     ▨   ▨   ▨

I would like to thank my newest friends, specifically, Paul Boccard of Crown Publishers, for spotting a diamond in a lump of coal. A singular thank you goes to my editor, James O. Wade, for the generou gift of his uncommon skills, his wondrously eagle eye, his valuable ac vice, and his liberating hold on the reins. Who says there are no suc cessful alchemists?

     ▨   ▨   ▨

I thank you for your voices, thank you,
Your most sweet voices.

William Shakespeare

The Sentry

The old man lay in the doorway of the cast-iron building absorbing the harsh sounds of an awakening city. He felt the pleasant early-morning coolness of the large marble step through his ragged sleeping bag and turned, allowing it to penetrate through to his warm side. He was still asleep, but it was a twilight sleep that allowed him to dream, yet be dimly aware of what was going on around him.

The street was still relatively quiet. He could actually feel the grinding gears of the nearby garbage truck vibrate the stone beneath him. The roar of a crosstown bus passing by, heading east, went almost unnoticed by his city ears.

He was young again and Maria was in his arms, caressing his face, whispering to him in that way she had, her lips brushing his ear, her breath warm, ticklish. He knew it was his dream then, but didn't care. It seemed real and that was enough.

He dreamed of his family. It was *that* dream and he let himself sink into it. He'd been dreaming it for so long, he could no longer remember when it had first started. Only that it began after he'd left. After his life fell apart. After Maria died.

In the dream he was whole again. His children laughed and ran to him at the end of a long day in the machine shop, where he worked on the parts he made better and more accurately than anyone else. Then Maria would come to him and kiss him and he would let his hand slip down the inviting curve of her spine to caress the warm round flesh of her backside. She would slap playfully at his hand and become red-faced, telling him that the children would see, that he was a crazy man, and he would smile and know he was a man who could still make his woman desire him.

In the lovely dream, he still cared. He still desired. He laughed and was satisfied.

The man wasn't very old, but it was beyond anyone's ability to guess his age. He'd been living on the streets of the city for the better part of twenty years and had learned the unwritten rules of survival. He'd watched as the rules changed over the years and the violence of living there took on a new and terrible tenor, making the simple act of sleeping, an act of faith. And sometimes, when what little faith remained in him seemed like only a flicker of memory, the sudden kindness of a stranger could still make him cry.

And now in his lovely dream he was in the tub in the bathroom and Maria was bathing him. He could feel her pouring warm water over his shoulders and feel it running down his belly and back. He was pleased but disoriented because he was sinking deeper into the dream and could not remember this part. This was new and he wanted to find out what happened, but it was all wrong.

Then, suddenly, the water began to bubble and boil, becoming scorching hot, a blowtorch on his skin, and his flesh recoiled in pain; Maria's face became a mask of horror and he stared dumbly at the roiling water in his dream, burning. And when the water burst into flames and began consuming him, Maria screamed for him to WAKE UP! WAKE UP! WAKE UP!

He awoke and the flames engulfed him and the small space of the doorway he lived in. He tried to rise, batting at the flames with his hands, but the action only fanned them and they grew larger, more intense. He fought his way out of the confines of his burning sleeping bag, tumbling blindly off the step, rolling to the street, tearing at the many layers of clothing he always wore, winter or summer, against the elements. Maria was still screaming, telling him to wake up, but he knew now that he *was* awake, and he got to his knees and managed to pull off two of the outer layers of sweaters. The flames licked his face and he felt the first reality of pain.

The old man rolled on the ground and beat at his head and face, grimy hands flailing frantically. He slapped and rubbed and rolled round and round on the sidewalk until finally he lay trembling in a steaming heap. He felt no more flames, but his flesh screamed silently in protest. No sound escaped his lips, but his mind howled in concert with the agony of a million nerve endings and Maria was screaming with him.

Then just before his mind shut down, passing into blessed, shock-induced oblivion, Maria stopped screaming, and he looked at his beautiful wife. Her large black eyes were filled with tears and he spoke to her, his lips saying nothing, yet knowing she heard, and he asked first, "Why?" and she did not answer, just stood, shoulders hunched, palms raised in a gesture of helplessness. He asked, "Who?" and the voice in his head was sad, resigned, as his sweet Maria whispered, "*El Centinela, mi amor.*"

2

The telephone rang at the other end of the upper level of the loft building once used as a Board of Education warehouse. Matt looked up from his typewriter, met his partner's bleary eyes and "Uh-oh" look as the phone man answered. Jonesy's muffled voice came to them across the outer squad room through the closed door. The lone, overworked air conditioner wheezed heavily in a valiant effort to keep the room livable. It failed. They couldn't make out what was being said, but it was easy enough to tell it was a job. Jonesy's clipped, short sentences indicated that he was repeating information as he copied it onto his log and work sheets.

Saturday night and Matt Kincaid and John Williams were manning the only car working the borough of Manhattan. They'd been running all night, three jobs in succession, and were dragging ass. It wasn't like working as a fireman, where you just put the fire out and went back to the firehouse. For marshals there was a lot more involved. By the time you looked a fire scene over, interviewed witnesses, and typed the report, even small, bullshit jobs took a couple of hours each to complete. The more important ones could take days, weeks; some, months or years. The name of the game was "case management," a euphemism for knowing which jobs could blow up in your face and which ones to shag and bag, close out and move on. And you had to walk a fine line. While a hallway fire in Harlem, where no one suffered physical injuries, was not going to get much attention, that same fire in a building in which a City Council member lived would be given major case status. It wasn't the way things were supposed to be, but there had been a lot of cutbacks. Even so, the Bureau of Fire Investigation—the BFI—was still investigating more than eleven thousand fires a year. You could only do so much.

It was 4:35 in the morning, still almost five hours till they got off, and more than ten and a half since they'd started at six o'clock the night before. Neither man was looking forward to going out again.

Matt started gathering papers and stacking them beside his typewriter, the one he'd brought in because the base supplied only one that worked. All reports had to be typed, but the FD didn't bother to order replacement ribbons for the one working machine they had. It reminded him of the biblical decree of Pharaoh telling the Hebrews to make bricks without straw. He decided to take a piss while he had the chance.

The bathroom was filthy; flies buzzed around his head, let in through the broken glass in the lone window. The window overlooked West Forty-fifth Street, which was lined with hookers in various states of undress, bending into car windows, fondling the johns, plying their trade, picking pockets, and holding up traffic. The street was wall-to-wall cars: horns blaring, drivers cursing, whores swearing back at the motorists. Pimps stood in the shadows of nearly every doorway and cavity along the sidewalk, watching the girls, making sure no one got too rough when they discovered that their wallet or cash had been lifted. Their hands caressed the knives and Saturday-night specials jammed into their pockets and belts, as they waited, itching for a chance to prove their manhood.

Matt finished and moved to the sink. He splashed cold water on his face and used toilet paper to dry himself. The fire department rarely honored their requests for paper towels. He tossed the soggy lump into an overflowing basket and looked into the mirror. He was feeling weary and it showed. Two small bits of toilet tissue dotted his cheek and he picked them off. He considered splashing more water on his face, but he looked at the toilet tissue and decided against it.

Matt Kincaid had the kind of face people trusted: A wide forehead and square jaw bordered a broad face highlighted by deep-set, pale, blue-green eyes. His dark complexion served to make his eyes appear eerie at times, as if they had the ability to see through things. His twice-broken nose betrayed his past as a street kid, and his dark brown, almost black hair was cut very short and combed straight back. The first gray of forty-something streaked his sideburns and peppered his neatly trimmed mustache. Dark, puffy, half-moon crescents hung beneath his eyes. He was tired and needed sleep.

Matt had just begun his eighth year with the Bureau. He'd fought fires in Harlem as a "truckee," a man who worked in a ladder company as opposed to an engine company, for the first thirteen years of his career. Away from the rigors of firefighting, he was out of shape, and his tall, muscular frame carried a slight paunch; he knew he'd have to start exercising if he didn't want to go totally to flab. His days of eating whatever he wanted and as much as he wanted were over and it annoyed him that this was so. He shook off the feeling of melancholy stealing over him and returned to the squad room.

The clopping sound of the phone man's untied shoes greeted his return. Lenny Jones, a third-generation Irish fireman on "light duty," assigned to answer the phones, opened the door leading into the squad room and stepped in. Matt liked Lenny a lot. They were about the same age, had come on the job at about the same time, and had both served in Vietnam. Lenny had an easy way about him that encouraged confidence and conversation. They had a running joke that it was their fate to be born in a loser's generation. Both had fought in the only war the country had ever lost, both had come on the fire department just in time to be laid off in the only FD layoff in history, and both had sustained major injuries while fighting fires. While Matt had more or less recovered, Lenny had been on light duty for the last five years.

"Lenny, you look ridiculous." Lenny's gray hair was uncombed and standing on end, and he was wearing only an oversized pair of boxer shorts. Matt called them "Hey, Abbot's," referring to one-half of the famous comedy team. The skin on his scrawny chest was almost translucent and bony knees poked out above a pair of untied boots, shoelaces trailing haphazardly. Lenny responded with a derisive snort.

"More good news, guys. It's a ten-forty-five code two. Someone set a homeless man on fire on Twenty-third Street. They took him to the burn center. Which one of you is catching?" Ten-forty-five was the code for a civilian fire injury; code two meant seriously hurt but not dead.

"I am." Matt reached out to take the carbon of the job ticket containing whatever details were currently available. The job came to them via the circuitous route of the fire officer or chief on the scene notifying the FD dispatcher that they were requesting a fire marshal response. The dispatcher then relayed that information to Bureau of Fire Investigation headquarters, and headquarters in turn determined which base was responsible for the area involved and assigned the job to that base. Usually, whoever answered the phone copied the information and gave the ticket to the duty supervisor, who was supposed to assign the jobs by priority. Jonesy had bypassed the supervisor in this instance because Matt and John were the only team working and were already at the base. There was nothing to prioritize.

Matt looked at his partner. "Just what we needed, huh, John?"

John shrugged, shook his head, and pushed himself wearily away from his desk. Matt read the address, trying to form a mental picture of the block where the incident had taken place. The address put it between Fifth and Sixth Avenues. He couldn't recall anything but commercial buildings on the block.

"Let's go to the hospital before we look at the fire," Matt said. "If they intubate this guy before we get there, we'll have to wait days before we can get an interview."

They gathered the gear they'd need and went down to the sweltering apparatus floor where they were instantly drenched with sweat. It was the first week of October, but New York was experiencing a true Indian summer. After a one-day frost in mid-September, the weather had settled into a monotonous, muggy warmth that had nearly everyone wishing fall would just get on with it and arrive. This building had been built to store books, not house cops, and the large space designated for the cars had neither heat in winter nor fans in summer.

Their clothes were a mix of business suit and practicality. While the job required that they wear jackets, ties, and slacks, they could never forget that several times during each tour, they were going to be trudging through fire-damaged buildings where coal-black water rained for hours after the fire was out, cascading down the stairs, forming pools of sludge on every landing. Everything in a fire building was filthy; the charred remains of wall joists and fallen ceiling beams, the contents of the apartments, even the air was a thick, palpable mass of oily soot. New men, just out of fire marshals' school, usually arrived at their first assignment wearing their best suit, only to find themselves cursing the ruin of it by the end of their first day. By week's end, the men had sunk into "wardrobe collapse"; one guy actually showed up in a polyester Nehru jacket. While Matt tried to dress better than most, he still had to balance the requirements of the job against the fact that he'd probably end the tour filthy. So most of the men settled into a sort of semicomfortable mix of sport jacket and tie above black denim pants that only partially concealed black construction boots. A man could go broke on cleaning bills alone if he wanted to look his best every day. The attitude had recently been best summed up by one of the newer men: Dressing up to go to a fire was like taking a shower to take a shit. Marshals often looked pretty shabby standing next to a PD detective wearing a three-hundred-dollar suit, but fire marshals were workingmen, guys who had to dig through the remains of ruins and could never seem to get all the dirt from under their fingernails. What they lacked in appearance usually faded into the background when their expertise was needed.

Still, Matt stubbornly refused to surrender to his work environment and prided himself on dressing a notch above the other marshals. His son was grown and on his own; his former wife had always worked, and he felt he could afford the luxury of a higher cleaning bill. He favored the bright, floral ties that were the current fashion, and was careful about his tailoring. John, on the other hand, had two children, a heavy mortgage, and trouble finding clothes to fit his large frame, so he settled on oversized rejects from the "big and tall" men's shops. Matt used to tease him that, if he ever needed a quick arrest, he could always bring in his partner for "violation of the Haberdashery Act."

While Matt was a big man, John Williams was a walking wall: big, beefy, and black. At six foot six and 245 pounds, none of it fat, John often made his partner uncomfortable by the unfamiliar sense of feeling *small.* He had that stance, peculiar to many oversized men, of holding his head bent down and forward, as if he expected to hit it on the next doorway he entered, or because he was trying to make himself less intimidating. Matt suspected it was the latter. John was a taciturn man, given to long silences and few wasted words. The mottled, angry-looking, pink burn scar marring his cheek stood out all the more in contrast to his dark, ebony skin, giving his face a sinister cast that disguised his gentle and thoughtful nature. He was self-conscious about the scar and wore a beard that grew in wispy, uneven patches and, rather than mask, sometimes served to accentuate the deformity. He had an awesome presence, and many a perp with trouble on his mind made the sudden transformation to model citizen after John Williams entered the room.

It was John's turn to drive and he eased his bulk into the unmarked

Plymouth. Matt went to the front of the building and opened the over-sized bay door. John pulled the car to the curb and Matt got in.

"We'd better use the lights and siren," Matt said. "I want to get there while the victim can still talk." He put the small, dome-shaped red light, called a "Kojak" light, on the passenger-side roof. While the rest of New York slept, their street was always backed up with cars and they had to ride the sidewalk to the corner while hookers waved and jeered; pimps nodding a wary acknowledgment. When they reached the corner, Matt turned the dial on the siren to automatic and John took off just as the first sound blared out of the "whooper."

They drove quickly but cautiously from the base on Forty-fifth Street and Tenth Avenue to Fifty-ninth Street, where they turned east to go crosstown. They stopped at all red lights briefly before proceeding. Driving headlong through red lights in New York City, even at five A.M., was an invitation for a body cast or worse. When they got to First Avenue, they headed uptown again until they reached Seventieth Street and turned right into New York Hospital–Cornell Medical Center. In the absence of traffic, the trip had taken ten minutes.

John took a spot in a no-parking zone outside the emergency room, then the partners headed inside and walked the short distance through the crowded waiting room. New York/Cornell housed the only true burn center in New York City, funded largely by the contributions of the city's firefighters. Doctors performed all triage and immediate treatment in the regular emergency room until a decision was made as to whether it was necessary to admit patients to the burn center on the eighth floor.

It was that slow time of the morning when the doctors did as little as possible before changing shifts at seven o'clock. Matt knew that unless you came in with something grave, your chance of getting quick treatment was close to zero. He'd spent many hours in emergency rooms and most often, at this time of the morning, a treatment cubicle was more likely to be occupied by an exhausted first-year resident trying to snatch a fitful hour of sleep than by a patient. Matt and John showed their badges to the hospital cop guarding the entrance to the treatment area and asked whether a burn victim had been brought in. The guard flipped a bored thumb over his shoulder at the triage room.

The treatment area was modern, spacious, and brightly lit, set up so that numerous cubicles could be partitioned off by curtains hung on ceiling tracks. An administrative section off to one side contained desks, chairs, and portable chart racks, and was where the staff worked when not tending to a patient. The curtains were all drawn back and only one patient lay on a treatment table, in the center cubicle. Even from where they stood in the administrative area, twenty-five feet from the patient, Matt and John easily saw the amoeba-shaped, red and pink burns surrounded by blackened, charred skin. Three nurses and two doctors sat or stood directly in front of them, reading or writing on medical charts. A woman in a white hospital coat, surgical mask, and gloves hovered over the patient, her face only inches from a particularly large burn, her hands manipulating an instrument near the wound. No one acknowledged the marshals' arrival. Matt showed his badge to the back of their heads and said, to no one in particular, "We're fire marshals." He indicated the cubicle. "Is he the burn victim?"

A short silence followed and Matt repeated the question before a nurse who'd been thumbing through a chart turned to answer. Her expression indicated that she considered dealing with the authorities to be one of the less pleasant aspects of her job. Her tone said, Let's get this over with. "Yes," she answered.

"Has he given a name?"

She walked over to a row of plastic, credit-card type identification cards and read the name. "Victor Hildaldo."

"Did he say how it happened?"

"Only that he was sleeping in a doorway and woke up on fire."

Matt looked at the victim, who was propped up in a half-sitting position. A nurse or female doctor—Matt couldn't see her name badge—worked on him, peeling loose skin from his chest and arms with an oversized pair of tweezers, not unlike the kind stamp collectors use.

"Does he speak English?"

"Yes."

"Is it okay to talk to him?"

The nurse looked past Matt and John to one of the doctors sitting at a desk, who looked up and shrugged.

"Sure, why not? You'll have to put on masks, though." She indicated a nearby tray. They each took one and tied them on as they approached.

They reached the foot of the gurney and a fusion of smells: Burnt flesh, disinfectant, sweat, and unwashed feet attacked their senses, making it difficult to inhale. Matt and John had seen more burns than most doctors or nurses would in their lifetimes. A quick appraisal told them the guy was pretty bad off. First-, second-, and third-degree burns covered his face and hands. His ears were partly burned away and blood oozed from the deeper wounds. The woman treating the victim gave them a cursory glance before continuing to work on the burns. The victim had watched their approach with hooded, shock-glazed eyes.

Matt addressed the woman. "Has he been drugged for the pain yet?"

"He was given morphine when he was brought in. Why?"

"I need to know how long I've got before he's unable to answer questions."

"Well, I'd say he'll probably start to doze in about five minutes." She looked at the tweezers, dropped the skin into a red plastic bag marked BIOLOGICAL WASTE, leaned forward again, and continued working on the wounds.

Matt spoke softly. "Mr. Hildaldo? Victor?"

He nodded but didn't speak.

"We're from the fire department. We're fire marshals. My name's Matt and this is my partner, John. We're here to try and find out what happened to you. Do you know what happened?"

The man looked at his feet and slowly shook his head.

"Mr. Hildaldo, did you see who did this?"

Again the man shook his head. Matt tried to hide the emotion that knotted his gut every time he saw someone burned. Most firemen had felt the pain of burns and had lain on the treatment table shivering while their wounds were treated, the affected skin peeled off layer by layer. While within the fire department, the resulting scars were considered badges of honor, there was no honor in this poor man's suffering. It was important that Matt sound calm, nonthreatening, but at the same time let the guy know that someone gave a damn. He forced his voice to remain steady but had trouble masking the intensity of his feelings.

"Victor, we'd like to make sure no one does this to you or anyone else again, but we need your help. Do you have any idea who would want to hurt you? I know you're in pain and I know it's difficult to think right now, but we need you to try."

Tremors racked Victor Hildaldo's body and he shivered fiercely. Matt recognized the signs of shock. Victor was naked except for his tattered, dirty undershorts. His teeth clicked, chattering uncontrollably as the frigid air of the ER brushed his toasted skin. Black soot lined his nostrils and dried mucus streaked his cheeks and chin. Matt turned to the woman treating the burns.

"Are you a doctor?"

She looked up, the giant tweezers suspended in midair, loose, blackened skin dangling from their tip. There was an edge in her tone when she answered, as if she expected to be challenged about her position.

"That's right."

Matt returned his attention to the victim. "What's your date of birth, Mr. Hildaldo?"

Victor told him and Matt quickly calculated that he was fifty-five years old. "How long have you been living on the streets?"

A pause, then, "About twenty years." The partners exchanged surprised looks.

"And how long have you been sleeping in that particular doorway?"

Victor's body was racked by chills. His answer came through chattering teeth: "I don't know."

"Take a guess."

"Two, maybe three years."

"Has anyone tried to do this to you before?"

Victor's eyes darted first to the doctor, then to the door, but they never met Matt's. "No."

"Have you had any arguments with anyone recently?"

"No."

Matt was getting nowhere and knew time was running out. He played his final card. "If you were to take a guess, who do you think would have done this to you?"

"I'm not sure."

Matt pressed. "Just take a guess."

Victor's eyes widened as fear replaced the pain on his face. He focused on the ceiling lights. For a brief moment he stopped shaking. His voice took on an eerie, faraway quality, tinged with what sounded like awe. He spoke slowly, haltingly.

"I don't know." His eyes started to close, then opened wide. "Maybe . . . I don't know, maybe *El Centinela.*"

Matt looked up to see whether his partner had understood what the man said. John shrugged as if to say, I didn't get it, either.

"Who?"

Victor's answer was a mysterious look followed by a conspiratorial whisper. "You know. . . . You know."

"No, we don't. What did you say?"

But Victor wouldn't speak again. His eyes said he was drifting off into morphine land, and Matt knew if they didn't get it now, it would be three days before they'd be back to work. He looked at the doctor.

"Do you speak Spanish?"

She shook her head. "No."

"Did you understand what he said?"

"I really wasn't paying attention."

He turned to John. "See if one of the hospital cops speaks Spanish."

As John headed out, Matt asked the doctor a question he already knew the answer to, but nobody cared about his medical opinion and the statement had to be official. "Will he be admitted to the burn center?"

"Yes, I'd say he'll be with us for a few weeks."

Matt was thinking that perhaps Victor had used what he called New York "Spanglish." He knew that many times people from other countries adopted a way of mixing their native tongue with English. Maybe what they'd heard was a combination Spanish and English word.

John returned with a young hospital cop and they explained what they were trying to find out.

"It sounded like he said, *'El Centinela,'* but we're not sure. Does that sound like Spanish?"

"Yeah, it could be. *Centinela* means like a guard or a watcher, something like that."

The young cop turned to Victor and spoke to him in a soft, melodious Spanish that Matt guessed didn't originate in Puerto Rico. Victor perked up at the sound of his native tongue. Matt had picked up some Spanish from working the streets and understood some of what the cop said. He repeated the word *Centinela* several times. Then they heard the word *Sentry* clear as day. The guard turned to them.

"He's telling me the same things you said he told you. I asked him to say the word in English and he said 'the S-e-n-t-r-y.' Does that help?"

Matt said, "Ask him if he means someone in some kind of uniform. A security guard or cop or soldier, anything like that."

The guard spoke briefly to Victor. Victor answered in two syllables with the same knowing look he'd given Matt.

"He just says, 'You know.' "

They questioned him until Victor's eyes started to close and the doctor told them he needed to sleep. If they had anything more to ask him, they'd have to do it on another day, upstairs in the burn center.

"We're gonna need his clothing to test for flammable liquid at the PD lab," Matt said. "You got a plastic bag and gloves I could have?"

The doctor pointed to a pile of filthy, charred clothing. Matt put on a pair of disposable latex gloves and stuffed the clothing into a fresh trash bag.

They thanked the doctor and security guard before leaving.

As they walked to the car, Matt turned to John. "Whatta ya think?"

"I couldn't begin to say. I mean this guy is *ste-range*. Says he's been living on the streets for the last twenty years? No wonder he seems so nonchalant about what happened to him. Can you imagine how many times this guy has been fucked with in that time? In *this* town?"

"Yeah, I know what you mean, man. But this 'Sentry' thing. I mean, do you have *any* idea what he meant? You think it could be something military?"

"I don't know, Matt. But while that hospital cop was talking to him, I remembered when I was working Red Cap in Queens with Harry Mondale a couple of years back, we had a fire in Flushing Meadow Park. You know, the old World's Fair grounds?" Matt nodded. "You remember the building where they used to have the water shows? The one with the Olympic-sized pool?" Matt said he did. "Well, it's abandoned now and people keep breaking into the building. We get there and there's all this shit set up like there'd been some kind of ceremonies there. Ya know, candle stubs all around—lots of signs that people use the place. There's even the remains of small animals that looked like they'd been burned." They paused at the front of the car. "Anyway, there's these writings and symbols on the walls. Things like that star in a circle with different symbols you see in the movies about devil worship. Shit like that. Well, after this guy started talkin' about 'the Sentry,' it struck me that one of the things drawn on the wall of that place was a smile face. Ya know, like in 'Have a Nice Day' smile face? Except it only had one eye, and written beneath it was something like, and I can't remember the exact wording, but it was something like 'The Sentry rules from within and below.' It was a weird place, man. We couldn't wait to get the fuck out of there. I mean, I was brought up strict Catholic, and that shit freaked me out. I never forgot that smile face."

John walked around to the driver's side and Matt paused, looking over the roof of the car before getting in. "You think there might be some connection between what you just described and the old man?"

John turned the key and opened the door. "I'm just tellin' you what I saw, partner. I don't know if there's a connection or not."

"Well, if we don't come up with something on this right away, I'd like to take a ride to Queens next day tour and look at that building. You said it was a couple of years ago. Maybe there's more there now."

They got in the car. John seemed preoccupied. As he eased away from the curb, he said, "Okay, but I ain't gonna like it."

■　　　■　　　■

They turned right off Second Avenue, heading west on Twenty-first Street. Marked and unmarked police vehicles, interspersed with civilian cars with police ID in their windshields, jammed the street, double-parked the entire length of the block. Matt and John lucked out as a patrol car pulled out of a double-parking spot only a few buildings up from the Thirteenth Precinct. John quickly backed the car in. They had opted for going to the precinct first, before examining the fire scene, because it was on the way and, since the fire had occurred outdoors, there was unlikely to be much damage to the building. The One-Three Precinct was a modern two-story building and they walked directly to the front desk. Wary looks and silence greeted their arrival. As soon as Matt identified himself, interrupted conversations picked up and the reception area resumed its normally animated appearance.

The desk sergeant looked as if he was barely out of college. "You here about the homeless guy who was set on fire?"

"Yeah, I've got to put in a sixty-one." A "61" was the PD's universal complaint form.

"I think it's already been done. The cop who got there first put it in. He's over there." He looked across the room and raised his voice. "Hey, Rodriguez, come over here a minute. The fire marshal wants to talk to you."

A cop even younger than the sergeant walked across the room to the desk. The old saying about how you know you're getting old when cops and priests look young, struck Matt with its sudden, ironic truth. He thought he must *really* be getting old. These guys looked like babies.

The cop came over and introductions were made.

"The sergeant says you already put in the sixty-one. What did you charge for the offense?"

"I put the top charge as arson."

Matt looked at John. Cops weren't supposed to do that, but he didn't feel like making a big deal out of it.

"My job ticket says it was an outdoor fire. Was there damage to a building?" There could be no arson without it.

"Actually, there was quite a bit of damage."

Matt's eyes widened in surprise and his voice reflected his puzzlement. "What kind?"

"The entire doorway was burned. You know, the frame of the door and the door itself. The fire got behind the metal sheathing on the frame. The firemen had to rip it off to get at it."

"Were you the first to arrive on the scene?"

"Yeah, me and my partner."

"Who was there beside the victim?"

"No one that I saw. The guy was standing on the curb naked from the waist up, steam and smoke comin' offa him. I can ask my partner if he saw anyone, but I didn't."

"Was the fire still going?"

"Hell, yes. The flames went to the top of the door frame, about ten, fifteen feet, I'd say."

"Did you smell anything? I mean like gasoline, kerosene, anything like that?"

"To tell you the truth, we didn't get too close to the fire. We called it in and helped the old guy out. I really couldn't say if there was an odor or not.''

''Did the victim make any statements to you? Did he say who did it? Anything that could be of help?''

''No, nothing. He was sort of incoherent, doin' a lot of mumbling. We were lucky to get his name.''

Matt took a moment to scribble into his notebook the cop's name, badge number, and command from the name tag and badge on his shirt.

''Do you remember what he was mumbling about?''

''Not really. It was hard making out anything specific.''

Matt turned to his partner to see if he wanted to ask anything. John shook his head, indicating he was ready to leave.

''Okay, thanks, Officer. Here's my card. If you should think of anything that might help or if you should hear anything on the street about the fire, we'd appreciate a call.''

''No problem.''

They were nearly out the door when the cop called out to them.

''Hey, Marshal? I don't know if it means anything or not, but I just remembered what the guy kept mumbling over and over. Something about 'the century' or 'sensory' . . . Something like that.''

''Could it have been 'the Sentry'?''

''Yeah, that's it, 'the Sentry.' Ya think he was talking about me? Ya know, the uniform and all. Sounds like a military term to me. But there's nothin' like that anywhere around here. Does it mean anything to you guys?''

''Yeah. A lot of extra work.''

On the way to the car, Matt asked, ''You think there could be something to a military angle?''

''I don't know, man. Could be anything, I guess.''

''We might have to check it out.''

John stopped and faced Matt. ''There's one thing I *do* know, m'man—I'm gettin' one *big* hinky feelin' about this one.''

''Yeah. Me, too, John. Me, too.''

3

John hit the brakes hard. Matt threw his hands to the dash to avoid being thrown forward. They were heading west on Twenty-third Street and had just passed through the intersection at Fifth Avenue.

"What the hell . . ."

"Matt, look at *that* asshole." John kept his hands on the wheel and pointed to the silhouette of a man halfway up the block standing on the sidewalk under a street lamp. The guy stood near the curb facing a doorway, just about where the address of the fire should be.

John eased the car to the curb and came to a full stop. The figure moved forward on the deserted street and paced to the entrance of the building, looked down, extended his right foot into the doorway, poked his toe in, then walked backward to the curb again, shaking his head, his attention trained on the doorway. Matt felt his hair prickle.

They were less then a quarter of a block away. The giant shadows cast by the buildings behind them kept the morning sun from fully lighting the street, but sunlight filtered through anyway, and from half a borough away, the East River sparkled in their rearview mirror. The figure reached the curb, paused momentarily, before repeating his little walk forward and toe-poking into the doorway. He was stepping backward again when Matt said, "Let's take him, John."

John accelerated along the edge of the deserted sidewalk. Twenty feet away, the figure turned and saw the blue Gran Fury. It was unmarked but clearly a police vehicle. Wide, surprised eyes glinted back at them: a deer caught in headlights, clearly wrestling with a "fight or flight" impulse. John had no intention of giving him either option. He pulled the car up next to him fast, slammed on the brakes, and, before the guy could move, jumped out and came around to the front, blocking the sidewalk. Matt leaped out and cut off any retreat to the east. The guy stood trapped near the curb, between the car and the two men who gave him a wide enough berth to allow for reaction time if he attempted to run.

"How're ya doin', m'man?" John said.

He looked to be in his early twenties, tall and slim, with shiny jet-black hair, cut medium length. A black leather biker's jacket, unzipped and wide open, revealed a skull's head belt buckle bracketed by a pair of stainless-steel handcuffs hung through the belt loops on either side of his fly. The short chain linking the cuffs hung like a noose under the chin of the skull. Lengths of chain dangled through flaps on his shoulders. Tight black denim jeans, black biker's boots, and a blue bandanna headband completed the outfit. Two buttons side by side on his left breast pocket. One said in bold letters, THE MEEK SHALL INHERIT SHIT. The other, one word printed under the other in capital letters: EAT. FUCK. KILL. More striking than all the paraphernalia he was wearing were the size and color of the boy's eyes. They were almost too large to be real and, even in the dim morning light, shined a pale, opaque blue. Framing the eyes were the longest eyelashes Matt had ever seen. His first impression was that the kid was either wearing mascara or the lashes were fake. If they *were* natural, the boy was sure to be the envy of every woman who saw him. At the moment, however, they were stretched wide with surprise and fear.

He stood stock-still, looking quickly from one man to the other, frantically calculating his alternatives and the odds of escape. When his expression changed suddenly and dramatically from fear and confusion to composure and serenity, Matt was momentarily flustered. The kid relaxed and faced Matt, speaking in a voice that tried valiantly to sound adult and matter-of-fact.

"How's the old homeless guy who was sleeping in the doorway?"

His head snapped around as John spoke. "He's burned pretty bad. What do *you* know about it?"

"Well, I was here. I saw it happen."

Matt felt his heart skip. "You saw *what* happen?"

The boy turned to answer Matt. "I saw him on fire. I helped put him out."

"Look, why don't you start from the beginning? What's your name?"

Though he was eager to hear what the boy had to say and didn't want to give him a chance to make up a story, something told him he'd better get the kid's ID before he tried to take off. He knew they had surprised him, arriving unexpectedly two hours after the fire. His clipped answers were a giveaway that the kid was stalling, his mind churning, trying to figure out what to say. Matt decided to get the bare essentials and proceed.

A long pause, then, "Eddie." His eyes swept the street, never looking at the men.

"Eddie *what?*"

"Eddie Cannell."

Matt took out his pad, asked him to spell it, and wrote down the name. "Where do you live, Eddie?"

"In Brooklyn."

Matt sighed. "Exactly *where* in Brooklyn, Eddie?"

"Canarsie." He gave them a street address on Flatlands Avenue.

"What's your date of birth, Eddie?"

"February 25, 1974."

Matt jotted it down and made a show of putting the pad away. The kid was twenty-one, a bona fide adult. Good. "Why don't you start from the beginning and tell us what happened?"

"Is the old guy gonna be okay?"

"They're not sure yet," John lied, "but maybe you can help us catch whoever did it."

"Sure, Officer, anything you want. I can't believe anyone would do something like this to a harmless old guy."

Matt was struck by the incongruity of the apparent concern and sincere tone, set against the background of his appearance, particularly the messages on the buttons. He said, "Eddie, we're not sure anybody did anything yet. How do you know he didn't set himself on fire?"

A puzzled look. "Why would anyone set *himself* on fire?"

"I don't know, Eddie. Why would someone *else* do it? Look, let's get to the point. Tell us what you saw and we'll work from there."

Eddie heaved a sigh and spoke in a resigned, almost matter-of-fact tone. Matt got the impression that Eddie didn't expect to be believed.

"I was in a cab with a friend and we passed what looked like a pile of papers on fire. Suddenly, it looked like the papers got up and started walking, until I realized it was a man. I say to my friend, 'Look, there's a homeless man on fire.' So I tell the cab driver to stop. I get out and run over to the guy and start slapping at the fire with my hands.'' Eddie shoved his hands in his pockets and continued. ''The homeless guy is rolling on the ground, pulling shirts off, and meanwhile another cab pulls up and someone gets out and uses a fire extinguisher on the guy and then to put the fire in the doorway out. Next thing I know, an RMP is there and I lead the guy over to the police. By that time, fire engines are coming down the street and they put the rest of the fire out with a booster line. A few minutes after that, the EMS arrives and takes the guy away.''

Matt and John were trying hard to conceal their surprise. The boy had used terms very few people knew, let alone used as casually as he had. While the term EMS was widely known, most people just said ''ambulance.'' But RMP was a PD designation for Radio Motor Patrol, a marked police car. It was rarely used by anyone but cops. Most amazing of all, though, was the boy's reference to a booster line. It was strictly a fireman's term and neither marshal had ever heard *anyone* outside the fire department use it. A booster line was the small-diameter red rubber hose wound on a reel at the back of a fire engine, used to extinguish small outside fires with the rig's internal water tank. They were intrigued that he had not only used it, but used it properly.

Matt also noted Eddie had said ''homeless man'' in his telling of the story. How would he know the guy on fire was homeless while in a moving cab? The cop had told them no one was around when he and his partner arrived, yet here was this boy claiming flatly that he had brought the victim over to their car.

Matt glanced at the spot where Eddie said the man was rolling on the ground. There was no fire extinguisher residue there or in the doorway. Most automobile extinguishers were dry chemical and they left a mess of white powder everywhere. The only way there'd be no residue was if the extinguisher was CO_2 or Halon, neither particularly good for outdoor fires. Nevertheless, it was possible. People didn't know shit about extinguishers.

Eddie looked over his shoulder and gestured to the blackened doorway. ''That's all I know.''

Despite the warm morning, Matt felt a chill. This kid was *weird*. While Eddie gave his version of the events, Matt used the time to better appraise him. He watched every movement of his face and hands, knowing a person's extremities told the real story. Matt recalled dozens of interrogations when the person he was interviewing was as polished a liar as could be imagined: smooth-talking, fully in control of his facial expressions. Yet at some point the body's extremities often revealed the telltale first signs of a lie: the nervous tapping of a foot, a leg pumping furiously under a table, a clenched fist on a lap, the nervous picking at a cuticle, drumming fingers, palm scratching, lint picking. None of which meant much by itself. After all, many people have nervous habits, especially when they're under duress, but in the right context, and at certain moments, such habits are as good as a polygraph test. And as useless in court. It fell into the realm of "intuition," a term courts and lawyers enjoyed deriding, but which any decent investigator learned to trust. Trying to read anything from a perp's eyes was almost always an exercise in futility. Practiced liars learn early on to look you dead in the eye. Besides, eyes can't kill, but a perp's hands could, so while developing the habit of watching a man's hands for signs of danger, Matt found that they could be fairly accurate barometers of what was really going on behind the words.

Eddie had his left thumb jammed into his jeans pocket, and while the fingers of that hand played and drummed incessantly on his thigh, his right arm was animated and jerky, dropping to rub his crotch from time to time. The material near the fly was worn pale from constant chafing.

Eddie continued, growing agitated, his voice taking on a decided edge. "Why would anyone sleep on the street, Officer? I mean, I worked in a men's shelter in Greenpoint awhile back. It was clean, with three squares a day. Even had cable TV, which *I* don't even have." He shook his head. "I don't understand why these people insist on sleeping on the street."

Matt looked over Eddie's shoulder at John. A raised eyebrow and a small shrug answered his unspoken inquiry, as if to say, I don't know what the hell to make of this guy, either.

Matt tried to sound sympathetic. "I don't understand it either, Eddie. You said you were in a cab with a friend. What's *his* name?"

"Jeremy."

"Look, Eddie, let's not go through this again, okay? I ask you a question, you give me a complete answer. Don't make this like pulling teeth. Jeremy *who*?"

"I honestly don't know. I just met him last night." He paused. "I'm not too particular."

This kid was full of surprises.

John interjected, "What is *that* supposed to mean, Eddie?"

The boy spoke huffily as he looked defiantly at the big man. "Just what it sounds like, I suppose."

"You mean you were on your way to have sex with this guy?"

Eddie's chin jutted out. "That's right."

"Where?" Matt asked.

"At his place."

"And where is *his* place?"

"I think somewhere on Fortieth or Forty-first Street. At least that's what I remember him telling the cab driver." The boy looked flustered. "Look, I'm not sure, okay? This thing really upset me and I'm not thinking straight."

"Where were you coming from?"

Eddie fixed Matt with a glare, his tone defensive. "Look, Officer, am I a suspect?"

"No. Right now we're just trying to find out what happened here. Do you feel like a suspect, Eddie?"

"No. . . . Well, yes. I mean, you're asking all these questions like I'm trying to hide something, and I've told you everything I know."

Matt tried another approach. His voice became soft, conciliatory. "Well, relax, Eddie. You're not a suspect, but we've got to try and determine what went on here. You were on the scene and you've become our best hope. Sometimes when people get excited, they see things they're not even aware of. Our job is to help re-create the situation and try to refresh their memories."

Matt affected a sympathetic tone. "I mean, I can appreciate how badly you must feel having your morning broken up by something like this. How horrible it must have been for you to suddenly see a man in flames. I'm sorry, but you're right. Sometimes my partner and I can be a little insensitive because we see stuff like this all the time and we forget how shocking it might be to someone like yourself." He touched Eddie's shoulder and took a breath. "Look, let's start fresh, okay? There are things we need to know. If I start coming on too strong, you just tell me. Do we have a deal?"

Eddie appeared to relax. Matt pressed a hunch. He was certain by the kid's use of service terminology that he was a major-league job "buff."

"Eddie, would you like to sit in the car while we talk?"

The boy perked right up, his large eyes widened. Matt knew he'd struck a nerve.

"Are you serious? I mean, would it be all right?"

"Sure, why not? It'll be more comfortable in the car, anyway." Matt stepped back, opened the rear door of the car, put the lock latch down as Eddie entered, closed it, and went around to sit beside him. John got behind the wheel.

"John, before we begin, why don't you start the car so we can monitor the department radio? That way Eddie can get a feel for how everything works." John started the car. The squawk and tones of the department radio were loud and John adjusted the volume before swiveling to face the back. He slipped the Glock nine-millimeter automatic from his shoulder holster, switched hands, and aimed it through the seat. Matt saw the move and faced Eddie.

"So where were we, Eddie? Oh yeah, I remember. You were gonna tell us where you were comin' from in the cab with this other guy, uh . . . Jeremy, I think you said his name was."

Eddie was gazing at the dash of the car when he heard the department radio send out a call.

"Hey, how come you guys are listening to the fire department frequency?"

John answered, "'Cause we're fire marshals, Eddie."

"But I thought you guys were cops."

"Well, we are," John said, "but we work for the fire department."

"How come you didn't tell me?"

Matt answered, "You never gave us a chance, Eddie. You just started asking about the old guy who got burned. Remember?" The kid was starting to aggravate the hell out of Matt, but he told himself to stay calm, that he hadn't gotten what he wanted yet and this boy just might shed some light on what happened. If *he* wasn't the one who did it, that is.

"But I thought . . ."

"Look, we'll explain all that after we talk. Right now we need to know what went on here. No more bullshit or stalling. Where were you coming from when you saw the guy on fire? And give us some details we can verify. Something that could get you off the hook so we can get on with finding whoever *really* did this.'' Matt's voice took on a sharp edge. "Like, exactly *where* you were coming from, Jeremy's full name and who you saw and what you saw and what you did when you saw it." He glanced at John, who was staring at Eddie, trying to figure out what the hell they had in front of them.

"I told you, I don't know his last name. I only met him last night."

"Well, where did you meet him?"

"A bar over on Twentieth near West Street."

"What's the name of the bar?"

"The Centurion."

Matt had seen the place in his travels, saw who hung out on the corner. "That a leather bar, Eddie?"

"Yeah, so what? That's what I'm into."

"No need to get touchy, Eddie. I don't care *what* you're into. It's strictly your business. So you meet this guy Jeremy. Then what?"

"We caught a cab to go to his place. When we passed this spot"— Eddie pointed to the building—"I see fire over in that doorway." Matt and John sat quietly as Eddie retold the story without any deviation from the original version. When he was finished, he said, "I was really upset and it's hard for me to figure out exact times."

John interrupted, "Can we see your hands, Eddie? Did you burn them putting out the fire?"

Eddie's tone turned defensive again as he shoved his hands out, palms up. They were clean, soft, and pink. "No. Hey, I was lucky. That a crime? After the flames were out, I asked if there was anything I could do for him and he just shook his head. I asked if he wanted a cigarette or coffee and he said no. What else was I supposed to do? I didn't know what to make of him." Eddie dropped his hands and shoved them under his thighs. "So after I handed him over to the cops, Jeremy surprised me by pulling up in the cab we were in—I'm like *really* flattered, ya know. I figure he must *really* like me to have waited all that time. So I decide there's nothing more I can do and I think, I still got a chance to save some of the evening. So I got in the cab and we went back to his place." Eddie paused, his expression pouty, as if he'd given them their cue to say something sarcastic about his lifestyle. Neither man took the bait and he continued. "After a while, I leave Jeremy's place and come back here. I was here about five minutes when you guys pulled up. And that's all there is to it.'' He turned and fixed Matt with a look that dared him to call him a liar.

He ignored the challenge. ''Okay, that's good, Eddie. That's good. When you saw the fire, did you see anyone on the street?''

''No. I mean, I don't know. It was late. The block seemed deserted. I think there might have been some kids on the other side of the street, but I can't be sure. I mean, I couldn't take my eyes off the flames on the guy. It was so fucking *weird*—excuse my language, but it was. It really upset me to think that someone would do something like that.''

Matt reassured him, ''I can see how it would, Eddie. It sure as hell would've upset me. How high were the flames when you saw them? Do you remember if they gave off any particular color?''

Eddie thought for a moment. ''The flames were *huge*. They were all the way up to the top of that door when I first saw them.'' He pointed to the doorway and Matt estimated fifteen feet. ''The flames on the guy were about two feet over the top of his head when he stood up. You couldn't see him at first. He was on fire from the waist up.''

''What about the color?''

''I don't know, man. They were flames. Yellow, I guess. Who can remember? Is that important?''

''Could be. It might be helpful if you can remember. Different fires give off different colors. Sometimes it's possible to get an idea of what was burning by the color.''

''Well, I can't remember no specific colors, man. I was shook up, ya know?''

John shifted in his seat. He looked impatient. He was still pointing the Glock at Eddie and would have liked to put it away. But the kid wasn't exactly volunteering information. Matt feared if he let him go, he might never see him again or he'd have time to make up a different story; maybe get in touch with this ''Jeremy,'' and get him to verify his alibi.

''Eddie, how long did you stay at Jeremy's apartment?''

''Not that long. We got there and we, ah, had some fun, and then I left.''

''By 'have some fun,' you mean you had sex?''

''Yeah. But it wasn't very good. I mean, *he* wasn't very good. I just couldn't stay there. I kept thinking about this poor guy on fire and I suppose I didn't stop going on about it and Jeremy didn't seem to really want to discuss it anymore. I thought it was pretty insensitive, ya know? Anyway, I left pretty quick and walked back here.''

"Where did you say Jeremy lived, Eddie?"

"On Fortieth or Forty-first Street, near First Avenue."

Matt looked skeptical. "That's some walk, Eddie. What, maybe . . ." Matt did some quick math, "seventeen or eighteen blocks and another, let's see . . . seven avenues to get here?"

"I like to walk. So what?"

"So nothing. But you must be exhausted."

"Like I said, I like to walk."

Matt made a dismissive gesture.

"Anyway, which was it, Fortieth or Forty-first, Eddie? Was the cab facing the East River or the direction our car is in now?"

Eddie thought for a moment. "It was facing the East River."

"Then it must have been Fortieth Street, Eddie. Odd-number streets run west."

"Okay, then, it was Fortieth Street."

"What side of the street was the building on?"

"I don't remember."

"Well, think. Did you sit behind the driver or on the passenger side? Did you have to walk around the cab or just step to the curb when you got out?"

"I sat behind the driver and had to walk around the car."

"That means the building was on the south side of the street. Was it at the beginning of the block, the end, or the middle?"

"I don't know. It was a fancy building, tall, maybe twenty or twenty-five stories high. I couldn't afford to rent the basement. I mean, it had *two* doormen and another guy at a desk inside. Why would anyone need two doormen?"

Matt ignored the question. "Think now. Did the driver stop just into the block, or did he drive to the end? Could you see a traffic light on the corner, or were you more toward the middle of the block? Was there anything distinctive next door to the building? Take your time and think."

The boy turned away and looked through the window at the burned doorway. His brow furrowed and Matt wondered if he was thinking of how to answer the question or how *not* to answer.

Matt had learned early on not to interrupt a suspect's thoughts. It was not an easy thing to do. Nobody in his line of work liked silence. He'd seen many an interrogation blown because the interviewer felt a need to fill the silence. Maybe it had happened like the kid said and the cop had been so fixed on the burned man that he didn't notice anyone else around. But how could *both* cops miss him? If he was lying, he was good. Details like the two doormen tended to make a story believable.

Eddie was still staring at the charred doorway when he said, "There was a church next to the building."

John asked, "Do you remember the name of the church? What kind of church was it?"

"Hey, man, I don't know. It was a church. How many fucking churches do you think are on the block?" He turned and faced the two men. "What's goin' on here? I mean, I stop and help a guy out and you guys are treating me like I done it. What's the deal? You think I set that poor guy on fire?" His eyes were blazing.

Matt's voice was smooth, quiet. "Hey, calm down, Eddie." He patted Eddie's arm. "Nobody's accusing you of anything. We're just trying to find out what happened. I know how our questions must sound, but you've got to understand our position. We *need* you, Eddie. We appreciate your cooperation. We *do*. Will you help us?"

Eddie looked at Matt with naked suspicion, but Matt felt the boy wavering. He kept his expression nonthreatening and waited him out.

"I don't know. I suppose so. But I don't feel like answering any more questions for now."

Matt took out his pad and prepared to write. "Okay, Eddie. Anything you say. But I've got to get some information from you in case we have to speak to you again. You got some ID? A driver's license, maybe?"

Eddie hesitated and Matt added, "Look, Eddie, I know you're tired of talking to us. Why don't you just give me your ID and I'll copy the information from that? You got ID, don'cha? I mean, you're twenty-one. Ya gotta have ID."

Eddie took out a wallet from his rear pocket, attached by a chain to his belt loop, and extracted a laminated photo-ID driver's license. He shoved it at Matt, a gesture clearly meant to convey his aggravation. Matt checked it carefully for signs that it might be a forgery, verified the information Eddie had given earlier, took down the license number, and handed it back.

"What's your phone number, Eddie?"

The boy gave it to him.

"By the way, Eddie, do you happen to remember what floor you got off on when you went to Jeremy's apartment?"

Eddie fixed him with a resentful glare. "Fifteen, I think. But I can't be sure. I told you, I was upset."

"I know, Eddie. I'm upset too, but we all gotta do what we gotta do." Matt smiled. "Listen, we'll be in touch, okay?" He reached into his jacket pocket. "I guess you can go, then. Here's my card. If you think of anything that could be helpful, give me a call, okay?"

"Yeah. Sure." Eddie glanced at the business card, stuffed it in his jacket pocket, and opened the door. Matt got out, came around to the front passenger-side door, and froze. Painted on the back of the leather jacket was a scull's head wearing a policeman's hat and insignia engraved with the numbers 666, the number from Revelations of the Great Beast, commonly used to signify belief in Satan.

"Hey, Eddie," Matt said, his tone matter-of-fact. "What's that mean on the back of your jacket?"

Eddie looked at him and spoke icily. "That's my tribute to Jack Bench." The boy turned, glanced at the ashes near the building, and walked quickly east, toward Fifth Avenue.

Matt watched him walk away, the low-hanging sun stretching his shadow on the sidewalk. He reached the corner, turned north on Fifth, and Matt found himself staring into the dawn light of what promised to be a bright, sunny day. A sense of foreboding enveloped him. Jack Bench was a rookie cop who had been ambushed and killed in a shooting in Brooklyn about nine months before. No motive for the murder was ever discovered and, despite a massive investigation, his killers had never been found.

■　　　■　　　■

By the time they arrived at the base between Tenth and Eleventh Avenues, Forty-fifth Street was drenched in sunlight and littered with used condoms. What had started out looking like a beautiful day was going to end up a scorcher. They'd stayed at the scene of the fire another hour and a half after Eddie Cannell had gone, waiting for the department photographer, who had to fight commuter traffic from his outpost in Brooklyn. There was fifteen minutes left before they got off at nine-thirty.

Their boss, Tony Morrison, was sitting at his desk in the small office that served as the supervisor's room, sipping coffee and filling out time sheets. He looked up when the men walked in. "How'd your job turn out?"

Matt answered, "Don't exactly know yet, boss. Give me ten minutes to call the computer room and I'll give you a rundown on our whole show, okay? I want to catch them in Brooklyn before the change of tours." Tony nodded and went back to filling out time sheets.

Matt walked into the squad room while John put on fresh coffee in the kitchenette. The day crew was coming in and a couple of the early birds were already catching up on their reports. Other guys were jammed around the table in the small eating area adjacent to the even tinier kitchen, drinking coffee and swapping stories. He nodded to the two men who were typing, took a seat at an unoccupied desk, picked up the phone, and dialed the number for the computer room.

"Computer room, Fire Marshal Hanson."

"Hey, Ricky. Matt Kincaid in Manhattan." Matt and Ricky used to work in the same battalion in Harlem when they were firefighters.

"Hey, Matt. How've ya been? Are you back to full duty?"

"Yeah. This is my first set, Rick."

"How long has it been, man?"

"Almost a year, Rick. How's things with you?"

"Same shit, different day, Matt. You know."

"Yeah, I sure do. Listen, I need you to run a name for me and I'd like to hold on while you do it. That okay?"

"Sure, no problem. Give me a second to bring up the right screen."

Matt listened to the faint clicking sound of a keyboard until Ricky came back on the line. He gave him the particulars he'd need to run Eddie Cannell through the criminal justice system computers, and lit a cigarette while he waited. John brought in two cups of coffee and gave one to Matt, who nodded his thanks as his partner moved to another phone. Matt heard the whir and chatter of the high-speed printer through the line and Hanson came back on.

"Well, we got a hit." A "hit" meant that the name came up with either a criminal record or a "want" on it. Matt felt his pulse quicken. "Let me see. . . ." Ricky paused while he scanned the page for particulars. "This is *not* a nice person, Matt." He began reading out loud from the computer printout. "January 1993—attempted murder second degree. Assault second degree, with use of a deadly weapon. Robbery second degree. Resisting arrest. Looks like he must have pleaded guilty to a lesser charge, though, and it looks like it was only his first conviction. The sheet says he got five years probation for the whole deal. That runs to 1998. No active warrants or anything. There's more. Do you want it?''

"I knew it. I fuckin' *knew* it.'' Matt put his hand over the mouthpiece and said to John, who was dialing the phone, "Wait till you hear *this* shit, John.'' He took his hand off and talked into the phone. "Let me have it back to '87 and send me the rest in the bag.'' "The bag'' was what everyone called the intradepartmental mail because, for as long as anyone could remember, it had been hand-delivered by messenger in a small white canvas bag.

"August, '89—another assault. Resisting arrest. February, '87—disorderly conduct. That's it up till '87. You want his social security number, address, and all that stuff?''

"Yes.''

Ricky read off the details as Matt copied them down. His mind was racing and he wondered if he had been wrong to let the kid walk away. Should he have kept questioning him? Should he have brought him to the precinct on some bullshit charge? He was tired and Monday-morning quarterbacking was self-defeating. Besides, he had no real evidence. What would they have accomplished by holding the kid, except make him more uncooperative? First, build the case, then bring him in. But there was more to Eddie Cannell than he'd have had them believe. Eddie was suddenly looking *awful* good. Matt forced himself to calm down as he finished writing the information Ricky was giving him.

"Hey, Rick, thanks a lot.''

"No problem, Matt. I'll send you the hard copy. You should have it in your box by tomorrow.''

"Great. Say hello to Diane for me.''

He hung up, picked up his pad and coffee, and walked over to John, who was in the middle of a heated telephone conversation with his wife. He caught his partner's attention and signaled that he was going into the office to talk to Tony Morrison. John rolled his eyes, pointed to the receiver, and made an "okay'' sign with his hand.

Morrison pointed to the other supervisor's desk as Matt came into the office. "Take a load off and tell me what you got." Matt sat on a corner of the desk and thumbed through the slim reporter's notebook in which he had made his hurried notes. The room was small for a boss's office; bright fluorescent lights accented the grime on the floor and walls and added to the sickly pallor given off by the drab, institutional-green paint. Black four-draw file cabinets lined one side of the room; two supervisor's desks, facing each other, occupied the other side. Dirty casement windows, their paint chipped and peeling, overlooked Forty-fifth Street. A large bulletin board abutted the doorway and filled the remaining wall. John came in just behind him, the situation at home apparently under control, and sat down on the chair behind the vacant supervisor's desk, put his coffee and feet on it, and leaned back as Matt began to tell Tony everything that had happened since they'd gone out. As Matt spoke, John would nod, occasionally add a comment to emphasize something Matt said, or give his own interpretation of the interview. Tony sipped his coffee and listened, stopping Matt twice to ask for clarification. Matt brought him to the point when he had Ricky Hanson run the kid's name through the computer. He rested his coffee on the desk and looked at Tony.

"Well, what do ya think?"

"Sounds good, Matt. The kid sounds prime. What do you plan to do now?"

That was what Matt liked about Tony. A lot of bosses would have started telling him what he *should* do before they knew what he was *planning* to do. Tony asked first, and only then added suggestions. If you covered all the bases on the first go-round, he'd tell you to run with what you had.

Matt proposed what he and John had worked out in the car on the way back to the base. "To start with, Tony, we'd like to flop our tours and work straight through today. At least until we can't stay awake anymore." Matt continued before any objection could be raised. "We took samples of the guy's clothing and we'll have to bring them to the PD lab for analysis. We don't want the trail to go cold on this, so we need to canvas the area as soon as possible. Maybe someone who lives nearby was coming home or leaving when the old man was being torched."

John nodded and chimed in, "We should also get into the PD computer and pull this kid's on-line booking sheet now that we know he's got a record. We can get a copy of his photo and see if we can find the cop who arrested him for the attempted murder. Maybe he can tell us something about Cannell that might be helpful.''

Matt took over with renewed enthusiasm, his fatigue vanishing for the moment. ''The victim ought to be reinterviewed, keeping what this kid said in mind . . . see if he remembers anything the way Cannell said it happened—hell, see if he remembers *Cannell*. He never said a word about anyone helping him, although he was kind of out of it and I don't remember specifically asking him if anyone did.'' Tony's face, while interested, gave nothing away as to whether he'd approve their request. Matt continued in earnest. ''I'd like to take a shot at finding this guy Jeremy, if he exists. We've got a pretty good idea where he lives, if Eddie was telling us the truth. If he's on that block, one of the doormen or security people should be able to tell us.''

Matt pushed his chair back, got up, and walked to the row of file cabinets. ''Also, we'd like to check out a lead at Flushing Meadow Park.'' He paused, then continued. ''I could go on, boss, but you get the idea. What do you say?'' He leaned on a cabinet and waited.

Tony put his elbows on the desk, joined his fingertips, and looked from man to man. ''It'd be nice if we could chalk one up for the good guys on this. I want you two to do whatever has to be done to catch this son of a bitch. Don't worry about the chief. I'll take care of him.''

Damn, it was nice working for a guy like Tony, Matt thought. He looked at John. ''I guess it's time to rock and roll, partner.''

4

Their footsteps echoed off the broken tiles of the dark, deserted building. The air was cool, but wet and musty, in sharp contrast to the hot midday sun outside. The sudden change in temperature accented their sweat-drenched clothing and made them feel cold and clammy. Smells of decay and rot mingled unpleasantly with the heavy odor of urine and defecation. John buried his nose in the crease of his arm, mouth-breathing through the sleeve of his jacket. It didn't help much, but he kept it there anyway and followed a step behind Matt, shining the beam of his flashlight a few feet ahead. They made their way past the entrance and drew their automatics, then walked carefully through scattered garbage, discarded remnants of furniture, mattresses, beer and liquor bottles. Matt's face reflected his revulsion as they sidestepped piles of human and animal shit and dark blotches of dried, reeking urine.

"Man, this is fuckin' horrible," he muttered. John kept his nose buried in the crook of his arm and followed reluctantly behind.

The three-story red brick building, built as the Aquacade for the 1939 World's Fair, was in the shape of a doughnut that looked as if it had had a bite taken out of it. The doughnut was an open area housing an outdoor pool and a semicircle of bleachers for viewing aquatic events. The city had recently decided that it was too expensive to repair and too dangerous to keep around. It was scheduled for demolition. Wide, dark tunnels, spaced about every fifty yards, led to the pool and bleachers. Matt looked ahead; thin shafts of sunlight coming through small cracks in the oversized, boarded-up windows lining the upper wall served more to accentuate the gloom than to light the area. Metal, scissor-type security gates backed up by plywood barred access to the pool.

They moved forward quietly, cautiously, guns in one hand, flashlights in the other, looking for a tunnel whose gate had already been breached. Matt played his beam around the high-ceilinged room. The scratching sounds of small creatures scattering along the edges of the walls unnerved him, and he stopped to listen. The thought of rat bites and rabies and hospitals and painful belly shots raced through his mind, and he swallowed nervously before moving on. Neither man wanted to accidentally corner some unsuspecting creature. Best to give it a chance to scurry away. John stamped his feet in warning and was rewarded by the flutter of wings as several pigeons took flight. Feathers grazed his head and he almost lost his balance ducking down quickly and painfully, a cramp knotting the muscles along his neck. He sucked in a breath, cursed and massaged the spot.

Matt paused long enough for John to recover, then continued to move toward the far wall. John regretted ever telling Matt about the place, and Matt thought that coming into the building was among the worst ideas he'd ever had. He was about to tell John to forget the whole thing, when a cough, sharp as a gunshot, reverberated through the empty room. Startled, they whirled around and dropped into a firing crouch, their flashlight beams dancing crazily on the walls and floor. The cough echoed off the tiles and broke up into a dozen smaller sounds, making it impossible to pinpoint the exact source.

The wall was a confusion of shadows cast by overturned boxes, garbage, and junk, making them acutely aware of their vulnerability. Their flashlights, while serving to light the way, also made them excellent targets; a shooter would simply have to aim down the beam. Matt held his flashlight at arm's length. John followed suit.

''Police!'' Matt yelled. ''Come out and keep your hands in front of you.'' He startled himself; the room made his voice sound like he was speaking through a megaphone.

They closed in on their best guess as to where the noise had come from. Matt shouted again. ''Police! I said, 'Come out!' No one's gonna hurt you. Just keep your hands in sight and come out slow.''

A scraping sound came from behind a crate directly in front of them. Matt sidestepped to get John out of his line of fire as they converged on the target.

Except for their footfalls, the place was quiet as a tomb. Matt quickened his pace. He forced himself to focus on the whole wall, depending on his peripheral vision to pick up any movement. He avoided looking at his partner, knowing that each glance at John's light diminished his ability to see in the dark. He cursed his own curiosity; wished instead that he'd decided to pass on this slim lead. He pictured himself and John dead, rats gnawing at their faces as they lay in piles of shit, knowing all too well how long it would take for anyone to find them. He tried to remember if they had told the day supervisor where their first stop would be. He wasn't sure, but it was unlikely he had. A loud thump at the other end of the wall, then a muffled "Son of a bitch" echoed and faded. John's flashlight beam zigzagged erratically, coming to final rest on the floor. Matt tasted the remains of his hasty breakfast.

"John? You okay? *John?*"

The silence was maddening. John answered in a cranky stage whisper, "Yeah, yeah. I just cracked my fuckin' shin. D'ya see anything?" he hissed.

Matt breathed, "Not yet."

The dim outline of the shipping crate grew larger with their approach. Nothing else between him and John could conceal a person. Their flashlights and weapons were aimed at the crate. Matt tensed. "Come out, you motherfucker! NOW! Move slow and show your hands."

A disquieting sound, extremely high-pitched, came from behind the crate. Matt cocked his head and listened. Williams tightened his grip on his gun. It started softly and grew louder, then louder still. It sounded inhuman, yet only a human voice could make it. It was the wail of a wild animal, a keening sound neither man had ever heard before. It was anguish and pain and fear and hate, and as it grew in volume and intensity, crying alternated with laughter, turning suddenly to pitiful sobs, until a steady, animal-like moan echoed unrelentingly off the concrete walls.

Matt finally found his voice and yelled. "Come out, goddammit! Come out. NOW!"

The moaning momentarily stopped, then began again. They could see each other's faces in the dim light. John's eyes were wide, standing out starkly white from his dark features. Matt's face glistened with perspiration and his jaw was set hard with tension when he indicated that he was going forward. John positioned himself in a way that put Matt out of his line of fire. Matt placed his flashlight on the rusted frame of a car body, thinking how odd it was that he would find himself wondering at a time like this how someone had gotten a car through the narrow doors. He aimed the light at the crate and advanced, all too aware of his shaking hands. He forced himself to relax, took a deep breath, and pulled at the edge of the crate. It gave way easily and tumbled backward, forcing him to scramble in order to avoid crushing his toes. The men were stunned into silence as they took in the small, curled form sobbing helplessly on the floor.

John was the first to find his voice, his words coming out in a breathy gasp. "Mo-ther of Je-sus! What the hell is this?"

Except for some sort of briefs or panties, the trembling figure was naked, his/her head lodged between tightly clamped knees. Even in the dirty yellow light, welts and sores could be seen covering almost all of the skeletal back, snaking around to a protruding rib cage.

Matt couldn't believe his eyes; the image before him had come so unexpectedly, his mind and body were so tensed for danger, that he was completely and intractably dumbfounded. He became aware of the gun in his hand, looked at it like it belonged to someone else, and watched as it floated of its own volition to his side.

His vocal chords betrayed him, and he barely managed a hoarse whisper. "Hey, it's all right." Swallowing hard, he said quietly, "No one's going to hurt you." Still no answer or movement. "Who are you?" He felt silly. His words sounded hollow, innocuous. His attempt to reach out, touch his or her shoulder and reassure, resulted in a cringing, muffled yelp.

Matt drew back as if he'd grabbed a hot poker, "Hey, take it easy. You're safe now. We're from the fire department. Everything's going to be okay. Can you move? Are you hurt bad?" The curled ball began shaking violently, convulsively. Matt regained control first. Twenty years of responding to tragedy showed itself in his level, businesslike voice.

"John, get on the department radio. Ask for an ambulance and a rescue company. When the dispatcher asks what kind of injuries we have, don't get too specific. Tell them they are undetermined and that we'll need a supervisor to respond ASAP."

John nodded and headed for the exit. His footsteps quickened as he got farther away. Matt removed his sport jacket, got down on his knees, and was relieved when he was allowed to drape it around the shoulders of the indistinct form. Even through the material of his jacket he could feel sharply protruding bones.

When a soft whimper gave way to full, wracking sobs, Matt could think only to maintain contact, whispering, "Shhh . . . shhh . . ." over and over, patting awkwardly with his fingertips.

Carefully sliding his hand down to touch the matted hair and then to cup the chin buried between bony knees, ever so softly, Matt drew the face toward him. The figure resisted before yielding to the pressure of his hand, and the body uncoiled slightly as the head came up and turned slowly toward him. Matt sucked in a breath as the glow of his flashlight revealed the deep hollows of eyes and cheeks. Then the unmistakable but delicate outline of small breasts and the fragile face of a young girl showed clearly as she straightened up, the jacket falling from her shoulders.

"It's okay, honey," he soothed. "Everything is gonna be all right now." Even as he said it, he knew how empty it must sound. Whatever this child had been through, nothing would ever be "all right" again. He replaced the jacket on her shoulders.

"If I help you, do you think you can stand?" He wanted her out of the excrement and garbage. He knew he should wait for the EMS to arrive before he moved her, but it seemed inhuman to let her continue to sit like that. He got behind her, placing his hands gingerly beneath her arms.

"Try and stand now. I'll help you. I promise I won't let you go or let you fall. Here we go. One, two, three . . ."

She rose quickly, faltered midway, and reached out a hand to steady herself. Matt heard a clanking noise. A thick-linked chain was secured with a padlock to a metal ring on the floor leading to her ankle. It was looped through a wide iron manacle, like the kind seen in old movies with dungeons. Her ankle was swollen and the shackle bit deeply into the flesh, which was badly discolored; dark scabs grew above and below the shackle. She must have struggled fiercely to cause that much damage.

He heard the far-off wail of a siren getting closer as he supported her with one arm and pulled a small wooden crate over. "Here, honey, sit on this." He lowered the shaking girl onto the crate and snugged the jacket firmly around her.

The siren was just outside the building. He used his flashlight to get a better look at her injuries. Her ankle was so badly damaged he doubted she could stand on it. Cuts and scabs and filth covered her entire body. Long thin lines of dried blood ran the length of her thighs. He suspected he'd find the same on her upper body, but he already felt intrusive and didn't want to chance scaring her by removing the jacket. He decided to wait for the EMS to check her upper body.

Matt didn't want to even think about emotional damage. It had to be horrendous. There were a million questions swirling through his mind, but he knew they'd have to wait. First, get help. Her injuries didn't appear life-threatening; his first priority was freeing her from the chain around her ankle. He knew Rescue could have her out in moments. The siren stopped outside the building and he waited anxiously for someone to appear.

Three helmeted figures came through the door and Matt yelled for them to bring a bolt cutter. One turned and spoke to another, who went back out. Flashlights advanced toward them. As they neared, a clawlike grip on his arm startled him. The girl, eyes wide with fright, whimpered deep within her throat. He laid his hand on hers. "It's okay, honey, they're here to help you. I'm not gonna leave you alone. I promise. No one is going to hurt you. I'll be right here. They're just firemen who are gonna get you out of here."

A lieutenant walked up with another firefighter and started to raise his light. Matt stopped his arm midway and said, "Don't shine it in her face." To his credit, the guy was a pro and asked the only pertinent question he could think of.

"What've you got here?"

"We're not sure yet, but her ankle is chained to the ground. I want to cut the chain first and get her out of here. Then you guys can work on the manacle outside if you think you can get it off without hurting her. Can you get someone to bring in some blankets?"

The lieutenant looked at the chain and talked into his radio. "Charlie, get the bolt cutter in here and bring blankets from the back of the rig. *Fast.*" Unable to stop looking at the girl's heartrending condition, he said to Matt, "What the hell is goin' on? Who is she? How did you find her?"

"I don't have any answers yet. Just questions like you. We just found her and she's not talking yet. I think we can assume she's in shock, but we'll know more when we get her outside. I don't know what her physical injuries are, but I think we better wait for the ambulance in case anything is broken or there's internal bleeding. Do you guys carry water on your rig? She looks dehydrated.''

"I'm afraid not. But the ambulance should. I'll tell my chauffeur to have the EMS bring some in when they arrive.'' The lieutenant spoke into his Handie-Talkie and gave instructions to his driver to pass on to the ambulance.

Another siren approached. "That must be the ambulance,'' Matt said to no one in particular. Two firefighters arrived carrying a bolt cutter and blankets, John behind them. They worked on the chain and she was free in seconds. The shackle was still secured to her ankle. Her grip on his arm was desperate; he covered her hand with his. They tried to remove Matt's jacket and replace it with the blanket, but she grabbed at the lapels and wouldn't let go. They settled for draping the blanket over the jacket.

Matt looked up to see John trying to catch his eye. He started to get up but the girl's grip on his arm was surprisingly strong. If this was a sign of trust, Matt didn't want to do anything to break it. He waved his partner over and John whispered in his ear, "Walter is asking why we need his response.''

"Goddamn him. Let me have the radio.''

Matt called the base, hoping the radio would transmit through the thick walls. The response was immediate but came in weak and broken up. Matt spoke in a slow, deliberate tone.

"We need the immediate response of a supervisor.''

The radio beeped and crackled. "What's the reason for the request?'' Matt recognized Walter Berry's nasal twang.

"We're unable to give that information on this frequency and we are nowhere near a land line. We request a supervisor response ASAP. We will explain upon his arrival.''

"We'll need more information before a response.''

Matt was ready to explode. The firefighters standing around him and the girl were looking at the radio in disbelief. He said, "Fuck it'' under his breath and spoke into the radio, dropping any semblance of radio procedure.

"Walter, you get your fat ass out here *now,* or you will be explaining this conversation for the rest of your miserable life. Forty-five Alpha, out.''

He looked at John. "I don't care if the prick responds or not. I had a feeling if we needed that scumbag, he'd pull some shit like this." When you "flopped" a tour, you worked for whichever supervisor was scheduled that day. Today it was Walter Berry, nicknamed "The Polecat" because of his strong body odor and minimal personal hygiene. He was five foot nine and 265 pounds of old-line supervisor who seldom bathed. His former partners had told him that spending a summer's day tour in the car with Walter was like sitting next to a three-day-old cadaver. The smell remained lodged in your nostrils for hours after the tour ended. Walter hated leaving the base and dragging all that weight around. He dressed as if he drove a taxi instead of supervised a squad of marshals, and was usually a source of embarrassment for any marshal who had to introduce him as his boss. Matt wished with all his heart that Tony was working today.

He gave the radio back to John. "If he calls again, don't answer. We'll tell him the radio wouldn't receive inside the building." The Rescue chauffeur told the lieutenant the ambulance had arrived. Moments later, two EMS technicians came in pulling a gurney and medical kits. As they neared, the girl made pitiful, deep-in-the-throat whimpering noises. She pulled away and gripped his arm tighter. Matt soothed her as best he could.

When the woman from the EMS team got close enough, she halted abruptly. A soft gasp escaped her lips, but she quickly recovered and reached for her bag. Even while she groped for what she would need in the bag, she began speaking to the girl, telling her she was going to be all right, that they were going to fix her up. Matt touched the woman's elbow.

"Do you have any water?" he asked her. "I think she's dehydrated. She hasn't said a word yet and she looks malnourished. She's got wounds and cuts that look infected and a shackle on her leg these guys will try to take off once we get her outside."

While her partner prepared the gurney, the woman opened a bottle and offered it to the girl. It was obvious she wanted it but made no move to take it. The paramedic took a step closer and put the bottle near her lips. As she reached around to support her head, the girl recoiled so violently that she and Matt almost toppled from the crate.

"Let me try." Matt took the bottle and presented it like an offering. When she didn't respond, he put the bottle to his lips. He discovered his mouth was dry as dust and took a long drink. He held it out again and the grip on his arm loosened.

''Go ahead. It's only water. It'll taste real good. C'mon now, honey, try some.'' He brought the bottle closer to her lips and, in the most tentative way, she opened her mouth to accept it. Matt thought she'd take the bottle and drink, but she seemed to expect it to be fed to her and made no attempt to take it. He awkwardly brought the bottle to her lips and tilted it, trying not to tip it too far. Once the water touched her lips, she drank greedily. He wasn't able to pour it fast enough for her. She released his arm and supported his hand, pushing up to tilt the bottle more. She wouldn't take it herself, only put her hand under his to help. When the water started seeping from the corners of her mouth and dripping down her chin, the paramedic said they'd better stop until they could get a better look at her.

The process was complicated. At each attempt to put her on the gurney, she cringed and pulled away, nearly choking on her fear. Finally, Matt just scooped her up in his arms and laid her down. She resumed her death grip on his arm and he had to walk crouched over her as they wheeled her out to the ambulance. He thanked the gods for the park being so remote. There were no onlookers and no questions to deal with as they came outside.

''Hey, Lou''—all lieutenants in the fire and police departments are called Lou—''could you have one of your men get on the citywide frequency and have the dispatcher get Car Sixty-one to respond?'' Car 61 was the FD Photo Unit. Matt knew he was going to have to document the scene. He was also trying to figure out how he was going to be in several places at once. He didn't want to leave the direction of the photographs to someone else because he was going to be responsible if it got fucked up or something was forgotten. He could trust John, but he felt he needed to be here in case he required special shots once the interior of the building was lit up with portable lighting. And he didn't want to leave the girl because she might make a statement once they got her condition stabilized.

The bright sunlight had a sobering effect on everyone. The girl looked even worse than she had inside the building. No one knew how long she'd been in darkness, but it was obvious the sun hurt her eyes. Her eyes were narrow slits and she was shielding them with her forearm. Her skin was sallow, almost translucent. The hollows in her cheeks and eyes looked like caverns in the light of day. Dark circles, bluish bruises, cuts and small scars covered her face and neck. Her hair had been chopped in ragged, uneven sections. It was matted and caked with filth; knotted and dull. Her face was young yet old. She could be twelve or twenty, there was no way to tell. Matt shivered at the thought of what they might find when they uncovered her body.

The lieutenant was looking at her leg and giving directions to his men. A medium-sized padlock secured the manacle. A bolt cutter could make short work of that. The problem was not getting the shackle off, but rather the condition of the leg around it. It had swelled to the point where it was protruding grotesquely out around the device. There was no slack and the skin looked like it had fused itself to the metal. A decision had to be made as to whether to remove it at the scene or to let the doctors do it at the hospital. Matt turned to the lieutenant.

"What d'ya think, Lou?"

"If we remove it, we may pull off some flesh. I don't think we should take the chance. If she starts bleeding badly, at least the hospital is equipped to deal with it."

"I agree. Let's get her out of the sun and into the ambulance."

They lifted the gurney into the back of the ambulance. Matt didn't know whether her clinging to him was healthy or not, but she wouldn't let go, even in the ambulance. When the paramedic attempted to unwrap the blanket, she sat bolt upright and tried to bite the woman's hand. The paramedic pulled back a millisecond before teeth grabbed flesh. A low, primal growl rumbled in the girl's throat. The thought flashed through Matt's mind that he was in way over his head. Nothing in his experience was going to be able to guide his actions here.

He took her by the shoulders and, speaking softly, guided her gently back down on the gurney. "Listen, honey, we've got to see how badly you're hurt, so we can help you. If you want, I'll go outside so you can have some privacy. Do you understand what I'm saying?" His words were met by a blank stare and a tightening of her grip on his arm. "Everyone is trying to help you. This nice lady has to look at you. We need you to cooperate so we can help." She tried to lift her head from the pillow, wasn't up to the effort, and fell limply back. She looked at Matt, her eyes sorrowful, as if trying to apologize for being unable to accommodate his wish. A lump formed in his throat. The anguish and pain in her face and eyes were like a shot to his heart. "I promise, no one is going to hurt you anymore. . . . I swear it." She relaxed enough for Matt and the paramedic to sit her up. Matt reached around her shoulders and took hold of the edge of the blanket. "I'm going to take this off now. Don't be afraid. We just need to look at you." He peeled the blanket and jacket from her shoulders. What they'd hidden was horrifying. A tight, vicious knot formed in his stomach.

The girl had been whipped. And whipped badly over an extended period of time. There were long slashlike scars everywhere. Some were old and healed, with raised, keloidal tissue crisscrossed by fresher wounds edged by scabs and dried blood. Crusted cigarette burns dotted her small breasts, some obviously infected. She looked like she'd been in a concentration camp. Her panties were filthy and ripped, and fresh blood stained the back of them. She sat with her arms folded across her small breasts, trying to hold on to a vestige of her dignity. Strong fecal odors permeated the closed compartment of the ambulance. Human waste was smeared on various parts of her legs and arms. The paramedic looked at him, her eyes expressionless. She reached above her head for a box.

"Better put these on." She handed him a pair of disposable latex gloves. "No telling what these wounds have been exposed to. I've got to lay her down so I can examine her. Help me." She turned to the girl. "Take it easy now, sweetheart. We're not going to hurt you. I need you to lie down so I can clean some of these wounds." The woman was concerned about the blood on the rear of the girl's panties. Together they eased her down, all the while whispering soothing words, murmuring softly, trying their best to reassure her.

When she was lying flat, the paramedic used a pair of scissors to snip the sides of the panties, then lifted her and slid them out.

"You might want to turn your head," she said to Matt.

Matt faced the back of the ambulance while the woman examined the girl. He felt the thin padding shift as the woman turned the girl and heard her swift efficient movements as she cleaned and dressed the wounds.

He felt queasy and took several deep breaths. He had to prevent any evidence from being washed away.

"You can examine her," he said, "but whatever you find may be the evidence we need to catch whoever did this. She cannot be washed until we can take samples at the hospital. You understand, don't you? Also, the panties need to be saved."

The woman's answer was sharp. "I'm doin' this eight years now. I know what has to be done. But some of these wounds need immediate treatment."

"Of course. I'm not implying you don't. But we can't afford mistakes that result from not communicating." His tone was placating and the paramedic accepted it. She returned to treating and cleaning the wounds, applying compresses. It was obvious the woman felt good about finally being able to do something solid, something she knew and could handle. Finally done, she turned to Matt.

"I've got to talk to you." She pointed to the front of the ambulance. The girl was covered with a sheet to her neck, one arm draped protectively across her chest. The other poked out to hold him. Matt placed his hand over hers and leaned down.

"I'm going to step away for a few minutes. I'm not leaving. I just need to talk to this nice lady." He tried to move away but she clung to him. He repeated what he'd said and added, "It's gonna be okay. I'm just moving to the front of the ambulance." He pried her fingers from his shirt. She whimpered but didn't look at him.

He moved the few steps to the front of the cab and huddled with the paramedic. Craning to look directly into his eyes, he observed that the woman's face was earnest, concerned. He noticed how young she was and wondered how this kind of thing affected her when she went home.

"She's suffering from malnutrition and dehydration," she told Matt. "The girl has been badly, and I mean badly, sexually abused. You can see the more obvious signs of physical torture yourself. But she's also bleeding from her rectum. No way to tell here what kind of internal damage there is. She has what appears to be dried semen all around her anus and vagina. Her labia is torn and there is evidence that she was burned there as well. She's missing several teeth and her gums are infected. Then there's the whip marks–some relatively fresh, others scarred over, covering most of her body." She paused and anger filled her eyes. "The pain must have been unbearable. Whatever scum did this should have their balls cut off before they're killed." Her voice cracked, her demeanor became resigned; she looked defeated, a victim of all she'd seen. "That's just the preliminary. I'm certain the list will grow with a thorough hospital examination. The only good news is that she's young, I can't find anything broken, and there's nothing life-threatening. Physically, she'll probably recover."

"How old do you think she is?"

"I can't really be sure until we clean her up. My guess is early teens. Maybe thirteen or fourteen years old. In her condition it's hard to say. No telling how malnutrition has affected her growth, but there's something basically immature about her bone structure and breast development. Still, she's so thin, it's hard to say."

Matt thanked her and returned to find the girl staring vacantly at the roof of the ambulance. He sat on a stool, took her hand, and stroked it for a time before speaking. It pleased him that she made no attempt to pull away.

"Hey," he said gently. "Can you talk to me?" Nothing. "What's your name?" Pause. "C'mon, darlin', just tell me your name." Again no response. He leaned forward slowly, pressing her hand a little tighter, wanting her to feel his presence. "Listen, why don't we introduce ourselves? My name's Matt. Matt Kincaid. This nice lady is . . ." He turned to the paramedic. "Nancy," the woman answered. "Okay, this is Nancy. Now it's your turn. What's your name?

"C'mon now. . . . You can say it. Just try. Would you like more water? Nancy, can you get our girl a drink?"

Nancy brought a small paper cup and gave it to Matt. He took the water, put his hand under the girl's head, and brought the cup to her lips. She drank greedily and finished in two large swallows. He lowered her to the pillow. She returned her gaze to the ceiling.

"That's enough for now. We don't want you getting sick." He put the cup aside. "Please, what's your name? You can say it. I know you can." Her eyes moved to look at Matt, but her head remained rigid. She tried to speak but emitted only a breathy rasping sound. "That's it, honey, talk to me. Try again." Matt lowered his head nearly to her mouth.

A dry whisper escaped from cracked, swollen lips. She winced in pain. "Ellen."

Matt felt elated at hearing her speak. "Ellen. That's a beautiful name. . . . Ellen what? What's your last name?" He cupped his ear.

The girl's voice was barely audible. "Ellen . . . Levy."

"Well, Ellen Levy." He tried to sound cheerful, upbeat. "It's my pleasure to meet you. Listen, Ellen, I need to know where you live. Are you from New York?"

Matt was rewarded with a small nod.

"Good. What's your address?"

Her forehead wrinkled in puzzled thought. An impotent little shrug said she was as surprised as anyone that she couldn't remember her address.

"Well, do you remember what borough you live in?"

A moment's thought and a small, negative shake of the head.

"Do you live in a house or an apartment?"

The girl's eyes widened a bit, seemingly glad to be able to remember something. "House," she whispered.

While her answer eliminated large chunks of the city, it left an equal amount to cover. He saw that Nancy was getting anxious, no doubt feeling Ellen should be on her way to a hospital. Matt fought the impulse to end the questions, let her go, but there was much to be done and he had to get what information he could before she left. He felt certain that Ellen wasn't going to like the idea of going to the hospital without him, and he might lose a lot of gained ground as a result. But he had to stay and try to make Ellen understand later.

He found himself wondering whether this whole thing had anything to do with his arson investigation, how it could possibly be related. He tried to put in order the facts of each case, but they resisted his attempt, spilling out in jumbled confusion.

Matt knew he was way outside his area of expertise, that the PD was going to have to be notified. They had special units that routinely dealt with trauma, and if this was in no way connected to his arson case, there'd be tremendous pressure to back off. His access to Ellen would be severely limited.

"Ellen, how old are you?" Her answer was an uncomprehending blink. "How old are you, sweetheart? Can you remember your birthday?"

The puzzled frown returned to her battered face. She was showing signs of agitation at not being able to answer this basic question, knowing she should. Her head jerked side to side, and smothered "Uhmm, uhmm" sounds rumbled in her throat.

Matt brushed her forehead. "It's okay, Ellen. It's not important. Just relax now. You'll remember. It'll just take a little time, that's all."

The questions would have to wait awhile longer. He assured her that he was coming right back, then stepped from the ambulance. The lieutenant, looking uncertain, stood surrounded by his men. Matt put his jacket on and motioned to him. The lieutenant joined Matt and they walked several feet away, where they spoke privately.

"Lou, I need a couple of favors." The fire department lieutenant's expression told him to go ahead and ask. "Can you accompany the girl to the hospital?"

"Yeah, we can do that."

"When you get there, it's important that before they get too involved in treating and cleaning her up, their rape trauma unit be brought in. They should know what has to be done, but sometimes they fuck up. I need you to make sure the girl is photographed as she is right now. It will be important later. Her condition has to be documented, even before they remove the manacle. Once they start to clean her up it will be too late. If we catch the scumbags who did this, without photographic evidence to present to a jury, it will be like it never happened. No one—not you, not me, or any doctor—is going to be able to adequately describe her condition. We need photographs. I have to stay here. I hate leaving her, but I don't see what else I can do." The lieutenant nodded and indicated that Matt should continue. "None of this may be necessary. I just don't know the hospitals in Queens very well. If we were in Manhattan, we'd have her brought to Bellevue, where they deal with trauma cases all the time and know the routine. I'm just asking you to make sure they do the right thing. Will you do it?"

The lieutenant considered a moment. "Okay, but aren't you going to call the cops in on this?"

"I'm doing it as soon as you and I finish talking, but they'll never be able to get to the hospital before they start to work on her, and it's important that no one makes any mistakes." He already knew that he was going to be accused of waiting too long to notify the PD.

A distant siren grew gradually louder. Either someone had already notified the cops or Walter had actually decided to respond. Matt walked to his car, started the motor, and radioed the Queens dispatcher. He gave his location and asked what precinct covered the park, then asked him to notify the cops and request the immediate response of a PD supervisor to the scene. As he finished speaking, a brown unmarked Plymouth eased to a stop at the curb. Its "Kojak" light flashing on the passenger side let Matt know that there was more than one man in the car. He recognized the license plate as belonging to a Manhattan base unit.

Matt replaced the handset, shut the motor, and moved to the new arrivals. As he approached, he saw Walter Berry sitting in the passenger seat wearing his customary cab driver's cap, plaid shirt, and navy-blue tie under a faded brown polyester sport jacket. The base commander, Deputy Chief Victor "Howcum" D'Aieuto, sat behind the wheel in a dark business suit, white shirt, and striped tie. Matt groaned. D'Aieuto wasn't the brightest man on the job. Among his many faults, he'd managed to achieve his position within the Bureau without ever having made a decision. He got along by delegating all authority to his executive officer, a bright young guy named Bob Sherry, the result of which was that Chief D'Aieuto didn't have a clue as to what was going on at his command. But he never failed to say, at any gathering of marshals, "My door is always open to you men." The fact was, his door was always closed and locked, and behind it you could usually hear the sound of a television, often tuned to cartoons.

He also had no friends in high places. He was basically a "second-guesser," someone who always knew what you "should have done" but never knew what you *should do*. The men called him "Howcum D'Aieuto" because he was always asking, "How come you didn't do this?" and "How come you didn't do that?" Between Walter Berry and the chief, Matt figured his bad day was about to get worse. D'Aieuto flung the door open and got out quickly.

Matt tried to sound casual. "Hello, Chief." He bent to acknowledge Berry, still inside the car, with a nod of his head. "Walter." He offered his hand to D'Aieuto, who looked at it as if he was being asked to fondle Matt's penis. His hand hung suspended a moment before he let it fall to his side. He followed the chief's eyes to Walter Berry and watched the fat man struggle to get his bulk out of the car. Berry swung his legs to the sidewalk, one hand on the roof, the other on the door frame. Two attempts to extricate himself failed and he rocked back and forth, trying to get the necessary purchase to pull himself up and out. He was snorting and sweating as if he'd run a marathon. Matt turned away and spoke to the chief.

"We've got a very odd situation here, Chief. Did Tony tell you why John and I flopped our tours?"

D'Aieuto nodded curtly and looked to Walter, who was still trying to get out of the car. The chief wanted Walter to get the briefing, preferring to see what action Walter took, rather than have to make any decisions himself. When Walter had come to his office flush-faced and sputtering, telling him what Matt had said on the radio, asking him to respond with him and put the son of a bitch in his place, he reluctantly agreed. If what Walter said was true, Kincaid was insubordinate. It was as good a time as any to show that he supported his supervisors. My God, he thought, Chief Cattalli himself could have been listening!

He studiously avoided looking at Matt while waiting for Walter to get out of the car. He *is* a fat son of a bitch, D'Aieuto thought with disgust. With a final great heave, Walter rocked his weight forward while pulling on the car frame and stood, finally triumphant. He kept one hand on the door for support, pulled a filthy, rumpled handkerchief from a back pocket and used it like a washcloth to wipe his dripping face. Matt hid his disgust. He wouldn't have used that thing to wipe his ass.

The firefighters watched the spectacle with amused contempt. Knowing firemen as he did, Matt was sure they were biting their tongues. The image of Walter trying to get his fat ass out of the car was sure to be the subject of firehouse humor when they got back. For now, the men stood gaping at the huge bulk wiping his forehead, trying to compose himself, and salvage what little dignity he had left.

"Like I was saying, Chief, we've got an odd situation here."

D'Aieuto glared at Matt, his voice dripping venom. "You can give your briefing to Walter here." He spoke coldly, trying hard to get just the right inflection, letting Matt know how little support he could expect.

Matt had been surprised to see the chief. D'Aieuto never came to a job unless he thought some bigwig was going to be there and he could score points. He preferred to stay locked in his office. Most times, he was as hard to get out of the base as Walter Berry.

There was bad history between Matt and these men. Matt had never forgotten or forgiven the fact that neither of them had come to the hospital voluntarily when his former partner and best friend, Larry Peterson, was shot. Tony Morrison had confided to him that when he called D'Aieuto at home to tell him about the shooting, his response had been to ask if Tony thought it necessary that he come. After all, if the man was dead, there wasn't anything he could do. Tony Morrison had been floored by D'Aieuto's reaction. Not only was it standard procedure for a chief to respond to any kind of shooting incident, but it was the human thing to do. D'Aieuto merely instructed Morrison to keep him informed by telephone of all developments.

When Chief Fire Marshal Carmine Cattalli came to the hospital and inquired as to D'Aieuto's whereabouts, Tony informed him that he had been notified and was still at home. Chief Cattalli exploded. He told Morrison to dial D'Aieuto's number, then he took the phone, asked everyone to leave the room, and closed the door. No one knows exactly what was said, but through the closed door Cattalli's booming voice could be heard shouting expletives. D'Aieuto arrived sheepishly an hour and a half later to a frigid reception. The word was that CFM Cattalli, who was known to have a long memory and a vindictive nature when crossed, had had him on his shit list ever since. The men loved it. "Howcum's" persistent lament was "How come the chief has it in for me?"

Walter finally waddled over, and Matt started to tell him that there was a girl in the ambulance in need of help. Still wheezing, Walter cut him off. "Who the hell do you think you are, talking to me like that on the radio?"

Matt tried a placating tone. "Look, Walter, we'll have time for this later. Right now, I think you ought to know what we've got here."

"Fuck what you've got here. You've always been overly impressed with your own importance. I don't give a shit what you've got here. I want to know where you get off talking that trash on the radio?"

Matt was trying hard to maintain his composure. He was concerned for Ellen and wanted to get back to her. He was tense and in no mood to coddle two assholes. But they were going to have to be dealt with, and it might as well be now.

He tried to sound conciliatory. "Walter, I know you're angry, but we've got a situation here that really can't wait. If you give me a minute, I'll explain. I think you'll agree our differences can wait till we get back to the base."

Walter was not to be soothed. He was building up a full head of steam and with each word was encouraged by the nodding head of Howcum D'Aieuto. Both men were glaring at Matt, and the sinking feeling he had was accompanied by the certain knowledge that he was going to get nowhere with either one. He suppressed his rising anger and was about to take another stab at trying to get them to listen, when a brown unmarked car coasted to a stop behind them. There were two men in the front seat. He figured they must be the precinct detectives. Great. Just fucking great, he thought.

His outrage increased as he pictured himself getting publicly reamed by these jerks. That would be all he needed to screw up his investigation, to be regarded as a guy without the slightest hint of support from his bosses. As it was, the firemen shifted uncomfortably each time Walter raised his nasal voice. It was a deeply ingrained feeling among the men of all uniformed services that ass-chewing never be done publicly. Walter was breaking the rule and no one liked it except the chief.

The reflection of the midday sun off the windshield made it impossible for Matt to identify the two men in the car. For their part, Berry and D'Aieuto were so consumed by their desire to take a chunk out of him, they hadn't bothered to turn around when the car approached. Just as Matt was determining how to put an immediate end to this, the two men got out of the car and, as recognition hit him, he gave an inward "Uh-oh." He was in deeper shit than he imagined. Why the fuck couldn't he learn to control his mouth? He started to speak but was cut off by the loud, indignant voice of Howcum D'Aieuto.

"Are you listening, Kincaid? Can you comprehend what is being said to you? Whatever situation you've got here is unimportant. What *is* important is that you know who you are dealing with. You cannot speak to your superiors any way you want, and you are going to pay a severe price for having done so. As soon as I get back to the base, I am instructing Supervising Fire Marshal Berry here"—he pointed without looking at Walter—"to file charges against you for insubordination, disrespect, failure to follow proper radio procedure, and anything else we can think of. You're gonna be burned and I'm gonna light the match myself."

The new arrivals had stopped about ten feet behind the small group, listening to the tirade without comment or movement. The chief had spoken loud enough for everyone to hear in order to get the full effect and to maximize Matt's humiliation. Walter wore a small spiteful smile, while D'Aieuto's face was frozen in just the proper, practiced mask of outrage. Matt was boiling inside but contained it and spoke through clenched teeth.

"Chief, if you'll listen to what's going on here, I think you'll understand. It's important that you know what's happened. This will surely make the papers and you're gonna need some answers."

Howcum answered, "How come men like you always think everything you get mixed up in is so fucking important? Marshal, nobody gives a fuck about what you've got.''

A flat, gravelly voice behind them said, ''I give a fuck.''

The two bosses wheeled around to see who had the audacity to interrupt them. Walter Berry turned to instant mush and Howcum D'Aieuto's tongue became a ball of cotton as soon as they saw the gray-bearded, chesty figure of Chief Fire Marshal Carmine Cattalli. Cattalli stood there with his hands on his hips, his eyes burning holes into the two men. The short silence was broken when he spoke again.

''What's goin' on here?''

No one answered.

''I said, what the fuck is goin' on here?''

◼   ◼   ◼

At a phone on the Lower East Side of Manhattan, at the intersection of Bowery and Delancey Streets, the handsome young man (actually more beautiful than handsome) held the spittle-encrusted mouthpiece as far away from his mouth as possible.

''I was questioned by fire marshals this morning,'' he said into the phone. ''I need to talk to you right away. They didn't get anything from me, but it's important we talk. You can reach me at the usual place in the usual way.'' He placed the receiver back on the hook.

At the other end of the line, a leather-clad figure sat flat-footed, erect, arms lying rigidly at right angles on the arms of a thronelike chair. Pinprick rays of sunlight poked through the heavy material of the closed, black drapes on the windows. Dust motes played in the beams and tossed in tiny swirls. Except for the sun's meager attempts at penetration, the room was completely dark. Unlit candles were positioned around the room at random locations, some grouped in batches, others spread haphazardly along the walls.

The man remained motionless for a long time after the boy hung up, then reached for the phone and punched in a number. It was answered after one ring. He spoke without preamble or emotion into the mouthpiece. ''Get over here. Now.''

He placed the phone delicately back on its cradle and resumed his former position. Only the closest examination would have revealed the single difference in his face. The whites of his eyes were veined red, the first telltale sign of a lethal anger.

5

Eddie Cannell hung naked from a metal pulley attached to a hook in the ceiling. He wore a black eyeless leather hood, laced securely at the back, with only a triangular opening for the nose and a sturdy brass zipper across the mouth. The zipper was open and an oversized rubber ball gag protruded from his stretched, gaping mouth. It very much appeared as if a grotesque black jack-o'-lantern was suspended above a human body. Eddie's feet were spread-eagled, toes just off the ground, ankles secured to rings in the floor so that his full weight was borne by padded leather wrist restraints. His captor watched him strain at his bonds and thought, There is nothing like the fear of certain death to make a person feel incredibly alive.

The Sentry marveled at the way the human animal, in these moments, became so sensitized, how the merest brush of a feather, along any area of the body, would send someone into spasms of shock. Deprived of sight, the victim would listen intently, trying to track the slightest movement in the room, nostrils twitching and flaring at the faintest odor, every nerve ending pleading for feedback. It struck him as wonderfully ironic that in almost every case his victims, despite knowing what awaited them at the end of the game, would become so elementarily alive, craving the ability to anticipate their fate.

He looked from his captive to the nearby table, where various instruments and devices were arrayed. Picking up a set of sharply pointed, caliper-type clamps joined by a chain about the size and weight of a small dog's choker collar, he fiddled with the wheels that opened and closed the clamps and adjusted them until the curved jaws were about a half-inch apart. He stepped within inches of the hanging boy.

"Eddie, Eddie, Eddie. What am I going to do with you?" The clamps were cold when he brushed the metal across Eddie's smooth, hairless chest. The boy jerked and shivered at the unexpected touch. His captor traced another line from his nipples to his belly. Eddie sucked his stomach in, trying to break the contact, but failed and, unable to sustain the weight of his lower body for more than a few moments, slumped as much as his restraints allowed. Rivulets of sweat ran down his body, though it was chilly in the darkened room. The light from a bathroom, just off the foyer entrance to the bedroom, and a large plumber's candle sitting on the table were the sole sources of light in the large space.

It pleased the Sentry to imagine that behind the mask, Eddie's eyes were wide with terror and anticipation. He felt an enormous sense of power and pleasure wash over him and settle in his groin as the first stirrings in his sex signaled that, before the day was out, he would have numerous orgasms. Not with this boy, of course. While he hated fags and lesbos, it excited him to work on either sex in preparation for his own release. And, so long as they obeyed him, as was the case with the young man before him, he'd tolerate whatever sexual preferences they had. The kid was into pain, but had only imagined the true meaning of the word. Until now.

He pressed a hand to Eddie's back to stop his swaying. Stepping to the side, he held one of the pointed clamps, allowing the other to dangle, and gathered the brownish flesh of a nipple between the thumb and forefinger of his free hand. Eddie struggled, but to no avail. The Sentry placed the pincers on either side of the nipple and slowly turned the wheel. A series of choked, muffled screams fought uselessly past the gag as the tips began to bite into flesh and pierce the skin, and droplets of blood oozed from either side. When the blood flowed steadily, he repeated the procedure on the other nipple. Eddie was shaking furiously, throwing his head from side to side, trying to shake the clamps loose. But his thrashing served no purpose but to bring more pain and a surer bite. The Sentry watched impassively as Eddie writhed and convulsed, waiting patiently for the pain to subside. Eddie was sucking deep, wheezing breaths through a nose clogged with mucus. It became increasingly difficult to breathe and his chest heaved spasmodically.

"Now, doesn't it feel better when you don't struggle, Eddie? Here," he said in an almost-kind voice, "let's make it easier for you." He brought a washcloth to Eddie's nose. "Now, blow."

Eddie tried to pull his head away. "You know I don't like having to repeat myself, Eddie. I said blow." Eddie obeyed and was ordered to do it again, and then again. The man's touch was like that of a kindly nurse. "Isn't that better now?" There was no response and his voice became brittle. "You always had trouble with instant answers, Eddie. I think it's time we cured you of that bad little habit."

The Sentry reached up and casually pinched Eddie's nostrils, bracing the boy's head with his other hand. He'd caught Eddie just after exhaling and there was no breath in him. Eddie's feet kicked out frantically within the small space his bonds allowed, and his arms bent and pulled at his weight. Back arched, veins and tendons protruding grotesquely, he tried desperately to gulp air through his mouth, but the ball gag prevented access. The Sentry patiently, calmly, held on through Eddie's struggles. It lasted surprisingly long, until he felt Eddie's body begin to sag. When the Sentry released his grip, Eddie's nostrils stuck together as he tried desperately, greedily, to suck air through them. Eddie wriggled and contorted his face until finally one nostril opened and then the other, and he sucked air deeply into his lungs through the much-too-small openings.

His tormentor watched and waited until Eddie's breathing returned to a semblance of normality before reaching up and nonchalantly pinching the nostrils once again. Eddie jerked in the air. He waited until he sensed imminent unconsciousness before letting go.

"Are you getting the idea, my dear boy?" The limp, exhausted Eddie responded with a weak nod while wheezing gulps of air. "It doesn't take a great deal of exertion on my part to make you wish you had obeyed me. Just a pinch of my fingers or the proper application of an instrument to the right place. Now, when I ask you a question, I expect an immediate response. Is that understood?"

Eddie's head bobbed immediately.

"Good. Now we're getting somewhere."

The Sentry's attention returned to the table and the arrayed devices. He chose what appeared to be a leather shoelace tied in knots at the ends. Two spring-loaded clamps formed loops that released and slid up and down when pressed, enlarging or contracting the size of each. He adjusted it and made a three-inch noose, approaching Eddie from the front. Reaching between the splayed legs, careful not to allow the thong to make contact with any part of the body, he looped it around Eddie's testicles and paused only long enough to savor the moment. Eddie thought he'd been struck by lightning when the Sentry jammed the clamp up hard around the base of the scrotum, closing the loop.

Shock and pain raced through Eddie's being as he bucked and fought in an attempt to dislodge the noose, screaming over and over in muffled agony behind his gag. A long time passed before he was able to subdue the tremors, and even then, small shivers continued to ripple through his spine. And then, almost as suddenly as the onslaught of pain had begun, he was calm. The pain was not so great as he had initially thought. It was more the unexpected suddenness of it that had shocked him. He'd felt similar but much worse pain, and knew instinctively that he hadn't been hurt in any permanent way. He forced himself to calm down and, to his surprise and despite his fear, felt a pleasant tingling in his cock and balls. Mixed uncomfortably with this feeling was the self-loathing he'd experienced from his earliest pubescent memories, a time when he discovered as he masturbated that it enhanced his pleasure to squeeze his testicles until they hurt. He remembered how it made him explode in a crescendo of pleasure/pain that later became first an obsession of mind and, as he grew older, a physical craving.

He hated himself because, despite this fear, despite his apprehensions of what probably awaited him at the end of all this, he felt his erection grow.

"Eddie, my boy. What have we here?" A wry grin crossed the Sentry's face. "You quite love this, don't you?" The young man's answer was a defeated nod, his chin coming to rest resignedly on his chest. His captor stepped forward and gently grasped the swelling penis. "You know, Eddie, I had no idea you were this large. It's really quite a handsome cock you have." He held the penis tenderly in his fist and felt it grow rapidly beyond his palm. He didn't stroke it, just squeezed rhythmically, delicately, as one might squeeze a peach, testing for ripeness. He thought, Still not fully hard and it's huge. I would love to have one like it. It is truly a waste to have put such a magnificent tool on such a stupid young man.

With a featherlike touch, he squeezed and pumped until Eddie became large and hard in his hand. The boy's cock grew hot and began to twitch and pulse of its own volition. The Sentry watched, using his free hand to bring the remaining loop of leather from between Eddie's legs to the head of his penis. When he felt the first twinge and sensed the impending first spasms of an orgasm ripple through his fingers, he quickly removed his hand, slipped the loop down the length of the shaft, and roughly jammed the remaining clamp up the thong's length. Eddie screamed behind his gag as pain raced like a high-voltage current from his cock into his body, the flow of semen and blood effectively dammed by the leather noose.

Eddie's body jerked in awkward concert with his cock, which was moving up and down like the wand of a spastic conductor. Two drops of cloudy white semen managed to escape, forming a stringy line. It hung suspended, mocking the predicament of its owner, until a spasmodic jerk whipped it backward, attaching it to his belly, leaving a sticky tightrope between his penis and his abdomen.

"Ah, Eddie. You are quite shameless, aren't you? I didn't want you to come just yet, and I suppose I should have told you. But you shall have to pay a price for it anyway, you know. This exercise is not about your enjoyment, but mine."

Eddie's penis was engorged and swollen, veins blue and bulging, the tip, a deep angry purple. The thong cut deeply into the flesh and it appeared all the more distorted at the center. The Sentry looked to his table of instruments and chose from among a line of triangular lead fishing sinkers, set up in order of size and weight. They ranged from small ultra-lights to a custom two-pound giant, each with a hook at the top and a loop at the bottom.

He picked one from the middle of the line and bent to peer under Eddie's scrotum. Finding the spot where the clamp trapped the testicle sac, he hooked the weight around the thong near the scrotum. He released the weight and allowed it to hang. Eddie moaned.

He selected a matching pair of half-pound weights, reached up and took an additional half-turn on the wheel of each nipple clamp. The flow of blood quickened as Eddie tried to twist away. The Sentry waited until Eddie settled again before hanging a weight on each clamp. Eddie fought his restraints for a long time before finally realizing that he was exacerbating his own pain; the more he moved, the more the weights jiggled and bounced. He forced himself to remain still, sucking air in desperate, shallow breaths.

The Sentry tried hard to be impassive as Eddie fought to come to grips with what was happening to him. But it seemed so comical. With each convulsive jerk, a crooked smile lined the man's sallow face. The term "St. Vitas Dance" kept intruding on his thoughts, and although he had never actually seen anyone go through it, he imagined Eddie's contortions to be a good approximation. He covered his mouth to suppress a giggle. Damn, he was feeling silly.

He'd already learned everything the young man knew. The two disciples who'd brought Eddie to him forced him to strip and kneel. They'd tied his hands behind his back, bent him over, head locked between the knees of one, while the other whipped his ass with a particularly wiry riding crop. Eddie had begged and pleaded and cried in great heaving sobs and related every moment of his experience with the fire marshals. The Sentry was infuriated that Eddie had told them anything at all. And why in hell had he returned to the fire scene against his explicit instructions? Once Eddie confessed his disobedience, his fate was sealed. But not before he had some fun. And not before the boy learned why.

His attention returned to the dangling boy and his mood changed. He felt a sudden icy stillness grip him and he thought, Now, my boy, it is time to get serious.

The flickering candle's elongated flame danced happily, as if mocking the silence of the room. The Sentry lifted it by its base and paused, his hand suspended over the table when the light captured the business card lying there. He picked it up, turned it to the light, and saw the gold shield beside the words "Matthew P. Kincaid, Fire Marshal, Bureau of Fire Investigation, NYFD." He gave the card a long, hard look before putting it back near the candle. He brought the taper in front of him. The walls became an eerie shadow-show as the candle's light shifted and flickered, casting a giant silhouette of the captive on the dark wall. The light pranced gingerly off the Sentry's sharply angled features while he waited for the flame to settle into stillness once more.

He sat on the metal folding chair, eyes level with the bound and swollen penis, and took a firm hold of the young man's shaft. He lifted it, exposing the underside and the stretched scrotum beneath, and looked up at Eddie's masked face with the dreamy look of a man on the edge of orgasm. He spoke in a husky, hoarse whisper as the candle's flame moved between the smoothly muscled legs, to a spot just below the hanging sac.

"Eddie?" he said, his voice a cajoling, warm caress. The young man cocked his head toward the voice. "Eddie. It is time you felt the fires of hell."

6

Chief Fire Marshal Carmine Cattalli had been returning from a meeting at the Brooklyn base when the radio interchange between SFM Berry and Matt Kincaid took place. Having worked with both men at one time or another, he recognized their voices. He thought Matt, who was a marshal under him when he was still a supervisor, an excellent investigator, but knew he didn't suffer fools gladly. Sure, he could be a hothead at times. Cattalli actually smiled while shaking his head as Matt made his "fat ass" remark on the radio. But he heard the frustration and concern as well. Cattalli instructed his driver to pull over, call headquarters from a public phone, and find out the incident location. Then he told him to drive directly to Flushing Meadow Park. His driver, a former partner and friend of Matt's, knew how the chief felt about Matt, but went to work on him anyway during the drive.

"Berry is a fucking asshole, Chief. You know that. I worked with Kincaid for eight months; he never calls for help unless it's something important."

"I know, Harold. You can stop defending the man. I worked with him, too. I'd just like to know what's going on, that's all."

When their car pulled up during the interchange between Matt and his bosses in Flushing Meadow, Cattalli was surprised to see D'Aieuto among the group. He thought, The shithead has finally done something right. But as he got out of the car and heard D'Aieuto chewing Matt a new asshole, he got pissed. The son of a bitch finally gets off his ass and out of the base and the only thing he can do is ream a man out in public? Cattalli had an innate dislike for that sort of behavior. He was a former marine, and it went against all he had been taught about leadership. It was part of the reason why, despite how angry he'd been at D'Aieuto when Larry Peterson was killed and D'Aieuto had chosen to stay at home, he had cleared the room before reading him the riot act. Now here he was, publicly humiliating Kincaid. Well, maybe it was time to see how Howcum D'Aieuto liked it.

"Victor, I asked you a question. If you make me ask it again, it's going to piss me off."

The chief fire marshal's presence confirmed D'Aieuto's theory that you couldn't get into trouble if you never left the base. He was silently cursing Walter Berry for involving him. *Now* look at this fucking mess. No way was this going to work out for him. Cattalli hated his guts. He turned to Cattalli and cleared his throat.

"Walter and I were instructing this marshal on the proper use of the Bureau radio, Chief." He knew it sounded lame.

The CFM fixed both men with an icy stare. "What's your complaint?"

D'Aieuto pulled his shoulders back and glowered at Matt. "He used profanity and was insubordinate."

Cattalli turned to Matt. "That true, Kincaid?"

"I suppose it is, Chief. I'm willing to take the rap for that, but we don't have a lot of time for this right now. Would someone please allow me to tell them what's going on here?"

"Yes, Matt, I would *love* to know what's going on here."

Matt shook his head and huffed sarcastically. "Terrific." Fuck 'em all, he thought. "I'll give you the details later, but briefly, Williams and I are investigating the intentional burning of a homeless man. We thought there might be a connection between that and some sort of devil worship or cult thing." He waved toward the pool building. "John remembered a case he had in this building where a phrase, similar to one the victim used, was written on the walls. We thought it would be a good idea to see it." Cattalli's nod encouraged him to continue. "Anyway, we get here, enter the building, and find a young girl chained to the floor. We don't know how long she's been here, but she's been severely tortured. We called for Rescue, an ambulance, and a supervisor. I suppose you heard the response we got. I didn't want to put this over the air or we'd have every reporter and weirdo with an FD scanner down our throats. The girl is in very bad shape. No telling how long she's been held captive, but she's been raped anally and vaginally, burned with cigarettes, whipped, and God knows what else. She's suffering from shock and some loss of memory as well. We'd like to get her out of here, but instead I'm over here getting a lecture on radio procedures.'' Matt couldn't resist the jab.

The CFM spoke to his driver. ''Harold, get on the radio and tell Headquarters I want every man from each of the bases' SIUs to respond here, ASAP.'' He turned back to the other two men, venom in his voice as he said, ''I'll get to you two later,'' then faced Matt, his voice struggling for control. ''Matt, show me what you've got. Let's start with the girl,'' he said, taking off toward the ambulance. When Berry and D'Aieuto started to follow, he spoke over his shoulder without missing a step. ''You two half-wits stay right where you are. I'll tell you when to move.''

Matt fell into step with the CFM and half-whispered, ''I'm sorry about this, Chief. I guess I blew my cool.''

A faint smile crossed Cattalli's weathered face. ''You always were a tactless son of a bitch, Matt. I suppose that's why I like you.'' Matt felt a great sense of relief. He was safe. At least for now.

They were nearing the ambulance. ''Chief, this girl is pretty fucked up. I've never seen anything like it. She seems to trust me, and right now I'm faced with the dilemma of staying here and documenting the scene, or going with her and trying to find out what I can. I couldn't see any way out of calling the PD in on this, so I did. They should be here any minute. I know they're going to want to take the case away. It'll soon be a three-ring circus and this young girl is not up to that. I need some advice.''

''I'm still trying to digest what you've told me,'' Cattalli said. ''I want to see the girl and the building. Maybe then I'll have some ideas for you. In the meantime, unless you have some objection, I'd be willing to stay here and supervise the scene. I've called for the Special Investigation Units, and that should be more than enough manpower to accomplish whatever it is you'd like to do. You can use them any way you'd like. This is still your case. I'll take care of the PD.''

''Chief, this means a lot to me. I owe you.''

Cattalli stopped at the back of the ambulance. ''You don't owe me anything, Matt. Not for doing my job, or for allowing you to do yours. Now, let's talk to the girl.''

Matt placed his hand on Cattalli's arm, restraining him momentarily. ''In the short time I've had with her, I've only been able to get her name. She doesn't remember where she lives, or who her people are, but I think she will, eventually. It looks like it's on the tip of her tongue, but something's blocking it for now. Name's Ellen Levy. With you here, I can go to the hospital with her and try to get more information. That would help a great deal. I was feeling a little like I was abandoning her by staying here. John Williams knows everything that's happened up till now. He can stay and answer whatever questions you have until I get back.''

Matt stepped up into the ambulance, glancing at Nancy, the EMS paramedic, as she moved to make room for them. He sidestepped to the gurney, Cattalli behind him. The chief saw the girl reach out for Matt and noted the look of relief that crossed her battered face. Matt smiled, leaned down, and held both her hands. The hair on Cattalli's arms bristled in response to the purring, animal sound coming from her.

Carmine Cattalli had been in the Bureau twenty-five years and the fire department for thirty-three. Back when he started out, the Bureau had only forty fire marshals, almost all civilians. They had no police powers or guns, no partners, and used public transportation to get to fires. He'd seen burn victims, murder victims, and other dead bodies in every condition imaginable and was long past the point where he thought he could be surprised. But even Cattalli wasn't prepared for the image before him. A momentary wave of nausea brought the cocktail sauce of the shrimp he'd had for lunch to the back of his throat. He thought about his own teenage daughter as he took in the pathetic sight before him.

''Jesus, Matt.''

Matt shot the chief a cautionary look. He didn't want Ellen any more upset than she already was. He certainly didn't want to talk about her as if she wasn't there.

''Yeah, I know what you mean, Chief,'' he said in a hushed voice. ''We'll talk outside, okay?''

Cattalli looked up, realized his mistake, and nodded. He was stooped over in the low-roofed ambulance and took a seat on the gurney opposite Ellen's, next to Matt.

The girl stared over Matt's shoulder when he leaned closer to speak. ''Honey?'' No reaction. ''Ellen?'' Turning to indicate the chief, he continued, ''This is my boss. His name is Carmine. He's a nice man, Ellen, and he's going to help me help you.''

Cattalli reached to touch her hand but drew back when her eyes widened with fear. "Hi, Ellen. You don't have to be afraid anymore. No one is going to hurt you. Do you understand? No one is going to hurt you again. I give you my word. We're going to get you fixed up, and before you know it, you'll be back home."

Matt half-turned, staring at Cattalli. He had never imagined the guy even *had* a soft side to him. The chief was always businesslike, gruff, and quick, but the voice of the man talking now was soft April rain, soothing to the ears, the voice of a loving father. Well, will wonders never cease. . . .

7

Matt held Ellen's hand throughout the ride to the hospital. They'd decided that St. John's would be a more pleasant place for long-term care than one of the public hospitals. He felt better knowing he'd be there to ensure that she was properly tested and photographed in the emergency room. He wasn't anticipating any problems but was prepared to bully the doctors if necessary.

Nancy radioed ahead and asked that a rape trauma kit be available, and that a photographer be summoned to the emergency room. As an extra precaution, Matt arranged for the fire department photographer to meet them there as well. He wanted backup photos in case the hospital photographer screwed up. He hoped to get him in and out of the ER before he would be missed at Flushing Meadow.

Matt tried to speculate about what was happening behind the girl's glazed eyes, which stared vacantly at the roof of the ambulance. They were unreadable—remote, ominous, like dark clouds drifting low and heavy in the sky. He continued to talk softly to her as the ambulance hurried through the streets of Queens, but she had shut down, lost in the rocking movement of the vehicle. Matt supposed he was comforting himself more than her by repeating soothing words and phrases, by stroking her fragile hands, but he needed to do *something.*

The ride and her silence provided the opportunity to assess the morning's events. Damn, but I'm tired. When was the last time I saw a bed? Thirty, thirty-five hours ago? Yesterday morning? It feels like my brain's been shot full of Novocaine. So many factors to consider. And how did they tie into his original investigation? The burned man, the girl, the PD. The PD . . . Now, that was something to consider. The last thing the chief had said was that he would handle the police.

Matt knew how ridiculous it sounded, but this girl, this Ellen Levy, was possibly the luckiest person in New York. When viewed as a whole, the apparently unrelated events that had conspired to see her saved were quite amazing. Neither Matt nor John would ever understand how the slim lead that led them to Queens and the abandoned pool building in Flushing Meadow Park, would result in finding Ellen Levy.

The short ride ended abruptly, throwing him sideways. The driver put the ambulance in reverse, backed up, and stopped again. Matt heard the front doors open and slam closed, and a moment later the rear doors were flung wide. The glass and slate entrance to the emergency room glinted at them, bright and shiny in the early-afternoon light. The driver and Nancy rolled the gurney to the end of the ambulance and together lifted it out so its legs extended and locked. A blast of cold, antiseptic air greeted their entrance onto the ramp leading to the emergency room. Matt kept a firm grip on Ellen's hand as he hung his badge from his jacket pocket and walked beside the gurney to the treatment area.

A nurse wearing green surgical garb looked up, said something to the doctor she was assisting, and walked to them. She spoke to Nancy.

"This the girl the paramedics called about?" Alert, intelligent cat-eyes, pale green with minute yellow flecks, looked piercingly at him. Her skin was smooth and the color of new ivory. Her jet-black hair was cut stylishly short, moussed in a feathered look, and to Matt's eye, she was exotically beautiful. Eurasian, maybe Filipino, he thought. When Matt nodded, she took the clipboard from Nancy, scanned the information and leaned down to make her own appraisal. Finding no life-threatening wounds, she relaxed slightly. She straightened, saw his badge, and fixed him with an appraising look. "Are you the one who found her?" She had the slightest hint of an accent, difficult to place. Matt felt certain she'd come to the country at a very young age, unable to erase the last trace of her heritage. He found it pleasantly exotic.

"Yes. Me and my partner."

"What animals would do such a thing?" She pronounced it "animuls."

"We don't know yet. Among her various injuries, she's suffering from some memory loss."

"Well, I don't doubt it. This is not unusual in trauma of this sort." She returned her attention to Ellen, leaned closer, and gave a radiant smile.

"Ellen, my name is Dr. Gold."

Matt's eyebrows arched at that double piece of information. She was not only a doctor but an Oriental named "Gold."

"We're going to make sure that you get well very quickly. Here, I want you to take my hand." When she didn't move, Dr. Gold took Ellen's hand and placed it firmly in her own.

"Now, squeeze my hand for me. Don't be afraid. Squeeze it. Go ahead, you won't hurt me." When Ellen didn't respond, she spoke more firmly, managing somehow to remain gentle. "Ellen, honey, I want you to squeeze my hand. Go ahead, do it now."

It took a second for Ellen to react, but then her fingers tightened around the doctor's.

"That's wonderful, dear. Just wonderful. I can see you and I are going to be good friends." She removed her hand and looked at Nancy. "Please bring her into the first examination room over there." She pointed to a curtained area to her left. The two paramedics wheeled the gurney away and Matt started to follow. Dr. Gold had come around to his side and put her hand on Matt's arm. She spoke to Ellen. "I need to borrow your policeman for a while, Ellen. Is that okay? He'll be right here where you can see him." She reached down, patted Ellen's hand, and gently pried her fingers from Matt's. "He'll be okay. I promise to take good care of him for you."

Matt thought it extremely astute of the doctor to have discerned the relationship he'd established with Ellen. He liked what he saw more and more. The doctor was obviously someone who knew her business and people as well.

Matt became acutely aware of the nearness of Dr. Gold as they watched Ellen being wheeled away. He could smell the faint scent of her perfume. Opium, he guessed, his favorite. She was tall for a woman, especially an Oriental, her head reaching the bottom of his nose.

He said, "Just so you know, Doctor, I'm a fire marshal, not a cop."

She turned to him. Matt thought he saw mischief in her eyes. "And what exactly is a fire marshal?"

Matt checked her face for sarcasm or mockery, but found only genuine interest. Her gaze was open and frank and he was a little taken aback to feel himself drawn to her. Her look had none of the arrogant self-importance he'd come to find in far too many doctors.

"I suppose the simplest way to explain it would be to say I'm a detective for the fire department," he told her.

"Sounds very interesting. But how does a fire marshal come into play on a case like this?"

"He stumbles onto it. Pure accident. We were investigating something else when we discovered her. You read what the paramedic found in her examination. There's still a manacle on her leg that's embedded into her flesh. Above all, it's important that we do right by her. She needs to be treated first as a victim of a crime and second as a patient. I don't mean to sound cold, because I feel for this girl, but her injuries need to be documented if we're ever to prosecute whoever did this. I hope you understand."

Her voice was suddenly hard and brittle, but Matt had the distinct sense it had nothing to do with him. "I understand very much, Fire Marshal. I was called to handle this case because I work the rape trauma unit, *voluntarily*. My normal field is orthopedic surgery. But I assure you, I would like nothing better than to see the people who did this punished. You will have no trouble here, I promise you."

He didn't know how, but he'd touched a nerve. Over the years, he'd become accustomed to the frustrating indifference of doctors, masked by a so-called professional demeanor. He'd come to think of them as lawyers with scalpels, and her fervor caught him off-guard. There was something very personal and vehement in her attitude. The doctor obviously harbored a few demons of her own. He decided he could trust this singular woman.

"Okay, then. The only thing I've been able to get from her so far is her name and that she lives in a single-family house. I haven't had a chance to ask much more and I'm afraid to push her too quickly. Any help you can give me in this area would be appreciated. Also, there's a department photographer on his way."

Though Doctor Gold appeared to have softened just a little, overall she remained cool and formal. "We usually shoot these things with a Polaroid, but if you think it will be helpful to have your own photos, then I have no objections. Just so we can get this part over with as quickly as possible. Even in her condition, she is very much aware of what is happening to her. I'd like to subject her to as few indignities as possible."

"That's fine with me. God knows, she's suffered enough of them."

She called to a nearby nurse. "Mary, would you please help me?" To Matt: "Would you mind waiting out here, Fire Marshal?"

"Not at all."

She started to leave, then stopped. "By the way, do you have a name to go with the title?"

Matt returned her small smile. "Yeah, sure. Matt . . . Matt Kincaid."

"Okay, Matt Kincaid," she said playfully. "Mine's Tracy. See you in a bit."

He rolled Tracy Gold's name around in his mind as he watched her walk away. She had a very un–New York woman's walk, certainly like no doctor he had ever seen. In his more chauvinistic moments, Matt bemoaned the fact that women in New York had forgotten how to walk. They were always in such a damn hurry, they'd adopted a stooped-over trudge that had lost all of its sex appeal. But Dr. Gold, even while moving quickly, gave the impression that she was gliding, shapely hips moving like a pendulum. It surprised him to see high heels poking out beneath the wrinkled green cotton operating-room pants. Very un-doctorlike indeed.

▨ ▨ ▨

George Elias, the department photographer, walked into the emergency room looking puzzled. Matt walked over and spoke quietly to him, giving specific instructions.

"The doctor is examining her in that room. As soon as she's through, we'll get you in to take the shots."

"No problem." George fiddled with the settings of the large, battered, old-fashioned box-reflex camera the department photographers favored for the low light shooting they specialized in. Matt had always been impressed by the quality of the shots they were able to get in near-total darkness. George was making the adjustments he'd need to shoot in bright fluorescent light when Dr. Gold came out of the examination room. Her expression was grim and her walk had none of the sexy sway of moments before. Her manner was brusque and her eyes were cool, green emeralds, her voice, dry ice.

"Is this your photographer?" she asked, indicating George with a tilt of her head. Matt nodded and felt suddenly intimidated by this completely different woman. "Well, let's get this part over with so we can get her settled in." She turned to George, her voice raspy and hard. "Go on in. The nurse knows what has to be done. Get everything. . . .

Every inch of her.'' George bobbed his head once in his peculiar bird-like way and headed off to the examination room. Tracy Gold looked Matt boldly in the eye, her tone all the more chilling in its matter-of-factness.

"I would like very much to see the people who did this deed."

Matt didn't know how to respond, and so said nothing for a moment. Then he slowly nodded in agreement.

"So would I, Doc. . . . So would I."

8

After Matt finished at the hospital, he was heading out of the ER when he bumped into Nancy, who was just returning from a bogus cardiac arrest run. Many of the city's disabled poor used the pretense of an emergency to get a ride to the hospital. Nancy's last run had been one of those. She offered Matt a ride back to Flushing Meadow and he accepted. The mood inside the ambulance was subdued as they rocked gently from side to side on the ride back, Matt deeply engrossed in his own thoughts, contemplating his next moves, Nancy respectful of his silence. When they pulled up to the pool building, it was overrun with PD crime-scene trucks, Emergency Service Units, the FD Searchlight Unit, and swarms of detectives and fire marshals. Cattalli was still at the scene and to Matt's relief, the bulk of the work was done. He spent much of the time before leaving, filling in the chief on the events leading to the girl's discovery, including the interview of Victor Hildaldo and his mention of someone called the Sentry. Eddie Cannell particularly intrigued the chief and Matt gave him a rundown of that interview, along with a full description, as well as laying out his criminal record. They spent some time discussing possible courses of action and an hour after Matt's return to Flushing Meadow, the pool building was as he had found it a million years ago that morning.

It was almost four o'clock when they returned to the Manhattan base. Matt had a pounding headache. He checked his pigeonhole, grabbed several scrawled messages, and thumbed through them on his way to the tiny kitchen. He took three aspirin from a cabinet, poured a cup of black coffee, popped the aspirin into his mouth, and gulped the coffee. The scalding liquid hit his tongue like a soldering iron. He raced to the sink, spit the partially dissolved pills out, and, using his hands as a cup, sucked in mouthfuls of cold water. A series of angry

"Goddammits" followed the brief respite the water provided. The bitter taste of aspirin coated his mouth and throat, and his tongue felt like he'd licked broken glass. He took another three pills, this time with water, before moving to the squad room while testing his tongue with his teeth.

Neither he nor John had eaten since breakfast and there were two hours left on the nine-to-six tour. He knew the headache was part tension, part hunger. There was a message from Chief Cattalli marked as having come in only five minutes ago, requesting that he call him upon returning to the base. Another was from an insurance rep inquiring about a case Matt couldn't remember, and a third: "Jeremy called about the fire you had this morning. Said he'd call back at 1630." Below was a P.S.: "I asked, but he wouldn't give a last name. Said you'd know who it was. —Bobby M." The time on the message was 1500 hrs., three P.M., and it was 1600 now. It took a moment before he remembered who Jeremy might be. It had been a long day, a thousand thoughts were racing through his mind, and connections were coming hard. He worried the inside of his cheek with his teeth as he considered the possibility of whether this Jeremy might actually call back. He wondered how he'd gotten his number, and whether he was calling to confirm or deny Eddie Cannell's alibi.

He walked into the squad room, nodded at the two men typing reports, and took a seat at a desk in the corner. He picked up the phone, dialed the chief's number, quickly reconsidered, and hung up before it could ring. He needed to organize his thoughts before he spoke to Cattalli, but his headache was acting like a synapse short-circuit. He dialed again. It was answered on the first ring by a female voice announcing that he'd reached the chief fire marshal's office. He told her that Chief Cattalli was expecting his call and was asked to wait a moment. Then the gruff voice of Carmine Cattalli came on the line.

"How're ya doin', Matt?"

"Okay, Chief. I just got your message to call."

"Listen, Matt, I'd like you to come down here with Williams and give me a full briefing on what's goin' on with the case. Ya know, from beginning to end."

Matt didn't like it. And, he'd just given the chief a full briefing at the park. In more than twenty years with the department, he couldn't remember a time when anyone had been called downtown for something good. They sure as hell never brought you to Headquarters to give you a pat on the back. If the chief needed to talk to him in person, it was unlikely to be anything he was going to like.

"Uh, okay, Chief. When do you want to see me?"

"How about now, Matt? If it runs past 1800, we'll see you both get overtime." Cattalli's voice was casual.

Things were getting worse, fast. The chief had used "we" instead of "I," and with all the cuts in the fire department, no one was giving out overtime, not even the chief fire marshal. He could easily have asked them to flop another tour and work the next day without costing the city a dime. This was definitely a bad sign.

Trying hard to sound casual himself, he said, "Sure, Chief. Is this urgent? I'm expecting a phone call at 1630. Can it wait until after that?"

There was a pause on the other end. He heard the muffled deadness that came with a receiver being covered. Then Cattalli was back on the line. "That'll be fine, Matt. Get here when you can."

Matt didn't like this at all. The chief was being too damned accommodating. "Chief?"

"Yeah, Matt?"

"Should I be worried?"

Another pause, this one very short. "Just get down here as soon as you can, Matt. We'll discuss everything then."

Matt found himself holding a dead line and wasn't happy with his thoughts as he returned the phone to its cradle. "What now?" he breathed.

John Williams wasn't thrilled to learn that he'd be staying late, and neither was his wife when he called to break the news.

Instead of following his normal routine of typing his report before going home, Matt decided the time would be better spent going through his notes and making an outline of the facts, and their actions up to this point. He'd include whatever this "Jeremy" had to say, *if* he called. He'd love to have a dollar for everyone who said they were going to call and never did. But he couldn't ignore this one. It might be important and he was curious as hell to know how this guy had gotten his name and number.

The next half hour was spent organizing his notes, but his curiosity about who constituted the "we" that the chief had mentioned kept interrupting his train of thought. He wished he had some idea of what he was walking into. Everything had seemed fine when he saw Cattalli after returning to the park from the hospital. Whatever had happened or changed occurred after the chief got back to Headquarters. He forced himself not to speculate, to keep his mind on what had to be done, especially the upcoming conversation with Jeremy. He looked at his watch. Four thirty-three. He wondered how much longer he should wait. Cattalli was waiting for him, and if the call never came, it would be something else he'd have to explain. He'd decided to give Jeremy ten more minutes when the phone man yelled that he had a call on line ten.

"Manhattan Base. Fire Marshal Kincaid speaking."

A male, sounding distant or, Matt thought, speaking through a cloth held over the mouthpiece, spoke without preamble.

"This is the person you know as 'Jeremy.' Not my real name, of course. I understand you'd like to talk to me." The voice was refined, but Matt thought he detected the remnants of a New York accent in it.

He covered the mouthpiece and snapped his fingers at John, who looked up from the opposite desk. He motioned for him to pick up his phone. Matt spoke as John lifted the receiver.

"That's right, Jeremy. What *is* your real name?"

"Please don't be cute. And you can tell whoever just picked up the other line that I don't mind. I won't be talking long."

"Nobody is listening in."

The voice was cold, sardonic. "Look, let's keep the bullshit to a minimum, my friend. I've got some things to say and not a lot of time to say them."

John lifted his eyebrows and shrugged his shoulders.

"Okay, Jeremy. What is it you'd like to say?" Matt asked.

"That's good, Matt. Right to the point. You don't mind if I call you Matt, do you?"

"Not at all, Jeremy. You don't mind if I call you Jeremy, do you?"

A small chuckle, then, "Well, here's the deal. I had nothing to do with that unfortunate old fellow getting burned. Eddie did it by himself. I wasn't even there."

"How'd you get my name and number, Jeremy?" Matt drew out and accented the name.

"Well, Eddie and I just had a long, fruitful talk. Told me everything he said he told you. Lied to you about almost everything, of course. All nonsense.''

"Oh, really. Where's Eddie now?''

A long pause was followed by something that Matt would have sworn was a bark. "Oh, you'll know soon enough. By the way, aren't you handling the case out at Flushing Meadow Park as well?''

Matt felt an electric sensation of alarm. This was bizarre. What could this guy know about Flushing Meadow? His heart palpitated as he looked across the desk to see the shocked look on John Williams's face.

"What the fuck do you know about it?" Matt asked. "Is the old man connected to that?''

The voice was calm, sardonic. "Everything in this world is connected to everything else, Matt. Life is all *very* cosmic.'' He uttered another short, barklike sound.

"How do you know about Flushing Meadow?''

"I know a great deal about a great many things, Matt. But that's not the point of this call. I called to tell you that, one, I didn't have anything to do with the old man. And B''—he allowed Matt a moment to get the old joke, then his voice took on a nasty edge—"you're dealing with a force you can't possibly understand. The message is, 'Back off.' ''

Matt felt his face get hot. He didn't know what this guy's angle was, but he didn't like threats.

"Hey, Jeremy, or whatever your name is, go fuck yourself. If you think I won't find you, you'd better think again. I love overconfident assholes like you. I'm gonna have you for breakfast *real soon,* shithead.''

"Ha! I like that, Matt. Shows gumption. Not much in the way of brains, but gumption. Maybe you'd better listen to me before you start making threats and spouting a lot of macho crap. You get yourself too involved in this and you'd better learn to see out the back of your head. You don't scare *me.* You aren't capable of it. Maybe you should take another ride out to the park and look in the pool building again before you try and threaten *me.*''

"Yeah, and what would that accomplish?''

"Just take the ride, Matt. I've got to go now. Maybe we'll talk again—after you've gone to the pool.''

"Who the fuck are you?''

"I thought a smart man like yourself would know that. Why, I'm your worst nightmare, Matt." He paused, very much aware of the effect his words would have. "I'm 'the Sentry.' " And then the barking sound again. Christ, he thought, it was the guy's *laugh*.

The line went dead. Matt sat with the phone to his ear staring at John in stunned silence. It was like looking in a mirror. They hung up and sat speechless, wondering what the hell they'd stumbled upon. Matt spoke first.

"I'd better call the chief. I don't think we should go to headquarters before going back to the pool."

John's expression told him there were a million things he'd rather do besides go back to that building, but he nodded and Matt dialed Cattalli's number. The secretary put him right through.

"Chief, I just got that call I told you about. This is even weirder than I imagined. The guy who called established a definite connection between the homeless guy and the girl at the park. He said that if we went back to Flushing Meadow we'd find something. And get this, he identified himself as 'the Sentry.' John and I think we should go back to the park before we see you."

There was a short silence on the other end. "There's no need to, Matt. Just before your last call, Queens Base caught a job at the pool building in the park. There was a burned body in the exact spot we found the girl—a young male. There were clothes piled next to the body. By the description you gave me of the kid you spoke to yesterday, I think it's him. There was also a note near the body. It said, 'Back off.' " Another pause. "It was addressed to you. That's one of the reasons I wanted to see you. Come on down here now, Matt. We need to talk."

Matt noted that the chief had said "one of the reasons." He wondered what the others were. How much crazier could this get?

9

Matt swung the car into the parking lot adjoining fire department headquarters. During business hours, all the spots went to the chiefs and bureau heads permanently assigned there, and at best, the lot accommodated only a few dozen cars. But because it was after regular hours and the lot was almost empty, the old security guard barely lifted his head as he waved John and Matt in.

At about the time the police department moved into brand-new headquarters at One Police Plaza, the fire department was forced to move from its convenient location at 110 Church Street in lower Manhattan to an old converted warehouse in the slums of downtown Brooklyn. One-ten Church Street had been close to City Hall and public transportation, and had its own parking lot. Two-fifty Livingston Street was hard to get to and impossible to park near. A trip to "250," as it was called, often wound up with the visitor explaining why his official vehicle had been towed away for illegal parking. It was ludicrous. There was no place to park within a mile of headquarters, yet the bosses felt obliged to put on the indignant act when a car was towed by the city's infamous "brownies."

Everyone knew the move to Brooklyn was politically motivated. The landlord was either a big contributer or a relative of a decision-maker. There could be no other logical explanation. But no one would dare try to prove it. Like everything else happening to the fire department these days, it was rammed down their throats without consultation. It was a dreary, unattractive building in a dreary, unattractive neighborhood, and was hated by everyone but the landlord who'd managed to pull it off. The hapless fire department was forced to make do.

They showed their badges, signed the log, got a peel-off lapel pass from the security guard, and walked past the station of the miniature lobby to the bank of two elevators. Both Matt and John resented the whole process of having to sign in and get a pass to enter their own headquarters. It was a recent change. The fire department used to be friendlier, more personal.

One of the elevators was out of service and an interminable time passed before the working one arrived. They got in, pressed eight, and were silent during the slow ascent. There was no one in the reception area of the chief fire marshal's office and the inner office door was shut. Matt tapped lightly on the frosted glass. The chief's voice came through clearly. "Come in."

Matt opened the door and stepped in, John just behind. The two men sitting opposite the chief turned to face the new arrivals. Matt closed the door, said "Hello, Chief," and nodded to the two strangers.

"Matt. John. These men are from the PD. This is Detective Sergeant Greg Townsend"—Cattalli indicated the younger of the two men—"and this is Captain Charles McDonnell. They're from the Office of Special Operations, working for the chief of detectives." Matt looked both men over carefully, sizing them up. It was clear that they were doing the same to him and John. Like rival dogs sniffing at each other, he thought.

Sergeant Townsend was about forty years old, with medium-length, wavy brown hair, parted casually on the side, and his expression was open and friendly. Although he was clean shaven, he had the kind of heavy growth that made him appear to always have a five o'clock shadow. His light brown eyes were alert and signaled intelligence. Physically, he was pretty much the picture of the all-American boy, and he wore the standard uniform of a NYC police detective—gray suit, white shirt, and black, Italian-style shoes—which gave away little in the way of personal taste. Matt was surprised to note that the shoes were scuffed and needed a shine. Townsend's only concession to fashion was a floral print tie, not unlike the one Matt was wearing, only much more subdued. He figured him for a working guy.

Captain McDonnell was wearing a perfectly tailored, charcoal-gray, three-piece pinstripe suit, powder-blue shirt with white contrasting collar, gold collar pin, and a silk paisley tie. The tie was knotted in an elegantly long knot and dimple that Matt had seen only in store windows and clothing catalogs but was never able to duplicate himself. It sat perfectly spaced in the collar and matched a handkerchief, lying flat above the breast pocket, three exactly spaced points looking like they had been pressed while in the suit. A gold and diamond tie-pin was spaced midway between the third and fourth buttons of his shirt. His conservative shoes held a luster to rival patent leather. McDonnell's face had a pink, freshly scrubbed look; his nails were glossy and manicured. A politician if ever I saw one, Matt thought.

They exchanged handshakes. The sergeant rose and offered a firm, dry hand and a small smile, while the captain remained seated, pointedly not offering a handshake and looking at Matt and John with studied indifference.

The only thing Matt Kincaid knew about the PD's Office of Special Operations was that he didn't know much. He'd only become aware of its existence recently, and from what he could gather, it was a highly secretive unit working outside One Police Plaza, away from prying eyes and ears. No one knew exactly what these guys' specialty was, if they had one, but it appeared that they were able to pick and choose from among any of the cases carried by any agency in the city. What criteria was used to decide what fell within their purview was unknown, but it was apparent they had clearance from the highest level, and that meant the mayor. The question now was "What are they doing *here*?" Although their case was certainly getting weirder all the time, it hardly seemed world-shaking in its implications.

Matt distrusted "special units," regardless of their organization or department. He'd spent a year working in the fire department's Manhattan Special Investigations Unit, the borough's major case squad, and found it staffed for the most part by men whose primary qualification was that they were politically well-connected. "Weight" in city service was known as having a "hook" or a "rabbi." One guy carried so much weight he'd only investigated one case in five years. He was very active in the Catholic Church, and the inside joke was that his "rabbi" was the Cardinal of New York, thereafter referred to by the men as "His Eminence, Rabbi O'Flannigan." Another man had been the then–Manhattan Borough Commander's partner in the old days, and now spent his days on duty giving racquetball lessons in a midtown gym, showing up at work only every other week, on paydays. There were some good guys and some excellent investigators in the unit as well, but enough bullshit went down that Matt had decided it was not for him.

So he'd left the unit to go back to working the streets, to the late hours, weekends, and holidays spent investigating shitty, run-of-the-mill fires that wore you down and burned you out. He'd done the proverbial cutting off of his nose to spite his face. After twenty years, he was still unable to believe that merit and civil service were natural enemies.

At Cattalli's request, they wheeled chairs in from the outer office and positioned them so they could face both him and the detectives.

Cattalli waited until they were seated before he spoke. ''I'm sure you're wondering why these men are here.'' He gestured toward the detectives. ''Well, you'll understand in a moment, but first, I'd like to hear a complete rundown of what you've got to this point, including the phone call you were telling me about.''

Matt took out his notebook, flipped to the last group of pages, and began giving them a comprehensive review of the case. He included everything but Jeremy's threat. John Williams noted the omission but said nothing. When he finished, he placed the notebook on his lap and focused his attention on the men across from him.

''So, how do two, high-powered guys like you figure into a case that, unless I'm missing something, seems a bit beneath your special talents?'' It came out more sarcastic than he intended.

Captain McDonnell almost sprang from his seat. ''Listen to me, Fire Marshal. The fact of the matter is, we have jurisdiction over any case we want. Nothing has to be explained to you. Your job, plain and simple, is to do what you're told.'' McDonnell punctuated his words with an index finger stabbing at Matt. His sharp, grating voice quivered with indignation. Matt thought the guy must be taking drama classes. Even with him seated, it was easy to see that the captain was an exceptionally short man. He suspected it might be the reason he had checked the impulse to stand. Although Matt remained deadpan during the short tirade, inside his hackles were rising. He spoke quietly through loosely clenched teeth.

''Captain, I've had a bad couple of days and, with all due respect, you are *not*—I repeat, *not*—my boss. If you ever use that tone with me again, you can expect to hear me tell you to go fuck yourself. Your muscle don't mean shit to me, and if you *can* hurt me, then give it your best fucking shot and let's cut this bullshit. I don't have the time or the patience for it.''

Cattalli was pissed. ''Matt! Don't say another goddamn word. You will apologize this instant.''

Matt looked into the chief's angry eyes, framed a quick response, and swallowed it. He looked past the chief to a plaque on the wall behind him. It showed a hog at a trough and said in bold letters, NEVER TRY TO TEACH A PIG TO SING. IT WASTES YOUR TIME AND ANNOYS THE PIG. He considered its appropriateness and forced himself to gain control while cursing his temper.

He took a couple of shallow breaths, turned to the captain, and forced a civil, if insincere, ''Sorry 'bout that, Cap.''

The captain was sputtering. ''That's not good enough. Not nearly good enough.''

Matt eyed him coldly, shrugged, and looked at the chief with an expression that said, I tried. What else can I do?

Detective Sergeant Townsend interrupted, palms up in a conciliatory gesture, his voice soothing. ''Hold on, now. Just hold on. . . . Everybody calm down. This isn't going to get us anywhere.'' He turned to the captain. ''Cap, I'm sure the marshal didn't mean what he said. He apologized and I don't think it will happen again. There's a lot of tension on all of us right now and there's no point in taking it out on each other.'' McDonnell was still obviously pissed off, but clamped his jaws shut and said nothing, focusing on a photograph of a raging fifth alarm hanging on the wall. Matt hated men who pouted.

Townsend faced him. ''Matt, I'm sorry, but you're taking the wrong approach here . . . jumping the gun. No one is here to hurt you or even to steal your case. That's not the way we operate. We're here to offer what assistance we can, not to take over. We have resources and manpower you could only dream of, and we're here to make them available to you. Our intention is to enhance your capabilities, not detract from them. Our unit does not make arrests. We leave that to whichever agency catches the case or the detective working on it. We have been set up specifically for situations like this, when it becomes obvious that local manpower and resources will not be enough. With that said, can we start over?''

Townsend exuded a sincerity lacking in his boss. Matt guessed he was the genuine article and decided to give him a chance. But he still didn't know why they were there and felt it was time he learned.

"Okay, Greg. That's fine with me. But what 'situation' is it we're talking about? As far as I know, nothing in this case warrants the attention of a unit such as yours. I must have missed something."

McDonnell was still staring at the photograph on the wall, so Townsend looked to Cattalli. The chief nodded for him to continue.

"Shortly before two P.M. this afternoon, the mayor's office received a threat. It was delivered by messenger." He reached for a folder lying on the edge of the chief's desk, opened it, and took out a flat, clear plastic Baggie containing a sheet of paper. He handed the Baggie to Matt. "It's already been checked for prints. There were none. We're trying to locate the messenger now."

Matt took the Baggie and examined the note. It was written with letters cut from newspapers and magazines pasted on and juxtaposed at odd angles. He almost laughed. This stuff only happened in the movies. It stopped being funny the moment he began to read:

MY DEAR MR. MAYOR,

TAKE FIRE MARSHAL KINCAID OFF THE CASE OR THERE WILL BE A MAJOR HOLOCAUST. YOU AND YOURS WILL SUFFER THE FIRES OF HELL. OBEY ME OR DIE. YOU CANNOT ESCAPE ME.

THE SENTRY

Matt finished, raised his head, and handed the note to John. Townsend met his baffled look with one of concern. "It seems you've really ruffled this guy's feathers, Matt. It's pretty obvious that he doesn't like you very much. Because, I'll tell you something. . . . It really isn't all *that* unusual for the mayor of New York City to receive an occasional threat. But here's the thing. . . . They have never, in anyone's memory, singled out a specific law enforcement officer. Is there anything you haven't told us that might explain this personal kind of message?" Townsend's tone was quietly probing. Matt guessed he was very good at his job.

He took the note back and read the threat a second and third time before responding, hoping to find some deeper meaning in it. He couldn't understand why this person, this "Sentry," whoever he was, was choosing to escalate what had begun as a routine investigation into something so large, so out of proportion. It didn't make any sense. And why *had* it become so goddamn personal? He didn't have a clue as to who the man was and, as far as he knew, had done nothing to bring about this kind of response.

He looked up. "No, I can't think of any reason. Hell, we've hardly begun and we have nothing so far. The only thing I can figure is, something we've touched upon is scaring this guy. Something that can reveal who he is. Only we don't know what yet." He had a chilling thought. "Unless it's the girl. Maybe she can identify him and he's scared. Maybe he's going to try to get to her." Panic crawled into the edge of his thoughts. He turned to the chief. "We've got to get a guard on her room."

The chief answered. "The captain has already taken care of that. There are two men assigned to her right now."

Matt exhaled. "That's good. I'm relieved." He turned to McDonnell. "I'm grateful, Captain." McDonnell barely acknowledged him. Matt addressed Cattalli and Townsend. "But this guy is no dope. He's well spoken and seems to know the system. He can't possibly believe his threats will do anything but intensify our efforts. He must also know we can't back down, stop investigating. What's on his mind? It doesn't figure."

Townsend was looking intently at Matt. "Maybe that's the point. Suppose he's *already* decided to do something and this is a way to set us up, so when it happens, whatever 'it' is, he can claim we were warned and brought it on ourselves. Because I'll tell you something, Matt, it sure as hell feels to me like he's already made up his mind to do something."

John Williams looked at the chief, his booming voice filling the small room as he asked, "Can you fill us in on what the guys from Queens found in the pool building? I got the feeling when Matt was talking to this prick on the phone that the whole connection starts there, not with the homeless guy. For some reason, even though he has no qualms about taking responsibility for everything else, he wanted us to believe he had nothing to do with that old man. Made a point of starting the conversation that way. Makes me wonder why this asshole, who doesn't seem to give a shit if we know about the girl, or Eddie Cannell, cares about whether we blame him for burning some 'nobody.' I find that pretty damn curious.''

''That's a good point, John.'' Cattalli moved a yellow legal pad in front of him. He summarized as he read, ''Marv Goodman and Spencer Johnson responded to the pool building when the local engine company was called to investigate an 'odor of smoke.' Upon arrival, they found a body smoldering in the building. They transmitted a 10-45 code 1 and a 10-41 code 1, asking for an immediate FM response. When Marv arrived and saw what they had, he remembered the earlier radio traffic concerning Flushing Meadow Park. He called in to see if there might be a connection. The four-to-two supervisor, Miguel Garcia, called me. I asked him to secure the scene. In fact, they're still there.

''Anyway, they found the body of a young male, burned to a crisp. They think it was done postmortem, but it'll take an autopsy to be sure. Next to the body, neatly folded, were what they believe to be his personal effects. No wallet or ID, but clothing. Specifically, a motorcycle-type black leather jacket, with a skull painted on the back, and two buttons on the lapels.'' He used his finger to trace a line on his notes. ''One said, 'Eat. Fuck. Kill,' the other, 'The Meek Shall Inherit Shit.' '' He looked at Matt. ''I remembered what you said about the kid and told them to do what they could, but not to leave the scene or disturb the body. About fifteen minutes after my conversation with Garcia, Captain McDonnell called and told me about the threat to the mayor. We agreed that we should meet and try to put all these pieces together.''

Cattalli looked meaningfully at Matt. ''By the way, I had all the bases check their records for the past year. Turns out there have been at least eleven other cases of homeless people being set on fire, citywide. There may be more, but so far, that's what they've been able to come up with.''

Captain McDonnell broke his silence. His attitude was civil but cold as he faced Matt squarely and said, ''Quite frankly, Fire Marshal, I was all for taking this case away from you *and* the fire department. But Greg and the chief convinced me that since this 'Sentry' person apparently has a personal thing going with you, you are our main link. Whether I like it or not, you have become *the* central figure in this case. You are 'in' because *he* wants you in. I don't know why. The chief does not know why. The mayor would like to know why. And it's become apparent that *you* do not know why. So the question remains . . . why? Because I'll tell you, Kincaid, it's hard for me to believe that you didn't piss this guy off in a very personal way. Are you sure there isn't something you're not sharing with us?''

Matt ignored the accusatory tone. ''I honestly can't say. It's as much a mystery to me as it is to you. I've told you everything that's happened to this point, and frankly, no one is more puzzled by this 'personal thing' than me. Until an hour and a half ago, I never spoke to the guy. Hell, I wasn't even sure he existed. He was just a couple of words from the mouth of a pathetic old man living on the streets for the last twenty years. We had no reason, until a little while ago, to think there was a connection between the homeless guy and the girl. *He* made the connection for us. John and I certainly never expected this case to escalate like this. It started out fairly straightforward and each twist has been more of a surprise than the last.''

He turned his attention back to the chief. ''But John has a good point. It probably starts with the girl. Finding her set something off in this guy. We don't know why yet, but she'll need to be interviewed again. Maybe she can give him to us if we can get her to remember anything. I spent more than two hours with her at the hospital and she couldn't remember any more than she did when we first found her. The doctor handling her case thinks she *will* remember with time, but it's likely we're not going to have the luxury of that information any time soon.''

Townsend interjected, ''We think we've located her parents. A team of detectives are on the way to the hospital with them now. If the girl is who we think she is, then she's been missing for almost two years. That would make her twelve and a half now. We pulled the reports on the case. According to them, Ellen Levy was last seen in Kings Plaza shopping center in Brooklyn. The mother claimed she turned to look at a dress in a store window and when she turned back, the kid was gone. Says she went crazy looking for her. Finally called the cops when she and the security guards failed to find her.''

Matt was stunned. ''Are you tellin' me that little girl has been going through this for *two years*? No way could she have stood that shit for so long. *No fuckin' way.* How long had she been in that building?'' A jumble of conflicting information raced through his brain. ''Something is very wrong. But if she's been held by this guy for two years, she might be in a lot more danger than we realize. She *must* be able to ID him. Maybe he's come to think of her as his property. Maybe *that's* why everything is so personal with him.''

Matt rushed on, unsure whether he was making any sense. ''It's clear the guy fears nothing, except maybe our finding out who he is. After all this time, maybe he figures no matter how careful he's been, she could somehow lead us to him. He's trying his best to taunt me for reasons only he knows, and has no qualms about threatening the mayor. He believes he can get to whoever he wants, whenever he wants. Why?''

No one offered an answer and Matt continued. ''Unless I miss my guess, we're being manipulated to act in a manner that he can predict. Like a chess game. I think he knew what our reactions to his little love note would be, including our putting guards on the girl. He hasn't given us any other way to go. Maybe he *wanted* us to put people on the girl, either to prove that he can get to her anyway, or because he *wants* her protected.''

Cattalli interrupted. ''Matt, that doesn't make sense. Why would he want to make it more difficult on himself?''

''I'm not sure, Chief. Maybe it's because, so long as we're doing what *he* wants, we're not able to do what *we* want. We really haven't had time to pursue other avenues. Despite his claim that Cannell didn't give us any correct information, suppose he did? Or suppose Eddie was too afraid to tell him what he *really* told us about where this guy lives—I think Cannell was actually stupid enough to use 'Jeremy,' a.k.a. the Sentry, as an alibi. Maybe there really *is* such a building and this Jeremy character actually lives there. And considering his other crimes, why the big deal about whether he burned the homeless guy? These things have to be checked out but we haven't had a spare minute.''

Greg Townsend answered. ''That's where our unit comes in, Matt. We *have* the manpower to do these things, no matter what he does. We have the people to follow up leads while you stay on top of this guy.'' He leaned forward, his expression earnest. ''As far as the girl is concerned, I don't believe he intends to try and get to her after alerting us like he has. He must have some other motive.'' Townsend sat back again. ''Yet, I also believe the girl is the key. I don't know why or how, but she is an integral part of what is happening.

We've got to get more from her." He paused briefly. "I understand
you've been able to establish a relationship of sorts. You'll have to
speak to her again. Stay at the hospital for a while if necessary. It's
our only real chance right now." He turned to Cattalli. "Chief? . . .
Chief?"

The chief, deep in thought, was flustered by the sudden attention.
"Oh, right." He gathered himself and looked at Matt and John. "Until
further notice, you two will be working straight days. I'm authorizing
whatever overtime you need to get the job done. Starting tomorrow,
you'll be attached to Captain McDonnell's unit and will take your direction from him. Sergeant Townsend will be your immediate supervisor." Cattalli held up a hand to check any protest. "I will still expect
daily briefings by phone, Kincaid. But the fact is, we need to recognize
that we're out of our league on this one and the PD is better equipped
to deal with it. It would be foolhardy to think that, with no experience
in this area, we could hope to do a decent job. Besides, the mayor wants
them to have it." The mayor's interest finalized the issue as far as the
chief was concerned.

Cattalli looked around the room to see if everyone understood, then
concluded, "If you don't mind, I'd like to talk with Fire Marshal Kincaid privately for a moment. You can give the details of where and
when you'd like my men to report to Fire Marshal Williams in the
outer office."

Matt remained seated while Townsend and McDonnell shook
hands with Cattalli and moved to the door. McDonnell exchanged
glances with Matt. His look reminded Matt of the story of the spider and the fly. He wasn't looking forward to entering the captain's
parlor.

The chief watched the men file out and waited for the door to
close. He kept his voice down but there was no mistaking the anger
in it.

"Matt, what the fuck is wrong with you? Are you intentionally
trying to fuck over your career?" He was exasperated, shaking his head
vigorously. "I mean, where do you come off embarrassing me like
that?"

"I'm sorry if I embarrassed you, Chief. It wasn't my intention. It's
just that the guy came off as such a pompous ass."

Cattalli's voice got harder. Matt saw the muscle on the side of his jaw twitch. "Don't give me that shit, Matt. He still outranks you and he was a guest in my office. You had no right to speak to him that way. I don't want to make a career out of bailing you out because you can't keep your mouth shut. I don't see you for months, and in one day you've managed to make enemies of a supervisor at your base, your borough commander, a police captain with direct links to the mayor, and, I might add, you're not doing so well with me. I want to know what gives with you."

Matt couldn't look the chief in the eye. He focused on his folded hands. The chief was right, of course. He was definitely fucking up.

"I'm sorry, Carmine." They went back a long time and Matt knew it was okay to use his first name in private. "I know you stood by me during some difficult times. I never thanked you for being there for me after Larry got shot." He still couldn't say the word *killed.* "I don't mean to be ungrateful, and I wish I could tell you why I do what I do, but honest to God"—he raised his head and met the chief's probing look—"I don't know myself. I want so badly to redeem myself, to put Larry's death behind me, but every time I turn around, I keep expecting him to be there." He stared at the corner of the desk. "I guess I lost it after Larry . . . went a little crazy. Jenny did her best, hung in there as long as she could, but even *she* couldn't cope with it anymore. I don't blame her for leaving. She tried longer than I might have under the same circumstances." He paused momentarily and Cattalli let the silence hang. Their eyes met. "Hell, Chief, I sound like some soap opera. I always hated people who felt sorry for themselves. I sure never wanted to become one of them."

Matt squirmed under Cattalli's steady gaze, but his eyes remained locked on the chief's. A long moment passed before Cattalli breathed a heavy sigh and spoke, his pace deliberate, resigned.

"You know, Matt, you're not the first guy to lose a partner. I've been knocking around a long time and I've seen it lots of times. Most men react in one of two ways. They either dwell on it so long they become useless, unable to make a move—afraid that if they act, it'll come out wrong and someone will get hurt or die—or they imagine a bullet coming at them from every perp they meet." He pointed a finger at Matt. "And that, my friend, is a prescription for disaster, failure, and possibly another death." Cattalli looked over Matt's shoulder to a spot on the far wall. "The other side of the coin is the macho asshole who refuses to be careful, he may be more dangerous than the guy who's scared. Fear is a wonderful monitor and, without it, a man becomes reckless, stupid. He starts to believe he's invincible. Well, you and I know better than that, don't we, Matt?" Cattalli picked up a pencil and seemed preoccupied with rolling it around in his fingers. "But there is a third way to react to what happened to Larry. Not many men are able to come back and be whole again, but I've seen a partner's death bring out the best in a man. I've seen men dedicate themselves to the memory of a fallen partner and use it as a springboard to do the best work of their lives. I always thought if something like that ever happened to me, that's how I'd want to react." He raised his head and looked deeply into Matt's eyes. "Because the truth is, 'the truth' has nothing to do with anything. By that I mean, even if there wasn't a cloud over the actions the two of you took that day, you would still be suspect in a lot of minds. This job has always been that way."

Cattalli's expression became melancholy, his voice lost its edge. "I remember when I was still a firefighter, I used to wonder why every time someone got badly hurt or killed, there were always other men who felt it could have been avoided. Like fire was some totally predictable force men could manipulate, and ceiling beams didn't just suddenly give way, and floors didn't unexpectedly collapse. Like accidents didn't ever just simply *happen*." He laid the pencil on the desk and leaned forward. "Then one day it struck me why that was." He raised his head, the sincerity evident in his face and voice. "It's because we're *scared*. Because we live with the constant possibility of death, we believe that if only we 'do the right thing,' we'll be safe. That's why, even if the job didn't affix blame, the men would. They'd do it so they can go out the next time, secure in the illusion that life can't be snatched away from them without warning . . . if they do the right thing, follow their training. The thought that death can be nothing more than a roll of the dice is terrible to them. So it always winds up as someone's fault, usually the deceased's, so the rest of us can go on without feeling afraid or guilty. But shit *does* just happen, no matter how good you are, how careful you are, how *anything* you are. Sometimes you run out of luck. Nobody's fault. You just simply run out of fucking luck.''

Cattalli pushed himself away from the desk, leaned back, and folded his hands on his belly. "I guess what I'm trying to say in my roundabout way is, I don't hold you to blame for what happened to Larry. . . . Never have and never will. Nobody with any street smarts does. So why do you?"

10

Matt looked up and was startled to find himself in the driveway of his home, with the broad, blue swath of the Hudson River, snaking its lazy way north to Albany, filling his vision. It was that sweet twilight time when a fading red sun reflected gently off the undulating surface, and the transfixed observer could be fooled into thinking he was seeing a river of glistening rubies. The lush foliage above the Jersey Palisades sported the first patchy changes of autumn, though it was still too early in the season for the breathtaking burst of color the area was famous for.

A disorienting sense of lost time, of how he'd gotten there or how long he'd been there, enveloped him. The magnificence of the scene was in stunning contrast to his dark, terrible thoughts, and he had to force himself to loosen his grip on the wheel.

The meeting with Cattalli had profoundly shaken him. He had just started back to work; almost a full year had passed since Larry's death. He didn't know if he could meet Cattalli's expectations. Anxiety and self-doubt gnawed implacably at the edge of his thoughts in sudden and unpredictable waves. And the past, like an uninvited guest, kept intruding and poking its nosy way into the present. . . .

※　　　※　　　※

Jenny Kincaid awoke to dazzling sunlight in her eyes. She brought a forearm up to shield them, rolled over on her side, and let out a lazy half-growl. She raised her arms and arched her back, snuggled further into the mattress, and indulged in the delicious feeling of a good morning stretch. It took her a moment to realize Matt wasn't in bed. The times had become few and far between when he was beside her when she awoke. A pang of guilt tugged momentarily at her for feeling so rested when she knew Matt had probably gotten no sleep at all, but it passed quickly as she yawned and stretched again, luxuriating in the warmth of the covers and the promise of the day.

The low murmur of the TV came to her from the living room. She cringed inwardly at the prospect of confronting another morning with a morose and taciturn Matt. The ten months since Larry Peterson's death had been a nightmare for both of them. But Matt was so self-absorbed, he was oblivious to the mounting damage exacted by his depression on Jenny and their marriage.

Nothing penetrated or alleviated his pain; Jenny's days and nights had become surreal. She hadn't known a human being could put himself through such suffering; she actually feared for his sanity. Their relationship was being eaten up in mean, vicious little bites and she felt helpless to stop it. Besides Matt's physical deterioration, he had become so depressed and dispirited that it was impossible to talk to him about the smallest things. They seldom made love; the man who slept beside her each night was becoming a stranger.

She padded to the kitchen after using the john, put a pot of coffee on, walked to the living room, and plopped down in her rocker. Matt ignored her "Good morning," and after a long, awkward silence, she took a stab at being cheerful. "Hey, babe, I have to go to the mall today. Why don't you give me a lift, and then we can catch some lunch at the Cockeyed Clam."

She was talking to the side of Matt's face as he sat watching a morning talk show. The host was laughing because the woman he was interviewing had written a book touting a diet that mainly involved eating huge quantities of grapefruit and sardines. Matt had taken to turning on the TV the moment he got up, watching a few minutes of a show and using the remote to flip incessantly through the forty or so channels the cable company supplied. At first she tried to sit with him, but the constant channel-surfing drove her crazy.

Stopping at the little pub on the riverfront in Nyack, the picturesque little town at the foot of the Tappan Zee Bridge on the Rockland County side of the Hudson, had once been almost a ritual during what Jenny had lately begun to think of as "the good old days." The little glow they'd get after a few cocktails would lead to an afternoon "nap" when they got home. That wasn't what was on Jenny's mind when she suggested it now. She just thought that getting Matt out of the house would do both of them some good.

Matt didn't respond. When she repeated her suggestion, he pressed the remote. The Weather Channel was giving the traveler forecast for around the world.

"Matt? I'm talking to you."

He hit the remote again.

Suddenly all the anger and frustration of the last ten months welled up inside her and burst out. She was so surprised by the depth of emotion she was feeling, she couldn't speak at first. A coldness gripped her heart and her hands became clammy. It was as if the remote in Matt's hand had flipped some switch inside *her*.

"Matt, I'm leaving you." Her voice was flat, unemotional.

His body visibly stiffened. He swiveled slowly around to face her. "What did you say?"

Her eyes and voice bore into him. "I said, 'I'm leaving you.'"

He looked befuddled. "Where're you going?"

"I don't know. It doesn't matter. I just know that I have to leave. I can't stay here and watch you kill yourself, and us. It's too much to ask of me."

"What are you talking about?"

"I'm talking about the fact that you've given up. That you've dug a grave for yourself and aren't content to just have me mourning—you expect me to jump in with you. I won't do that, Matt." She couldn't contain her frustration any longer. "Ever since Larry's death, you've refused to be consoled. You've wallowed in self-pity and self-hate for ten months now."

She stood and moved to the side of his chair, her wide brown eyes hard and her normally pleasant face a mask of anger. "Do you remember the story you told me about the prisoner of war you interviewed in connection with a case? Remember how he told you about how the North Vietnamese tortured him by tying his arms behind him and hanging the rope over a ceiling beam and pulling on the rope until his arms almost popped from their sockets? You were really affected by that story and I've heard you retell it a dozen times. You asked him how he survived such treatment, how he could live knowing that each day they were going to come for him, tie him up, and stretch his arms beyond the limits of human endurance. Do you remember what he said? You told me he looked at you for a very long time and then said, 'You learn to love the ropes.' '' She paused. ''Well, Matt, I think *you've* finally learned to love the ropes.''

Matt wearily closed his eyes. An involuntary shudder, a gigantic sigh, and he seemed to shrink before her eyes. Looking down at the floor, he whispered, ''Please don't leave me, Jenny.''

Much of the sharpness left her voice. ''I have to, Matt. I don't know what else to do. I don't want to go, but I can't stay and watch what you're doing to yourself. I'd rather live with the memories of what we had than watch it slowly turn to dust.''

Matt raised his head and looked pleadingly into her eyes. ''I'll die without you, Jenny.''

''Don't do that to me, Matt! It isn't fair. You're dying *with* me. I can't stay here because of guilt or pity. The old Matt wouldn't have wanted it. You've become someone I don't know anymore. I've hung on because I love you; I just kept hoping you'd come out of this . . . this,'' she groped for the words, ''monstrous thing you're doing to yourself.''

Jenny turned and looked outside, barely noticing the inexorable flow of the Hudson winding past their picture window. Her whole body had become rigid, her tone implacable. ''Don't ask me to stay here without hope. . . . Without any chance that you'll ever be yourself again. Without being able to believe that I'll have my life back. No more, Matt. No more. I just can't take any more.''

▨   ▨   ▨

The sun had set by the time he entered through the kitchen of the carefully restored old house. The town of Stony Point was rich in the history of the Revolutionary War, and many of the houses of that era had survived. Finding this early-nineteenth-century gem in the old section of town at an affordable price had been one of his and Jenny's triumphs. They'd had to fix it up bit by bit, modernize as money became available, but it had been a true labor of love. The house had a character and charm impossible to duplicate with modern construction. Jenny had wept when the sale almost fell through and it appeared they would not be able to live there. But Matt had been determined to see them in the house and had persevered through the bullshit the bank and the former owner put them through.

The house sat on the crest of a small hill overlooking the Hudson River. A front porch with tall wooden columns served as a perfect place for guests to sip their coffee or after-dinner drinks and admire the wide panorama of the Hudson Valley before them. Inside, ten-foot ceilings gave a sense of space and openness; fireplaces in the living room and master bedroom offered a warmth well beyond the mere heat of the flames. Matt and Jenny had installed a picture window that took up almost the entire northeast wall facing the river and porch so they could enjoy the view when it was too cold to sit outside. The breakfast counter faced a rear yard filled with flowering shrubs and three towering oaks that had been young trees at the birth of a nation and had matured and grown through the countless trials of the people who'd lived there before Matt and Jenny.

Matt groped for the wall switch, half-expecting Jenny to call out a greeting from another room. When his hopeful thoughts were met only with silence, he walked despondently through the house, turning on lights and opening windows, pretending he wasn't hoping that she was somehow there, about to walk out from another room. But his movements only served to underline the emptiness of the house.

The message light was blinking on the answering machine in the bedroom. He sat wearily on the edge of his bed, pressed the rewind button, and kicked off his shoes as the machine squawked. He knew there was a way to guage how many messages were on the tape, but had never been able to figure out how. He lit a cigarette and waited, hoping one of the messages was from Jenny. It was two months since she'd moved out and rented a small carriage house up in Rhinebeck, but Matt refused to accept the finality of a broken marriage. Hope and denial were all he had left.

The first two beeps preceded annoying lapses, background noise and the sound of someone breathing but no message. He knew many people refused to talk to a machine and he considered it unreasonable, until he remembered that before he bought one of his own, he used to leave the same annoying gap on other people's machines. Still, he wondered who had called.

The third beep was followed by a message from Jenny's college roommate reminding her that they hadn't seen each other for a while and asking Jenny to call so they could meet for lunch. The message drove home how short a time had lapsed since Jenny left, and how much he missed the more mundane parts of their life together, like the sound of her puttering in the kitchen, or the lingering scent of her perfumes and powders in the bathroom. A bout of guilt and self-pity filled the gap before the next message, then another beep and a soft, female voice penetrated his reverie.

"Hello, Matt. It's seven-fifteen, so I guess you're working late to-night." Matt looked at the digital clock on his bureau, wondering whose voice it was. It was seven-forty. "This is Tracy Gold. I'm calling from the hospital to tell you our girl's parents showed up with two detectives. I was sort of taken aback by that. Didn't know what it meant. Are you off the case? Those two guys wouldn't say anything. Said I shouldn't worry about it." A short pause. "Anyway, Ellen didn't seem to recognize her parents, which I thought was unusual. I think I expected that once they showed up, we'd see some sort of breakthrough. Or maybe it's just what I was hoping for. But she hasn't said anything since you left. We've got her physical condition stabilized, but I don't know about her mental state. She's been set up for a psychiatric eval-uation tomorrow." Her tone became slightly annoyed. "Look, this ma-chine is going to hang up on me in a second, so why don't you call me? I'll be here about another hour and then I'm going home. My number here is 555-4312, and home is 914-555-7766. I probably won't get there until nine or nine-fifteen. Speak to you later. Bye."

Matt jotted the numbers on a pad. His thoughts lingered on Tracy Gold and the warmth of her voice and the inexplicable tenderness she elicited in him, making him almost miss the first part of the next mes-sage. By the time his mind deciphered what his ears were hearing, his smile and good feeling had already disappeared. He stared numbly at the machine as the muted yet clear voice filled the room like a bad odor. He was suddenly afraid.

"Have an interesting day, Matt?" A brief pause. "I guess you know who this is. Are you wondering how I got your not-so-carefully-guarded home number?" A short, barklike laugh was followed by "Men like you amuse me. You think you're so well insulated, so well protected. Well . . . obviously you're not. Are you?" The caller let that sink in. "Oh, how I wish I could see your face right now. Does it frighten you to know that I have your home phone number? Is panic setting in because I know where you live? Does it make you feel vul-nerable? Oh, yes . . . I'm certain it does and, I have to admit, I abso-lutely love it." Matt heard genuine delight. The voice was taunting now. "Are you perhaps wondering what happens next? Isn't the suspense just *killing* you? Oops, bad choice of words." Another sharp, barking laugh was followed by a short pause. "I can't talk much longer, Matt. After all, nobody's going to take care of all the little details if I don't see to them myself. But please don't be disturbed by the police being brought in. I wouldn't dream of allowing them to take you off the case. It's going to be me and you—to the end." His "goodbye" was that peculiar laugh that left Matt feeling like he'd just chewed aluminum foil.

He stared at the machine, stunned. For the first time in his life, he thought he knew how a woman felt after being sexually violated, because for those few moments before he got really angry, he *did* feel vulnerable, violated. He cursed the empty room. "You rotten cocksucker! I'm gonna rip your fucking throat out." He got up, stormed around the bedroom, and kicked the side of Jenny's small padded dressing chair. The chair slid across the wood floor as he rammed his big toe into the hard mahogany leg. The pain sped up his leg like a striking viper, and he was instantly, and silently, cursing his own stupidity as he hopped to the bed, sucking air through his teeth in short, wheezing gulps. He toppled down on the mattress, grabbed his toe, and writhed in pain. Rubbing only made it worse, so he settled for just holding it gingerly in his palm. It struck him that he might have broken it and he shouted, "You fucking idiot, you could've broken your goddamn toe!"

Matt's reaction to physical pain was to laugh, but it was not, in any sense of the word, a happy laugh. To those who had observed it, it seemed to be the laugh of the truly demented. Still, it was a laugh, nonetheless. In his youth, he'd bought into the lie that crying was unmanly and had never succumbed. But while laughter served as an outlet to alleviate physical punishment, he'd developed no mechanism to deal with emotional pain. As he sat now holding his injured foot, absurd chuckles escalated quickly to hysterical laughter, as if the recent series of tragedies and events—Larry's death, Jenny's leaving, his mother's suffering before she died, and the frustrating sense that he had lost the ability to control any aspect of his life—seemed to culminate in that moment, in that injury, and his laughter took on a new, foreign tenor that was not laughter at all.

He massaged his toe until only an occasional, throaty chuckle shook him, and he continued to rock on the bed. Then, as suddenly as it began, the laughter stopped, and his anger returned in a violent rush, tinged with ice this time, instead of fire. A wave of hate washed over him, flooding his senses, stilling him, freezing the moment like the crisp, crystal clarity of a winter's morning. He knew what he had to do.

The winking red eye of the answering machine mocked him as he searched for the spot on the tape where the last message began and listened to the message twice more. He erased everything else and removed the cassette. He spoke, his voice cutting the silence like a razor.

"If you give me the slightest chance, I'm going to kill you, you sick son of a bitch."

Matt sat on the edge of the bed, one leg up, kneading his toe. He thumbed through his phone book, found John's number, and dialed. A young girl answered on the second ring. Matt couldn't remember her name.

"Hi, is your daddy home?"

"Yes, who may I say is calling?" Very formal, very polite, very cute.

He answered just as formally. "Please tell him Matt Kincaid is calling." Her polite, little-girl voice lost all decorum as she shouted like a lumberjack for her daddy. John and Ruth Williams were doing a fine job with their children. Matt remembered the big man bursting with pride when he told him his boy had been accepted at Stanford as a premed student. Even with the partial scholarship, and his son working while attending, it was a heavy hit. He took a second mortgage on the house and was working a second job as well. It would be a long time before John could even begin to think of retiring. His partner's bass drum of a voice interrupted his thoughts.

"Hello?"

"Hey, John, it's me. Sorry to interrupt you at home, but I thought you ought to know our little maniac left a love message on my machine."

Silence was followed by an incredulous "Holy shit, man! Are you kidding? How the fuck did he get your home number?"

"That's what I'd like to know. I called you, because if he got mine, there's a good chance he got yours as well. Anybody call your house today while we were working?"

"I don't know, man, I just got home. Let me ask Ruth." Matt

listened as John asked his wife if she'd received any strange calls, or if anything unusual had happened that day. He heard Ruth reply from a distance but couldn't make out what she said. John came back on.

"She says she doesn't remember anything like that."

"Well, just so you know. Remind your children not to talk to strangers. It may just be me he's fixed on, but it can't hurt to be careful."

"Matt, who *is* this fucking guy?"

"I don't know, but he just made it more personal than he should have." He chose his words carefully. "John, I don't think this guy is gonna go down easy."

There was a short silence before John spoke. "Man, what are you saying? No, never mind. Don't tell me anything more. Just remember, Matt, this ain't the wild, wild West. Don't do anything stupid. No perp is worth losing everything for."

"Well, it seems to me the alternative is to sit back and wait for him to make a move. I can't think of anything else but to go after *him*. Hard." He drew a breath into the silence. "Look, John, I know this is a lot more than you bargained for. It sure as hell is a lot more than I expected. But right now, you've got more to lose than I do. If you want my honest opinion, I think you ought to ask to be taken off the case. No one would blame you. You can bet your ass I won't. Get out while the getting is good. If they won't take you off, go sick. Tell them your back went out again. This is one demented scumbag, John. Ask to be relieved. I would in your place."

"You're full of shit, Matt. No way you would ask for that."

"Yeah, well, I don't have a family to worry about. How do you know what I'd do if I did?"

"Look, let's stop this crap. I'm not asking to be relieved and I'm not going sick, and that's that. We're in this together. I say, let's get this motherfucker."

Matt's voice was resigned, but deep down he knew he was going to breathe a little easier because his partner wasn't bailing out on him. "Okay, John. Then I'll see you in the morning and you can hear the tape. We'll see what we can do."

He hung up and called the base and asked to speak to Tony Morrison, who quickly came on the line. If he hadn't swapped tours, he'd be at work himself. It struck him how much had happened since he'd last spoken to Tony. He brought his boss up to date on what had gone down since then, emphasizing that whoever the maniac was, he'd gotten his home number. He asked Tony to try to find out if anyone had called trying to get information. Tony told him everyone who worked the day tour was already gone but agreed to call them at home and get back to him.

Matt hung up, then dialed again. Two rings and then the soft voice of Tracy Gold said, "Hello?"

"Doctor Gold? This is Matt Kincaid. I just got your message."

Her tone was playful. "Are we back to 'Doctor Gold'? I thought we were past that by now. . . . It's Tracy, remember?"

"Uh, right. I remember. How are you?"

"I'm fine. How are you? Is something wrong? Your voice sounds different. You sound tense."

Matt was again impressed by her perceptiveness, but he lied. "No, nothing is wrong. Just tired, I guess."

"Well, if you need to talk, I'm available."

Matt thought it an odd offer to make. After all, they'd only just met. What made her think that if he needed someone to talk to, he would choose her?

"Thanks for the offer, but I'm okay." He shifted subjects. "Your message said Ellen's parents came to the hospital and she didn't recognize them. Did you get a chance to speak to them?"

"Yes, I did. And it was the oddest thing. . . . Their reaction, especially the mother's, was entirely out of sync with what I imagined it would be. I guess I really didn't know *what* I should have expected, but I can tell you I didn't think it would be what it was."

"Why? What happened?"

"I guess it wasn't so much what *did* happen as what didn't. The whole time they were there, Ellen stared at the ceiling. Never once acknowledged their presence. I was hoping that seeing them would snap her out of it, let her know that everything was going to be okay."

"Is that really all that unusual in a case like Ellen's? I mean, she's been through hell."

"No. *Her* reaction wasn't the problem. It was the mother. She stood in the room and could barely bring herself to give the girl a hug."

Matt considered that. "Look. As far as the parents knew, she's been dead for the last two years. They would've had to have come to that conclusion, or at least forced themselves to believe it as a simple matter of self-preservation. It must have felt like they were looking at a ghost. Don't you think?''

Tracy's tone indicated she was unconvinced. ''Well, maybe you're right. Maybe it doesn't mean anything. But something felt wrong.''

''Look, Trace . . .'' Matt surprised himself. He didn't know how he'd suddenly gone from Dr. Gold to Tracy to Trace. It just seemed the natural thing to do, as if she encouraged familiarity. ''I'm not saying you're wrong, but you can't base an investigation on feelings and impressions. Not that you're not being helpful—you are. You've raised a new issue that will have to be explored. Please don't feel I don't appreciate what you're trying to do, because I do. I really do. Frankly, it's refreshing to meet someone in your position who really gives a damn. In fact, *you're* the most refreshing thing to come along in some time.'' Oh, Jesus, he thought, why the hell did I say that?

Tracy Gold was suddenly coy. She focused on Matt's last statement as if nothing had come before it.

''Oh, you think so?''

Normally, ''coy'' annoyed the hell out of him, but she was so disarming, so unabashed in the way she homed right in on his compliment, he was charmed by it. ''Uh, yes, I do.''

''Well, I think you're pretty refreshing, too.''

''Now you're making fun of me.''

''Not at all, Matt. It's the nicest thing someone has said to me in a long time. It was, well . . . *refreshing.*'' Her voice gave away her smile on the other end.

He was feeling foolish, didn't know how to take this woman, thought he was still being made fun of. ''Look, I'm sorry. I had no right. I should have kept it strictly business.''

A long, awkward pause followed before she spoke, her tone earnest. ''Are you always this sensitive, or is it me? I'm not mocking you. I *liked* what you said. Truly.''

Damn, he liked this woman . . . liked her a lot. He knew she expected a response, some encouragement, but he was at a loss for words. She waited patiently for him to sort through his feelings.

''Look, Trace. There are many things you don't know about me. For one, I'm recently separated from my wife of sixteen years. My partner was shot and killed a year ago and I've been an emotional basket case ever since. That's one of the reasons my wife left. But if what you want to know is, am I attracted to you, the answer is yes. I have to wonder, though, what you could see in a guy like me. Normally, I'd consider someone like you out of my league. You're not *crazy* or anything, are you?''

She didn't laugh. ''No, I'm not crazy, Matt. Just someone who trusts her instincts and generally knows what she wants. I'm sorry you've had so much trouble in your life recently. I'd like to help if you'll let me.''

His pause was only a heartbeat and he felt suddenly like a teenager. ''So, uh, Trace, what are you doing for dinner tomorrow?''

She laughed. ''Why, I'm having dinner with a tall, dark, and handsome fire marshal.'' They agreed Matt would call the hospital or stop by to see Ellen some time the next day and they would work out where and when to meet then. His ego was flying as he placed the receiver on its cradle. The phone rang the instant he hung up.

Tony Morrison's voice burst his bubble. ''Well, there's no mystery to how he got your number. No one knew anything about it until I called Dave McPherson. He said the phone man was at lunch when the call came in. Dave was covering the phones when a guy called and identified himself as a fireman from your former company. He said they were having a promotion party for one of your old buddies. . . . Told Dave that they'd lost your phone number and address and wanted to know if he could give it to him. Dave said he didn't think anything of it. Just gave the guy the info.''

''Damn, Tony.'' His toe throbbed. He sank back on the bed and shoved a pillow under his foot.

''Hey, wait a minute, Matt. You know he wasn't trying to fuck you over. That kind of shit happens all the time. . . . One of the brothers calls looking for a former member of the company, you give him the number. We've all done it. There was no way he could know the guy wasn't the real McCoy.''

Matt calmed down. Tony was right, of course. He'd done the same thing himself. There would be no reason not to give a number to a fireman. ''Okay, so he's got my address and number. Now what?''

''Well, it's a little worse than that. He asked for John's number, too. . . . Said he and John came on the job together.''

''Oh, shit. I just got off the phone with him. I'll have to call him back.''

"I already did. Before I called you. He said, 'Fuck him.' "

Matt smiled. "That's John, all right. Listen, thanks for making the calls and for getting back to me. I appreciate it, boss."

"No problem, Matt. But watch your ass with this guy. He's obviously smart. And I don't have to tell you how dangerous he is. Don't turn your back for a second."

"Thanks, Tony. If I recall, that's exactly what *his* advice was, 'You'd better grow eyes in the back of your head.' "

He hung up, the glow from his conversation with Tracy Gold already a dim memory. A dry, metallic taste, as bitter as his thoughts, coated the back of his throat. He resisted the urge to make a drink and settled for a glass of milk. He hobbled out to the living room, turned on the TV, and flopped into his favorite chair. A sense of ennui gripped him and he succumbed to it. The images on the screen had no meaning and the volume was turned down low. He was numb and stared dumbly into the flickering screen as if it were a crystal ball, but the blurred, disjointed images appearing one after the other in his mind did not come from the screen.

The car's skin vibrated in a dull, metallic hum, as the windswept October rain beat an irregular tattoo on the roof and hood. Inside the car, it sounded like it was raining raisins. The chill outside combined with the heat from their bodies and steam fogged the windows. Smeared hand prints created uneven rivulets on the door and dash. It was like trying to see through waxed paper. They couldn't run the motor for fear the exhaust would give them away, so they had to leave the windows open a little in order to see out. Matt's shoulder was soaked from rain entering through the slit he'd allowed.

Larry Peterson was peering intently through the narrow opening in his window and Matt wanted to yell at him to leave, to start the car, simply drive away, before it was too late. But he was a prisoner of the dream-script, powerless to affect its course, or its outcome.

The man they were hunting should have been there hours ago. Three hours and twenty minutes of waiting. They talked while they peered out and waited, but his partner's voice was elongated and slow, like a 45 record playing at 33⅓. "How long we gonna wait for him?"

"We'll give it another half hour. If he doesn't show by then, we'll head back to the barn." But in his mind he was shouting, "Drive away now! Now! Now!"

"Sure, Matt. It's just . . . Matt! Give me the picture, quick!" Except in the dream, nothing was quick, and he reached for the photo of Abdul with the speed of ketchup. Larry took it and Matt leaned over to see what his partner was looking at.

"I think it's him, Matt. He raised his head and I saw his face."

The figure on the other side of the narrow street floated toward them, hands jammed in the pockets of an orange, Day-Glo ski jacket, head and shoulders braced against the rain.

As he neared the liquor store, Matt said, "Let's take him on the way out."

The eerie sense that he was part of the scene yet also an observer dogged him as they drew their guns and raced to opposite sides of the store entrance. He poked a wary eye around the edge of the metal, scissor-type security gate. The figure was talking to the clerk behind the bulletproof glass. Larry's face was a question mark as Matt turned and saw the rain dripping off his partner's head and face. He tossed a thumbs-up to Larry but shivered in apprehension as he turned to look inside again.

The man paid and the clerk twirled the lazy-Susan partition that fed the bottle to the front. Matt jerked back as the suspect scooped his change and bag from the counter. He looked at Larry and nodded. Matt was astonished when Larry's feeble, resigned smile, his nod of acknowledgment, his whole demeanor, seemed to say he *knew*. He knew, and it was okay. But Larry couldn't know. Because it was Matt's dream and he was helpless to change a thing.

The suspect exited the store, his hands shoved deeply into his pockets. The twisted end of a paper bag poked out above the cuff of one sleeve. His neck was drawn into hunched shoulders and he seemed preoccupied with keeping warm and dry, oblivious to his surroundings. Matt wished he could see his hands.

Larry stepped out from the nook and came face to face with the suspect. Matt moved behind him so neither was in the other's line of fire. He took a combat stance.

"PO-LEECE, DON'T MOVE!"

The suspect stopped abruptly and Matt sensed the movement of his right hand. Matt lunged and grabbed for his pocket. The contour of a short-barreled gun met his fingers and he groped for the cylinder to prevent it from firing. He twisted the shape, forcing the barrel down as his gun arm wrapped around the suspect's throat. The suspect's resistance increased along with Matt's sense that he was losing his grip on the gun.

Larry darted forward and poked two fingers into the perp's eyes. His scream of agony and rage was cut short as Larry swept the man's legs from under him with one of his own. Matt rode him down in a slow-motion ballet, a death-grip on his pocket, as the suspect slammed into the ground. Larry jammed the barrel of his gun into the man's about-to-protest mouth. His words were harsh, dangerous: "If you move, I'm gonna blow your fuckin' brains out."

Matt felt the perp's body stiffen, then sag, as resignation replaced resistance. He gagged on the barrel of the gun. Matt reached into the suspect's pocket, pried his fingers loose, and handed the revolver to Larry, who tucked it in his belt.

Larry holstered his own weapon and, working together, they turned the suspect facedown. The man tried to speak, but Matt kneeled heavily on the back of his neck, pressing his cheek into the pavement, cutting off his ability to speak. They twisted his arms behind him and Larry quickly cuffed him. Matt was winded but managed a smile when he looked at his partner. "Where'd you learn the two-finger move on the eyes? The Moe, Larry, and Curly School of Self-Defense?"

Larry grinned sheepishly but otherwise ignored his partner's jibe.

"You blinded me, you motherfuckers. You fucking blinded me."

Larry spoke to the back of the suspect's head as he patted him down for weapons. "Hey, Abdul, why'd you want to shoot us?"

"Who the fuck is Abdul, man?"

The partners looked at each other. Matt's smile disappeared and sudden doubt hung between them like a foul smell. They ignored the cold, driving rain and their heavy, soaked clothing, as the possibility of having the wrong guy on the ground tugged annoyingly at their thoughts.

Larry continued his pat-down. "Don't bullshit us, motherfucker. *You're* Abdul."

The suspect whined, "Man, I knew this was jive shit the minute you stepped out. I ain't Abdul, whoever the fuck *he* is. Now, get the fuck offa me, goddamn it! You ain't got the right to do this shit. I ain't the motherfucker you be lookin' for. I don't even *know* nobody named Abdul."

Larry's search turned up a four-inch switchblade, no ID, and a thick roll of cash inside the suspect's coat. He whistled as he removed the rubber band from the roll and played his thumb off the edge. "The smallest bill in here is a fifty, Matt." He looked at the suspect. "You a collector for the Red Cross? Look at this shit, Matt. There must be a few thou' here. Where'd you get the dough, bigshot?"

"Ain't none of your fuckin' business, pig. And don't think I don't know how much is supposed to be there when this is over. 'Cause I do. Now, you got the wrong man, so get me outta this fuckin' water and take these cuffs offa me.''

Matt looked at Larry, suddenly aware that they were in the middle of the sidewalk getting drenched.

"Let's get him up and into the car.''

They lifted him by his elbows and led him across the rain-swept street. His eyes were very red, blinking frantically, as if he were sending Morse code through his tears.

Matt climbed in the back with the suspect while Larry eased behind the wheel. Their wet clothes added to the steamy oppressiveness. Larry started the car and turned the heater on full blast. Matt turned to the man suspected of setting fire to his girlfriend's apartment.

"Yolanda says to say hello.''

"Who the fuck is Yolanda?'' Blink. Blink . . . blink. Blink.

Matt sighed. "Let's start at the beginning. If you aren't Abdul, then what's your name?''

"Fuck you, pig.''

Matt was getting angry fast. "I said, 'What's your name,' asshole.''

"Fuck that 'asshole' shit, man. You got no right to talk to me that way. You the asshole, 'cause you got the wrong man.''

"Tell you what I'm gonna do, *asshole*. I'm gonna read you your rights and then we can talk.''

"I ain't sayin' nothin' till I speak to a lawyer.''

Matt pulled his Miranda card from his pocket and read it. He put it away and looked expectantly at the man.

"I told you, man. I ain't talkin' till I got me a lawyer.''

"If you haven't done anything, why do you need a lawyer?''

"So's I can sue your motherfuckin' ass for false arrest. Tha's why.''

Matt's anger was rising. "First of all, you little prick, watch your mouth. Secondly, you ain't suin' nobody.'' Matt started ticking points off on his fingers. "Third, me and my partner both saw a gun sticking out of your pocket when you went into the liquor store and we decided to investigate to make sure you weren't goin' to hold the place up.

"Four, you *do* have a gun on you *and* a knife *and* a roll of cash that we figure you owe an explanation for.

"Five, you exactly fit the description of a suspect in an arson case and you don't have any ID on you. As far as me and my partner are concerned, unless you prove otherwise, you're him.

"And last, but not least, if you don't shut that shithole of a mouth, *right fucking now,* I'm gonna plant my foot so far up your ass, you'll need surgery to get it out.

"Now, I'll ask you one more time. What's your name?"

The change was immediate and dramatic. The suspect's shoulders sagged while his voice took on a tone of subservience.

"Roger."

"Roger what?"

"Phillips."

"You know a woman named Yolanda Watkins, Roger?"

"No, man. I *told* you that already. Man, don't do this to me. I didn't do nothin' to you guys . . . didn't start no fires. I'm tellin' you true. I ain't no fuckin' ar-sen-ic."

There was a short pause, then Larry, who was facing the backseat, looked at Matt and laughed so unexpectedly, it hurt his nose.

"You're a funny guy, Roger," he said between deep chuckles.

Matt was smiling and shaking his head. Phillips was smiling too, although he didn't know why. "No, man. I never did no fire shit. It ain't my bag. I got a beef with someone, I confront the person. I don't burn the fucking building down."

"Is that why you carry a gun?"

"Hey, it's a rough neighborhood, ya know? There's a lot of bad people out there. A man's got to protect himself." A sly smile played on Phillips's lips, pleased with his attempt at humor. Matt ignored it.

"You wouldn't lie to us, would you, Roger?"

"No way, man. Look, I didn't do no fire. That's the main thing, ain't it? I told you, this is bullshit."

"Where do you live, Roger?"

"The Bronx."

"How come you got no ID on you?"

Roger's cockiness returned. He sneered. "I guess I forgot my wallet home."

Matt pointed to the roll of money on the seat between them. "Where'd you get the dough?"

Phillips's demeanor changed. He looked grim as he turned to peer through the steamed window. "I told you. I ain't talkin' no more until I see a lawyer."

Matt decided he'd listened to enough bullshit. He turned Phillips by his shoulders, his voice a harsh whisper. "Roger, or whatever your name is, you're beginnin' to piss me off. If I don't start gettin' some believable answers to my questions, well, I don't think anyone saw us pick you up out there. . . . Too wet and nasty for anyone to have been looking out of their windows." He pointed to the empty street. "I mean, you could probably drop off the face of the earth and the only ones who'll know you're gone or where you went will be me and my partner. And we're not likely to tell. You gettin' my drift? I mean, who's gonna miss a piece of shit like you?"

Phillips started to protest but Matt poked a stiff finger into his chest. "Now, I'm gonna explain something to you, and I want you to listen good, 'cause I'm only gonna say it once. Me and my partner are *fire marshals*. That means we investigate fires and arson. It also means that we don't give a shit what else you're into, drugs or whatever, so long as you don't break our balls. But we've got to know. That means if you're straight with us, you can go about your business, whatever it is, with no trouble from us. It also means we can help minimize the trouble you're already in, *if we want*. We can write it up and approach the DA so that this little episode looks like baby shit, or we can make you look like Adolf-fucking-Hitler. That's up to you, but we've got to know."

He gave Phillips a chance to digest the little speech, watched as he turned it around in his mind. Matt forced himself to be calm, reasonable. "Now, you ever been arrested for a felony?"

Phillips nodded a subdued response.

"How many convictions?"

He spoke softly, matching Matt's tone. "Twice, man, but I was set up."

"Well set up or not, this would make you a three-time loser and a predicate felon. That's life in this state, Roger. No parole, no early release. What were you convicted of?"

"Once for armed robbery and once for felony possession."

"You on parole?"

"Yeah."

"You ever go by the street name Abdul?"

"No, man. I told you already, I ain't the one you lookin' for."

"What're you into, Roger? I mean, where'd a guy on parole get the kind of dough you got on you now? And remember what I said, we're fire marshals, not narcs.''

''Man''—Phillips was shaking his head in aggravation—''I just deal a little weed, tha's all.... Just weed.''

Matt's voice hardened. ''You're lyin' to me again, Roger. I ain't gonna keep warnin' you. There ain't that kind of money in weed. Unless you're sellin' by the kilo. You dealin' weight, Roger?''

Phillips looked like a caged animal as his eyes pleaded for understanding. Matt's face was set in stone, so he turned to Larry.

''No, man. I'm tellin' you true. Look, I sell some pot, a little coke, nothin' big. Man, you know how it is. I mean, who's gonna hire a two-time felon? You gonna give me a job? *Hell, no.* But I gotta eat. Gotta feed my family.''

Matt tapped Phillips's shoulder. ''Look at *me* when you answer, Roger. You're breakin' my heart. Do me and you a favor, okay? Stow the bullshit. You're mistakin' me for someone who gives a shit. You want sympathy, you'll find it in the dictionary between 'shit' and 'syphilis.' Matt shook his head. ''I mean, does it look to you like I just fell out of a fucking coconut tree? Get real, man. You're a two-time felon. You're dealin' drugs, you just got caught with a piece on you that you were gonna use on us, and, as far as I'm concerned, you haven't said a goddamn thing that would lead me to believe you're not the guy we're looking for.'' He paused and drew a breath. ''Where were you livin' last September? And don't be fuckin' lyin' to me. It's gettin' old real fast.''

Phillips thought for a moment, then brightened. ''Hey, I was in the joint last September. You can check with my parole officer.'' For the first time in his life, Phillips was glad he'd done time. ''That's right, man, you can check. I was in the fuckin' joint last September.''

Matt was unimpressed. ''You just violated your parole, Roger. How much time you got to serve on your sentence if you go back in? I wouldn't even need a conviction to violate you. You'd have to do the rest of the time and I wouldn't even have to go to court.''

Phillips sounded pathetic. ''Man, don't *do* this to me! I didn't do nothin' to you guys, didn't start no fires.... I'm tellin' you *true*. Okay, you're right. I done some shit in my time, but Jesus, I didn't do the fire you're talkin' 'bout.

Larry's tone was sardonic. "I know, Roger. You ain't no 'arsenic.' "

Matt, serious again, said, "You know, Roger, I'm beginnin' to believe you. Maybe you're *not* the guy we're lookin' for, but what do we do about the shit that went down today? Plus, I got to get a positive ID on you before we do anything else. You got a street name, Roger? I know your friends don't call you Roger. And you still haven't told me how much time you got on your parole."

Phillips perked up at the prospect of getting off. "I got three years left, man." His voice became wheedling. "Hey, don't 'violate' me on this. Look, I may be able to help you out on somethin' you be workin' on. I know a lot of people, man. I could help you guys."

Matt showed mild interest. "How's that, Roger? How can you help us?"

Phillips thought a moment, then looked ingeniously at Matt. "You know the fire in the social club about three months ago? The one up in the Heights?"

Matt feigned nonchalance but his mind raced. He and Larry had caught the fire in Washington Heights that had killed six people. Because it was a homicide, jurisdiction passed to the PD, but Matt and Larry had pursued the investigation anyway, without the Bureau's blessing or knowledge. And up till now, had drawn a blank. Everyone knew it was drug-related but were afraid to talk for fear of winding up as victim number seven.

Neither partner saw any reason why they should be locked out of the investigation. Detectives hated arson cases because they knew so little about them. Plus, it meant they might have to enter the fire building and get their suits dirty. However, the deaths made headlines and the PD never let anything newsworthy go to another agency.

Matt deadpanned, "What do you know about that fire, Roger?"

"Listen, man, these motherfuckers don't fuck around. If I tell you anything, you got to keep me out of it. You got to promise me no one will ever know I told you. And I got to know right *now* that I slide on anything that went down today with the gun."

Matt made a decision. "Roger, if you give us righteous information on that fire, the gun will disappear along with our memory of you. But you lie to us, man, and I'll hunt you down like a fuckin' dog. I'll see to it you *never* get out of the joint. Are we understanding each other?"

Phillips nodded enthusiastically. "Good. You ask around on the street about me and my partner and you'll find out we deal square. You'll also find out we never forget it when somebody fucks us. Now, what can you tell us about the fire?"

"Okay, but I don't have nothin' definite, man. Just talk and shit. You understan' what I'm sayin'?" He paused, looking from one man to the other. Matt shot him an exasperated look.

"Okay, okay. There's this Spanish dude, I think he's Colombian or Dominican or somethin', deals weight in coke and crack up in the Heights. The word is, the owner of the club that caught fire did a number on him with some cash. The fire was this dude's way of sendin' him the bill."

"Where'd you hear all this?" Matt asked.

"Around, man. . . . Around. Shit, *everybody* knows this guy. He's a crazy motherfucker. Thinks he's Tony-fuckin'-Montana from *Scarface.* They say the day after he saw the movie, he had two of his dealers wasted for the hell of it. I can't believe you guys never heard of him."

"What's his name, Roger?"

"I don't know his real name, man. They call him 'El Venero.' Supposed to have come up from Miami to take over for the dudes down there."

"What the fuck does 'El Venero' mean?"

"This Spanish guy I know told me it means 'The Sauce.' "

"The what?"

" 'The Sauce'—ya know, like in 'spaghetti sauce.' I always thought it was a weird fuckin' name, too."

Larry burst out laughing. He had done a stint in Panama in the army and was fluent in Spanish. "You mean 'The Source,' s–o–u–r–c–e"—he spelled it out—"don't you?"

"Tha's right, man. The Sauce."

"I'll tell you, Roger, you're beautiful. I'm *really* beginning to like you. Don't you like Roger, Matt? He's fuckin' beautiful."

Matt smiled. "Yeah, he's beautiful, all right. But listen to me, Roger, you better not be sending us on some wild-goose chase, 'cause it will drive me absolutely crazy if you do."

Phillips's head swiveled between the men, unsure if he was supposed to be laughing with them.

Matt became serious. "Where does this El Venero hang out?"

The car had become a Turkish bath. Even with all the windows cracked and the defroster going full blast, their wet clothes and heavy breathing after the struggle had made the interior unbearable.

"Look, man, I don't know for sure. This dude is way out of my league. I never even saw him. They say he has an office in the back of one of them health-food stores that sell weed, on One hundred fifty-eighth Street—between Amsterdam and Broadway." Phillips shifted uncomfortably, the cuffs beginning to cut into his wrists. "Hey, I gave you everything I know, man. How 'bout takin' these things offa me and lettin' me go? And my fuckin' eyes are killin' me, too."

"Soon, Roger, soon. What'd you say they call you on the street?"

"Man, they just call me Roger. Tha's all, just Roger. Don't got no street name."

Matt didn't like that answer at all. In his experience, no one did time without getting a handle. Hell, everyone in Harlem seemed to have a street name. He'd conducted interviews with people who'd known a perp all their lives and couldn't tell him the person's real name. And no one walked around in the joint with a name like Roger, even if he had to give *himself* a better name.

"Well, Roger, we just got to check a couple of things out and then the gun will be gone and so will you. That okay with you?"

"Sure, man, I ain't got nothin' to hide."

"Good, 'cause now we're gonna take a ride to the precinct and my partner will stay with you while I make a few phone calls. After that, you'll be on your way."

Larry put the car in gear and pulled out into the street. The Three-Two precinct was around the corner and Matt asked Phillips for the information he'd need to run him through the computer: his full name and date of birth. Larry pulled into the spot marked for the precinct commander, killed the ignition, got out, and opened Matt's door. Matt slid out and Larry took his place.

The rain had tapered off to a light, sporadic drizzle and blue sky was poking through the clouds above the Gothic spires of City College to the west.

Matt bent over and spoke into the open rear window. "This shouldn't take long. I'll be right out. Roger. You behave yourself while I'm gone and don't give my partner any shit. You understand?"

Phillips nodded.

Larry looked meaningfully from Matt to Phillips. "Don't worry, Matt. Me and Roger have an understanding. Don't we, Roger?"

Phillips nodded again. Matt dismissed the strange, fleeting look that passed for the briefest of moments in Phillips's eyes, attributing it to the fact that he was sitting there handcuffed in front of a precinct, while two strangers determined his fate. He'd probably be feeling a little hinky himself in the same situation. He, on the other hand, was feeling pretty good about the way things were going as he trotted up the steps of the precinct. Trading a gun charge for a chance to solve six homicides was not a bad day's work.

He responded to the suspicious look of the desk sergeant by draping his badge over his jacket pocket, explaining that he was going to the 124 Room and then up to the squad. The sergeant relaxed and waved him on. Paranoia was definitely a cop's disease, he thought.

The "124 Room" is what cops call the room where "61's," complaint and incident forms, are taken from civilians and cops alike. The name "124" is a holdover from the old days, when cops used to do the job civilians do today. The rules governing their responsibilities were contained in Section 124 of the *Patrol Guide*. The name stuck after the section had been superseded. Matt walked in and smiled at the two matronly black women seated at the only two desks in the small space.

"Can I use your phone to call my base?"

"Sure, you can use that one over there."

He could've made the call from the detectives' squad room, but they always eavesdropped. Matt preferred to tell them only what he wanted to, and not feel obliged to answer unwelcome questions. He dialed the fire department's computer room in Brooklyn. Hank Schneider answered.

"Hey, Hank. Matt Kincaid. How're you feeling?"

"Okay, Matt. Could be better, could be worse," the reedy voice on the phone answered. "What can I do for you today?"

"I need to run a name but I can't wait too long. My partner's got the guy out in the car. We're at the Three-Two. Can you run the guy and get back to me in the squad?"

"Yeah, no problem, Matt. What's the name and DOB?"

Matt gave him the information and added, "Listen, Hank, I need a little extra on this. The guy says he's on parole. I'd like to know for what, and I want to know any known aliases. I know we normally don't get that info, but could you dig a little deeper? It's important.''

"No problem, Matt. What's the number there?''

Matt covered the receiver and turned to the older of the two women. "Ma'am, what's the phone number for the squad?''

He repeated the number and hung up, thanking the women before heading for the stairs.

The squad room was a spacious rectangular area with two holding cells set into the long wall opposite the windows facing the front of the precinct. There were two prisoners in each cell sitting morosely on the metal benches. The walls were painted two-tone institutional green, and bulletin boards with neatly tacked department notices and union newsletters were the only decorations. The room was orderly and clean, the antithesis of the filth and disarray at his base. Five detectives sat at desks lined along the wall opposite the holding cells. Another notable difference: There were many more desks than detectives, and an IBM Selectric on each. Two men were on the phone, two were typing, and the fifth was reading the *Daily News*. The newspaper was open to the movie review section. Wary eyes gave him the once-over until they noticed his badge. The detective reading the paper said, "What can I do for you today, Fire Marshal?''

"My name's Matt Kincaid. Is Danny Amato around?''

"No, it's Danny's RDO.'' Regular day off. "Where d'ya know Danny from?''

"We worked a case about three months ago. Some guy did a fire to cover a burglary/homicide.''

"I remember that. Maybe I can help ya. Danny and I partnered for more than two years. My name's Bill O'Connell. What is it you need?''

O'Connell didn't have a lot of respect for investigators outside the PD, but information didn't cost him anything and you never knew when you might need a favor from the strangest places. He was enough of a politician to know that having IOUs out on the street never hurt.

"I need to know if you got a card on file for a mutt named Roger Phillips. He's done time on an armed robbery and felony possession. My guess is, he was arrested in this precinct. Also, I'd like to look at your alias file. This guy says he's got no street name, but I don't believe it.'' Matt looked at his notes. "And last, if it's possible, I'd like to know what Narcotics has on a dude, supposed to be a heavyweight dealer in Washington Heights, with a street name of El Venero.''

From across the room, one of the detectives held up a phone. ''Are you a fire marshal? Pick up on one-nine.''

Matt pressed the flashing extension button on O'Connell's desk.

''Fire Marshal Kincaid.''

''Matt? It's Hank Schneider.''

''Hi, Hank. Thanks for getting back to me so fast. What've you got?''

''This guy's sheet took five minutes to print. He's been into everything since he was twelve years old. Even been arrested for arson twice. Hardly ever did any time though.''

Matt's heart was thumping. ''You get those aliases, Hank? I need to know quick. The rest can wait.''

''Yeah, here they are. He's got several. Goes by the names Roger the Dodger, Flash, Akim Phillips, Abdul Akim, and—''

Hank was cut short by the crash of the phone hitting the floor. Startled detectives watched Matt run to the door and fling it open hard enough to rattle the frosted glass. He raced down the stairs two at a time . . . except he wasn't running at all . . . he was high-stepping through molasses.

⬛   ⬛   ⬛

Inside the dark blue Plymouth Gran Fury, Larry Peterson was fighting for his life. The fogged windows revealed only hazy shadows moving furiously within. No one on the quiet street heard the muffled shot ring out. A hole appeared in the smooth roof of the car, protruding from the metal like puckered lips kissing the sky. A louder shot shattered the rear window. Two pairs of entwined arms crashed through the spidered glass, one black, one white, a gun arcing violently at their apex.

Matt heard the third and fourth shots as he took the last few stairs of the precinct two at a time. He tried to move faster but something was pushing into his chest, holding him back. Cops were moving toward the door as he ran by, his four-inch Colt Python pointed toward the street. Someone yelled ''Hey!'' but he didn't hear.

The rain had stopped. He came through the door, leaped the three stone steps, and swallowed the scene in one encompassing glance: the shattered rear window, glass lying across the trunk of the car, rear door opening, and Abdul emerging. Matt caught a glimpse of Larry lying slumped against the far door, unmoving, his head leaning against the glass, blood soaking the front of his shirt. Abdul was almost out of the car now, his head coming up, his gun arm rising, one foot on the ground.

A cold fury gripped him. Matt's mind was crystal clear as he stopped, took careful aim, and fired into Abdul's emerging form. His shots were well spaced, controlled, and he took a step forward with each. The first bullet crashed into Abdul's chest, throwing him into the open door. The second pierced his Adam's apple. The next three tore gaping holes in his belly. His body sank to the ground, legs askew, back against the door, head lolling to one side. Matt stood above the bloody figure, his weapon pointed at the top of Abdul's head, a foot away. The last round blew the back of Abdul's head off, and red and gray brain matter exploded onto the door, splattering Matt with blood and fragments of bone. He squeezed the trigger twice more before realizing his gun was empty. Reaching down, he grabbed the wet, slimy front of Abdul's shirt, dragged him from the door, and dumped the body into the rushing water at the curb. Abdul lay in a twisted heap, half on the curb and half off, his wounds pouring blood, turning the water a sickly pink.

Cops streamed out of the precinct, guns drawn, surrounding the car and Matt, who knelt on the rear seat, his gun thudding to the carpeted floor.

"Larry?" he called, softly. Nothing. "LARRY!?" Larry's finger twitched and Matt bellowed, "SOMEBODY CALL A FUCKING AMBULANCE! NOW!"

The desk sergeant pushed a young policeman into the precinct and told him to get an ambulance, ASAP, there was an officer down.

Matt reached for the Handie-Talkie and depressed the transmit button. His voice cracked, "Four-nine Alpha to Manhattan. This is a ten-thirteen transmission." Ten-thirteen was the code for both fire marshals and cops, signaling that an officer needed immediate assistance. It was reserved for the direst of emergencies. "Any unit receiving this message, acknowledge."

His boss, Tony Morrison, was the first to respond. "Four-nine to Four-nine Alpha, what is your location?"

The veil of fog descending on his brain made him sluggish, his thoughts disjointed, but he was able to respond. "Four-nine, transmit a signal ten-thirteen. Fire marshal down in front of the Three-Two precinct. Repeat, fire marshal shot and down in front of the Three-Two precinct. Suspect is dead but I need help. Can you respond?"

"Ten-four, Matt. I'm on my way."

"Get the dispatcher to get an ambulance and Rescue over here fast. Larry's hurt bad."

"You got it, Matt."

He dropped the Handie-Talkie on the front seat. As he turned to Larry, he heard Tony calling every available unit to respond to the scene. The wail of sirens through the speaker filled the ominous silence of the car as units acknowledged. His mind's eye saw them hurtling through the city's streets, lights flashing, sirens piercing the air, converging on the Three-Two. There'd be hell to pay later, but for now, help was on the way. He knew there was little they could do, but some instinct had urged him to gather the tribe, to have his own around him, other marshals, his brothers. And they were on their way.

Larry's chest was making a sucking sound and Matt's hand quivered momentarily over the gaping wound. He pressed his handkerchief onto it and felt for the pulse in his friend's neck. Larry's eyes fluttered open, unfocused, searching, and then they found Matt's, and a fragile smile played at the corners of his mouth. A coughing spasm that sapped the last of Larry's reserves shook the seat and blood spewed through Matt's fingers. As his frightened gaze met Matt's, bewilderment swept across Larry's anguished face. A sharp, drilling pain deep within his soul filled Matt with agony. He tried to speak, to say something reassuring, soothing, his lips forming and reforming words that wouldn't come. He gestured helplessly as the light in his friend's eyes dimmed and then, for a fleeting second, brightened. And in that moment, before they went blank, Larry winked at him.

"Hang in there, partner. Please. Don't you die on me, you crazy bastard. Just hang in there. Help is on the way." A boulder lodged in his throat as he reached for his partner's hand; a lifetime of hidden emotions welled up behind his eyes, threatening to spill over. He tried to force himself to let go, but the blessed relief of tears never came. Only pain.

12

While Matt was having his phone conversation with Tracy Gold, three men met in a dark apartment in the Alphabet City section of lower Manhattan. Two of the men stood facing the third, their leader, who was sitting formally upright in a high-backed chair, his demeanor aloof, commanding. His two followers were both over six feet tall, thin and gaunt. Long silk hoods were folded back neatly to reveal their faces. Candles, cupped within their palms, were held forward as if in supplication. Flickering light danced in the black voids of their eyes, and played on their pale, lifeless faces. All three wore black leather, differing only in the type, location, and number of zippers and chains adorning them. Sensing that something important, something they'd been awaiting a long time was about to happen, the two stood erect, tense, their posture not unlike that of wolves anticipating food.

The leader scanned the faces of his men. Zealots both, devoted to their Master. He had seen to that, kept them carefully separate from the others, nursing their hates, their fears, their pain and paranoia. It hadn't been easy searching among the dregs and disenchanted to find the whole pure grain of absolute dedication; from teenagers fighting parental reins to the dozens of morons who flocked to the call of anyone willing to lead. Total, unquestioning obedience—absolute belief. And before him stood the distilled essence of that work: Pure. Simple. Undiluted.

He sensed their anticipation and let them wait, knowing the effect it had. Then, when he knew they could wait no longer, when the tension in the room felt like an enormous pressure threatening to suffocate them all, he lowered his voice and spoke. Uncharacteristic emotion filled his words, resounding in the barren room like the crack of a small-caliber weapon.

"It is finally our time," he said quietly. "It is time for us to fulfill the destiny we have worked so hard to achieve. Time to leave our hiding places, reveal ourselves, and make the world tremble." He looked directly into his disciples' eyes. "You two will be the instruments by which they will come to know our Master. We have husbanded our resources, built our networks, hidden ourselves before the very eyes of our enemies. Our bodies and minds are hard and firm. It is time." He paused, looking beyond them to something only he could see. His voice became flat, emotionless. "Anyone who stands in our way must die. Anyone who defies the will of our Master must die. The plans and hopes and dreams of all of us rest on the absolute obedience of those who claim to be 'one' with us." His tone became challenging. "You will serve as both leaders and reminders to those who fail in their sworn duty to Him. No mistakes will be tolerated. No failure of wills. No going back. Death to anyone who falters or betrays us."

In the ensuing silence, even the candle's flames stood at rigid attention, still as a pond. A mass of energy steadily, inexorably grew, until finally the harnessed rage of the men shot across the space like a lashing whip, coiling around their leader. He reveled in it. His head fell back, eyes closed, mouth agape, tongue licking the air, tasting it like a serpent. Almost faint with power, he struggled to regain his charismatic hold on the two men staring hungrily at him.

"Satan is our Master and I am His Sentry. Guardian of His Way, Keeper of His Gate," he intoned.

The men raised their candles in unison and began to chant, "Satan is our Master and You are His Sentry. Guardian of His Way, Keeper of His Gate. . . . Satan is our Master and You are His Sentry. Guardian of His Way, Keeper of His Gate. . . ."

The Sentry rose, arms outstretched in a grotesque mockery of a sacramental gesture. "My friends"—a thin-lipped smile played at the corners of his mouth—"the hour has arrived!" His head lolled back dreamily and his laugh sliced stilettolike through their chants.

13

When Matt arrived at the PD's Office of Special Operations at exactly eight A.M. on the day after his meeting with Cattalli and the two detectives, he was favoring his injured foot. Tired and stiff from sleeping in his chair at home, he was wiped out mentally as well by the vivid nightmare that had replicated the horror of his former partner's death. He stretched and yawned in the elevator, studiously avoiding his reflection in the polished stainless steel.

Matt was habitually early to work, but this time it wasn't just a matter of simple promptness. Besides not wanting to give Captain McDonnell anything to complain about, he wanted to get the lay of the place, see how it felt and who showed up when. The office, which was located in a well-maintained but nondescript building on the west side of Broadway, between Fifty-second and Fifty-third Streets, occupied an entire corner of the large floor. There was a digital combination lock on the door and Matt had to ring to be let in. Greg Townsend, whom he was not surprised to discover was the first one in, greeted him. The office was much larger than he'd expected. Without any real reason, he'd formed a mental picture far removed from the room before him, full of computer terminals and high-tech gear, including, in one corner, a locked cage containing what looked like sophisticated radio and surveillance equipment. He'd been expecting back-office boiler room and had instead got Star Wars. It was a long way from what he was accustomed to.

Greg laid aside the case folders he'd been thumbing through before Matt arrived. His being there so early reinforced Matt's initial judgment of the man. This was a guy you'd literally have to get up early in the morning to beat. He wasn't quite sure why, but he liked him better for being there before anyone else.

Greg offered Matt a friendly smile and warm handshake before showing him where the coffee was. He poured two mugs and then led Matt to the desks he and John would be using. Matt sat down while Greg made himself comfortable on the edge of the desk. They traded small talk, Greg trying to make Matt comfortable before getting down to business. He asked the usual: Did he have any trouble finding the place? How long did it take to get there? Matt remarked on the high-tech look of the office. When they were both feeling more relaxed, Greg asked Matt what he thought needed to be done next. Matt was pleased. He'd worked with the PD before but never with a unit like this. He didn't know what to expect, but he'd known marshals who'd worked with so-called "elite" units of the PD and had ended up being buried where they could do no harm *or* good. He was determined to see that that didn't happen to him and John. Leveling with Greg Townsend right off the bat might be one way to get a feel for how he was going to be used, so when the small talk dried up, Matt told him everything: the phone call to his home, the Sentry's threat, and Tracy Gold's evaluation of Ellen's parents. If they were going to be effective, he would need someone he could trust. He decided to see whether Greg Townsend could be that man. His instincts told him that he was a straight guy, but he'd been fooled before. I'll play it by ear . . . see how much I get in return, he thought.

Matt took the cassette from his pocket and asked for a tape player, and Greg got one from his desk. Matt loaded it and hit the play button. Greg listened without interruption, staring intently at the machine throughout the playback. When the message ended, Matt rewound the tape, looked at Greg, and answered the question written on his face.

"He called my base," he said with a shrug, "told the marshal who answered the phone that he was a firefighter from my old company. He got John's address and phone number the same way. Said they came on the job together."

Greg shook his head. "This is bad, Matt. What do you think he's up to? I mean, first, in his threat to the mayor he wants you off the case. Now he's saying he won't allow you to be taken off. What's the deal?"

"My guess is, he *knew* that mentioning my name would *ensure* I stayed on. He knows a hell of a lot about how we operate. I believe he recognized from the outset it would have sounded ridiculous to ask to have me *on* the case, and he knew if I was taken off at his direction it would look like we were scared—we'd lose face. Think about it. He gets to have me on the case and establishes a motive for whatever shit he pulls. He can say we didn't give in to his demands. It's actually pretty clever. And perverse. I'd say he's really getting his rocks off on this.''

Greg looked disturbed. ''This is freaky stuff, Matt. And believe me, this unit handles all kinds of nutty cases. The question remains, though, why such a personal interest in *you?* There *has* to be some reason, some connection you're not thinking of. Have you given it more thought?''

''Yes, I have, Greg. But for the life of me, I don't know what it is.''

''Well, if we find that connection, we've found our man. We should run a check on the whereabouts of every arrest you've ever made. Does this guy fit the profile of anyone you can think of offhand?''

Matt thought carefully before responding. ''No, not at all. It's the logical place to start all right, but I figure this guy to be a white male. Frankly, I haven't arrested very many white males. Most of the shit I get takes place in the ghetto; crimes of passion or druggie stuff—boy burns girl, girl burns boy, drug dealers sending a message. . . . Lots of drug stuff. Revenge for almost anything. Sometimes the fires are set to cover another crime—usually burglary, occasionally homicide. The white males I've arrested were primarily into insurance fraud, commercial fires. But kidnapping? Torture? And the other shit this guy is into?'' Matt shook his head. ''Don't ring no bells for me.''

They sipped their coffee in silence, each lost in his own thoughts until Matt finally spoke. His voice sounded loud and hollow in the empty office. ''Okay, look. I've got a few ideas, things that need to be done today. First, I'd like to get a voice-print analysis of this tape. Because leaving this message may be the biggest mistake he'll make. How long do you think it will take? I mean, does the lab give you guys some priority?''

''Yes, I'll get it to the lab first thing. We could have something in a day or two.''

''Good, then John and I would like to verify what the Cannell kid told us. He seemed pretty definite about where his alibi lived. I find it hard to believe he made it *all* up. We caught him by surprise and his description was too specific. It shouldn't take long to determine if he was lying. Either the guy lives there or he doesn't.'' Matt placed his mug on the desk. ''I'd also like to speak to Ellen Levy's parents.''

Other detectives began filtering in and Greg introduced them to Matt. No one paid any particular attention to him. He got the impression that they were used to working with outsiders and he was grateful for that.

John came in three minutes before nine o'clock. As a matter of principle, he hated giving the city extra time, major case or not.

"Hey, brother. How's it going?"

John said hello to Matt and shook Greg's hand.

Matt told John what he and Greg had been discussing, but it was obvious that his partner was preoccupied, and the conversation ended without any input from him. Greg used the lull to refill his coffee mug. John waited until Greg was well across the room before whispering to Matt. He spoke so softly, Matt had to ask him to repeat it.

"I've got to talk to you alone."

"What's wrong, John?"

"Not here. Outside," he whispered, nodding toward the door.

Greg returned with his refill and a mug for John, then excused himself and went to his office with a detective who'd asked to speak to him privately.

Matt turned to his partner. "What is it?"

"I don't want to talk here. Let's take a walk."

They left word for Greg with one of the dozen or so detectives now sitting at their desks that they'd be back shortly.

Broadway was a mass of people hustling to get to work and they had no opportunity to talk as they weaved through the crowds and headed south. Matt's slight limp forced him to move more slowly than usual, but even so, he found himself walking alone several times, turning to catch John stealing furtive glances up and down the street, pausing at store windows, whirling to eyeball traffic. The blocks were short and the first four went by quickly. The buildings got older and more weatherworn and the neighborhood got a little seedier as they entered the forties. Triple-X-rated movie theaters and peep shows began appearing. John's behavior was driving Matt nuts, but he held himself in check. If it was that important, he wasn't going to press him. As they prepared to cross Forty-seventh Street, the light turned green and Matt stepped off the curb. He was stopped by John grasping his arm. John jerked his head, indicating the doorway of a residential apartment building off the corner. They stepped into it and John's distress was immediately evident in the deeply etched furrows on his forehead.

"I'm going to ask to be taken off the case," he said.

Matt wasn't surprised. When John said he wanted to talk, he suspected something like this. He didn't know what it was, but it was obvious that something had happened between their conversation last night and his arrival this morning.

"Okay, John. Tell me why."

"I can't, Matt."

Matt's eyes bore into his partner's, his voice hardened. "John, don't give me that 'I can't' shit. My ass is on the line here also. If there's something going on that changed your mind overnight, then I've got to know what it is. My fucking life could depend on it. You don't have the right to withhold anything pertaining to this case."

John looked down at the street and muttered, "I can't, Matt. I just can't."

Matt eased off. "Look, let me guess. I can only imagine this change has something to do with your family. It's the one thing the son of a bitch could do to make you want off the case. So, why don't we start with that. Did he get to them? Was it Ruth? Your daughter? Are they both okay?" He looked for confirmation that he was on the right track.

John looked startled and confused but shook his head and barely breathed. "No."

"What does that mean, John? No, what? No, he hasn't made threats? No, he hasn't hurt anyone? No, you won't tell me what's going on? What? . . . Speak to me, goddammit!" Matt's voice rose and passersby glanced their way. He grabbed John's arm and led him into the small vestibule of the building. John, looking forlorn and lost, wouldn't meet his eyes. Instead, he shifted his attention from the chipped checkerboard of the ceramic floor tiles to the small bank of mail boxes and door buzzers on the wall.

Matt laid a gentle hand on his friend's arm. "John, you owe me an explanation. I can understand if you want out. Dammit, I was the one who proposed it to *you* last night. But you've got to tell me *why*. This doesn't affect just you."

John straightened up and peered out to the street through the small glass panels, first one way, then the other. Satisfied that no one was paying any particular attention to them, he met Matt's imploring look. Matt had never seen him so shaken.

Spitting out the words, an expression of distaste turning down the corners of his mouth, he answered, "Okay, Matt. I'll tell you *why*.

'Why' is because when I got up this morning, I went to the bathroom, and when I came out, I see a note taped to my little girl's door." He shook his head. "I thought I swallowed my fucking heart, man. I almost broke the door down before I realized it wasn't locked. She's lying in bed and I can't tell if she's breathing because the air conditioner is on and her head is under the covers. As I approach the bed, I see a Polaroid taped above the headboard. It's a picture of my daughter sleeping, the covers pulled back, with a hand holding a dagger over her chest. It was shot in low light and it's not very clear, but there's no mistaking what it is. I pulled the blanket down and she opens her eyes and I swear to God, Matt, I died ten times in those few seconds. The motherfucker was in my *house,* man. My fucking *house!*"

Matt was stunned, almost unable to find his voice. "Holy shit! Is she all right?"

His voice was resigned, defeated, and when he spoke, his words came slow. "Yeah, she's okay. Never even knew anything happened. I took the picture off before she could see it. But the fucking note, Matt ... The fucking note made it clear if I stayed on, he was going to kill her first." He shook his head. "I can't take the risk. *Nothing* is worth that to me. I know you'll probably think I'm a coward, but if it was just me, I'd find and kill this motherfucker and gladly tap-dance on his grave. But he ain't important enough to endanger my family."

John's face pleaded for understanding, his hands flailed helplessly. "Shit, you know as well as I do, we can't protect *anyone* if some maniac decides to get at them. Hell, they can't protect the fucking *president* once someone makes up their mind to kill him. And he's got people who do nothing *but* protect him. I can't lock my family in the house and stand guard twenty-four hours a day." He held up his hand to keep Matt from interrupting him. "And no, there aren't any out-of-town relatives to send them to, and even if there was, how long could that go on? There's no guarantee we're ever gonna catch this motherfucker. We already know how rough he plays. Matt," he said, his voice reflecting his sense of defeat while disjointed images of Ellen Levy filled his mind, "this ain't the goddamn movies." He pointed a shaking finger at him. "You're not Mel Gibson, and I *sure as hell* ain't Danny Glover. This is for fucking *real,* man."

Matt Kincaid was motionless and silent. His thoughts were on the essential truth in what his partner was saying, yet it made him angry that this maniac could intimidate him. John Williams was no coward, that was for certain. He'd seen him in action too many times to even entertain the thought. But the message he'd send if he backed off was bad. Real bad. Matt was afraid it might embolden the crazy son of a bitch even more. He tried to imagine the power trip this guy would go on if he thought, even for a moment, that he could intimidate the police. Every cop knew and feared the possibility that something like this could happen. Fortunately, it almost never did. But it sometimes *did* happen, and how could any of them ever feel safe if John allowed the Sentry to control his actions? He had to find a way to protect John's family *and* keep him on the case, or no one would be able to feel safe. Then he had an idea.

"Let me see the note, John."

"That's part of it too, Matt. I wasn't supposed to tell anyone about it. I was supposed to destroy it."

"John, I know you too long. There's no fucking way you'd destroy something like that, no matter who told you to. Now, let me see it."

John, shamefaced, said, "Okay, but not here. Let's go back to the building and find an empty room someplace, maybe in the basement."

"Fine."

Despite his limp, Matt took off at a quick pace and John had trouble keeping up as he kept turning to check the streets. They arrived back in half the time it had taken them to reach Forty-seventh Street, Matt's emotions a swirling tempest. He was feeling grim, determined, and sorry for his partner all at once. The lobby felt deliciously cool as they waited for the elevator. An awkward silence filled the cab during the short descent to the basement.

Except for a building crew receiving a delivery, the basement was deserted. At the end of a long, clean, gray-painted corridor, they found an alcove and stepped in. John reached reluctantly into his breast pocket and pulled out a letter-sized manila envelope folded once.

"Be careful. I've only handled it by the upper left corner. I'm sure there aren't any prints, but you never know."

The Polaroid fluttered to the floor as Matt used his thumb and index finger to pull the page from the envelope. Both men stooped to pick up the picture. Their hands met. John quickly drew back and rose as Matt lifted it by the edges and gave it a hard look before standing back up. He tucked the photograph back in the envelope and read the note constructed from similar cut-out letters as the one sent to the mayor only utilizing smaller type:

NIGGER,

 NEXT TIME SHE'S DEAD. GET OFF THE CASE NOW AND SAVE YOURSELF AND YOUR FAMILY. THERE IS NO PLACE YOU CAN HIDE THEM IF WE WANT THEM. DE-STROY THIS AND TELL NO ONE ABOUT IT OR ELSE.

 DO IT TODAY!

THE SENTRY

 As Matt stared at the note in the dim light of the alcove, what John saw in his partner's expression frightened him almost as much as finding the note on his daughter's door. He believed the thin line Matt had been walking since Larry's death was being stretched to its limit and worried that this would make him snap. Matt's eyes were unfocused, wide. He stared at the note without seeing it, his empty hand clenching and unclenching. But when Matt finally looked up, John wondered if his imagination hadn't been playing tricks on him. Matt's expression was calm, and his tone, when he spoke, almost matter-of-fact.

 "John, whether you pull out or not, this guy is going to try to use you. If he can't get to me, he'll still go after you, maybe directly or maybe through your family. 'Cause once he sees *I'm* not stopping, he's going to try another tack. You're the link to me. He'll know I won't want anything to happen to you and he's not going to stop because you pull out. He's just gonna get worse." Matt slipped the letter back in the envelope and held it out for his partner to take. "In your heart, you've got to know that. He has to be stopped. *Now.*"

 John reached for the envelope but didn't take it. Their eyes met. John pushed the envelope back at Matt, his voice resigned. "You keep it. I'm sure you won't find anything, but you might as well have it checked. Maybe they can find out something in the lab. Maybe the kinds of magazines he's using utilize a special kind of typeface—something." His expression was resolute. "But Matt, I'm not coming back. I'm taking my vacation time and staying home with my family until this is over. This prick could've killed all of us last night, and I'm not gonna give him another chance."

 Matt grabbed his partner's arm in an almost painful grip. "So, what are you gonna do, John? You never gonna sleep? Walk around the house pointing a gun at every sound? You just finished telling me that you couldn't stand guard over them twenty-four hours a day. Think about it, partner. You *were* home last night, and he got in and out without you ever knowing it.'' He continued, his tone urgent, trying to make Williams understand the logic of his reasoning. ''You're right, of course. He *could* have killed you *and* your family. So you're being home wouldn't have stopped it. You've got to sleep sometime, just like everyone else. And what about your family? Are they going to be your prisoners until this thing is over? Come on. Think. That's not the solution, either.''

John pulled his arm away and shot back, ''Well, goddammit, what *is* the fucking solution? You got one, you let me know. Otherwise, that's the way it is. I may not be able to do what I need to do, but I sure as hell can try. I don't see the City of New York breaking its ass trying to make sure my family doesn't get hurt.''

''That's just the point, John. I think I *do* have a way to keep you on *and* protect your family.''

An excited buzz of voices greeted them as they stepped from the elevator and got louder as they approached the door to the Office of Special Operations. Matt and John exchanged puzzled glances, wondering what all the excitement was about. The room became silent as the dozen or so detectives standing in a semicircle behind Greg Townsend, peering over his shoulder, looked up from the newspaper he held to watch them enter. It was as if a conductor had waved his baton to end the noisy tuning of instruments prior to a performance.

Matt groaned, knowing two things instinctively: It had something to do with him and he wasn't going to like it. The long uncomfortable silence was broken by Greg when he closed the paper, walked to the door, and held it out to them. Matt saw it was one of New York's daily tabloids, its banner headline screaming in red, THREAT TO MAYOR, CITY. Below, in smaller type: "WE'RE TAKING IT SERIOUSLY": PD.

John looked over Matt's shoulder as they read the accompanying text. Alongside it ran a photograph of the note sent to the mayor. The note had been sent to the city desk by someone identifying himself as "the Sentry" and was followed by a phone call. The article went on to speculate about who this person was and the chronology of events leading up to the threat. Next to the article was a small ID photograph of Matt, which the department must have released to the newspaper. There was no other way to get it. Matt's heart sank.

John was dumbstruck. "Who the fuck *is* this guy?"

"Why don't the two of you come with me?" Greg headed for his office. The detectives broke up and drifted to their desks, some casting commiserating looks their way. Fucking great, Matt thought. We're not here an hour and we're already objects of pity. The buzz of voices resumed as the door closed.

Greg seated himself behind his desk and waved them into chairs. "We need to gain control of this investigation. We can't allow this crazy bastard to call the shots."

John spoke. "How? We don't have a fucking clue who he is. Now this."

Greg dismissed John's query. "This shit in the paper has nothing to do with us. It was bound to come out sooner or later, anyway. Sure, it's easier to work if reporters aren't hounding your ass, but his choosing to go public should have no impact on our actions. It's all bullshit and hype. God knows what his motives are, but we can't let this nonsense distract us. That's exactly what he'd like." He pointed to the paper on Matt's lap. "In the larger scheme of things, the newspaper means nothing."

John's voice was uncharacteristically soft. "I have to tell you, Greg, this guy scares the shit out of me."

"Hey, no one blames you for that. He's a scary fuck. You'd have to be as crazy as him not to be worried. But if we can take a moment to be objective, in an oddball way, he's been very predictable, even when you take into account that this investigation is little more than a day old. Think about it. If we tried to anticipate his actions instead of trailing them, we would have seen a pattern." He pointed to the newspaper. "Maybe not specifics, but a pattern. While there's no way we could have anticipated what happened to the Cannell kid, a pattern is there; escalation, a threat to the mayor, a phone call to Matt, threats of future problems, and now making it public. This guy is enjoying every minute of this. Almost as if he'd been waiting for just such an opportunity. I don't think he could have anticipated the two of you specifically finding the girl, but he had to believe *someone* eventually would." He turned to John. "The only thing still surprising me is that *you* haven't heard from him yet." His expression reflected the doubt in his voice.

John squirmed. Matt turned to his partner as well, hoping he would volunteer the information. When he made no move to answer Greg's unasked question, Matt spoke, his words hushed, hesitant. "Well, that's no longer true."

John slammed his fist on the arm of the chair, his face a mask of stone, the muscles in his jaw locked, protruding noticeably. "Goddammit, Matt. Don't do this."

Matt glared at his friend, his tone hard, unyielding. "John, I told you how I feel about this. I think I have a way to stop it, but we can't do it alone. Greg's the man. He's telling you he suspected this guy would contact you. Are we supposed to sit here and lie? Maybe he can help." Matt shifted in his seat and tried to calm down. "Look, your way is no good. He'll get to you anyway. You've *got* to know that. John, don't make me go through the whole thing again. You know what's being said here. Give us a chance."

John sat granite-faced, unmoved. Greg let a moment pass before speaking, his tone reasonable. "John, I knew something was wrong the minute you showed up today. Did you think I couldn't tell you were carrying a load? Jesus, man, do you think I believed this guy got your address and phone number and wasn't going to use it? For that matter, did *you* think he wasn't going to use it?" He leaned back and spoke decisively. "Matt's right. No matter what you do, you're part of this in his mind. If he can't get to Matt, he'll get to you. Don't play his game. Let us help. Alone, you're no match for this guy. There are too many ways he could come at you, and you can't know which one it'll be. Tell me what happened."

Faint beads of sweat appeared and glistened on John's smooth black skin as they waited for his response. A facial tick jerked his burn scar. Matt was afraid he was going to get up and walk out. His answer was a long time coming, but finally, he turned to Greg and said, in a low, tired voice, "Let Matt tell you. . . . I can't."

Greg listened quietly as Matt related the story and showed him the letter and photograph. When he was finished, Greg whistled softly.

"I'm sorry, John. I had no idea it had gone this far." He turned to Matt. "If you have any ideas on how to handle this, I'd like to hear them."

"First of all, I want to amend something I've been saying." Matt paused, trying to find the words. "I told you I had no idea who this 'Sentry' person is, and I don't. But I've been listening to his tape and trying to remember the first phone call. The one where John listened in? Well, there's something about his laugh. It's almost like a dog's bark. Each time he did it, I got like a . . . I don't know, this weird feeling, like I'd heard it before, a long time ago. Yet the harder I try to place it, the further away it seems to get. It nags at me like a dream you want to remember and can't. I *know* I've heard that laugh before. . . . You guys have heard it." He had their undivided attention. Even John, who was clearly preoccupied by the threat to his family, turned to catch what he was saying. "It could be nothing, nothing at all. But it's so fucking"—he fished for a word and came up lame— "distinctive." He looked from Greg to John, his shrug indicating that he wished he could do better.

"What are you saying," Greg prodded him, "that you have gotten close to this guy without knowing it? That you've maybe even met him before?" He was leaning forward, hands clasped tightly in front of him.

"I don't know. But that fucking laugh haunts me."

Greg thought for a moment, clasping and unclasping his hands several times, a gesture Matt was beginning to think of as his trademark. "Okay, let's get back to this idea you've got."

Matt leaned forward, his expression intense. "The way I see it, our first priority has to be keeping John's family safe. Now that you know what's going on, Greg, it should be easier. You told us that you guys have resources that we could only dream about. Well, you must have a safe house, or maybe the feds do for such a situation. John and I don't want protection, we just need it for his wife and daughter. That has got to be arranged—and before the end of the day." He looked at Greg and waited.

Greg toyed with a pen, then put it down and glanced at Matt before fixing John with a penetrating look. "Okay. We can do that. But once they're safe, John, you cannot visit or go near them until this is over. In fact, it would be best if you didn't know where they were. It could lead him right to their door. We can arrange phone calls at selected times, but that's it. You understand? Can you live with that?"

John nodded in dull comprehension.

"Okay, then. I'll get to work on it the minute we're finished here." He looked at Matt. "What else?"

Matt picked a piece of lint off the leg of his trousers and began to lay out his idea. "This part's a little trickier. Remember what I just told you about his laugh being familiar? Well, I believe he's somehow connected to my past. I don't know how yet, but he is. And the important part right now is that he knows *me*, not whether I remember *him*. And he's got to be wondering when I'll make the connection. Except for our purposes, it isn't important that I actually remember him, just so he thinks I do, or am about to."

Greg looked skeptical. "And how do you propose we do that?"

"We could leak it to the press, same as he did. We say that his personal attraction to me is just that, personal. And we further let on that in order to remember, I'm willing to subject myself to hypnosis or chemical regression."

Greg quickly shook his head. "I'm gonna tell you right off that I'm dead set against leaking anything to the press. Once that's done, it becomes impossible to control, and the press has a way of making a case take on a life all its own. It's like opening Pandora's box, and the tactic rarely works. Tight security is the key here, not loose lips." He paused, picked up his pen again, and tapped it lightly on the desk. "But your hypnosis idea has merit."

Matt sat back and waved him off. "No way, man. I was just saying we could let him *think* that's what I was doing. I'm not letting anyone fuck with my head."

"Why not, Matt? If you were a civilian who we thought could remember this asshole, isn't that something we might consider? If Ellen Levy doesn't come around soon, wouldn't one of us eventually try to get the doctors to go along with some type of hypnosis? Or whatever drug they're using nowadays instead of sodium pentathol." Matt felt manipulated by his own words and his sullen look reflected his annoyance. Greg finished, "So what's so far-fetched?"

Matt wasn't giving in. "But I wasn't proposing that we *really* do it."

Greg was smirking. "Why? You're the one who brought it up, and now you want to drop it. I say that's bullshit. It's worth a try."

"That's not what I was saying! I only thought he should *think* that's what we're doing."

John turned to Matt and smiled for the first time that day. "Greg's got a point, m'man. Why is it such a good idea in theory and not for real? Suppose it worked?"

Matt shifted uncomfortably. "You're loving this, aren't you, John?"

"Well, now that you mention it . . . Yes, I am."

Matt had trapped himself. "Fuck you, bro."

John held his hands up in mock defense. "Hey, it was your idea, not mine. Don't blame me."

"Hey, I still haven't agreed to do it."

"Well, *I'd* like you to do it," Greg said, "because we hope it will help you remember where you heard the laugh. But I am definitely nixing any release of information to the press." He continued, "I think we can all agree this guy's on a power trip. Maybe he fully expects that you will remember him sooner or later anyway and he just doesn't care. Maybe he'd just like the chance to rub our faces in shit while we try to find out who he is."

John was unconvinced. "You could be right, Greg. But can't you see what he's doing? Dictating our actions. Matt and I were going to do follow-ups today. Instead, here we go dancing to this guy's tune."

"I don't see it that way, John," Greg said. "It will take at least a full day to set this up. Meanwhile, we go about our business like we planned—that is, Matt and I do. *You* need to go home and get your family ready and stay with them until I can set them up." He turned to Matt. "If it's okay, I'll partner with you today and we'll do the follow-ups."

"Sure. I think it's a good idea." Matt was liking Greg Townsend more and more—especially after his latest experience with *his* bosses.

Greg stood up, indicating that the discussion was over. He pointed to John. "Right now, you need to be home. I'll send one of my men with you to help out, after I make some phone calls. Call your wife and tell her you'll be leaving here soon and to get some things packed. Nothing too elaborate—say, enough for a week. If you need more, we'll arrange it later." He gestured to Matt. "Why don't you figure out the places you want to get to this afternoon? I'm gonna need time to make the necessary arrangements."

They rose and turned to leave. Matt was opening the door when John stopped, turned back, and extended his hand to Greg Townsend. "Thanks. I won't forget this."

Greg stood there with John Williams towering over him. As his hand was being swallowed whole by the big man's, the fleeting hope crossed his mind that John knew his own strength. They shifted uncomfortably for a long moment. "Get the fuck out of here. Both of you."

15

John had been a different man when he emerged from Greg Townsend's office. His step was lighter and he seemed to have made up his mind to go the distance. His family was going to be safe. Now he could focus his energies on finding this bastard—this animal who had violated his home and threatened his child. He couldn't remember a time when he felt such hatred. Not in the years he attended Catholic school as the only black kid among white, middle-class kids. Not in his four years in the Marine Corps, when he'd come home from Vietnam to a country in turmoil, embittered, lost, and angry—used, really. Haunted by the memory of his friends, young black men who'd left their blood and futures in the soil of Southeast Asia. The Civil Rights movement was in full swing as he sat out the last two years of his enlistment at Camp Lejuene, North Carolina. The resentments of the past paled against the hatred he felt now. He knew if given the opportunity he would kill this man.

Matt Kincaid left the meeting feeling anything but light or loose. The enormity of the responsibility he'd taken on when he'd assured John of his family's safety, and even the fact that he'd convinced John to stay on, sat like a bowling ball in his gut. And realistically, his "plan" didn't really seem like much. He sat down at the desk Greg had assigned him and tried to organize his thoughts.

He'd played off John's pride and offered straws to a drowning man. The truth was, he had only the vaguest notion of a plan, and the discovery that the case had become headline news had changed that. He hadn't been sure Greg would go along with the "safe house" idea, but was gambling that he would be wise enough to see that it was in everyone's best interest to protect John's family.

What prompted his proposal was the growing awareness that he'd heard that distinctive laugh before and it was only a matter of time before he'd be able to match it with a face. It was also his firm belief that John's bailing out would send the worst possible signal. But should he have let John take himself off the case? Did he have the right to change his partner's mind about something so important? John would be in real danger now. There was no doubt that whoever this Sentry was, he would try to prove to John that he should have followed his instructions. After today, Matt intended to glue himself to his partner. Whoever came at them would not have the luxury of picking them off one at a time.

He thumbed desperately through his notes, wondering what he'd missed. His temples pounded and his neck was stiff with tension. How had it become such a mess? It seemed incredible that it had only been two mornings since the homeless guy was set on fire. Events were far outpacing his ability to deal with them.

The chance to prove that he was back and fully functional seesawed with the knowledge that he felt lost and disjointed, far from competent. But he couldn't blow it. If he fucked this up, he'd be marked as a man unable to cope, washed up as an investigator.

Greg's hand on his shoulder startled him. "Matt, you ready to go?"

Matt glanced at his watch; Greg had taken a full hour to make arrangements for a safe house and coverage. "Yeah, sure."

"Where do you want to start?"

"I'd like to try to find the apartment Eddie told us about. See if there *is* such a person as Jeremy. Then over to Brooklyn to talk to Eddie's and Ellen's parents. I spoke to his mother and she said they'd be home all day. She was pretty distraught, naturally, but sounded like a nice woman. We can play it by ear after that. Okay with you?"

"Sounds good to me. We'll take my car."

They gathered their things and took the elevator down to the indoor garage where about a dozen brand-new unmarked Chevy Caprices were parked along one wall. As Greg moved to the driver's side of the one nearest them, Matt remarked, "No budget problems in your outfit, huh, Greg?"

Greg chose not to answer, instead got in, hit the power locks to open Matt's door, and started the car. He turned to Matt, and smiled. "Where to, partner?"

"Fortieth and First. Let's see if Eddie was a liar."

Greg pulled out of the garage exit on Fifty-second Street and turned east before stealing a glance in Matt's direction. Matt was staring distractedly through the open side window. The day promised to be another scorcher, but the streets still clung to what remained of the morning cool. Whenever possible, Matt preferred to have the windows open, to maintain contact with the street and its sounds. He liked to drive with the A/C going full blast and the windows rolled down, which used to drive Jenny crazy. They'd gone a few blocks before Greg broke the silence.

"You did the right thing back there, you know."

Matt spoke without turning. "Right thing? What's right, Greg? If something happens to John or his family, will you still feel the same?" He turned to face him. "I know I won't."

"But it isn't like there's a choice here now, is there? What are the alternatives? You know what could happen if we let John do it his way."

Matt took his time answering. "Yeah, well, it's not much in the way of consolation. He'd have liked to have kicked my ass when I told you what happened at his house last night. I guess he sees it as a betrayal. I don't know. I just know *his* way would play right into the bastard's hands."

Greg swerved to avoid a car pulling out from the curb. "Matt, he's in no position to make rational decisions. It became too personal the minute he found the note and photograph. Nobody makes good decisions under those circumstances. He'll eventually thank you."

"You think so?" Matt squinted into the sunlight. "Maybe."

They drove the rest of the way in silence. Greg turned onto Second Avenue and then Fortieth Street. He slowed to a crawl as they looked for a church and a building that fit Eddie's description. There were no churches and none of the buildings had lobbies resembling the one Eddie had described.

Greg pulled over to the curb. "Maybe he was lying."

Matt's face was set. He wasn't buying it. The kid's description was too specific. He told Greg to turn left on First Avenue.

"Let's do all the even-numbered, one-way streets in the forties."

They turned left and drove uptown on First past Forty-second Street. The gaily colored flags of the United Nations snapped smartly in the shadow of the huge, gray monolith. Forty-second and First acted like a vacuum for the wind, sucking the breeze off the East River and funneling it in the only direction it could go, west. The flags of the U.N. rarely hung limp. Matt wondered if the designers had suspected that would be the case when they decided to surround the building with them.

Greg weaved slowly through the streets of the forties, widening their search from Third Avenue to the river, skipping Forty-second because it was hard to believe Eddie Cannell wouldn't have known he'd been on one of the city's busiest and most identifiable streets. Neither man saw anything fitting Eddie's description.

Greg pulled over to the curb again at the corner of Forty-eighth and First and turned to Matt. "Looks like the kid was lying, Matt. What d'ya want to do now?"

"Let's try Forty-second, Greg."

"What's the point, Matt? Forty-second is two-way. Don't you think the kid would've known that? Even a tourist could point you to Forty-second Street."

Matt thought a moment. "You're right. But it can't hurt to look anyway. Could be our boy realized he told us too much and at the last minute decided to give us the wrong street. He seemed certain that he was facing the East River. Well, Forty-second Street also ends at the river."

Greg shrugged, put the car in gear, turned onto Second Avenue, and made another left when they reached Forty-second. The three monstrous smokestacks of the Con Edison plant, on the Queens side of the river, were visible in his rearview mirror. He hugged the row of parked cars and cruised slowly along the wide, tree-lined street, past a park on the south side bordered by a mature oak and some maple trees. The car inched its way under a narrow overpass bridging the north and south sides of Forty-second Street where the first buildings began, at the end of a wide, granite-faced wall. The first building to the south was about twenty stories high and sported a long, broad, forest-green awning, overhanging a mahogany and glass doorway. The building's name, The Walden Arms, was written in white letters on the canopy. The marble was elegantly weather-stained, and long, blackish teardrops ran from the joints wherever four stones met. Greg looked ahead. Another building, no more than ten stories high but just as well kept, abutted a two-story brick church that sat recessed some distance from the sidewalk atop a small hill, dwarfed by the structures around it and hidden unless you stood directly in front of it. It looked very old and weary, its steeple peeking out above and behind a drab stone wall. The copper spire, long since turned green, was probably once meant as a focal point for the church's parishioners. Time had turned the brick a brackish color, and only a few speckles of its original red dotted the surface. The wall was topped by a black iron picket fence and, at each spot where the fence was bolted to the wall, long, wide columns of rust ran down to the street, slashing through the name of the church cast in black iron letters: THE CHURCH OF THE BLESSED VIRGI. Any indication that there used to be an ''N'' at the end of the last word had long since disappeared. Greg stopped the car and pointed.

''There's a church, Matt. But the fancy high-rise is two doors away. What d'ya think?''

''Let's check it out.'' Greg made a U-turn, double-parked in front of the entrance, and threw his NYPD vehicle identification on the dashboard.

A man wearing a pale blue uniform adorned with epaulets and trimmed with gold piping opened the interior door of the building and eyed them suspiciously. The lobby was large and elegant. Dark oak, crystal chandeliers, and Persian rugs complemented the antique furniture and red velvet ropes guided the visitor to two double-sized mahogany elevators. Despite its size, the space radiated comfort and subdued invitation. A circular teak desk sat equidistant between the foot of the stairs and the elevators to the rear. A uniformed attendant was perched on a stool behind it. To the right of the station, a medium-sized counter of burnished oak traversed a wall painted tastefully in the palest of blues. Another uniformed attendant manned that counter, his back to them, putting mail into gleaming wooden mailboxes. A janitor was polishing a brass plate housing the buttons of one of the elevators.

''May I help you gentlemen?''

Matt showed his badge and ID to the guy at the desk, who'd risen when they walked in. The doorman followed just behind them. ''Yeah, we hope so.'' He turned to the doorman. ''Why don't you come up here so we can talk to both of you at once.'' The concierge was no less wary than the doorman. ''We're trying to find a guy who was mugged the other night. He gave this address to the police officer who took the report, but then decided not to give his full name. All we got is 'Jeremy.' Anyway, for a change, we think we caught the mugger. We'd like to see if this 'Jeremy' can identify the guy.'' He looked from man to man. ''It'd be nice just once to put one of these assholes away, don't you think?'' His expression conveyed the message that he was speaking as one New Yorker to another—not as a cop, but as yet another victim fed up with all of the city's bullshit.

The concierge leaned on his forearms. ''Well, 'Jeremy' isn't a heck of a lot to go on. I mean, we call most of the tenants by their last names. What's this guy look like?''

''I guess you'd say that his distinguishing feature is that he wears leather, chains, and boots. You know the look we're talkin' about.'' He leaned closer and lowered his voice. ''Look, not for nothin', but between you and me, I'm told the guy is probably gay, if that helps.''

''It doesn't ring any bells for me. But I'm the day man. Most of the people I see are dressed for work.''

Matt turned to the doorman. ''How about you?''

''I think I know who you're talking about. But I don't know his name or what apartment he lives in.'' He jerked a thumb toward the counter along the wall. ''Maybe Richie knows. He's been here the longest and he used to work nights.''

Richie was sorting mail into the open boxes behind the long counter against the wall. The doorman rapped his knuckles on the counter. ''Hey, Rich. What's the name of the guy who wears the leather getup when he goes out at night?''

Richie turned. He was clean-cut, mid-twenties, medium height, with dirty-blond hair. His lips looked like they were stuck in a perpetual pout. He glanced at Matt and Greg but spoke to the doorman. ''Who are these guys?''

''They're cops, man. They said the guy was mugged, but left before he could give his last name. Said they think they caught whoever mugged him.''

Richie looked at the two men and spoke politely, his voice in direct contrast to his petulant expression. ''We're not supposed to give out the names of our tenants.''

Matt smiled. ''Hey, I understand. Except we're here to help the guy, not hurt him. We just need to talk, see if he can identify the bastard who mugged him and hopefully get him to press charges.

Maybe put away the scumbag who did it. Opportunities like that don't happen every day in this town.''

Richie was torn between obeying the rules and doing something helpful. He shrugged his shoulders. ''The guy you're lookin' for is Jeremy Patterson. Apartment 15C.''

Matt tried to sound disinterested. ''Do you know if Mr. Patterson is home now? Does he work days?''

''I'm not sure. I hardly see him during the day.'' He spoke to the doorman. ''How about you? You see him leave today?''

''No, but that don't mean nothin'. Lots of tenants use the garage exit. It lets them out closer to the corner.''

''Just as a little background,'' Matt asked, ''what's the deal on this guy? You know, the leather and all?''

Richie became wary. ''What's that got to do with anything?''

Matt waved it off. ''Nothing, Rich, we just like to know who we're dealin' with whenever we can. Naturally curious, that's all. Don't want to get to the door and find out the person we're talking to is some kind of nut if we can avoid it. Do you know how many cops get hurt by the people they're trying to help? We're not asking you to give away the guy's secrets. Just what kind of a person he is.''

Richie looked nervously toward the elevator and up to the balcony. Greg broke in. ''Hey, Rich, is there a room where we can talk?''

''Uh, yeah.'' He pointed to a door beside the row of pigeonholes. The doorman and concierge started to follow.

Greg turned to them. ''Thanks, guys. We appreciate your help. We'll see you on the way out, okay?'' Matt and Greg followed Richie to the small office. Greg closed the door.

The small room was sparsely furnished; a scarred desk, a comfortable but worn executive chair, and two stiff-backed folding chairs constituted the furniture. The desktop was tidy; an old black rotary-dial phone, an ink-stained blotter, a desk spike with a stack of notes impaled on it, and a pad and pen near the phone were all symmetrically arranged. Matt guessed that the furniture had been thrown away by tenants. Now that they were in his office, they noticed a subtle change in Richie. Small and unattractive as it was, this was his domain. Richie waved them into the chairs, reclined comfortably in his, and put his feet up on a worn section of the desk.

''Now, what is it you want to know?''

"Well, like we said, what kind of a guy is Patterson?"

Richie looked at them slyly. "You're not here because he got mugged, are you? You want him for something."

Matt was ready with an answer and leaned forward, his voice earnest. "You're a perceptive guy, Richie. But we're not after him for something he did. He witnessed a crime. We're hoping he'll be willing to talk to us now that a couple of days have gone by."

"What'd he see?"

Matt leaned back, resigned, apologetic. "I'm afraid we can't talk about that. You know how it is. But he's not wanted for doing anything wrong; we simply want to talk to him. The reason we wanted to know what kind of a person he is is because we were hoping you could give us some insight into how best to approach him. But you saw right through us. I'll bet you're real good at your job." Matt shook his head in admiration and looked at Greg. "This guy is sharp."

Richie beamed. "I'm on the list for the PD, ya know."

"You're kidding! I knew it." He looked at Greg again. "I knew this kid was on the ball." He turned back to Richie. "When are you supposed to be appointed?"

"Pretty soon. Maybe the next class or the one after."

"Greg, your brother is an instructor at the Police Academy, isn't he?"

Greg nodded solemnly. "Yes, he is."

"Well, if Richie gives us a call before he goes in, do you think you might be able to do something for him?"

"I don't see why not." Greg turned to Richie. "I think I could swing it so you get almost any assignment you want after you graduate. How does that sound?"

Richie was all ears. He was like a puppy promised a treat. His excitement was palpable, his mind toying with images of becoming a detective right out of school. But Greg didn't have a brother, let alone one who worked at the academy.

Matt became serious, almost grave. "Of course, it all depends on how well you do for us now." He gave Richie a meaningful look. "So what's the deal on this Patterson guy?"

In his mind, Richie was already a fellow police officer, a member of the "long blue line," a brother in arms. He was suddenly thrust into the role of a player in a very old game: cops and robbers, good guys and bad guys, cowboys and Indians. He was ready to give up his parents if necessary.

He removed his feet from the desk and sat forward. His voice was heavy with conspiracy. "The guy is weird, ya know what I mean? A stone-cold fag, if you ask me. During the day, he looks normal enough, although I don't think he goes to a job. But at night . . . Man, you should see this guy!" Richie looked for comprehension to appear in their faces and, finding none, continued. "Look, here's a guy who doesn't seem to work, right? At the same time he lives in a place like this. Do you have any idea what a two-bedroom apartment goes for in this building?"

"No, Rich. How much?" Greg asked.

Richie emphasized each syllable. "Fifty-two hundred dollars a month."

Matt whistled in appreciation. "So where does he get his dough? Does he come from money? What kind of people visit him?"

"Man, the guy dresses pretty casually most of the time, all Levi's and T-shirts—except at night when he wears the leather. Expensive leather. The soft kind, lambskin, I think. In this building, the men all wear Armani. You know—two-thousand-dollar suits, five-hundred-dollar shoes. Hey, tell me the truth, is he wanted for something?"

Greg waved, dismissing the question. "We already told you the truth, Richie. The guy's a witness, not a suspect. Anyway, go on. What does he look like?"

Richie wasn't buying it. He was playing the "great game" and no way were these two guys asking all this about a witness. Well, no matter. They had to do what they had to do. He'd play it any way they wanted, but he was making damn sure he got a phone number before they left. Man, what a stroke of luck. A cop with a brother instructing at the academy!

"Tall and skinny. I mean, *real* thin. Gaunt, ya know? Looks like a fucking skeleton. Very pale complexion. Medium-length black hair, no part. Combs it straight back. About thirty, thirty-two years old."

Matt was writing in his pad and looked up. "Does he have any facial hair? A beard or mustache?"

Richie's brow wrinkled. "No. But he has those thick eyebrows connected in the middle, like it's one long eyebrow. Looks like a fucking caterpillar walking across his forehead."

They laughed. "How about scars or tattoos?" Greg asked. "Glasses?"

Richie licked a finger and rubbed at a spot on the desk. "I never saw any scars or tattoos and I've never seen him wear glasses."

"Does he ever talk to you guys?"

"Almost never. Pretty much minds his own business. I sort all the mail for the building, and the only stuff he gets is addressed to 'tenant' or 'occupant.' You know, the generic stuff. Nothin' addressed to him personally. If he's getting mail, it's being delivered someplace else, maybe a P.O. box."

"Oh yeah? Which post office services this building?"

"I'm not really sure. But the mailman was already here. You want me to ask him tomorrow?"

"Yeah, thanks. Then give us a call and let us know. Okay?"

"Sure, no problem."

"Anything else you can tell us about this guy?" Greg asked. "Does he have visitors?"

"Well, not during the day. I mean, all visitors have to be announced. Sonny, the doorman, could tell you more about that. But when I used to work nights, he'd sometimes bring men home. They'd all be dressed the same as him—leather and chains, I mean."

Greg looked at Matt. "You got anything else?"

Matt shook his head, rose from the chair, then thought of something. "Oh, yeah, I forgot. You ever hear this Patterson guy laugh, Richie?"

Richie looked puzzled, trying to figure out how a man's laugh could have anything to do with what they'd been talking about. "No, can't say that I have. Is it important?"

Matt extended his hand. "No. Just curious is all. Hey, Richie, thanks a lot. You've been a big help." He took a business card from his wallet, crossed out the number for his base, and wrote the number for OSO on it. "Call this number when you get the post office information. If we're not there, just leave it with whoever answers the phone." He gave him the card.

"What do I do when they call me for the academy? Should I call you guys?"

Greg took a small blue phone directory from his sport coat. "Give me my partner's business card, I'll write a number to call on the back.

But don't call until the day before you go into the academy. They don't like to be bothered until it's time. Okay?'' He copied a number and handed the card back to Richie.

"Hey, thanks, guys," Richie said. "I really appreciate it."

"No problem. Just don't use it until they call you. And Richie? One more thing. We'd appreciate it if you kept our conversation just between us."

"I will."

Matt opened the door and almost tripped over the bent figure of a janitor polishing the doorknob. The small man looked up and Matt noticed he was Indian or Pakistani. "Sorry, bud. Almost ran you down there." On the way to the elevator they repeated the need for confidentiality to the doorman and concierge.

As the elevator doors opened and they stepped in to face the front, Matt turned to Greg. "What phone number did you give him?"

Greg smiled. "The police department chaplain's office. The kid's gonna need it."

◼   ◼   ◼

Like the lobby, the fifteenth floor was a study in low-key elegance: diffused clamshell lighting on the walls, print carpeting, and brass lions' head door knockers.

Greg nudged Matt. "Let's talk a minute first." They found the stairwell and ducked in.

"Whatta ya think?" he whispered.

"I don't know, Greg. He could be our guy. But this is awful easy, man. If he turns out to be this 'Sentry' asshole, I'll be amazed. But it all fits, doesn't it?"

"Well, how do you want to play it if he's home?"

"I'm not sure. I definitely want to get a look at the guy. Hopefully he'll let us in and we can check out how he lives. See what he's got to say. We certainly don't have anything to bring him in on. As far as we know, he's exactly who Eddie said he is."

"Well, let's be careful. If he is our man, he's one dangerous motherfucker."

"You got that right."

They found 15C and took positions on either side of the door. Matt slipped his two-inch Smith & Wesson into his jacket pocket. They listened at the door and heard nothing. Greg knocked several times, and when no one came, he removed a business card from his wallet, wrote a brief message to please call on the back, and slipped it into the door near the knob.

He looked at Matt. "We'll come back."

■   ■   ■

While Matt and Greg were deciding what to do next, a telephone call was placed from the basement. The small man Matt had mistaken for Indian or Pakistani, but who in fact was a native of Sri Lanka, dialed a number he kept hidden in his wallet. The numbers were in a simple but effective code that took only a moment to decode.

The phone was picked up on the second ring. "Yes?"

"The men you asked me to watch for are here. They are asking questions about the man in 15C. What do you want me to do?"

"Nothing. Thank you. Your reward will be under your door to-night." The little man hung up the phone, retrieved his rag and metal polish, and walked from the room smiling. Ah, America, he thought, truly the land of opportunity. Where else could money come so easily?

16

Back in the car, Matt hesitated. "Let's not leave yet. I need a minute to think. Something doesn't feel right and I don't know why."

Greg took the car out of gear and swiveled in his seat. "Okay. What's bothering you?"

"I don't know yet"—Matt looked thoughtfully at the marble entrance—"but I'd like to run this building in the FD computer and find out who owns it. Maybe we can go to the landlord's office and get some info on the guy in 15C. He must have signed a lease, which should give us a Social Security number, a date of birth, maybe more. Then we find out if he has a record. I hate to leave here without starting the ball rolling on who this guy is. I can write a subpoena to the phone company and get a list of his calls for the past month. Longer if we need it."

Surprised, Greg said, "What do you mean you can write a subpoena? Don't we have to see a judge?"

Matt smiled. "Well, my friend, one of the little-known and few advantages we fire marshals have over the PD is that, as long as we don't abuse it, we can write our own subpoenas in this city. It comes in handy sometimes. . . . Like now."

"I didn't know that, man. That's great. Saves us a lot of trouble. And I agree. We should know as much as we can about Jeremy Patterson before we come to see him again."

"Let's find a phone."

They decided to drive to the nearest precinct to make the necessary calls, rather than deal with a public phone. They went up to the squad, identified themselves, asked a detective if they could make some calls, and took seats at empty desks.

While Greg called the office to see if there were any new developments and to find out if John had checked in, Matt called the FD computer room.

Matt was off the phone first and waited for Greg to hang up. "They're gonna call me right back. How're things at the office?"

Greg didn't look happy. "Nothing's going on, but John hasn't called in. How far away does he live?"

"Not far. Hollis, Queens. Does Burroughs have a beeper?"

"Good idea." Greg thumbed through his notebook and punched in the series of numbers.

As he hung up, Matt snapped his fingers. "Speaking of beepers, I've got to make a call." Matt had just finished dialing the beeper number Tracy Gold had given him, when a phone rang across the room. A detective answered and called to them, "One of you guys a fire marshal?" Matt felt a black sense of having lived this scene before.

"That's me."

"Pick up on three-six."

He depressed the flashing button. "Fire Marshal Kincaid."

It was the computer room. Matt recognized the man's name but didn't know him well. There was no small talk as he copied the information and hung up. Greg watched as Matt read from his notes.

"The building is owned by Belzier-Stone Realty," Matt told him. "I've got their address and phone number."

Belzier-Stone was one of the largest real-estate companies in the city. Unlike Trump or the Helmsleys, Belzier-Stone kept a low corporate profile. They were known for buying, building, and managing expensive, high-quality real estate, and enjoyed the reputation of being good corporate neighbors, giving generously to charities and the arts. They managed to be on the winning side of political elections by maintaining a strict policy of neutrality and giving judiciously to candidates from both major parties. Their properties suffered few fires and none were due to the negligence of the building owners. When they did occur, they were routine, the kind one would expect to find in any apartment building in New York, resulting from an unattended pot on the stove, an electric blanket gone bad, that kind of thing. Their tenants were carefully screened for money, power, and stability; the nouveau rich and famous—actors, sports figures, and public personalities—need not apply. Belzier-Stone buildings employed the latest fire-detection and

-suppression devices, along with top-notch security. Repairs were instantaneous.

Their attention was drawn to the detective answering the phone. "It's for you again. If you're gonna stay, you're gonna have to hire a secretary." He shook his head, annoyed, and returned to his typing. Matt punched the flashing light.

"Fire Marshal Kincaid."

"Hi, Matt."

Matt turned away and lowered his voice. "Hi, Trace. How are you?"

"I'm fine. Just fine. I was waiting for your call. Are we still on for tonight?"

"Sure, assuming nothing crazy happens. In fact, I was planning to stop at the hospital today to see Ellen but didn't know if you'd be around."

"Oh, I'll be around all right. Why don't you have them page me when you arrive? We can have a cup of coffee together."

"Great. I'm in the middle of something now and I probably won't get there till late afternoon. That okay?"

"Whenever. I'm not going anywhere."

"Okay. See you then. Bye."

"Matt?"

"Yes?"

"Please be careful."

She hung up and Matt savored the warm feeling brought on merely by speaking to her. She made him feel lucky and, under the circumstances, he knew he shouldn't. But that's what a woman could do, make you feel lucky. . . .

When he hung up, Greg was smiling. "What's so funny?" Matt asked.

"Oh, nothing. It's just, I was watching you fidget while you spoke. You reminded me of my son when he's on the phone with a girl."

Matt flushed. "Well, I hope you enjoyed yourself. Next time I'll put you on the extension so you won't miss anything."

Greg chuckled. "That won't be necessary. It's more fun trying to guess what she's saying."

"Very funny. If I knew you were such a funny guy, I would have worn my Emmett Kelly costume."

The good humor on Greg's face suddenly vanished; Matt followed his gaze to several detectives gathered around a PD radio. They walked over and Greg tapped the detective who had been answering the phone.

"What's going on?"

The detective, bothered by yet another interruption, answered curtly, "Some detective in Queens just phoned in a ten-thirteen. His partner is down but there aren't any details."

Greg's face was ashen when he asked, "Where in Queens?"

The detective, surly now: "Hey, what am I, the fucking *World Book Encyclopedia?* How the fuck should I know?"

Greg grabbed his arm and twisted the material of his jacket. "If you still want to be a detective tomorrow, you'd better curb your tongue and find out."

The younger man looked at Greg, then Matt. When he responded, the transformation was dramatic and he answered respectfully, "I'm not exactly sure. The address sounded like Queens Village or Hollis, someplace near there."

Greg picked up a phone and asked the dispatcher for details and the location of the shooting. He was given the address but told they had no further particulars and that units were en route to the scene.

As they bolted for the door, Matt heard Greg whisper under his breath, "Please, God. Please let them be okay."

17

When John left the PD's Office of Special Operations on Broadway with Bill Burroughs, the detective Greg had teamed him with, he was feeling better than he had all day. A subdued but nonetheless certain sense of renewed confidence had replaced the paralyzing fear he'd felt for his family. He'd considered not going in to work at all after finding the photograph and note, but his sense of duty and obligation overcame his anxiety and he decided it would be okay to leave the house long enough to have himself removed from the case. After all, if this guy, this Sentry, wanted to hurt him and his family, he could have done it during the night, while he had the chance. He'd also have to know that John would need time to withdraw from the case. John had every intention of following the guy's instructions and believed his family would be in no danger during that brief period.

Matt's reaction had taken him by surprise. While they'd known each other for many years and had worked on individual cases together, their steady partnership was new, begun only after Matt had returned to full duty. John had his reservations about Matt's stability since his former partner's death. When Matt returned to full duty, Howcum D'Aieuto was against his going back to the field. He wanted him to work in the office pushing paper because he was afraid that he was a poor risk. Matt had gone to Tony Morrison and pleaded with him to give him a chance, told him office work would drive him crazy. He felt his past record had earned him an opportunity to prove himself and Tony agreed. It was Tony's appeal to D'Aieuto, along with a promise to take full responsibility, that had put them in the position they were in now. One of the conditions of Matt's return was that he find someone who would work with him, and that's when he came to John, asking if he'd agree to be his partner. It was clear he needed a friend and John found it impossible to turn him down.

And things weren't as bad as he'd thought. They were going to work out. His fury at Matt for telling Greg Townsend about what happened that morning had faded, replaced by the sense of relief he was feeling now that he was doing *something* constructive. He was en route to his home with Bill Burroughs and he felt a hell of a lot better. His family would soon be safe and he could get on with catching this bastard.

■   ■   ■

Bill Burroughs was a streetwise, case-hardened detective who was hand-picked to work in the Office of Special Operations by Greg Townsend because, as a uniformed patrolman, his arrest and conviction rate was among the highest in the department. Unlike many police officers, he hadn't been made cynical by the years of daily interaction with the scum of New York City; he remained an unusually decent man and a dedicated cop.

Things didn't go well on the ride to John's house. They were halfway through the Queens Midtown Tunnel when a car fire broke out near the exit on the Queens side, quickly filling the tunnel with smoke. Burroughs killed the engine; without the benefit of the air conditioner they were drenched in no time. While John believed Ruth and Stephie to be in no immediate danger, he was nonetheless anxious to get home. It was two hours before traffic started moving and by the time they reached Hollis, John was a wreck.

Hollis is a predominantly black, middle-class, residential neighborhood of mostly private, wood-frame homes and neatly trimmed lawns. Fords and Chevys are the transportation of choice and the homes are owned by people who make the city run: Cops, firemen, Con Edison workers, and railroad and postal employees form the backbone of the relatively stable neighborhood. Were it white, Archie Bunker would love it.

After turning into his street, John pointed to a small, yellow, wood-frame house near the middle of the block. Burroughs pulled to the curb in front. John waited impatiently on the sidewalk for him to come around. The brown shutters and trim were set off nicely against the yellow of the house. It looked newly painted.

"Nice house," Burroughs said.

John quickly led the way up the driveway to the rear of the house, the only entrance the family used. He stopped in his tracks. The screen door was wide open, pressed flat against the side of the house. The kitchen door was ajar. His warning words to Ruth to keep the doors locked rang in his ears. His hands shook as he drew his revolver and signaled to Burroughs to wait on the steps. Burroughs drew his weapon as John pushed back on the kitchen door and poked his head in.

"Ruth?" No response. He stepped into the area they called a mud-room, really only a landing between the kitchen and the basement. He raised his voice. "Ruth?" Her name played off the kitchen walls and came back empty. He knew before he called out that they weren't there, like sometimes when you make a call and the phone rings, sounding hollow and empty on your end, and you know immediately that no one is home, even though there is no explanation for how you know. And he was more afraid than he'd ever been in his life. He ignored all his training, all precautions, and rushed through the kitchen into the living room, not caring what might be awaiting him. Burroughs was more cautious, moving behind, gun ready, trying his best to cover the corners. John stopped as though he'd hit a wall in front of the large mirror over the couch, his face contorted in horror, his eyes transfixed.

"Oh, my God . . . Oh, my God. No . . . Please, God, no."

Bill Burroughs was chilled to the marrow as he read the words written on the glass. They were runny, red, and appeared to have been written in blood.

> I WARNED YOU. I HAVE YOUR WIFE AND DAUGHTER. KILL YOURSELF BY 5 O'CLOCK TODAY AND I WILL RE-LEASE THEM UNHARMED. LIVE BEYOND THAT AND THEY SUFFER, THEN DIE. THE DARKER THE BERRY, THE SWEETER THE WINE. I CAN HARDLY WAIT TO TASTE YOUR WIFE AND DAUGHTER.

House sounds John had long ago become deaf to became loud, disturbing intruders. The clock ticked, the wand of a venetian blind announced the breeze against the window frame. Their own bitter silence permeated the room, throbbing, alive. Suddenly, the room was filled with the shrill, insistent sound of Burroughs's beeper, and startled, they jumped, fully disoriented, unable momentarily to figure out what it was. Finally, Burroughs pushed his jacket aside, unclipped the beeper, and read an unfamiliar number from the small LCD screen.

"It's probably Greg. We should let him know about this."

John looked at Burroughs as if he had just stepped off a spaceship.

He spit out, "We're not calling anyone. Are you fucking blind or just plain stupid? He's gonna kill my family and you want to compound what I've done! I should have never listened to anyone. He warned me. He fucking warned me. He told me what would happen if I didn't listen, and this is all my goddamn fault."

Burroughs reached out tentatively to comfort him. John pulled away angrily.

"John, it's not your fault. This guy is crazy. He didn't leave you any choices. No *real* choices. You couldn't let him dictate what you did. He'd always want more. He'd have owned you."

John's voice came from a deep well of pain. "Well, he owns me now, doesn't he?"

Burroughs shook his head. "I know what a jam you're in, buddy, but we've got to call Greg and Matt and let them know about this. Maybe they've found something in the meantime that will help us find this guy."

John was a study in menace, his voice deadly flat. "You call them and I'll kill you."

Burroughs became angry. Anguished or not, he couldn't take that kind of threat. "Hey, don't be talking that shit to me, man. You forget who we are? Who *you* are? What the fuck is wrong with you? Look, man, don't go crazy on me." Agitated now, he paced back and forth, working up steam. He thumped the wall with his fist, talking under his breath. "Gonna threaten me! You fuckin' nuts or what? I'm just tryin' to help, goddammit!" He whirled and looked at John, whose normally very dark skin was gray, drained. He looked like he was already dead and the gun in his hand pointing at Bill was steady as stone.

John sounded like a robot. "I told you, if you call them, I'll kill you."

Bill Burroughs was scared. He'd seen men endure all kinds of stress, but none who'd reacted like this. He raised his hands, wanting terribly to convey to John that he meant no harm. He had to clear his throat twice before he could speak.

"Take it easy, man," he said, his voice soft, cajoling. "Calm down. I'm not gonna do anything you don't want. Just take it easy. Let's think this out. We've got a little time, John. Don't have to make no decisions just this minute. Let's just think this out."

But John Williams was gone, replaced by a zombie, beyond hearing or response. He was looking through Burroughs, his mind somewhere in another dimension.

"You don't want to hurt me, John. I know you don't. I'm not the enemy. This isn't the way to do it. Don't do this. *Please*. For your family's sake. They wouldn't want this. Think about it. You *know* they wouldn't want this."

Burroughs's appeal struck a chord and a flicker of humanity, of recognition, crossed John's face. Burroughs used it as a wedge, hoping to bring him back. "That's right, John. Think about *them*. Would they want you to hurt someone because of them? You know they wouldn't. They'd never be able to live with it. Think, man. Take a minute and think."

John was a baleful presence in the room. Burroughs saw his gun hand relax, the barrel beginning to drift down. He took a hesitant step forward, lowered his hands, and reached out, his tone cautious.

"Give me the gun, John. Just give me the gun."

The vacuous look on John's face changed to one of puzzlement as he looked at his weapon, as if surprised to find it in his hand. Burroughs advanced and suddenly the gun was pointing squarely at his chest.

"Stay there, Bill. You're right. I don't want to hurt you. But don't come any closer."

Burroughs stopped, showing the palms of his hands. "That's cool, man. Just relax. Don't do anything we'll both regret."

John was looking over Burroughs's shoulder to the bloody writing on the mirror: off in never-never land again. Burroughs figured no move was better than the *wrong* move, so he stood stock-still. He couldn't penetrate the blank stare, but knew the stalemate couldn't go on forever. He made another attempt to get John to give up the gun.

"Listen to me, John. We can't stay like this all day. You know you don't want to hurt me, so let me have the piece." He advanced, but was brought up short when John stiffened and tightened his grip. The black hole staring at him from the barrel of the gun looked huge. He retreated a step. John appeared to relax slightly, looked at Burroughs, then at the bloody message. He said slowly, "This guy has us wired. He knows everything we're gonna do, even before we do it." He bent his elbow and the gun was pointing at the ceiling. Burroughs cautiously lowered his hands. The gun continued its arc until it was pressed against John's temple.

The leviathan that was John Williams looked at Burroughs, his face suddenly serene, his voice soft and composed as he said, "Tell Ruth that I love them all very much." Bill lunged forward, waving frantically, shouting "NO!" but he was too late.

John Williams pulled the trigger. The explosion sounded nuclear in the quiet room as Bill Burroughs watched the side of John's head detach itself and splatter onto the mirror, the blood mingling with the letters of the message until they merged, blocking out much of it. It happened so fast, John didn't fall right away. He stood teetering for several moments, his arm poised like a mannequin at his head. And then, like the toppling of a giant oak, his body crashed to the floor.

18

Matt, stunned and subdued, seemingly incapable of speech, sat in the passenger seat as Greg drove like a man possessed, bullying and pushing his way through traffic and red lights. The siren seemed much louder than usual and its shriek even more insistent, more incessant, as if knowing that this was no ordinary run. Greg pounded the steering wheel and dash, pushing the car and safety to their limits, careening around corners and slow-moving traffic, cursing anyone who failed to yield or move fast enough. He had tuned the PD radio to the Queens frequency and turned the volume way up. Radio traffic concerning the shooting was hectic, as more and more units acknowledged and responded until finally the first unit to arrive gave a preliminary report: A fire marshal was shot and apparently DOA.

Matt was a distant observer of the hairpin turns and red lights, taken without so much as an easing up on the accelerator. He had no strength to protest or care. He was simply numb. His only concession to reality was to stiff-arm the dash to keep from being tossed around.

The signal 10-13 had brought out the troops in force. The block was jammed with RMPs, PD Emergency Service units, FD Rescue units, and EMS ambulances. People milled about on the sidewalks and in the street, talking in hushed tones from yard to yard, leaning on fences. All attention was focused on the neat, newly painted yellow house with brown trim. Greg zigged in and out of the randomly parked official vehicles and got about midway down the street before screeching to a halt and jamming the lever into park. He and Matt jumped from the car and ran toward the house. Greg was livid when he saw how it had been overrun by the horde of uniformed men.

A police captain stood on the small front lawn talking into a cellular phone, two aides holding clipboards at his side. Greg, flushed and out of breath, stopped in front of him, showed his badge, and began to speak.

The captain cut him off, covering the mouthpiece. "Can't you see I'm on the phone, Sergeant? I'm speaking with the mayor's office."

"I'm *with* the mayor's office, Captain . . ." he read the name plate on his shirt, "Kajinski. The fire marshal and detective in that house are working for *me*. This is my case. Check it out with whoever it is you're talking to, but in the meantime, a crime involving the death of a police officer may have occurred here and I want everyone not directly involved out of the house and away from the building. They've already screwed up any chance we might have had to recover footprints, and they're totally trashing a crime scene. Unless it stops immediately, the mayor will want to know why."

The captain, red-faced and flustered, not used to being talked to like this by a mere sergeant, was about to bring Greg up by the short hairs when he thought, Let's see just how high this guy is hooked.

"What's your name, Sergeant?" Greg told him. He spoke into the phone. "There's a Sergeant Townsend here. Says he works for the mayor. Claims to be in charge."

The captain listened, said good-bye, and handed the phone to an aide.

"Looks like you've got it." He pretended nonchalance as he spoke to his aide. "Peter, have the house and this area cleared immediately. No exceptions. I want everyone out. *Now.*" The aide took off like he'd been shot in the butt.

The captain spoke to Greg. "I didn't realize we were dealing with a *crime scene,* Sergeant. Looked like another cop *suicide* to me," he said sarcastically. Greg strained to hold his temper. Men began streaming out of the house and backyard as the captain's orders spread. A large crowd of uniformed men and detectives began milling about in the street, talking among themselves. The aide came back and spoke quietly to the captain, who turned to Greg.

"There you are, Sergeant," he said with a mock flourish. "Everyone's out. Now what?"

"Where's the detective who was here during the shooting?"

The captain waved toward a command truck parked opposite the house. "In there. The shooting team is interviewing him."

"Please have them bring him out. I need to speak with him."

"Listen, Sergeant, the shooting team has priority on a thing like this. You know that. Why are you trying to create problems?"

Greg was struggling for control. "Captain Kajinski, I am here to *solve* problems, not create them. As for who has priority, perhaps you'd better check with City Hall again."

The captain wasn't about to let Greg know that when the deputy chief inspector he'd been speaking to heard Townsend's name, he'd instructed Captain Kajinski to cooperate fully, render whatever assistance was requested, because, for all practical purposes, Sergeant Townsend was in charge. When he got back to the precinct, he'd make some calls and find out exactly who this pissant was. But he hadn't risen to his rank in the department, with every expectation of rising further, without getting a damn good grip on the politics of power.

His tone still held a trace of reluctance as he spoke. "I suppose if you feel it's so urgent, there's no reason why the shooting team can't wait awhile." He turned to the other man attending him. "Paul, get the detective from the command post and bring him here." He smiled at Greg. "My aides . . . Peter and Paul. I was going to get a relief for them named Mary." He chuckled. "Ya know, like the singing group. But I think I like the simple biblical significance of 'Peter and Paul' better."

And I suppose that makes you Jesus H. Christ, you silly prick, Greg thought. He was furious, knowing this pompous ass had not properly secured the scene. His hopes for finding any significant clues were sinking.

The aide scurried to do Kajinski's bidding and Greg turned to Matt, his anger muted by his concern for John's partner. "Maybe you shouldn't go in. We don't know how bad it is in there. Why don't you wait in the car."

Matt was grim. He shook his head slowly, determined. "I'm going in."

Bill Burroughs walked across the street accompanied by the captain's aide. His clothes and hands were covered with drying blood. Greg cursed Kajinski under his breath. He hadn't even allowed him to wash up. Scumbag, he thought.

Burroughs reached them and Greg searched his face. Burroughs was often teased about the fact that he looked and acted like a recruiting poster for PD detective. He was a sharp dresser and meticulous about his grooming. He was a black man whose light skin and green eyes had caused his teen years to be filled with fistfights and confusion. The blend of black and white features made him an extremely handsome man and, to his constant embarrassment, women of all races pursued him. Burroughs could care less. He was devoted to his wife and two boys. But the man who walked listlessly to where Greg stood with Matt was anything but a poster boy. His pale-green eyes were bloodshot and red-rimmed, his skin a dull gray, and his eyes were fixed on the ground. He looked on the verge of shock or tears.

Greg's tone was exasperated as he spoke to the captain. "Has the department trauma unit been sent for?"

Kajinski looked at both aides and received no reply. "I don't know. I mean, no, not that I know of."

"Why? Isn't that standard procedure when a man's partner has been shot? Isn't he supposed to be examined by a doctor for shock, psychological effects?"

The captain spoke with the sincerity of a whore saying she loves you. "Well, yes, I suppose it is. But everything's been so hectic, we haven't had a chance. I'll see that they're called now. It was thoughtless of me."

Townsend snapped at him, "Do that, Captain." He knew he was bordering on insolence and was also aware that there was only so much he could get away with, mayor or not. The old-boy network of the command ranks was patient and nobody stayed mayor forever. Politicians and hooks and rabbis came and went, but the basic bureaucracy remained the same. A promising career could turn on a dime, leaving a man as a sergeant in charge of other fallen angels, setting sawhorse barricades out for parades. Greg signaled for Matt and Burroughs to follow, and turned on his heels before Kajinski could respond.

Greg wanted to hear Burroughs's version of what happened before he looked at the scene. As they entered the rear yard, he stopped him. "Now, real slowly, Bill, tell us what happened. Start when the two of you left the office." They were near a neatly stacked woodpile a few feet from a redwood picnic table and benches. Burroughs looked like he was about to lose his legs and Greg guided him to the table where he eased himself down gratefully on the edge. Matt's eyes were riveted on the rear door of John's house. His wooden expression offered Burroughs neither compassion nor help, but Burroughs did find sympathy and encouragement in Greg, and he sighed heavily before he began to speak, his words coming haltingly, like a man trying hard to remember something that happened a long time ago.

He was groping for words, and his hands were shaking until he finally shoved them in his pockets to still them. Greg allowed him to settle some before asking again, "What happened?"

Burroughs's voice was hoarse, uncertain. "I don't know. It all happened so fast. One minute we were in the house and the next his brains were on the wall."

"What are you talking about? What do you mean, 'his brains were on the wall'? Who did it?"

Burroughs looked stunned. "You mean you don't know?" He looked at the rear door, but what he saw was something well beyond it. "Oh, my God. You don't know?"

Greg took him by the shoulders. "We just got here. We don't know anything yet. What happened? Who did it?"

"He did, man. . . . He did. He just put the fucking gun to his head and blew his brains out." He began sobbing, shoulders heaving uncontrollably. Greg put his arm around him, squeezed, said something soothing, innocuous.

Burroughs looked from one to the other, anguish and pleading in his eyes. "I couldn't stop him, man. He was gonna shoot *me* if I tried. Oh, my holy God." Matt's face was a stone wall; the veins of his neck were distended, pulsing.

"Why?" Matt's tone sobered him; his eyes drilled into the distraught detective.

Burroughs answered softly. "They took his *family,* man. We got here and there was a message on the mirror. It was written in *blood.*" Bill Burroughs broke down; his handsome face contorted into a wretched grimace and tears started again in the corner of his eyes.

Greg wanted to comfort the man, but he needed to hear the rest. He patted Burroughs's shoulder, urging him to continue. "What *exactly* did the message say?"

Burroughs barely managed to get it out. "It said, 'I warned you. I have your wife and daughter. Kill yourself by five o'clock today and I will release them unharmed. Live beyond that and they suffer, then die.' There was a little bit more, but I forget what."

Matt's response was a cold, blank stare.

Bill Burroughs pushed himself away from the table, turned and walked several steps to face the rear fence and a row of beautifully groomed rose bushes. Matt and Greg barely heard him whisper, "I tried to stop him. I did. I tried to stop him." But they understood that the words were not meant for them.

At Greg's urging, Burroughs related the story: how Williams seemed fine when they left the office, even cheerful; to the traffic jam in the Midtown Tunnel and the discovery of the open rear door and the bloody message on the mirror; then the weapon pointed at him, and finally, the moment when John Williams put his gun to his head and pulled the trigger.

Matt moved decisively toward the house. Greg released Burroughs's shoulder and roughly grabbed Matt's arm. "Matt? Wait! Don't go in there. . . . I'll handle it."

Matt looked at Greg, then Burroughs, then the rear door. He pulled away and was up the two steps and into the kitchen before anyone could stop him.

"Matt! Don't go in there. You don't need to see it." But Greg was too late and had to scurry to catch up. Burroughs followed but lagged behind. Greg drew up next to Matt and they surveyed the kitchen. Everything was neat, clean, except that muddy footprints marred the white-tiled floor. Greg cursed the captain again. He knew that while everything appeared okay, the place would be a disaster forensically. There was probably not a common surface that hadn't been touched by the swarm of cops allowed into the house. What could Captain Fuckhead have been thinking?

Matt walked tentatively to the doorway of the living room, paused, gathered his resolve, and walked purposefully into the room, stopping just inside, Greg at his elbow. Burroughs remained in the kitchen.

The blanket wasn't long enough to cover the body and John's legs poked out from the shins down. The big man took up most of the floor. There was blood everywhere; bits of flesh, skull, and globs of grayish substance splattered the front wall and large mirror. Matt walked to the body, crouched down, and reached for the blanket.

Greg tried to stop him. "Don't, Matt. It isn't necessary. There's nothing to be accomplished by looking."

Matt whispered, "I have to."

Greg stepped aside as Matt drew the corner of the blanket back.

The shattered, bloody head assaulted his senses, and a wave of over-whelming nausea gripped his belly in a vise. He rose on unsteady legs, looked quickly around, and raced for the front hall. He found the light switch behind the door of the bathroom and threw himself to his knees at the bowl. Someone had urinated and Matt silently cursed the cops as he flushed, gagging into the swirling water. Spasm after spasm wracked his insides and went on for a time after his stomach was empty. Sweat-soaked, his shirt clung to him as he loosened his tie and unbuttoned the collar. He fell back and pressed his face against the cool porcelain of the sink. He was spent, without the energy to even pick himself up off the floor.

Greg heard Matt's struggle and fought through the nausea threat-ening to make him sick as well. He looked away, reached down blindly, and re-covered what used to be John's face. He felt like a total failure. A hundred thoughts flew through his mind as he tried to work out how he could have prevented this. He should have anticipated that the Sen-try might try something. They could have had a patrol car sit outside his house until John arrived. They had been fools for underestimating him. He swore to never make that mistake again.

Greg looked at the mirror. Whole sections of the message were ob-scured by blood and fragments of bone. He tried filling in the missing letters. He'd have to ask Burroughs exactly what it said again. He walked to the kitchen; Burroughs was standing where they'd left him, looking lost, out of it. Greg moved to him.

"Bill, I need you to write down exactly what was written on the mirror. Go to the command post and call Crime Scene. Have them respond ASAP. Then call the PD lab and ask for Terry French. Give him our location and tell him I need him and his team here right now. If he's not there, tell them to get him on his beeper. Remember, Terry French. No one else. Stay there when you're done." He hoped that giving Burroughs something produc-tive to do, until he could be relieved and sent home, would take his mind off the suicide. Burroughs didn't move or seem to compre-hend. Greg turned him around and gently nudged him toward the door. "Go on," he said softly, "there was nothing you could do to prevent this. It's not your fault."

As the screen door banged closed behind him, Burroughs heard Greg say under his breath, "It's mine."

█   █   █

The Crime Scene Unit arrived. The streets had been cleared of emergency vehicles save for two patrol cars to ensure that no one tried to enter the house or grounds. The captain had gone back to his precinct house after telling Greg he'd like an update on the progress of the investigation when they were finished at the scene. As far as he was concerned, it was just another cop suicide. Every year more cops died by their own hand than in the line of duty. When it was revealed that John Williams was a fire marshal, it changed nothing for the captain. He was a police officer, wasn't he? And so John had finally gotten the recognition of being one of *them*. Only it was too late, and it was from someone who didn't give a shit.

Matt notified Chief Cattalli, who arrived and asked if there was anything he could do. He extended his condolences and offered to meet with Matt the next day. Howcum D'Aieuto showed up, but he was very late, and stayed only long enough to get a cursory briefing from the Queens supervisor. Greg notified Captain McDonnell, who didn't show up at all.

The work was methodical and tedious. Burroughs had been able to remember what the obliterated parts of the message on the mirror said, and as the sun hit its apex, Matt and Greg couldn't help thinking about John's wife and daughter. But there was nothing to be done at the moment except hope that the maniac kept his word. They had no clue as to their whereabouts, and their only hope was that Crime Scene would turn something up that could lead them to the Sentry. It was a slim hope.

Lieutenant Terry French had been complaining nonstop about the captain who'd allowed *his* scene to be trashed. A committed bachelor, French couldn't imagine time away from his work. He was tall and gangly, with skin color that matched the pallor of his fluorescent work environment. Light blue veins were so clearly visible on his face and arms that he resembled the human anatomy model used in high-school biology classes. His neatly trimmed black hair was combed to one side and parted so crisply, it looked like a toupee. Thin, wire-frame glasses constantly slipped down his almost-bridgeless nose, and after fifteen minutes of watching him habitually push them up, you wanted to grab his hands and hold them still.

Lieutenant French was the ultimate nerd, one of those people born to spend his life in a laboratory.

Greg had met French during an investigation of a series of stranglings and had been enormously impressed by his work. Although he wasn't really a "field man," his instincts were excellent, and he was the most thorough person Greg had ever met. His one major failing was that he was myopic about his work and, even when excited, his voice was a monotonic drone. Greg teased him by saying that he was the only surefire cure for insomnia he'd ever known. Two minutes into a conversation with Terry French and your eyelids started to droop.

After the body had been photographed and its position marked, Greg authorized its release to the medical examiner. The room was still a mess, but it wasn't so grim once John's remains were gone. His size had required them to constantly step around him, so once the body was removed, the work sped up. One of the first things Greg requested of French was that he take samples of the blood used to write the message on the mirror and have them walked through the lab. The writing bothered Greg from the moment he'd seen it. If John's family was to be returned unharmed, then whose blood was it? If it belonged to his wife or daughter, then he feared that he was already dealing with multiple murders. But he didn't think so. If they had been killed in the house and their own blood used, then they would have found traces of it somewhere in the house. But they didn't. And if they were killed elsewhere, why would the killer bring their blood back to write a message that promised they'd be returned unharmed if John complied? No, Greg thought, something was definitely not right.

Terry French took samples, notified the serology lab, and gave the samples to a Crime Scene detective to hand-deliver there and wait for the results. Greg looked at his watch. The detective had been gone more than three hours. It was five P.M., the deadline the message had set for John's death. He looked at Matt, who was leaning against the wall, staring at a photograph of John and his family. The phone rang and Matt snatched it up, visibly deflating as he held it out to Terry French.

"It's for you."

Matt walked to a corner chair and sat down. It was an oversized recliner and well-worn. Judging by its size and the comfortable impression in its seat, Greg was certain it was John's. He moved closer to the monotone of French's voice. French hung up and turned to Greg.

"It's not human."

"What's not human?"

"The blood. It's some sort of animal blood, not human. They haven't typed it yet, but it's definitely not human. The serologist is gonna type it and get back to us. That takes longer, maybe tomorrow morning or early afternoon."

It was exactly what Greg had expected. John had been fooled into thinking he was looking at his family's blood. Had he been able to be objective, he might have had the same reservations as Greg had about that possibility. But Greg could only imagine the terror John must have felt, believing his family had been harmed. He knew he wouldn't have been thinking so clearly if it was his own family that had been kidnapped.

■   ■   ■

During the time they awaited the results from the serology lab, Matt had sat in the recliner, feeling very alone amidst the swirl of activity around him. He rationalized his inaction by assuring himself that he had nothing concrete to contribute to what was already being done. He was aware of how passive he must appear to the other men, especially Greg, but he didn't care. He had some thinking to do. A plan was forming in his mind and he didn't want to be disturbed, so while physically he appeared withdrawn, inwardly his mind was working quickly, coldly.

He would call Cattalli first thing in the morning. He doubted that anything he asked for at this point would be denied, and he intended to take advantage of that. Cattalli would want this bastard caught as much as he did. His reasons would be different, but he'd want it nonetheless. He didn't dare tell the chief what he really had in mind, but it wouldn't matter. So long as he cooperated.

As Forensics went about the business of dusting for prints, gathering and labeling every item that might offer a clue, Matt remained immobile. He heard voices, but they sounded disjointed and surreal and seemed to come from far away. Men appeared, then reappeared elsewhere in the room. While Greg quietly issued orders, Terry French continued to fuss about the screwed-up state of the scene.

They'd taken prints from John's body before it was removed and figured the best place to get samples of his wife's and daughter's would be upstairs in their rooms. When the lab report came back negative for human blood, Matt was as unsurprised as Greg. An hour and a half had passed since that call and each minute beyond five o'clock left them less and less hopeful that John's wife and daughter would be returned unharmed. Yet there was something not quite right about the whole thing. Greg Townsend sensed it and so did Terry French.

French pulled Greg aside. "I don't know about you, buddy, but outside the mess in this room, I can't detect any signs of a struggle or anything unusual. Whatever happened here happened without violence."

Greg looked concerned. "I agree. I can't find anything, either."

A woman's screams pierced the quiet and sent them scrambling for the front door. Matt arrived at the doorway first and stopped suddenly just beyond the entrance, the men behind pushing against him, straining to see. Two policemen assigned to watch the street were restraining a well-dressed black woman and a young girl clinging to her skirt. She was struggling fiercely with them.

"Let me go! I *live* here. This is my house. What's wrong?" She yelled, "John? John? What's happening?" She spotted Matt and renewed her struggle. "Matt! Tell them to let me go! Where's John? Matt? Matt?"

Matt stepped forward, Greg alongside. "That's John's wife and daughter," Matt told him. "Tell them to let her go."

The officers were looking over their shoulders for direction from inside. Greg motioned to the cops to let her go. Ruth Williams ran to the front stoop and tried to push her way through the wall of detectives. Matt caught her and held her. She struggled in his arms, imploring him to answer: "What's happened? Where's John? Why are all these men in my home?" She pulled away from Matt, her eyes wet, on the verge of tears, looking both defiant and scared.

Matt tried to put his arm around her shoulders but she twisted angrily away. "Never mind that. Just tell me what's going on."

"Ruth, I want you to walk to the back of the house with me."

"No, goddammit! I don't want to go to the back of the house. I want to know what's going on."

Matt managed to choke out the awful news. "I'm sorry, Ruth. John's dead."

Her wail of anguish filled the quiet street. She fell forward and Matt caught her, wrapping his arms around her. Her daughter was clinging to her, sobbing. Instinctively, she pulled her daughter closer and Matt encompassed the child in his embrace as well. Wracking sobs shook Ruth Williams's body and she cried uncontrollably until the front of Matt's shirt was soaked with tears. No one spoke. The men in the rear backed into the house one by one, until only Matt, Greg, Ruth, and the young girl remained.

"Ruth?"

She looked suspiciously at the stranger.

"My name's Greg Townsend. John was working for me."

She blinked and wiped her eyes with the back of her hands.

"I know this is a terrible time for you," Greg said, "but I have to ask you a couple of questions. I'm afraid they can't wait." He reached to touch her shoulder, make some sort of contact, transmit the pain he felt along with her. But she'd have none of it. She wrenched away from him and glared with hate-filled eyes.

"What happened? Why is John dead?"

Matt gently turned her to face him. "Ruth, where have you just come from?"

She looked at Greg and then Matt again as if he'd just asked the most stupid question she'd ever heard. "We were shopping. Just like you told us to."

They were dumbstruck; nothing registered. Matt broke the silence. "What do you mean, 'just like *I* told you'?"

Her frustration spilled out. "Well, not *you* exactly. But the detective who called this morning. He said that John told him to call, and that the plans had been changed. He said John wanted us to stay away from the house today, go someplace public, someplace filled with people, until around six-thirty. I figured what better place than a mall?" Her face reflected her puzzlement that they didn't already know this, that they *should* know this. "He called about a half hour after I spoke to John. When I told the detective that I'd just gotten off the phone with my husband, he said he knew it, but that John had something important to do first and couldn't come right home."

Greg asked, "What was the detective's name?"

She hugged her sobbing daughter, patting her shoulders. "I don't know. . . . Cantell? Cantrel? Something like that. He said he was working on a case with Matt and John."

Greg offered, "Was it Cannell?"

"Yeah. That was it. *Cannell.*"

The news that she had been safe all along stunned them. And it hadn't begun to really sink in just how diabolical this nightmare was.

There was no way to get anywhere in the house without passing through the living room and Matt didn't want Ruth or her daughter to see the gore or the message on the mirror.

"Greg, they can't go in the house. Let's take them to the car."

Ruth pulled away when Matt tried to lead her down the walkway. "Why can't I go into my own house?" She was almost screaming. "It's time for *you two* to answer some questions. What happened? How did John die? Is he in there?" She pointed at the house and then tried to break through the two men blocking her way. Matt grabbed her around the arms. She struggled but he held firm.

"He's not in there, Ruth. He's been taken to the medical examiner."

The mention of the ME renewed the reality of John's death and she slipped from Matt's arms and slumped to the stoop. Her daughter sat beside her and they held each other and sobbed, undisturbed by the men. Matt felt awkward standing over them and knelt beside them.

"I'm so sorry, Ruth. I can't begin to say how sorry I am. I loved John. I think you know that. He was one in a million, and there'll never be anyone like him." He put his arm lightly on her shoulder and was comforted that she accepted the gesture.

The sun had just dipped below the horizon and the western sky glowed a reddish orange, an omen for a beautiful tomorrow. They sat lost in the memory of their friend, their husband, their father, each filled with the terrible tragedy that had befallen them. Ruth finally looked up.

"You haven't answered me. How did he die?"

"Ruth, please. Stephie doesn't have to hear this, does she? Let's go someplace and talk. Is there a relative nearby? A close friend?"

"She's old enough to hear. It was her father, and we never kept any secrets in this family."

"But this is different, Ruth. Let's talk about it, and if you still feel she needs to know the details, you can tell her yourself."

Ruth thought for a moment. "Okay, fine. There's a neighbor down the street where we can talk. Her daughter is best friends with Ste-

phanie. We can go there." She pushed herself off the stoop, ignoring
the helping hand offered by Greg, and took her daughter's hand. "Stephie honey, we're going to Charlene's house." Stephie, who hadn't said
a word through it all, grabbed her mother in a move so desperate, so
anguished, that it took Ruth by surprise.

"Where's Daddy? I want my daddy. Please . . . God, please give me
back my daddy."

Ruth patted her softly, her little girl's need momentarily surpassing
her own. "There, honey. It's okay. I know, baby. I know. You cry.
You just cry." After a few moments she met Matt's dejected eyes and
said softly, "Let's go."

When they arrived at the Walters' house, Ruth sat stoically as Matt
and Greg told her what they'd been able to piece together. She asked
few questions. When they were finished she slumped on the couch, a
cup of coffee growing cold on the table in front of her. Matt didn't like
the fact that she was so listless and docile. The Ruth he knew was a
good woman, a good wife, and one tough bird. The Ruth he knew was
the woman who arrived home earlier and demanded answers. When
they left Ruth and Stephie in the care of the Walters, she was unresponsive, just sitting and holding her daughter tightly.

When Matt and Greg got back to John's house, Terry French was
in the basement. He called to them to come down.

"Did John or his wife smoke?" Matt told them he knew John
didn't, that he always complained about Matt's smoking. He'd never
seen Ruth smoke either and couldn't imagine John liking it if she did.

"Well, someone's been smoking down here." He indicated a work-
bench in the corner. "Look at this." He pointed to residue on one edge.
There was none on the floor. French surmised that the ash had been
brushed into someone's hand and disposed of along with the butt.

"How do you know that it's from a cigarette?" Matt asked.

"I don't, for certain. But it's an extremely fine-grain ash, not like
you'd get from paper or anything else. We'll be able to tell for sure in
the lab."

Greg said, "So, if it *is* from a cigarette, it means somebody came
down here and stayed long enough to smoke one."

French considered that, pushed his glasses up on his nose. "Yes,
but I think there's more to it than that. Remember what you told me
about the break-in here last night and the perp leaving Williams a note?

I think there's a distinct possibility that he never left. *Someone* was in the house when John left for work this morning, and was still here when Ruth got the call from the bogus detective.''

French ignored their doubtful expressions and became uncharacteristically animated as he continued. ''Look, whoever gets in here last night takes the photo of the girl, tapes the note to the door, and instead of leaving, comes down to the basement. Maybe he has a two-way radio equipped with an earpiece. John gets up, finds the note and photograph, and leaves a short time later. The perp radios his accomplices that Williams has left and waits here for him to call home, knowing that the odds are he won't call again after that. Then they have the phony detective call, and Ruth leaves as instructed. He waits to make sure she isn't coming back and sneaks a smoke. That's why I believe it was only one guy who stayed behind—I don't think an accomplice would allow his partner to smoke. Sneaking a smoke is the kind of thing a man alone would do. The advantage of never leaving the house in the first place is it saves the trouble and obvious risk of being seen by a neighbor during a daylight break-in.''

Matt Kincaid seemed interested in the investigation for the first time since seeing John's body. Greg Townsend was running his fingers through his hair, unmindful of his disheveled state.

French led them to a small closet in the far corner of the room. ''Take a look at this.'' He opened it carefully and knelt down. ''This is one of those closets we all have in our basements or garages. It contains our least-used tools and things. Stuff we should throw out but always think we're gonna need some day.'' He aimed his flashlight. ''Look at the buildup of dust on the floor. Now look at the center.'' There, easily discernible, were scuffed footprints.

He looked over his shoulder. ''Now, why would anyone stay in a closet if no one was home? My guess is this is where he hid until after Ruth Williams left. Then he comes out and smokes a long-awaited cigarette. He probably put it out under water in the mop sink over there, taking the butt with him. I'm gonna have one of my guys look it over. As for the blood for the message on the mirror, he had it with him when he arrived.''

French stood up and faced them. ''And there's another reason why I believe this guy never left.'' He jerked his thumb toward the stairs. ''One of my men removed the kitchen door lock. It's a common double-cylinder house lock; it needs a key from either side to be opened. We won't be certain until we can view it under a microscope, but from what the technician can see with just a magnifying glass, it appears that the lock was picked from the outside and shimmied from the inside. There's one clean scrape mark on the inside striker plate and door edge, and one small indentation on the inside of the striker.''

Greg asked, "Look, Terry, put it in plain English, would ya? How did he get in and out, and how can we tell if he did it more than once?''

French's voice took on the tone of a schoolteacher tutoring a student. "Okay, look. By eliminating the fact that he didn't have a key and there are no force marks on the outer part of the door or lock, we can pretty much assume that he picked the lock getting *in*. Locks are designed to keep people *out*. So, once he's in, it's a heck of a lot easier to use any curved, pointed object to get out, rather than bother finessing the lock with a pick-set again. Almost anything will do the job—a nut pick, a dentist's probe, even an ice pick would work fine. They all leave a small dot on the striker, like the one my man found. He says that judging by the scrape mark on the paint, the handle of the instrument probably had knurling or tooling on the shaft. That would be consistent with a dentist probe or nut pick.''

Greg still wasn't satisfied. "So how does any of this show that he only broke in once?''

"Well, it doesn't, exactly. We can't tell if a lock has been picked more than once within a few hours, but what the marks clearly show is that he almost certainly only broke *out* once. Which is almost the same thing.''

Matt wasn't convinced either. "Why couldn't he have just left the door ajar the second time, so as not to have to worry at all about how to get out?''

"That's a good point, Matt, but it's been my experience that a pro doesn't worry about locks or getting past them. Especially house locks. He opens them quicker than you and I could with a key. He closes the door behind him because it's not smart to leave a door open. A neighbor stopping by would wonder why the door wasn't locked with no one home. Any number of scenarios make it a dumb move to leave a door open behind you after you've broken in.''

Matt looked puzzled. "Look, I'm not denying what you're saying, but that would mean they knew what John would do all along.''

Greg faced him. "Or what *you* would do, Matt."

"What's that supposed to mean, Greg?"

"Maybe it's *you* they've got a handle on. Maybe they knew you'd never let John walk off the case under those circumstances. Nothing against you, Matt—you know I believe as you did that it would've been the wrong thing to do."

Matt didn't want to believe he was so easily read, so predictable that plans could be drawn up based on his anticipated movements. He tried to invalidate the argument, but the physical evidence spoke too strongly and French's suppositions seemed too logical. If it didn't go down just as French said, it was probably damn close.

Well, let's see if the demented son of a bitch can predict what I'm about to do now, he thought.

19

Matt was numb, his mind as yet unable to deal with John's death. He filled a tumbler half-full with vodka, added an ice cube, walked dejectedly to the living room, turned on a lamp, and slumped into his beat-up La-Z-Boy. The house was stiflingly hot but he made no move to open a window or remove his jacket. He took a long pull on the vodka. Beads of condensation slid down the glass, dropping unnoticed onto his already-soaked shirt. The ice cube popped and cracked in the glass, the refrigerator compressor recycled, and the house made its usual, small creaking sounds as outside, the evening cooled. Slouching lower in the chair, he tried to wrap himself in the illusion of peace the quiet offered, but the day continued to pass through his mind in a series of appalling images. He tried to force himself to cry. He *owed* John some tears, but they wouldn't come, and because he couldn't pay even that small homage, it intensified his feelings of guilt and self-disgust.

Perspiration traced a path from his forehead to his chin and he became sluggishly conscious of the airless heat of the living room. He ignored it. Beyond the large window the Hudson River was defined by the lights lining its shores. Stars twinkled above the palisades, reflecting off the black sable surface of the water. A string of bare bulbs highlighted the perimeter of a barge being pushed south toward the ocean by a dimly lit tug.

The crunch of wheels on gravel at the side of the house and the sound of a motor shutting down was followed moments later by a light rapping on the glass of the kitchen door. The knocking became more insistent but he remained immobile. A muffled female voice came through the pane.

"Matt? . . . Matt?!" The voice was unfamiliar. "Matt, it's me, Tracy. Please open the door."

Tracy? How the hell did *she* get his address? I can't see her now. I just can't. Why can't people just leave you alone when you want to be left alone?

"Matt, I know you're in there. I'm not leaving until you talk to me."

He felt as ancient as the Mariner as he put his drink on the end table and pushed himself heavily out of the chair. The kitchen door seemed far away, looming like the Great Wall, until he gathered the resolve to pull it open. Matt never so much as glanced at her, just turned and walked back to the living room, dropping like a stone into his chair. The screen door slammed loudly. He picked up the tumbler of vodka and cradled it to his chest, leaving a large puddle on the wood end table.

Tracy had followed him to the living room but stood at the entrance, hesitant to enter. "I called to see why you didn't show up at the hospital," she said. "Sergeant Townsend told me what happened." She paused, hoping for a response that might assuage her unease or hint that she was even a little welcome. She hid her disappointment. "I'm so sorry, Matt. I want to help. Tell me how I can."

He didn't recognize the hollow, tinny sound as his own voice. "There's nothing you can do. Nothing anyone can do. You can help me by leaving."

"I don't want to leave, Matt. I want to help. I want to be here with you."

Resignation and fatigue weighed like anchors on his thoughts. His speech was heavy and slow. "Look, I appreciate it. But can't you see I'm in no mood for company? Just go. I'll call you sometime. But go."

She was suddenly kneeling beside him, her scent blossoming in the narrow space between them. Her featherlike touch on his arm accented the nearly imperceptible squeeze of compassion. Drawn to her humanity, her warmth, he almost succumbed before pulling sharply away. She gasped, recoiling at the violence of his reaction.

This is wrong, he thought. I don't deserve to be comforted. If I knew what the hell I was doing, John might still be alive. If I hadn't been so goddamn sure of myself. No, I don't deserve to be comforted. I deserve to be in John's place.

"Matt, please. Look at me. Just look at me."

His tone was flat, mechanical. "I told you. I don't want you here. I appreciate it, but I don't want you here. I can't make it any plainer than that."

The quiet seemed a tangible thing: thick, gelatinous. When, at last, the futility of her presence struck her fully, she slowly rose. Unable to find her voice or the words that might unlock the silence, her hands miming a helpless entreaty, she hovered uncomfortably at his side.

She backed away, sadness and regret coloring every word. "You know, Matt, the first moment I laid eyes on you, something clicked inside me. I don't know what it was, but it felt good." She struggled to find the precise words that could convey how she felt. "It felt like I'd just come home after being away for a long time. When you came to the ER with Ellen . . ." She sighed, then shrugged. "I've never felt that way before. You seemed familiar to me. Comfortable. Like I'd known you all my life. You felt"—she suppressed a smile—"I don't know, like . . . like a favorite shirt." She stepped hesitantly back into the room. "I know that isn't very romantic. Nobody wants to be an old shirt. But I think you know what I mean. It just seemed *right*. . . . *You* seemed right. And I think you felt it, too." No response. "Or was it all just in my head?"

He remained unreachable and she surrendered. Whatever vitality had been in the room deflated with her. She looked at the man she liked so well and decided that she was simply wrong. Maybe she'd put too much emphasis on *her* emotions and only imagined he felt the same. But it was clear he didn't want her there. It was also clear that she wasn't going to be able to help him. She bit her lip, struggling to control the sense of frustration and disappointment threatening to make her cry.

"I'm sorry, Matt. I didn't mean to intrude. I thought I could help. Good-bye." She turned and walked woodenly to the door, grasped the doorknob, and paused, torn momentarily by indecision. Finally, she took a breath, straightened her shoulders, and turned the knob.

Matt's hand covering hers startled her, and she froze.

His voice was husky, fragile, and seemed suddenly very young. "Please don't go."

A bolt of pain hurtled the gap between them, slamming into her as a physical force as she turned to face him, reading the world in those three simple words. Open agony was etched deeply on Matt's face. Her heart pounded, threatening to pummel its way out of her chest. All of her experience as a doctor couldn't help her now. There were no prescriptions, no healing arts to draw upon that could ease this pain. And so she did the only thing she could. She put her arms around him and pulled him close.

He let himself be drawn to her and her hand played a light, helpless rhythm on his back. He fell to his knees, burying his face in her belly. She held his head and stroked his hair. His arms encircled her waist, gripping her tightly, his breath hot through her blouse. Then, slowly at first, almost imperceptibly, his body began to heave, growing in intensity until full, rending sobs shook them both. His pain entered her, attaching itself to a spot somewhere at her core, feeling like a throbbing open wound. Yet while his anguish tore bits of her heart away, she soared beyond the agony to feelings so powerful that she had to open her eyes to regain her equilibrium.

Tracy Gold held Matt even tighter, stroking his head, slowly falling to her own knees, Matt clinging desperately to her. When he laid his head on her shoulder, the motion was so like a little boy's, it nearly made her cry. And then, without really knowing why, she did cry.

Even, after a time, when his anguish receded and his sobs became an occasional soft hiccup, when only a sporadic tremor shook him, they remained locked in place, unwilling to break the bond. The clock ticked loudly, a car's headlights swept the room from the street, and they became acutely aware of the beat of their hearts. Then Matt stirred, loosened his grip, and, holding her at arm's length, studied her face. His own was tearstained; the once-hard lines, soft and yielding. Her cheeks were streaked with mascara; her hair, damp and pasted to her brow. She looked at him looking at her and brushed a hand self-consciously across her forehead.

He almost managed a smile. "Why the heck are *you* crying?"

"Because I think I love you, you big idiot." She punched his shoulder and he laughed lightly and drew her to him. His lips brushed her cheeks and a strong hunger washed over her. She found his mouth and kissed him deeply, pressing herself against him. He held her even tighter before removing her hands from around his neck and standing up, pulling her to her feet as they kissed again. The kiss was more insistent this time, more desperate; their need overpowering. He pulled away, his face asking the question. Total understanding flashed between them and he bent and scooped her up. She was light and Matt savored the way she fit him as he carried her to his room. She lay her head on his shoulder and a feeling of contentment she had lost hope of ever finding embraced her, wrapping her heart in a warm cocoon. Under her breath she whispered a message not meant for him, but for another she loved, who was gone.

"I think I'm home, Momma. I think I'm finally home."

20

Despite the night of passion and blossoming feelings for Tracy, Matt awoke depressed. Their lovemaking, which had begun soft and tender, had grown fierce and desperate as the night wore on. He'd found himself clinging to her as if she were the source of light in a bleak, dark landscape, and in a way, that night, she was. He'd never felt as despondent or alone. Her lips, her arms around him, the warmth of her flesh, acted as an affirmation of life over death. No one would ever know how close he'd come to ending it all.

Tracy had awakened first, found the coffee, and set it brewing. Matt's eyes opened to the sound of toneless humming coming from the shower. He padded to the kitchen, where the sound grew louder, poured himself a cup of coffee, and sat at the breakfast bar facing the rear lawn, listening. He had to use the can but decided to let her finish.

She luxuriated in the heat of the shower, making minor adjustments in temperature until the scalding-hot needles of spray reddened her skin. Steam condensed and ran down the wallpaper. The ingredients of Matt's scent were everywhere—in the shampoo, the soap, the towels—and she breathed them in deeply.

The range of Matt's emotions that night had left her bewildered. At first, he'd been so intense, so incredibly needy, and then at some point, a strength emerged from a hidden well within him, which made her feel suddenly delicate and fragile. His physical size may have been part of the reason—she felt small and protected in his arms—but no, it was more the *force* of him. Mournful and disconsolate as he was, something—an energy, an anger, she couldn't say for sure—changed his lovemaking from tender, almost delicate, to rough and frenzied, as if he had a desperate need to bury himself inside her. Tracy felt as if she'd stood at the lip of a dormant volcano come suddenly to life. And the intensity of his need released instincts of her own she'd kept buried for far too long. When they were spent and he became quiet, withdrawn, she asked him what he was thinking. It took some time before he answered, "I'm thinking about what you said at the hospital." She asked him what he meant, and he said, "About wishing the men who hurt Ellen were dead." But he would say nothing beyond that.

She came out of the bathroom toweling her hair, wearing one of his white shirts she'd found draped over a chair in the bedroom. He swiveled around as Tracy entered the kitchen. God almighty, she's beautiful. Her thick, black hair glistened with moisture and her face, devoid of makeup, made her look very young. The shirttail barely covered her buttocks and the front of the shirt was wet in spots. One dark nipple, clearly visible, clung invitingly to the material. She stepped to him and slid her arms around his neck and lifted her face to kiss him, but instead of feeling natural, it felt clumsy and strained for both of them. They fumbled until she dropped her arms, turned away from him, and poured a cup of coffee to cover her awkwardness. She wondered why he seemed so distant. Absorbed as he was in his own anxieties, the moment served to kindle his growing confusion.

He wasn't working that day. He didn't know what kind of leave he was on; the fire department didn't have a contingency for a partner getting shot. Cattalli had just told him not to come in, that he'd take care of it. One thing's for certain, he thought, I'm not going to curl up in a corner and die on this one. Unlike when Larry was murdered, this time the people responsible were still out there, still unpunished. And they were going to pay.

It was this mounting resolve to see justice done that Tracy had interpreted as renewed strength in the night. He would do whatever it took to find John's killers (for that's how he saw them). Hypnosis, drug-induced regression, whatever—nothing was going to stop him. He'd tell Greg today to make an appointment with the PD shrink. If that didn't work, he'd do the drug thing. He'd pick through the records of every case he'd ever handled, locate and speak to every person he'd ever arrested, every victim who'd felt cheated by justice. But he would not roll over on this one.

He looked up to find Tracy leaning against the sink, sipping from her mug, holding it in that uniquely feminine way, using two hands, studying him over the rim.

"What?!" he said in mock annoyance.

Her eyes widened innocently, a hint of mischief playing at the corners. "Oh, nothing. Just doing a little mind reading is all."

"Really? Am I that transparent?"

"Not at all. I'm just a good mind reader. No reflection on you *or* your mind," she said, grinning.

"And what have you come up with?"

"See? There you go, wanting to know my business. If I told you what *you* were thinking, then we'd both know, wouldn't we?"

He laughed. "Well, you've got a point there. We wouldn't want *me* to know what *I'm* thinking, would we?"

"Nope. Next thing, you'd want to know what *I'm* thinking. And then everybody would know everything and all the mystery would be gone. And boom, just like that, it'd be over. And we've hardly just begun."

The remnants of a smile still lingered on his face but his tone was serious. "Are we, Tracy? Are we just beginning?"

Her fingers tightened on the mug. "I'd like to think so, Matt. Why? Is something going on that I'm not aware of?"

"No. It's just that there's a tension in the room that wasn't there last night."

Tracy placed her cup deliberately on the counter and faced him straight on. Her tone was playfully astonished. "Last night? Are you kidding? You call what happened last night *relaxed?* Relative to what? A nuclear holocaust?"

He didn't know what to say, so he bought some time by sipping his coffee.

She spoke before he could respond. "Look, Matt, I told you. I like you. Last night doesn't put either of us under any obligation. I promise I won't ask you to marry me before I leave. But what did you expect? We hardly know each other." She looked away from him, out the window to somewhere far beyond the lawn. "Maybe your expectations were greater than mine. I don't know. But I'm not complaining." Her attention was suddenly back on him, her eyes riveted on his. "I thought parts of last night were magical."

He suddenly felt very young and vulnerable. He gazed blindly into his coffee, a warm flush of blood coloring his face. "I thought so, too."

She brightened and, sensing how difficult it was for him, tried to change the subject. "Hey, I've got an idea. Why don't you come over tonight and I'll cook dinner?"

And then he was in front of her, taking her by the elbows and drawing her close. Whatever uneasiness remained, melted away as she floated into his arms. Their kiss was soft, sweet, unhurried. His hands slid under the shirt and cupped the warm flesh of her buttocks. She pressed against him and held his face in her hands and peppered him with small, delicious kisses, until her lips found his mouth again and met his longing with a hunger of her own. She broke away and took his hands, her eyes bold, wanton, enticing, as she tugged insistently.

"Let's go into the bedroom. I need to feel you inside me."

21

Jake Morgan sat comfortably, feet up, hands behind his head, at his desk in the small windowless room of the Special Investigations Unit at FD headquarters on Livingston Street in Brooklyn. His boyish, lightly freckled Irish features were fixed in a self-satisfied grin; he was feeling rather good about himself. Jake's face had somehow managed to escape damage from the inferno that had trapped him as a young firefighter with only two years on the job, but large, smooth, square and rectangular-shaped skin-graft scars covered almost every other part of his body. His face had escaped unscathed only because his mask had miraculously failed to melt in the fiery basement that might easily have become his tomb. The doctors at the New York Hospital–Cornell Medical Center Burn Center had worked for months on the rest of his body. Despite the scars on his hands and arms, he remained a handsome man. The plastic surgeons had been able to rebuild the tips of his ears fully. The grafts at the back of his neck were covered by reddish-brown hair worn slightly longer than was the current style. He had thick, bushy eyebrows that were slightly darker than the rest of his hair, and his warm brown eyes were nestled comfortably beneath them. Jake was quick to laugh and his eyes lit up when he smiled.

The reason he was feeling so good was because he had been a key player in the largest arson indictment in the history of the Manhattan DA's office. Yesterday had been a day of great personal and professional satisfaction. A combined force of fire marshals, cops, and troopers from two states had swept through the five boroughs, Long Island, and New Jersey, arresting forty-eight defendants. And much of it had been because of him. The case had taken more then two years to develop, requiring extraordinary patience and perseverance from all those involved. But when the payoff had come, it came Big-Time. His photograph had appeared in every local newspaper and on every local news broadcast. Friends and family hadn't stopped calling to say they had seen him and were proud.

The headquarters' Special Investigations Unit was the best SIU to serve in, but even Jake would admit it wasn't necessarily the *best* SIU. They had more resources than the remaining two base SIUs and worked directly for the chief fire marshal, whose office was just down the hall, and because they worked for him, they operated without many of the constraints imposed on other marshals. It was a pretty sweet deal, and though Jake felt he had earned his spot, there was nonetheless a lot of petty jealousies to contend with from other marshals.

But for now, none of that mattered. He was lost in the joy of his moment in the sun. Jake Morgan had waited at the courthouse as each of the defendants was brought in to have the charges against him read. He couldn't remember ever feeling such a deep sense of professional satisfaction. Some all-too-rare justice was being dished out, and he thought back to how it had started with a casual remark to his former partner.

Matt Kincaid was senior to him, with more time as a firefighter, and had already served four years in the Bureau when Jake was promoted to fire marshal. When the class of new marshals graduated from the Fire Academy, Jake was assigned to Matt's squad and their supervisor made them a team. At first Matt resented the younger man. Partnerships resembled marriages in many ways, and while Matt had been through a series of less than satisfactory partners, at least those men had been able to conduct their own investigations. New marshals had to be told *everything*. Things taken for granted with an experienced man had to be explained to a new one. It could be exasperating and you usually wound up doing the new guy's work as well as your own.

But it didn't take long for Matt Kincaid to realize that Jake Morgan wasn't just another new guy. He was streetwise and sharp, never had to be told anything twice, and had an instinct for what to say and when to say it. Matt found himself having fun again. It had been a while since he'd enjoyed coming to work, but he was discovering that, despite their age difference, he and the younger man had many things in common. Unlike most marshals, both had some money to burn. Jake's wife was a top copywriter in an advertising agency and earned nearly twice what Jake made as a marshal. They had no children. Matt's son was grown and Jenny was making good money as the assistant to the chairman of a specialty wire company. And because money wasn't a problem, Jake and Matt were able to enjoy some of the better restaurants Manhattan had to offer. Their often oddball, caustic senses of humor complemented each other and so, despite the heavy work load, they managed to spend much of their time laughing. In retrospect, both men looked at their two-year partnership as the best match they'd ever had.

Their breakup came when Matt was offered a spot in Manhattan's SIU and Jake Morgan took his position at headquarters. They knew that partnerships didn't last forever and both agreed that this was the best way to end theirs, before they were forced to do it anyway by another class of graduating fire marshals, or because the city thought they were making too much overtime from their many arrests.

Matt's stint in the Manhattan SIU didn't last more than a year. Larry Peterson became his partner after Matt requested a return to the field, dissatisfied with the paper-pushing and political bullshit of the SIU. After Larry was killed, Jake visited and called at least once a week, trying to pull Matt out of his funk. Matt remained unresponsive through it all but Jake never gave up.

While they were a team, Matt enjoyed the intense commitment Jake Morgan had for his job. After four years, the job had been getting stale for Matt, and Jake's enthusiasm inspired him to recapture some of his own old energy.

The two years Jake spent in and out of the burn center prior to becoming a marshal changed him forever. The fire that burned over forty percent of his body had been determined by the fire marshals to be incendiary. The perp was never caught.

Jake developed an all-consuming hatred for arsonists, would do anything to catch them. This obsession became both his main asset and his main fault. His search for certain fire-setters sometimes became personal vendettas that skewed his objectivity. Not even Matt could talk to him about it. As far as Jake was concerned, jail was much too good for them, though he never did say what he thought *would* be good enough for them.

It was that vengeful passion that ultimately caused him to throw caution to the wind and go charging into a vacant building to chase a suspect he and Matt thought they had cornered. They had approached a man who fit the description another junkie had given them of a guy named Paco, who was suspected of having started a series of arson-for-pay fires throughout the South Bronx. When they came upon him, Paco's back was against the wall of a vacant building. Neither Jake nor Matt saw the hole in the brickwork of the wall as an avenue of escape, but Paco was a junkie and had scored his crack in that very building many times. The perp saw them approach and darted into the building through the hole in the wall. Matt wasn't quick enough to stop Jake, who dashed through the hole in hot pursuit.

Inside, the building was shadows and dark forms, illuminated only by the cracks and breaks in various window boards. But Paco knew it well. Jake was following the man's footfalls up to what remained of the second-floor landing when a step gave way and he plunged through. As he dangled precariously, supported only by his arms on the stair treads, the junkie, just ahead of him, looked back and saw Jake hanging there helplessly. Jake watched wide-eyed, sure that he was seeing the final moments of his life as Paco reached under his sweatshirt, smiled an almost-toothless smile, and pulled out a snub-nosed pistol. He took careful aim; Jake clenched his eyes shut and gripped what remained of the stairs. The sound of the shot surprised him and he was sure he was dead, until he heard Matt yelling, asking if he was all right. Paco's body was sprawled on the floor next to Jake, his bloody head a foot away. Using only the hazy back-light of the stair-landing window, and forced to shoot from an impossible angle at the bottom of the stairs, Matt had somehow managed to put a third eye in Paco's forehead. Jake Morgan still believed it was the best shot he'd ever see. Matt never told him he'd been aiming for Paco's chest.

Now, on the day of his greatest professional triumph, as Jake sat savoring the delight of sending forty-eight coconspirators to jail, he remembered that it was Matt who made the vital link that connected all the fires. They'd been playing a round of golf up in Yonkers and Jake mentioned that he'd been handed a thick folder containing twenty-seven separate cases where the fires had occurred in foreign-owned leather-goods manufacturers. Matt told him that he had handled two of the cases while assigned to Manhattan but had been pulled off of them before getting the chance to really get into it. Still, he'd be willing to bet that if Jake checked, he'd find that all the companies used the same insurance agent. The next day, Jake did check and, sure enough, there he was, Gino Bestani, insurance man. The case escalated, the circle of suspects kept widening, and before long, the police departments of three jurisdictions were involved. The Manhattan DA's Rackets Bureau took over as the lead agency, which led to wiretaps, stakeouts, and a long paper trail to follow. Jake Morgan loved every minute of it. And although he was the main player, he always credited Matt as the guy who had set him on the right path.

Because he'd been in the field making arrests, Jake hadn't heard about John Williams's death until after all his arrests had been processed and he'd returned to headquarters. He would never have figured a guy like John for suicide, had always thought of him as a tough guy with a thick hide. John's death coming so closely on the heels of Matt's return to duty had him deeply worried.

He picked up the ringing phone on his desk expecting it to be another friend or relative offering congratulations.

When he realized it was Matt, he let out a long breath but kept it light, not wanting to make a big deal out of how concerned he was about his former partner's state of mind. "Hey, Batman. You okay?"

One of the less inventive marshals at the base had given them the nicknames Batman and Robin after their brush with death at Paco's hands. It had spread and stuck and become a joke between them.

Matt's voice was strained, low, and terse. "I need your help, Jake."

"Sure, Matt. Anything."

"No, Jake. This is different. Don't agree until you know what it is. I can't talk to you over the phone. I need you to meet me as soon as you can break away."

■   ■   ■

The restaurant was noisy, brightly lit, and short on decor; it was strictly blue collar, its customers working stiffs. Those few in business suits or dresses came from the windowless anonymity of cubicles in the city's endless departments and bureaus. Steam rose in great clouds behind the counter as three cooks struggled to keep up with the onslaught of eat-in and takeout orders. Cheap paneling covered the walls, the booths were out of a 1950s diner, and prints of the Polish countryside were hung helter-skelter throughout. The help was friendly but spoke little English. The waitresses wore multicolored peasant outfits that hadn't been seen in Poland since before World War II. The owner, a short, heavy, jovial man in his mid-sixties, made off-color remarks to every woman entering or leaving the place. He let them all know he'd been married five times and knew how to please a woman, telling them that, although he was no longer a young man, he still knew what to do. When women would ask him why, if he knew how to please a woman so well, all his wives had left, Lenny Shumulski would smile and give a devilish wink. "I wore them out," he'd say and point to his tongue, and the women would giggle or punch his arm. Lenny was a man who could make the most sexually explicit remarks without either the women *or* the men they were with taking offense. Everyone knew Lenny was a character and totally harmless.

When Matt walked in, Lenny rushed out from behind his post at the register to welcome him. He threw his arms around the much taller man and laid his head on his chest. He spoke in heavily accented English, pronouncing his *A*'s and *I*'s as *E*'s.

"Matthew, you son of a bitch. How come I don't see you no more?" It came out, "Metthew, you sonovebeech. Ow come E don't see you no maw?"

Matt stood awkwardly, arms pinned to his sides, smiling despite himself. The other patrons looked at him with crinkled eyes and half-smiles, probably having found themselves in that very position at one time or another.

"Lenny, if you kiss me, I'm going to kill you."

He spoke so only Matt could hear. "Fuck you, Matthew. I'm gonna listen to a schmuck? I'm still young enough to handle a big schlemeel like you." He released him and took Matt's face in his hands, stood on his toes, and planted a wet kiss on his cheek. "So there, you big bastard. Kill me, why don't you?"

Matt couldn't help smiling. Lenny simply forced you to respond to his warmth. "You're a sick man, Lenny."

"I'm sick? I'm sick? *You* look like a bag of shit, and *I'm* sick? You haven't been eating Lenny's food, so you look like hell." He tugged Matt's sleeve. "Come, I'll get you a table in the garden." He started to lead Matt to the rear of the restaurant.

"Lenny, I'm meeting my old partner. You remember Jake?"

Lenny bobbed his head and pulled Matt's arm again. "Sure, I remember Jake. Don't worry, I'll have him brought out to you." He rattled off something in Polish to a nearby waitress.

They weaved through the randomly placed small tables, then passed through a rear exit door to "the garden," a small backyard between two tenements that had been made into Lenny's version of an outdoor café. Round Cinzano umbrellas poked through the center of rectangular picnic tables. Suspended overhead, cheap plastic Chinese lanterns bordered and crisscrossed the garden. A wood fence, its paint badly chipped and peeling, separated the area from the rear yards of the adjoining tenements. Matt never understood why he was so fond of the place, but he knew it was Lenny who drew the crowds.

A young couple occupied a corner table, the only round one in the yard. Matt knew if they stayed together, this would become a place they'd reminisce about in their old age—when money was no longer a problem and the kids were grown, when they wouldn't be caught dead eating in a place like Lenny's. "Remember that ugly little Polish restaurant with the crazy owner?" she would say. And he would remember. And they would smile and bask in the glow the memory brought. It was that kind of place.

Lenny led Matt to his favorite table. It amazed Matt that Lenny remembered little details like that. He sat facing the entrance to the garden and Lenny took a seat opposite him.

They lapsed into an easy patter and Lenny commented about a new waitress, "I cannot convince that one that it is in her own best interest to allow me to schtup her. Ah, what she's missing!"

"You know, Lenny, if all of these women you hit on ever took you up on it, you'd be dead in a week."

"Ah, yes. But what a way to go!"

They laughed and then sat quietly for a moment. A young waitress with an open, fresh face and ready smile came over with coffee and a menu. Matt picked up the menu and Lenny snatched it from his hand. "You don't need no menu. I'll tell you what's good today."

"Okay, but I'll wait for Jake."

Lenny took a firm hold of Matt's hand. "Matthew, what's wrong? I don't see you in here for what, a year? You don't like Lenny no more?"

"No, Lenny. It's not that at all. I haven't worked in a year, since my partner was killed."

Lenny was visibly shaken; his animated face became alarmed. "What partner? Larry? Larry was killed? My God, when? I didn't hear nothing about that. I'm sorry, Matthew. I only read the Polish newspapers. They don't cover a lot of local things. Dammit . . . Larry . . . My God. That's terrible.''

Matt's eyes were glassy when he looked away. ''Yesterday, my new partner killed himself.''

''God in heaven!'' Lenny didn't say anything for a while, just patted Matt's hand. Matt thought that Lenny was one of only a few men capable of holding another man's hand without either of them feeling awkward.

''I'm very sorry, Matthew. No wonder you look this way. Is there anything I can do for you?''

''No, thank you, Lenny. But thanks for offering.''

Lenny's chest heaved and he pushed himself back from the table, as if by doing so he could push the bad news away. He brightened his tone. ''Well, at least I can see that you eat decently. You come here two, three times a week and I'll make you healthy again, put some meat back on those skinny bones.''

The waitress came through the door, trailing Jake behind her. He spotted them, waved, and maneuvered his way through the hodgepodge of tables. They stood as Jake arrived, then Lenny grabbed him in a bear hug and put him through the same embarrassing ritual. But at least now they were nearly alone. He gave his seat to Jake.

''I'm gonna leave you two alone now. I got customers and women who need my attention. I'll order for both of you. You'll love it.'' He hurried off.

''I see Lenny hasn't changed much.''

''No, Jake. Lenny is the one of the few constants in the world.''

Jake looked across the table with undisguised concern, but kept his face from betraying the shock he felt at the terrible shape his friend was in. Matt's normally clear and alert eyes were cloudy, bloodshot, and underscored by dark circles. He needed a shave, his clothes were wrinkled, and his skin was a sickly yellow. Man, the guy is aging right before my fucking eyes.

''So, partner, how're you holding up?''

Matt lit a cigarette and Jake noticed how unsteady his hands were. Matt caught him looking and closed the old Zippo he always carried. ''I didn't get much sleep last night. It's catching up with me.'' Jake's face reflected his skepticism and Matt tried to make light of it. ''Hey, it ain't like we're ever gonna find a picture of *your* ugly face on the cover of *Playgirl* magazine.''

Jake Morgan laughed and raised his hand in a placating gesture. ''Hey, I didn't say anything.''

''No, but you were thinking it.''

''So sue me. You look like you spent a week bobbing for apples in a Porta-John, and I'm not supposed to notice?''

Matt looked at him hard, then grinned. ''Hey, Jake, don't hold anything back on my account. Go ahead and be honest. I wouldn't want you to feel repressed.''

Jake smiled back. ''That's what friends are for.''

''Yeah. Then we wouldn't have to work so hard at making enemies.''

The waitress brought fresh coffee, a plate piled high with three different kinds of Polish sausage, another with pork chops smothered in sauerkraut, and still another piled high with a stack of pirogi, an East European version of ravioli.

Matt looked at all the food and then at Jake. ''Lenny's idea of helping me live longer. This meal could take four months off your life.''

Jake dug in. ''Yeah, but as Lenny always says, 'What a way to go.' '' They laughed and both men felt it, the easy way they had fallen into their former patterns, how each knew without speaking what the other was thinking; the comfortable feeling that comes with being totally understood. That was what had made them great partners and it was what made them great friends. Matt had almost forgotten how good it could feel.

Although he had no appetite when he'd arrived, the smell and look of the food had started his mouth watering. They ate ravenously; the food was too good and the moment too special to be spoiled by words. Matt considered it the height of understanding when two people could sit without talking and not be uncomfortable.

After he'd had enough, Matt pushed his plate away and looked at the serving dishes still piled with food. How could Lenny think any two people could eat all of that? He was stuffed and feeling better. He waited for Jake to finish eating before lighting a cigarette. The waitress refilled their cups and Jake lit up, too.

''So how can I help you, Matt?''

Jake was surprised to see Matt look suspiciously around the nearly empty garden. He'd always made fun of cops who'd developed the habit. But he also understood. "You're not paranoid if someone's really out to get you," Matt used to say.

"Do you know what I'm working on, Jake?"

"Not really. Only that you've been assigned to work with a special unit of the PD. I assumed it was a 'heavy,' certainly something to do with the headlines yesterday and your name in the paper." Matt nodded and Jake continued. "I asked Cattalli, but he refused to give me any of the details and told me in so many words that it was none of my damn business."

Matt looked around again. "Well, it's 'heavy,' all right. I don't even know where to begin."

"Well, I got time. Why don't you begin at the beginning."

It took thirty minutes to recount the events that had brought them to Lenny's restaurant. Jake sat quietly sipping coffee, interrupting only for clarification from time to time. When he was through, Matt signaled the waitress for a refill and lit another cigarette.

Jake Morgan wasn't sure where he came in. The story was amazing, eerie in fact. Though he said nothing, he had felt his hackles rising from the moment Matt told him a homeless man had been intentionally set on fire. He knew what burns felt like, and the thought that someone would subject another human being to that kind of pain simply for fun enraged him. If Matt said nothing else, he would have wanted "in" for that reason alone. Then Matt told him the rest—the torture of the young girl, the threats to Matt and the real story behind the headlines and the way John had been manipulated into thinking he was saving his family by taking his own life.

Jake could barely contain himself when he asked, "How can I help? You name it."

Matt was overwhelmed by the sense of kinship he felt for his friend. He was touched by the quick offer to help, to be "in," by the affection that passed silently between them and the display of unquestioned loyalty and trust.

"I was hoping you'd say that. Right now, I believe I'll have carte blanche with Cattalli on whatever I need. I want to tell him I need *you.*" He looked into his former partner's eyes. "I want you to know up front, Jake, if you do this with me, we're gonna be breakin' a lot of rules. It could be both our asses if we get caught. If you decide you'd rather not be involved, I'll understand."

"Fuck that, Matt. I'm in. Let's get this motherfucker, nail the bastard to a cross." He extended his hand and Matt took it. Their eyes met. Unlike Lenny, with his unabashed displays of emotion, neither man had ever learned how to be comfortable with strong feelings, especially the more tender ones. Maybe, because the warmth and understanding hanging awkwardly in the air seemed almost feminine, out of character, they dropped their hands and looked away from each other. Neither would ever say it, or even try to define it, but in a more enlightened time and place, when it would be okay to feel strongly about another man without being suspect, it might have been described as love.

Matt cleared his throat and lifted his head decisively. "It'll probably take a couple of days to set up. Greg Townsend has arranged an appointment for me to see the PD shrink tomorrow. You and I will start the day after."

22

Matt awoke with a gasp, hands clawing the air. Where the fuck am I? His thoughts were jumbled and, in his confusion, the episode at John Williams's home seemed to have ended only moments before. He was lying on a leather couch in a dimly lit room, and his skin and clothes were pasted to the leather. Books lined a paneled wall behind the large oak desk in front of him. A voice spoke from behind him.

"How do you feel, Fire Marshal?"

Matt craned his neck and saw the shaved head and Ben Franklin spectacles of Dr. Alfred Warren, the PD psychiatrist. The doctor was leaning forward in a high-backed brown chair that matched the couch. Matt took his time answering. He wondered how long he'd been under, had, in fact, no sense at all of having been hypnotized. Rather, it seemed he'd been asleep and merely dreaming. Dreaming . . . Mickey . . . The beating . . . The kid . . . The laugh. *The fucking laugh!* That was it! *That* was what he'd forgotten.

Matt studiously avoided thinking about the past; couldn't bear to even listen to "oldies" stations on the radio because of the uneasy emotions they dredged up. And while he'd never forgotten the beating he'd taken back then and the revenge he'd extracted, he rarely thought about it. But he'd entirely forgotten the *laugh.* That incident became a part of him he'd tucked away in the attic of his brain alongside many of the other horrors of his youth: his father's death when he was eight, the several fathers he'd been forced to know after that, the beatings he'd had to watch his mother endure, the shame of being too young to stop it, the poverty and the indignity of growing up a victim. But he was remembering now. And what echoed through the corridors of his mind, like the scraping of nails on a blackboard, was that *fucking laugh.*

How much did he say out loud? He sat up and found that his lips were gummy and stuck together and his tongue felt thick.

"You got some water, Doc?"

Dr. Warren poured from a pitcher and handed the glass to Matt, who drank greedily, then held out the glass for more.

"What did you find out?" Matt asked him.

"I'm not sure. You regressed well and everything was fine until you told me you were standing outside a school yard as a boy. Then you internalized."

"What do you mean, 'internalized'?"

Dr. Warren lifted his spectacles onto his forehead, massaged the bridge of his nose, leaned back and crossed his legs. "Well, you stopped talking. Your face and body said that something traumatic was going on, but you wouldn't say what it was. I was afraid to push you too hard. I figured it would be best if I let you go through it, then wake you and hope you remembered what it was. Do you?"

Matt drank, set the glass on the table in front of him, and briskly rubbed his face. "No. I don't."

Dr. Warren scrutinized Matt's face and gave him a long, skeptical look. Matt's mind was racing to assemble the revelations of his hypnosis and patch them into his knowledge of the present. They began to meld like drops of mercury sliding toward a concave center, joining, forming a whole much larger than its parts. Already, certain facts had surfaced. He knew now exactly *who* the Sentry was. Whoever had called the base saying that Jeremy Patterson and the Sentry were one and the same was lying. The description the workers in Jeremy's building had given him and Greg said specifically that he was no more than thirty-two years old. The Sentry was older—Matt's age. "Well, we can try another time. Sometimes it takes more than one session for these things to work out."

Matt thought, I'll never, ever do this again. Not in this lifetime, Doc.

He looked sincerely at the doctor and said, "Sure. Anytime. Whenever you think we should." And then, as he replayed the scene in his mind, old musty feelings of hatred and revenge came alive, dusted themselves off, and coursed through him, dragging him down into the graveyard of misplaced memories.

▨   ▨   ▨

The school yard of P.S. 68, taking up the entire block between 170th and 171st Streets on Gerard Avenue, was empty save for two groups:

two boys in ragged jeans playing an intense game of one-on-one at one end, and another, larger group at the other. The hoop pointed down at a forty-five-degree angle, a present from those less respectful of the game, who made a habit of hanging on it. It didn't seem to affect the boys' concentration or their game. Most, if not all, the hoops in school yards in the Bronx were bent at a similar angle. You adapted.

Sixteen-year-old Matt Kincaid stood outside the chain-link fence looking in, his fingers hooked through the diamond-shaped holes. But he wasn't looking at the players or their game. At the opposite side of the yard, seven boys had formed a semicircle around a younger boy, whose back was pressed against the aged and dirty red brick of the school.

It was midafternoon on a humid, bright summer day and the streets around the school were deserted. A lone, thin, wispy cloud stretched unmoving along the horizon. When the line ''Only mad dogs and Englishmen go out in the midday sun'' was penned, the author forgot to mention kids.

The group surrounding the younger boy was laughing. Their leader, a tall, gaunt boy of sixteen, had a broom handle in his hand that had served as a stickball bat until he and his crew had taken it away from other youngsters who were playing with it. Their current victim had come along just after that happened, while they were still swelled with pride at their ''victory.'' He had wandered into the school yard with his worn-slick basketball under his arm, hoping to find a game with someone his age. His ball was now being whipped two-handed against the wall above his head, forcing him to duck. His eyes were wide with fear and he attempted to escape twice, only to be grabbed and thrown back against the wall.

Matt didn't know why he was watching. It was none of his business, and if he wasn't careful, he might find himself the object of their attention. Although he'd seen the kid around the neighborhood and in school, he didn't really know him. Matt was two grades higher. From what he had observed, the kid was a loner. Without older brothers or anyone else to act as a guardian angel in the neighborhood, he was shark bait. Matt thought, Well, the little shit should have known better than to come here alone. This is the Bronx, and you'd better not walk around with your head up your ass if you knew what was good for you. Yet Matt continued looking through the fence.

The boy with the basketball aimed it closer and closer to the youngster's head. Finally, and stupidly, the kid decided he'd had enough and was going to show he had guts. The next ball went straight for his head, but this time he didn't duck. The ball hit him flush in the nose, causing his head to snap back into the wall. Even from where Matt stood, he heard the double *splat* as the ball hit the boy and then his head hit the wall. As he went down on one knee, Matt heard him start to cry. He was doubled over, holding his bleeding nose, kneading the back of his head, and checking his hand for blood. The others were laughing. The leader thought it was hilarious.

Matt ran into the yard but slowed his pace when he neared the group. He forced his voice to sound calm, detached. "Let him go. He's had enough."

They turned to see who had the audacity to challenge them. The leader stepped forward. "Hey, Matt. This is none of your business. We're just having a little fun is all." He waved a hand toward the boy. "This little shit came in here and didn't want to pay like everyone else. You know the rules. Why are you sticking your nose in where it don't belong?"

Matt looked past them to the boy. Blood seemed to be everywhere. "The way I figure it, he just paid," Matt said. "Let him go."

"Or what, Matt? Me and you know each other a long time. What is it you think you're gonna do?"

"That's right, Mickey. Long enough for you to know that no matter what happens here now, I'll get even. We know each other since we were kids. You ever know me not to even a score?"

Mickey didn't know what to say to that and so he just glared. Matt continued, "Look, you had your fun. The kid's learned a lesson and you got his ball. He's bleedin', so he's paid in full. Let him go."

"He's paid when I say he's paid, Matt. You know that." He backed away, handing the broom handle to the nearest member of the group. They closed in.

Matt's avenues of escape were limited. His hand moved to the sharpened buckle of his thick leather belt and undid it. The belt was off and wrapped around his left hand before any of the group could stop him. He reached into his rear jeans pocket and came out with a thick wool sock, one-third filled with lead shot.

"This ain't necessary, Mickey," Matt said to him. "You can still call it off."

The leader backed further away. "Sorry, Matt. No can do." He waved his hand at the other boys, but before they could move, Matt attacked the kid carrying the broom handle. He slashed and hit, first with the belt and then the sock. The boy fell, groaning in pain. The buckle had opened a thick gash on his head and the makeshift sap caught him on the side of the face. Matt bent quickly and tossed the stick to the youngster he'd come here to defend, who was now at his side.

"Get against the wall and swing at anyone who comes near you," he told him. Matt backed away and moved closer to the boy, weapons ready. The youngster seemed to draw courage from his rescuer and held the bat out in front of him. Matt looked at the group. He was mad now and didn't care what happened. He'd made up his mind that regardless of the outcome, he was going to take a bunch of them with him. At least they'd know they'd been in a fight. In a situation like this, it was the best you could do.

"Okay, assholes. You wanted a piece of me. Well, here I am. Come and get it."

The first boy went down after two shots to the head with the sock. The second and third covered their heads, bent down, and charged in. Matt beat one off but the other managed to pin one of his arms. The fourth, fifth, and sixth each got bloodied, but by that time the outcome was certain. The youngster beside him was game, swinging wildly at anything in reach, but was no match for their viciousness and was quickly disarmed. In less than a minute, Matt was on the ground trying to cover his vital parts while feet, fists, sticks, and even his own sap beat a steady tattoo on his body. He thought it would never end. As darkness spread like an oil spill over his consciousness, he wondered, almost idly, how long they would beat on him after he conked out. The last thing he heard before the engulfing blackness took him was something he knew he'd never forget. Confused and disoriented as he was, it made him shiver inside. At first he thought he was hallucinating. It struck him that the sound was pure evil. A nature film he'd seen about animals of prey flashed in his mind and he knew that that was where he'd heard it before. Mickey was laughing. And it was the sharp, barking laugh of a jackal.

■   ■   ■

The beating had put him in the hospital for five days and he couldn't leave his house for two weeks after that. He'd suffered a concussion and multiple fractures, including a hairline fracture to his sternum, and was black and blue everywhere. The younger boy had suffered less serious injuries. Maybe because of his age or because Matt was the one who had challenged them, or simply because they had exhausted themselves beating on Matt, the kid had escaped with a broken arm and some stitches on the back of his head. He visited Matt in the hospital on the second day, bringing him a corned beef sandwich from a kosher deli. Matt was touched by the gesture. It smelled great but his lips were swollen and painful and two of his teeth were loose. He managed to nibble on it for a while and then offered it to the boy, who had been looking at it hungrily. Matt liked the way the kid obviously wanted the sandwich but refused to take it, until Matt told him that it would be a shame to see it thrown away. Only then did the boy, who told him his name was Arnie Shapiro, gobble it down.

"Hey, save me the pickle, okay?"

"Sure, Matt. Here."

Matt bit into it and delighted in the taste for about two seconds before the acid and salt seeped into a large cut on his lip. The next thing he knew, his mouth was on fire. Arnie stood by helplessly as Matt poured water on his face, soaking the pillow and bed. Arnie couldn't stop apologizing until Matt convinced him that it wasn't his fault. Then they laughed. The more they thought about how Matt looked when he bit into the pickle, the more they laughed. A nurse came in and told them to quiet down, that they were disturbing the other patients, and that made them laugh even more. They finally made Arnie leave and Matt told him where he lived and that it would be okay to come by. He felt sorry for Arnie. He seemed like a nice kid but had no real friends. Arnie visited him at home every day during his recuperation.

The cops came to the hospital the first day, but he told them and his parents nothing, only that he'd been jumped by a group of unknown guys for unknown reasons. But for those two weeks, he thought about nothing else.

He knew it was going to take time to recover. The small fracture in his sternum prevented his taking a deep breath. The doctor said it might be six months or more before he could expect to be entirely healed. Matt had no intention of waiting that long. As soon as he was able, he and a friend who wanted to enter the Golden Gloves trials rented a basement room from an old woman who was a building superintendent in the neighborhood.

He and Howie Barbassi bought some equipment, scavenged some, stole some, and made most of the other stuff they thought they'd need. A duffel bag filled with sand hung from one of the sturdier steam pipes and served as a heavy bag. They skipped rope with clothesline and did incline sit-ups on wood planks stolen off a park bench. The basement was always damp, airless, and smelled of mold, but it was theirs and they used it faithfully.

When he recovered sufficiently, he started to spar with Howie. He'd gone in with him on the basement so that he could build himself up. Matt had no intention of boxing, but had agreed to help Howie achieve his goal. So he worked out on the heavy and speed bags they'd rigged, skipped rope, and sparred without any thought of the Golden Gloves. Matt had always been a street fighter. He couldn't see any need to add rules to something that entailed your survival. Survival *was* the rule. Whoever walked away won. But he found that he had a knack for boxing, and that ability, combined with his natural ferocity, made him a tough kid to beat. Howie was soon urging him to enter the Gloves tryouts with him, but Matt wasn't interested. He had other uses in mind for his newfound skills.

Weeks, then months passed uneventfully. Occasionally, Matt would see the gang and their leader, but he always gave them a wide berth. His chest still hurt a bit when he got winded or took a very deep breath, and his nose had a bump that hadn't been there before, but otherwise, he was in better shape than he'd ever been.

And then one day, after a tough workout in the basement, when Howie wound up on his ass in a sparring match, he knew he was fully healed and it was time.

■   ■   ■

Mickey Stone and his friends hung out in a poolroom on 170th Street between Clay and Morris Avenues. "The Snakepit," as everyone called it, was a convenient destination for the young hoods who met outside the school yard of John Quincy Adams High School, diagonally across the street, and decided to cut school. The Snakepit never closed and they'd pick up an egg sandwich on a roll and a cup of coffee on their way. There was no sign in front and no one ever thought to ask what its real name was, and no one could recall a time when it wasn't there and wasn't the Snakepit. You entered by walking down two flights of stairs. Inside, spectators watching the action in large, high-backed chairs became mere shadows along the wall, as the only light in the large room was cast by the hanging table lamps. Charlie, the guy who ran the place, was also a bookie and the only one who knew for sure who was, or wasn't, in the room at any given time. There was a heavily reinforced back door that led to a below-ground-level alley that had seen many a scurried exit on a signal from Charlie. The Snakepit was home to some of the best pool hustlers in the Bronx and big-money games were a near constant. When fresh meat walked in the door, it was like watching a school of piranha jockey for the privilege of taking the first bite. In its own inimitable way, the Snakepit was famous. It was also a place in which you kept one eye on your wallet and the other on your back.

Mickey was a good pool player, a *real* good pool player for his age, but his chief attribute wasn't his skill with a cue stick, it was his ability to psyche out better shooters and make them play poorly. He'd hustle an unsuspecting kid into giving him a spot, though he could've beaten him straight up. Or he'd have his gang surround the table and glare intently at the competition, or cough, or move at just the right moment. Complaints about any of it held the inherent risk of having your cue stick literally shoved up your ass.

Much of Mickey's power came from the fact that the entire Stone family was made up of bad-asses. His father was on parole after serving five years for a botched armed robbery, and his older brother, Philly, was the undisputed toughest guy in the neighborhood. Philly Stone's gang had advanced from petty theft to armed robberies and selling protection to the local merchants. He was trying to make a name large enough to become ''connected,'' and he was doing a damn good job of it. The local wise guys thought of him as a kid with a future.

Mickey wasn't above exploiting his brother's rep when things went badly for him. When all else failed, the name could work miracles. Everyone knew Philly was fond of his brother. Everyone knew he would kill you if you crossed him. The local pundits liked to say Philly was a ''Stone'' killer. Of course, they never said it within a mile of Philly.

◼   ◼   ◼

Matt Kincaid waited in the shadows of the recessed doorway of the shoe repair shop across from the Snakepit. The illuminated clock inside advertised Cat's Paw Heels and Soles, and read slightly past one A.M.

He folded his arms across his chest and slapped his biceps with gloved hands, hopping from foot to foot, trying to chase the cold from his bones. The late November wind slapped his face raw and he tucked his chin deeper into the collar of the faded navy pea jacket. Neighborhood guys never buttoned their coats. It was uncool. But the street was deserted, he was damn cold, and he just plain didn't give a shit about being "cool" anymore. After tonight, none of that would matter anyway. Almost two hours had passed and the tension and cold were wearing on him. I'll be a fucking stiff if I wait much longer, he thought. That'd be just my goddamn luck, freezin' to death while waitin' for Mickey. It was a school night and Matt knew that while Mickey rarely attended classes, he always left his house in the morning as if he was going to. He hoped Mickey planned to leave the pool room early. Matt stepped out of the doorway and surveyed the street. Except for an occasional car turning off Morris Avenue toward the Grand Concourse, past the fifteen-foot fence surrounding the track and playing field of Adams High on the corner, the streets were empty. Good.

He was back in the shadows of the shoemaker's shop when four figures emerged from the Snakepit and stood under the bright lone bulb of the gooseneck fixture hanging above the doorway. Sharply angled shadows elongated and shrank as they gathered, shoulders hunched, their hands jammed into pockets, under the lamp. The sound of voices and easy laughter faded in and out on the crisp wind and Matt watched as finally the group slapped each other "five," split up, and headed home. Matt's eyes drilled holes into Stone's back as he broke away and began a lazy saunter toward Clay Avenue. He slid from the doorway and ducked into the alley leading to Clay and the direction he knew Mickey would turn. Light spilled from the few windows facing into the alley, highlighting the darker areas, revealing some discarded tires, and glinting off of broken beer and soda bottles. The smell of rotting garbage made him crinkle his nose in distaste. A baby's insistent wail, a man's voice raised in anger, and the heavy baritones of "The Duke of Earl" echoed in the narrow space. He picked his way carefully and quickly through the debris. He saw the street ahead and quickened his pace. The mouth of the alley was positioned between two street lamps, which did little more than define the edges of the entrance. Matt pressed himself against the building and chanced a look around the corner. Mickey had just turned into the block. Matt reached into his pocket and slipped a set of brass knuckles over the fingers of each gloved hand. Then he leaned heavily against the cold brick, trying desperately to control his racing heart and labored breathing.

Doubts raced through his mind and he dispelled each one in turn. It was the only way. He was leaving for the Marine Corps in the morning; this would be his last chance to even the score. His life wouldn't be worth a dime in the neighborhood after tonight. Philly Stone would see to that. There'd been two other nights of waiting in the shadows, but something always saved Mickey from his wrath. Today was payback day. He remembered reading a saying somewhere: "Revenge is a dish best eaten cold." He snorted. He was cold, all right. He was fucking freezing.

The approaching footsteps refocused him and he listened, his body a coiled spring. The footsteps were odd: step, slide, step, slide. Matt grinned. Mickey was "bopping." He saw him in his mind, walking that cocky, arrogant walk every prospective bad-ass in the neighborhood had adopted. Even with no one around to impress, Mickey still felt the need to walk tough.

Matt held his breath as Mickey shuffled by. The moment he passed, Matt came out of the shadows, closed the small distance between them, and threw a devastating punch into Mickey's kidney. Mickey, clutching his side, went down like a sack of cement, the air knocked out of him. He fell to one knee, teetered for an interminable moment, then toppled sideways to the ground. Though he was injured, Mickey's street instincts kicked in and he went for his jacket pocket. Matt expected him to go for a weapon and took his time, carefully aiming a heavy, booted foot into Mickey's pocket. The muffled sound of cracking bones was unmistakable. Before Mickey could cry out, Matt kicked him viciously again, this time in the mouth. Blood flowed and puddled beneath Mickey's face. Matt looked at the damage he'd inflicted and was surprised to find himself nauseated. But he wasn't through. Not by a long shot. He hadn't suffered and waited for as long as he had for Mickey Stone to walk away with a broken hand and some missing teeth. But he was having trouble viewing the boy lying at his feet as a threat anymore. Mickey moaned and rolled over, and Matt watched recognition appear in his eyes. Even in the light of the street lamp, he saw hatred and the seed of promised vengeance growing in Mickey's eyes.

"You're dead, Kincaid." Mickey's jaw wasn't working right; it sounded like he had a mouth full of cotton. But Matt knew what he said. He leaned down, hovering just above Mickey's head.

"Mickey, what makes you think *you're* coming out of this alive?" He punctuated his words with two quick rights into Mickey's face, breaking his nose, the sound a sharp report in the still night. He pulled Mickey's limp hand from his jacket pocket, reached in and removed the spring-loaded stiletto he'd been trying to get at.

"Planning to use this on me, Mickey?" Matt pressed the button and the knife shot out like a bolt. He held it up. Light glinted evilly off the blood-gutters on either side of the blade, and both edges were razor sharp. It was a knife with no purpose but to hurt or kill. Matt brought the point of the knife to Mickey's cheek. Mickey looked defiantly into Matt's face, his eyes filled with hate, his expression unafraid.

"You don't have the fucking balls to kill me, Kincaid. And if you don't, you won't see tomorrow night. This was really dumb. My brother will see you dead. You know that." Mickey spit a glob of blood-filled phlegm into Matt's face.

Matt felt completely detached as he wiped the spittle from his cheek with his sleeve. Mickey had no warning when, quick as a whip, Matt swept the knife deeply across his face. Blood gushed from the five-inch gash in his cheek. Matt stood up, towering in his anger. He looked down at Mickey Stone, knowing that these few moments were going to change the course of his life, that he would have to leave his friends and family, stay away, probably for years, before he could even think of coming back. And that infuriated him even more. This piece of shit lying on the ground was a predator, an animal that fed on the weak and helpless. Unless he killed him . . . Stone was right. Unless he killed him, he'd be hunted and, despite his plans, maybe caught. But if he killed him now, who would know he'd done it? No one. Not a fucking soul. Five months had passed since Mickey and his friends put him in the hospital. How many others had met the same fate, before and since? There'd be a long, long list of people who'd like to see Mickey Stone dead. But then he reasoned, no, death would truly be too good, even if it meant he'd have to run.

"Hey, Mick. You're right. I'm not going to kill you. I'm just going to make it so you wish you were dead." He laid the knife aside and, stooping over him, began delivering powerful and deliberate punches into Mickey's face, the brass knuckles making sickening thuds as he drove them home, snapping bone and tearing flesh, until Mickey was out cold and unmoving. His gloves were blood-soaked as he slipped off the brass, reached for the knife, and used it to cut away the belt of Mickey's pants. Unzipping the fly, he gripped the sides of the trousers and pulled them down, cutting the underwear away until Mickey lay totally exposed, his penis flopped limply to the side. Matt lifted it, took a breath, and slashed the knife across the place where the scrotum met his cock, severing the sac from the base. He used Mickey's shirttail to wipe off the handle of the knife and laid it gingerly on his chest, stood, took one long look at what he'd done, and whispered hoarsely, ''I told you I'd get even, Mickey,'' then turned and walked briskly to where he'd stashed his travel bag.

Seven hours later, Matt Kincaid, seventeen years old and running for his life, was on a train heading for Parris Island, South Carolina, and four years in the Marine Corps.

23

Seventeen months after boarding the train headed for Parris Island, and nine months after touching down in Da Nang, while other eighteen-year-olds were busy pondering the all-important question of who to take to the prom, Matt Kincaid was wondering how much longer than the two months it had already been would it be before he'd be able to take a shower again.

The past few days were filled with bad omens and bad luck, and today, a cloudless and oppressive 106-degree day in early April of 1968, was no different. His company of marines, like everyone and everything, had been dug in and living underground at Khe Sanh Combat Base since early January, when sixty-five thousand North Vietnamese Army Regulars had surrounded and attacked the five thousand marines defending the base and airstrip. They were taking a pounding: thirteen hundred rounds of incoming mortar and artillery fire a day. Young men were wounded and dying with numbing regularity.

When Matt Kincaid and Charlie Company of the 1st Battalion, 9th Marine Regiment, landed four days after the start of the New Year, the base was already under full attack. Initially, reinforcements, including Matt's unit, were flown in as fast as the enemy and daylight allowed. Mortar and artillery fire were so intense, and the range to the runway so well plotted by the North Vietnamese, that the planes could never stop moving. The massive C-130 transports landed and kept rolling as the men spilled out at a full run, then spun quickly around to take off again. That lasted only days, as the toll of destroyed planes mounted quickly, and daily parachute drops of food and ammunition were all that stood between the marines and total isolation.

The 1st Battalion, 9th Marine Regiment, was a spearhead regiment, and their casualty rate was such that they had come to be known by marines everywhere as "The Walking Dead."

◼   ◼   ◼

Corporal William "Preacher" McDaniels was the sort of young man you'd want your boy to grow up to be. He was tall and thin without being gangly, moving with a natural fluid grace that seemed to make no noise. He had the often startling ability to suddenly appear at your side. His skin was unblemished and radiated a healthy, rosy-cheeked glow while his open face invited conversation. His amber eyes crinkled in a merry, Old St. Nick way when he smiled, and seemed to always ask "What can I do for you?" Like everyone else, he wore his blond hair cropped short. Among young marines with whom cursing came as naturally as breathing, he was never heard to do so. It wasn't just because, at twenty-four years old, he was older than almost everyone except the officers and senior non-coms, that the men looked up to him. There was an aura of moral decency surrounding him. He was deeply religious and the Protestant lay preacher for the platoon, hence his nickname. And because there weren't any Catholics willing to lead a Sunday service, he served as the unofficial chaplain for the whole platoon.

During mortar or artillery attacks, when everyone else was diving into foxholes and bunkers, Preacher would remain standing, unconcerned and unprotected by anything other than his God. He believed so strongly that his life was in God's hands that he felt it didn't matter what you did; if the Lord wanted you, he would take you. Two schools of thought developed within the platoon: Preacher was either the luckiest man alive, or he was right.

On patrol, the moment they fell under attack, Preacher was the first man charging. Others followed, not because he necessarily inspired bravery, but because no one wanted to be accused of having allowed Preacher to get hurt. The irony was that, while his squad took an inordinate number of chances, they suffered few casualties. He seemed to live a charmed life, and marines from other squads were constantly requesting transfers to Preacher's.

Lance Corporal Matthew P. Kincaid was the leader of the machine-gun team attached to Preacher's squad. The two had been together since boot camp, and while Matt was not particularly religious and did not attend any Sunday services, there was a deep respect and affability between them.

As their bond grew and as other men they'd come to know and care for were shipped back to the States in body bags or on stretchers, neither felt entirely comfortable on patrol without the other. And as the platoon took on more and more replacements, Matt and Preacher became like talismen to the rookies. The word was, if you wanted to live, you'd attach yourself to one of them. Until one day when Alpha Company, 1/9, hit the shit.

※　　　　※　　　　※

As they moved en masse to assist a pinned-down Alpha Company, radio traffic became more desperate. It reported heavy casualties; the dead and wounded were too close to the enemy to request supporting artillery fire or even to use their own lightweight mortars without hitting their own men.

The tropical sun was brutally hot, relentlessly punishing the two-plus companies moving much faster than was normally considered safe, toward the unnamed hill. Their clothes were black with sweat by the time they'd gone one hundred meters; small-arms fire and explosions mounted in tempo and volume as they closed the distance. Though it took more than an hour to reach the base of the target hill, Charlie Company was ordered without respite to form a single column and begin the climb up the narrow, snaking path. Preacher's squad was the last of three in the long, strung-out column.

As each squad reached the crest, they were ordered to form a line and sweep across the hilltop, raking it with automatic-weapons fire.

It was an ideal ambush site. Matt's platoon was stalled. The first squad to reach the crest was met by a hail of AK-47 fire backed up by Russian-made machine guns and mortars. The marines were mowed down almost before they could get started. The second squad, more hesitant, called for confirmation of orders before being led on the attack. By the time Preacher and his squad reached the crest, a few bloody survivors had crawled back and stumbled to the relative safety of the slope.

Preacher grabbed a short black marine in full flight tumbling down the hill. "What's going on up there?" he demanded.

The young marine, tears streaming down his cheeks, pulled away roughly and continued down the hill, crying out, "They're dead, man! They're all fucking dead. Get up there! They're dyin'."

Preacher turned to Matt, his face grim. "I want you to set your gun up at the corner of the ridge and give my squad covering fire as we do our sweep."

When they were in position, Matt tapped Pete Leighton, his machine gunner, on the shoulder. "When I give you the word, give 'em a full belt, Pete. All one hundred rounds. Then twenty-round bursts after that. And don't stop for anything." The gun was designed to fire controlled six-round bursts. Too much, and the barrel would turn white-hot and melt. Fuck the barrel, he thought.

Matt snuck a look over the edge of the hole. There were bodies lying everywhere, all marines. He was sure some of them were alive and said a silent prayer that they'd stay down as his team opened fire. Preacher's squad was lying on their bellies in a line at the crest of the ridge. He looked up and Matt knew he was going.

"Give it to 'em now, Pete. Now! Open fire!"

Preacher raised his arm, threw it forward, and yelled, "Charge!"

It was surreal. "Charge?" No one said that anymore, did they?

The moment Pete started firing, the NVA sent a fusillade of small-arms fire, showering their position with dirt, rocks, and ricochets. They ducked down and Pete fired blindly, holding the trigger and moving the gun from side to side. It didn't matter. There were no targets to shoot at.

As Preacher's squad moved forward, a barrage of automatic-weapons fire preceded five quick mortar explosions in and around them. They'd advanced no more than fifteen feet when Matt poked his head above the edge of the crater and saw no one standing or moving.

"Jesus! Oh, Jesus."

Matt scurried to the lip of the crater. Two more mortar rounds exploded just in front of him and small-arms fire peppered the area around the hole. He pressed himself against the side of the crater and cupped his hands to his mouth.

"Third squad! Preacher! Anyone! Can you hear me?"

The firing stopped, as if the NVA were as eager as Matt to hear whether anyone responded. Rifle and mortar fire from Bravo Company's side of the hill was all that broke the sudden calm. Matt yelled again. Then again.

Everyone *couldn't* be dead. They're just afraid to give away their positions, he reasoned.

He spoke to Pete. "I'm gonna crawl along the ridge line and see if I can establish contact with anyone. Don't stay down too long. Take turns looking over the lip or you're liable to find them up your ass." Pete nodded solemnly.

Matt unclasped the bandoleers of machine-gun ammo from his chest, laid them beside the gun, took off his field pack, checked the magazine in his M-16, and scooted to the far end of the crater.

"Pete, give me a twenty-round burst for cover."

A hail of automatic-weapons fire raked the edge of the crater the moment Pete's gun opened fire. Matt rolled out of the crater and slid ten meters down the hill. He was below the ridge line, pretty certain he couldn't be seen, unless the bastards were hidden in underground spider traps.

Within three meters of the crest, he stopped to look and listen. The muted pops of sporadic fire from the top of the hill sounded far away. Pete opened up with a six-round burst to his left. Just doing what he was told. Good.

Matt tumbled into a small bomb crater. Another explosion rocked the hilltop just in front of his gun team's position. Please let them be okay, he thought.

He pressed his hands to his shaking thighs to still them. Goddammit, he thought, get *through* this! Get the fuck up there and get it over with. He scrambled to the top and noticed movement through the field of motionless bodies. Shit! What do I do *now*?

He inched ahead, wishing with his very being for a cloak of invisibility to blanket him and make him part of the earth. Hold on, buddy. I'm coming. Hold on. Just a little bit more. I'm coming.

He fought back a powerful urge to turn around and get back to cover, to forget he'd seen a guy move. Live, he thought.

A soft, low moan became more audible as he crawled closer until finally he recognized the pain-wracked face of Pedro Martinez, one of Preacher's men.

He drew up alongside him and put his lips to Martinez's ear. "Pedro! I'm here, man. It's me, Kincaid. How bad are you hurt?"

But Pedro wasn't hearing. A deep grimace distorted his features, but his eyes stared vacantly at the clear blue sky. Matt tried to locate his wounds. A loud groan escaped Pedro's blood-caked lips and Matt put his hand over the man's mouth.

"Pedro, you gotta keep quiet. You'll get us both killed." Blood soaked the ground around Pedro's legs. Matt could see earth through the shattered kneecap. He grabbed Martinez's rifle, unsnapped the sling, and, as carefully as he could, slid it high on Pedro's thigh.

Kincaid unhooked Martinez's utility belt, took the morphine from the first-aid kit, and plunged the nearly weightless tube through Pedro's shirt, into his arm. He removed a battle dressing and held it over Pedro's mouth while he cinched the belt tightly around the wounded leg, pressing hard against his mouth to muffle the screams.

It took a long time for Pedro's body to stop convulsing.

Matt picked up sudden movement off to his right. He snatched his M-16, twirled around, and took aim over Pedro's chest.

Two men were lying in a shallow, narrow trench about twenty meters to his right. One man appeared to be tending to the other. Matt called out in a stage whisper, "Hey, marines. I'm over here."

He was both happy and scared when a blood-soaked Preacher McDaniels turned around. Preacher couldn't see him. Matt ventured a raised hand.

"Over here, Preach. It's me, Matt."

Preacher signaled weakly that he wanted Matt to come to him.

Matt spoke to the unconscious Martinez. "I'm coming right back, buddy. I'm not leaving you. There are other guys wounded. I promise I won't be long." He finished tying the dressing, patted his arm, and began to crawl.

It took forever to traverse the relatively short distance through dead bodies and rough terrain, and when he finally tumbled into the shallow depression, Preacher barely glanced at him, intent as he was on helping the wounded marine. His voice was weak and straining to sound calm. "Welcome, my friend. Mi casa et su casa."

"Are you hit, Preach?"

Preacher tied a final knot in the dressing and fell back against the side of the trench. "They got me a couple of times, Matt. I know they got my leg. And I think I took some shrapnel in my side."

Matt moved to assess the damage. He looked for Preacher's first-aid kit but the case was empty.

Preacher jabbed a limp thumb toward the other marine. "I already used it on Albert."

Matt pulled at the snap of his own kit and asked, "Is that who that is? Reggie?" Preacher nodded. Reggie Albert was a black marine, an amiable giant from Chicago. Matt asked, "How bad is he?"

"He's bad, Matt. Gut shot. I tried to put his intestines back in, but they won't stay." His hands waved helplessly. "They keep popping back out through the bandages. My hands ain't working right. You'd better take a look at him."

"I will, Preach. After I've looked at you." Preacher pushed his hands away when Matt tried to examine his wounds.

"No, Matt. Look at Reggie first. I'll be okay. See what you can do for him."

Preacher was clenching his side and sucking air through his teeth. But Matt knew there was no point in arguing with Preacher McDaniels. The guy was stubborn as a mule. He turned to Albert and began adjusting the battle dressing.

"Matt, we've got to get these guys to the base of the hill. A medivac might be able to land down there."

Matt finished retying Reggie's bandage. "Let me look at that." He pushed Preacher's flak jacket aside and gently pried his hands from the wound. Blood spurted alarmingly from a large, irregularly shaped hole just below his ribcage. He was shot in the left thigh as well and Matt found another hole in his left shoulder.

"Preacher, I'm gonna try to get you back. Then I'll see if I can get someone to come back with me to get Martinez and Albert."

Preacher shook his head. "No, Matt. That's not the way we're gonna do it. First you take Martinez. Then Albert. Then me."

Matt shook his head. "Look, we don't have time to argue, but that doesn't make sense. These guys are wounded bad, Preach. I don't think they're gonna make it. But at least you can help me a little. You ain't dead weight."

Matt sighed when he saw the tightly compressed set of Preacher's lips.

"I'm not leaving these guys here, Matt. And that's all there is to it."

Matt's anger was rising. "No. That's *not* all there is to it. I'm the one who's making the decisions here."

Preacher coughed, and a trickle of blood oozed from the corner of his mouth. "Since when? When did you start outranking *me*?"

"Since you became wounded and delirious."

His voice became a soft plea. "Matt, don't do this to me. I wouldn't want to be saved if it means leaving these guys behind. You've *got* to do what I say."

Matt looked at Reggie Albert, then out to where Martinez still lay before turning back to Preacher. "Can you still fire a weapon?"

"Sure. I think so."

"Okay, then. I'll leave you here with Albert. I'll try to get Martinez back and come back with help for you and Reggie."

Preacher sank back heavily. "Thanks, Matt. You're doing the right thing."

Matt smiled, squeezed his friend's arm, and rolled out of the shallow depression. It was slow going. By the time Matt reached him, Martinez had regained consciousness.

"How ya doin', buddy?"

Pedro's words were slurred and barely audible. "Not so good, compadre."

"You're gonna be okay, man. But we gotta get out of here. Can you move at all?"

"I don't know. I can't seem to feel anything below my waist."

"That's just the morphine, man," Matt lied, looking furtively around. "Do you think you can help me?"

"I'll try, Matt."

Matt grabbed Martinez under the arms and pulled. After moving only a few feet, he was exhausted. He allowed himself the luxury of a respite and lay there panting.

Matt gathered his remaining resolve, grabbed Martinez again, and began pulling with all his might. He prayed to God and swore to somehow repay the debt, if only He would let them live. His legs felt like jelly and his arms threatened to pop loose from their sockets. But they were close to safety. Can't stop now.

Matt didn't hear the single, expert shot that peppered Pedro Martinez's skull and brains and blood onto his face like a load of twelve-gauge buckshot. He was still pulling with all his might when the top of Pedro's head disappeared. A chilling shudder passed from Martinez through Matt's hands, and he blinked uncomprehendingly at the bloody mass of meat and bone where Pedro's head had been only a moment before.

Revolted, he scrambled backward, legs and arms pumping furiously, tumbling over the crest line, rolling several feet before he regained control of his fall. He swiped desperately at the gore on his face and gagged.

Rebellious thoughts and images raced helter-skelter through a mind nearing its breaking point. Fuck! What the fuck do I do now? Preacher. Oh, God, Preacher. I can't go out there again. I can't. I don't want to die, and what's the sense of both of us dying? I'll wait here until help arrives. They've *got* to send help. I can tell them where Preacher is and we can *all* go out and get him. He's okay. Oh, shit. Oh, fucking shit. What do I do? What the fuck should I do?

But then, after a while, he remembered something Preacher said. What was it? That he couldn't live with his conscience if he left his men behind. He thought about how Preacher would never leave him, how he never for a moment considered if he would live or die when Matt left him in that hole. Shame washed over him like a waterfall of sludge. He suddenly saw himself for what he was: a filthy, fucking coward, unworthy of a friend like Preacher McDaniels.

Matt set aside his fear and checked his weapon. It was caked with dirt and dust. He used his shirttail to wipe it, blew into the receiver, and did what he could to make sure it would work.

He slid out of the hole and onto his belly. Fuck it, he said under his breath, and, crouching low, moved rapidly under the line of the hill. He made good time, and when he was near the trench, flopped down and made a beeline to Preacher's position. He froze as he heard the unmistakable clank of a weapon being moved into position. Holy shit, he thinks I'm a gook.

"Preacher?! It's me! Matt. Don't fucking shoot!"

Matt scrambled in, laid back against the dirt, gasping for air. He surveyed the trench. Albert lay absolutely still. Preacher was ghostly white; his eyes glassy, faraway, when he said, "How's Martinez?"

Matt brushed at his rifle. "He's dead." His voice boomed inside his head. "They put a bullet in his head three feet from the crest."

Preacher spoke slowly. "I'm sorry, Matthew. But you did the right thing."

"Yeah. Well, if I had left him where he was, he'd probably still be alive."

Preacher's face was almost serene. "No. You did what had to be done." He closed his eyes. "God will help us, Matthew."

Matt's anger and frustration welled up and spilled out bitterly. "Oh, yeah? Well, I always meant to ask you, Preach. Just when the hell did God take the fucking Pledge of Allegiance?"

Preacher opened his eyes, strained to lift his head, and glared at Matt. His voice was weak but his words were hard. "Don't you dare talk to me like that. God will help us, or he won't. That's up to him. But don't you ever talk that crap to me again."

Matt was already sorry before Preacher finished speaking. He averted his eyes and his tone was soft, conciliatory. "Okay. Okay, I'm sorry, man. It's just that . . . It's just that, I don't know what to do."

Preacher slumped back and sighed. "I don't know either, Matt. Right now, though, you've got to take Albert back."

Matt shook his head in a gesture of resignation, but moved to Albert's side. He was very still, and barely breathing. This was stupid. He'll never survive being dragged across the hill. The guy was huge and Matt didn't think he could pull him all that way. He felt shitty for considering leaving Albert behind, but taking Preacher was the smart thing to do, the logical thing. Matt was being forced to go against his instincts and that bothered him even more.

He took a final, and what he knew to be a futile, stab at talking sense to Preacher. "I don't know if I can carry him, man. He's not gonna be able to help, and I don't think I have enough strength left to get him all the way."

"If you ask, God will help you, Matthew."

Matt's body slumped in defeat. There was no arguing with *that*. For the first time since he'd known him, he resented Preacher's faith. Faith over logic. Great.

Albert's weight sat on his back like a side of beef. At first he couldn't move, but after a few false starts, he began inching out of the hole. The slight upward incline might as well have been the Matterhorn. He felt like he was suffocating but pressed on and focused on a single thought, repeated monotonously, rhythmically, superstitiously, over and over: "God is good . . . God is good . . . God is good . . ."

The sound of another mortar round leaving its tube came from somewhere behind him. He reacted instinctively, rolling Reggie off him and covering his body with his own. Oh, fuck. Oh, God.

Every nerve ending in his body shared the anticipation of being blown to smithereens. He began to count, one Mississippi, two . . .

He was still covering the upper half of Albert's body when the explosion cut short the count of five, at that very moment when he began to think that he had only imagined the sound. It rocked the ground but landed safely off to the right, and he allowed himself to breathe. He lay on top of Albert another full minute before he dared move, then rolled off and swiveled to eyeball the hilltop. "I think we're gonna make it, Reggie. Just a few more feet, man. Just a few more feet. Reggie?"

He felt for a pulse. Nothing. Reggie's eyes were open, staring blindly into the scorching midday sun, and his expression reflected his final moment of surprise when he awoke to find his would-be savior's body smothering the life from him.

"Oh, no. Oh, fucking no." He roughly shook the lifeless form. "Wake up, man. Wake-the-fuck-up!"

Matt slumped to the ground, clenched his eyes shut, and bit into the fleshy part of his palm until he drew blood.

He waited for the nightmare to end, but when he looked, Reggie Albert still lay beside him. The sun still beat relentlessly down. And the top of the bleak hill still held the smell of bodies rotting in the tropical sun.

He thought of Preacher. *You* made me do this, you son of a bitch. I didn't want to take him. You made me do this and now he's dead and I killed him. *I* killed him. And it's your fault. If you just hadn't insisted. If you had just let me do things my own fucking way, he'd still be alive. Where's your God *now*, Preacher?

Matt closed Albert's eyes and started to crawl back to the hole where Preacher waited. "I'm sorry, Reggie. I'm very, very sorry."

A few meters from the trench, he called out, "Preacher, it's me."

No answer. He lunged for the hole, rolled in, and fell against his friend. Preacher's eyes were closed, but Matt's rising panic was cut short when his eyes fluttered open. He smiled meekly. "I guess I dozed off. You think they'll court-martial me?"

Matt let out the breath he'd been holding. "Man, you scared the shit out of me! I thought you were dead, you son of a bitch."

"Well, the reports of my death are entirely premature. How's Albert?"

Matt looked at his rifle and brushed at the caked dirt. "He didn't make it."

Preacher's eyes probed Matt's downcast face as he said, "May God rest his soul."

Matt bowed his head for a moment and then said, "I'm gonna have to put you on my back like I did Albert." His face flushed deeply as he said Reggie's name.

If Preacher, who had been watching Matt closely, noticed, he didn't let on. He said merely, "Can you handle the weight again, Matt?"

Matt recovered quickly. "Do I have a choice?"

Preacher looked into Matt's eyes. "Well, yes. You could leave me here. I'd understand."

Matt snorted. "Yeah, sure. And have you haunt me the rest of my fucking life? No, thanks."

Preacher wasn't as heavy as Albert, but Matt was using reserves long since depleted and the effort made him queasy. He had to stop repeatedly and was on the verge of blacking out when the heavy thumping of his team's M-60 machine gun went off about forty meters away. The sound was like an adrenaline boost and he veered toward it with renewed strength, hoping Pete had the sense not to shoot *them* as they approached. Thank God they're still alive.

Twenty meters from safety, Preacher became dead weight.

"Preacher? Preacher?! Answer me, goddammit!"

The silence was ominous. He rolled over, roughly tossing Preacher in a heap. Matt checked for a pulse. He was unconscious but still alive.

He pulled and tugged on Preacher's arms and implored God to, just this once, let them get back, let Preacher be okay, give him the strength to keep going and not let anything happen. He resorted to bribery: Please, God, if you get us through this, I'll buy you the coldest case of beer you've ever had. Please, Lord, just this once. Please. . . . Please.

When finally they were close to the gun's position, Matt looked for cover, a place to rest and plan their final approach. There. About eight meters to the left, a bomb crater. He summoned the last of his reserves and hauled Preacher to the rim of the hole, rolling him into it as gently as he could. He allowed himself to fall to the bottom. He had never been so tired. Would this day ever end? He propped Preacher up against the wall as best he could, closed his eyes, and collapsed.

"Matt?" Thank God. Preacher was conscious and looking across the crater with tired, hooded eyes.

"Yeah, Preach. How do ya feel?"

His voice was barely a whisper. "I'm tired, man. Never felt so wasted in my life. Ya think I could have some water now?"

Despite the warnings in their first-aid classes about not giving water to someone with a belly wound, Matt knew that at this point Preacher stood as much chance of becoming dehydrated as anything else. He needed water to survive.

"Sure. But you gotta sip it, man. Don't gulp. Okay?"

Preacher nodded.

Matt unsnapped a canteen and put it to his friend's cracked lips. "Remember, just a little, now."

Preacher took a sip and rolled the warm liquid around in his mouth before swallowing. It took a great deal of self-control, but Preacher wasn't going to make it any harder on Matt. Matt gave him another sip and took a few swallows himself.

"Thanks, buddy," Preacher said. "Are we close?"

"Yeah, I think so. But the gun hasn't fired in a while. I figured I'd wait till it did, to see if I can pinpoint them."

Five minutes passed before the heavy thumping of the M-60 went off, just ahead and to the right.

"Sounds like we're almost there, Matt."

"Yeah, it does." As far as he was concerned, twenty meters might as well have been twenty miles.

Preacher, hearing the desolation in Matt's voice, said, "I think it would be best if you leave me here and go the rest of the way yourself. Then you can come back with help. It's not that far, Matt. You can make it."

"I ain't leaving you, man. No way. We'll go together."

"Yes, you are, Matthew. It's the thing to do. But before you go, I want to say something to you." He struggled to sit upright, wincing as he did. Matt tried to help but Preacher wouldn't have it. The effort cost him, and he had to take several deep breaths before continuing. His speech was halting. "We've known each other a long time, Matthew. And we've been through a lot together. And in all that time, you never attended a single one of my services. I have never seen you pray and the only times the name of God crossed your lips, 'damn' followed.'' Matt tried to protest, but Preacher's expression stopped him. ''But, you know, I never minded. Because I always knew you were a good guy—a good man. Lots of men came to Sunday services who were not sincere.'' A grimace brought Matt to his side. He adjusted the dressing and made a study of avoiding his friend's eyes as Preacher continued. ''Since boot camp, I've seen you in what, a couple of dozen fights? But it was always for the right reason. You were sticking up for someone or for something you believed in. You wear this hard, outer shell that won't let anyone in, and yet God is with you. You act like the tough guy, but I've seen you risk your life for others, and that is what a man of God does.'' Matt was obviously uncomfortable, but Preacher went on. ''You curse and blaspheme, but I know that it is only to hide your fears. But you needn't be afraid. Because God *is* with you.''

His words brought a lump to Matt's throat.

Preacher grabbed Matt's sleeve, his tone urgent. ''I want you to do something for me when you get back to 'the world.' I want you to stop hating yourself. I want you to be proud of yourself. I want you to live a little of your life for all the good men who have lost theirs. And I would be honored if you lived even a little bit of it for me.''

At that, Matt snapped, ''Hey, what the hell are you talking about? You can live your own fucking life. We're *both* gonna get out of this.''

A look of resignation touched by sadness accompanied Preacher's announcement. ''I don't think so, Matt. I think my time has come. I think God wants me.'' He held up a hand to ward off Matt's protest. ''I could be wrong. But that isn't the point. I think we owe these men something. We owe them a good life. Promise me you'll give something for them.''

Matt was sputtering. ''I'm not promising anything. I'm gettin' us outta here, and you can do whatever you want with your life.''

Preacher was insistent. ''Promise me.''

Matt caved in. ''Okay, fine. I promise. If I get out of here, I'll be a good boy.''

''Matthew, don't mock me. I will be watching you from wherever I am.''

Matt took his friend's hand. His voice was quiet, sincere. ''I promise.'' But then he quickly let go and said, ''But it won't matter, because we're gonna be fine.''

Preacher's eyes probed Matt's face. ''What *really* happened to Albert?''

Matt couldn't meet his gaze. ''I told you, he didn't make it.''

''How did he die, Matthew?''

Matt was tired of all the talk; his voice rose angrily. ''I killed him. Okay? I fucking killed him. They threw a mortar at us and I jumped on him and I killed him. You satisfied? Are-you-fucking-satisfied-now?''

Preacher's voice was quiet. ''You were trying to save him, Matthew. God knows that.''

''Yeah? Well, God don't know shit. If God is so good, how come Albert's dead? How come all the rest of these fuckers are dead? What the hell did any of *them* ever do to God?''

Preacher's voice was very tired. ''It doesn't work that way, Matt. He has his own reasons for doing things. Maybe they died so that you could live.''

Matt was exasperated. ''I don't want to talk about this anymore. It's gonna be dark in a couple of hours and I don't want to be sitting in this hole arguing with you. Now, let's get the fuck out of here. You can tell me all your theories some other time. And if I have to, I'll knock you out and carry you.''

Preacher's strength was fading, but before Matt knew what was happening, Preacher had drawn his .45, cocked the hammer, and aimed it at Matt's chest.

The flat, lifeless tone of Preacher's voice sent a shiver through him. ''Get out of here. Now.''

Matt stared uncomprehendingly at the weapon, until a deep sense of indignation filled him, and he spat out, ''You point a weapon at me? You're threatening me? ME?!''

''That's right. And I'll use it on you, too, if you don't take off in the next ten seconds.''

Matt's face contorted in rage and he said through gritted teeth, ''I drag your ass all this way, and you point a weapon at me?! Threaten *me*?!'' His fist punched the air at Preacher. ''Then, fuck you, man. FUCK YOU! I'm outta here. Save your own fucking ass.''

He grabbed his rifle, tumbled out of the crater, and scrambled to-

ward his team's position. He stopped ten meters away, knowing god-
damned well he just couldn't do it. The son of a bitch was *trying* to
get me mad, he thought. He'd already started back to Preacher's position when the pop of a mortar round leaving its tube forced him to
bury his face in the dirt and cover his head. This is it, fuckhead. This
one's for you, for leaving Preacher alone. Hail Mary, full of grace, the
Lord is with you . . .

The explosion lifted him into the air and tossed him backward like
a rag doll. He choked and spit and coughed and tried to breathe, and
when finally he rubbed the dust from his eyes, a cloud of acrid, gray-
blue smoke hovered over the crater where Preacher's body lay twisted
and limp over its rim. Matt clawed his way to his friend. Blood spurted
from dozens of holes in Preacher's body. Matt slid into the crater and
dragged Preacher in behind him. He cradled his friend's head on his
lap and stroked frantically, helplessly, at Preacher's face.

"I'm sorry, man. I'm sorry. I didn't mean it. I didn't fucking mean
it, Preach. No . . . Oh, no . . . Oh, God. No." He looked at Preacher and
was stunned to see him staring back. "I'm gonna help you, Preach.
Don't worry. I'm gonna get you out of here."

Preacher's lips moved, but Matt couldn't make out what he said.
He pulled him closer and put his ear to his mouth. "What, Preacher?
What'd you say?"

Preacher tried to raise himself but failed. His last words wheezed
fitfully out. "I love you like my brother, Matthew."

A wounded cry of anguish lodged somewhere in Matt's soul, bursting forth in a howl of unbearable pain. "Noooo!!" He rocked fitfully
back and forth, his tears spilling onto the best friend he had ever
known. "Don't die, Preach. Don't die. I promise to do anything you
want. I'll live for you, or anyone you want me to. Just don't fucking
die, man!"

The last thing Matt remembered before waking up aboard the hospital ship anchored off the coast of Da Nang was getting up, grabbing
his rifle, and running, firing blindly into the underbrush surrounding
the crest of the unnamed hill.

24

When Mickey Stone awoke to a sky of haloed silhouettes and brain-numbing pain, his mind toyed momentarily with the possibility that he was in purgatory, and that the shadowy figures hovering over him were angels. But as the hum of voices grew louder and the veil of confusion lifted from his mind, he saw that the angels were only people, that the coronas of light surrounding them came from the streetlights behind them, and that the pain was coming from inside his own body. He fought to swim to the surface, and as he burst through to full consciousness, more pain, like a white-hot spike driven into his brain, threatened to send him back to the angels. He tried to move but razor-sharp talons gripped his left kidney. He screamed and firm hands pressed into his shoulders.

"Don't move, son, an ambulance is on the way."

An ambulance? Why? He struggled to remember. The fight. Kincaid. Brass knuckles. He tried to lift his arm to his face but his hand felt limp and numb. He willed it to move. It wouldn't. He moaned. His face hurt and a breeze accented the sticky wetness on his face and neck. He realized he was panting and tried to breathe through his nose but gagged on the liquid running down his throat.

He felt a thick wad of material being pressed onto his groin and wondered who the fuck was touching him down there. And why. He was remembering the fight in photographic flashes, but out of sequence and disjointed. He felt frustrated that he couldn't comprehend what was happening. People were talking; he heard the approach of sirens and saw the crowd separate. Two men in white knelt beside him. One opened his shirt while the other rolled up his sleeve. He struggled to make out what they were saying. One told the other to start an "eye-vee," whatever that was, then asked, "How does it look down there?" A long pause before Mickey felt the cool night air on his groin. The voice said, "Better get him outta here fast. Somebody sliced his balls." Mickey's head was filled with the sound of his own voice screaming, cursing, swearing revenge and death, and then nothing, until he awoke immobilized by casts and bandages.

■   ■   ■

His recovery took much longer than Matt's, but eventually Mickey's wounds healed. Reconstructive surgery took care of most of the outer damage. His cheekbones were rebuilt, his nose repaired, and a bridge replaced his missing teeth. Aside from the five-inch scar on his cheek that tended to turn a shade of purple when he got angry, six months after the attack, only the close examination of an expert would have revealed that he had been beaten to within an inch of his life. His scrotum was reattached with no permanent damage. The doctors told him that nothing vital had been severed; he could have sex, and eventually children.

But his inner scars were another matter. His brother, Philly, told him that Matt was nowhere to be found, and by the time Mickey recovered enough to leave his house, Matt's family had moved.

Sooner or later everyone in the neighborhood found out what had been done to him. He was humiliated. And he didn't believe the doctors. If nothing permanent was wrong, then why couldn't he get a hardon? At first he wasn't too concerned. After all, it still hurt and no one could be expected to get a boner while there were stitches in his balls. But long after the stitches were removed, when he'd been discharged from the hospital for several weeks, he tried. And failed. He looked at his penis, lying limp against the stubble of itchy hair that remained after the operation and seemed to be taking forever to grow back. It looked forlorn and useless and he swore on every saint, every god he knew, on his parents, his family, and ten stacks of bibles, that he would exact his revenge on Kincaid. No matter how long it took.

Mickey prided himself on his virility, his ability to attract girls. He was at the age when teenage girls did everything wrong for themselves. He was the "bad boy" their parents told them about, which only served to make him all the more interesting and attractive. He was the forbidden fruit, a symbol of their independence. It was that stage in life when every "good" boy was baffled by the ability of the bad ones to get the best-looking girls.

As the days grew into weeks and the weeks into months, his hatred seethed. He still got the girls, only now they wondered what was so "bad" about him. Except for the lousy way he treated them, he wasn't bad at all. When he didn't try anything sexual, they began to wonder, and soon began to leave. In 1967, as the sexual revolution was shifting into high gear, Mickey was stuck in neutral.

Until the day he wound up at Karen Davidson's house. They had cut classes and, since her parents worked, decided to go there to watch TV and drink some beer. Karen wasn't from the neighborhood. She'd moved to the Bronx from Ohio three months before when her father was promoted and transferred to the main office of his company in Manhattan, and they lived in a building on the Grand Concourse—definitely not part of the neighborhood. Mickey was intimidated by the fancy buildings on the Concourse, with their doormen and large, well-furnished lobbies. It was a source of constant irritation to him that their lobbies looked better than his home.

Karen had never known a boy like Mickey. She had made no real friends since moving in, but had heard girls talking about the legendary Mickey Stone in the school hallways as he passed by. His brooding good looks and tough swagger, even the scar on his face, reminded her of the pirate in her childhood fantasies. And beneath her demure exterior and cheerleader face, Karen was wild. As far as her parents were concerned, her father's promotion couldn't have come at a better time. Karen had seemed determined to screw every boy in Canton, Ohio, before she was eighteen. Her parents had tried sending her to psychologists, psychiatrists, and social workers, but by the time she was seventeen, Karen was a veteran of two illegal abortions. She had cost her father thousands of dollars and several years of his life.

So when she saw Mickey Stone standing alone, leaning against the wall under the awning of a sandwich shop, hands stuffed into his pockets, a cigarette dangling arrogantly from his mouth, she went right up and introduced herself.

Mickey wasn't at all surprised. He'd seen her around, ogling him in the halls, trying to catch his eye. He knew the type. Good girl, good family, expensive clothes. The first time you tried to touch her, she'd get insulted, ask you what kind of a girl you thought she was, and then start to cry, or worse, try to slap you. He wasn't in the mood for all that crap. So when she asked him if he wanted to cut school, get some beer, and party at her house, he was less than intrigued. But he didn't want to go to school and he didn't want to walk the streets either.

"Sure," he said, "but I got no dough." "That's okay," she said, "I've got money." They went to a deli where Mickey knew they wouldn't ask for ID and bought beer and chips.

Mickey was unhappy from the moment they stepped foot in the door. The building had gone up during the housing boom following the end of World War II, when everyone was flush with cash. It was ornate and employed a doorman and elevator operator. Mickey was used to none of it. Jeez, you could fit my whole fucking apartment in the living room of this place, he thought. But he'd never let her think she was better than him. He acted nonchalant. Everything in the apartment appeared expensive and he felt uncomfortable and out of place. So, she's a rich bitch, he thought. Don't mean *nothin'* to me! He plopped down on the plastic-covered couch and helped himself to the Hershey Kisses and M&M's on the coffee table. While Karen went to the kitchen to open a couple of beers, Mickey surveyed the room. All the furniture was covered in vinyl, a large gilt-edged mirror hung above the couch, brown shag carpeting covered the floor. Ceramic figurines filled every nook and a large floor-model TV sat next to a blond-wood stereo console facing him. Probably color, he thought with contempt. She probably thinks she's better than everyone else because her parents got money.

Everything in the room was in contrast to the way he lived. He thought of the shabby little apartment in the tenement on Clay Avenue, a railroad flat without privacy. He shared a room with Philly, but as far as Philly was concerned, it was *his* room and Mickey was an interloper. Their room was the next to last in the line adjoining their parents', separated only by double glass doors. He'd spent his life listening to his father grunt and his mother moan in the next room. They always thought he was asleep, but he would lie awake waiting for them to come to bed, listening as they passed through his room, stumbling in the dark, trying to be quiet so as not to wake the boys. He'd hear the squeak of the bed as they lay down and the muffled whispers followed by a brief silence. It was during that time that he'd take hold of his penis and position the tissues he brought to bed. Then he'd wait.

■   ■   ■

Victor Stone was a crude and cruel man. He was worse when he was drunk and that was almost every night. Mickey couldn't count the times his mother had turned away to mask the result of violating one of his father's rules. Or perhaps she just hadn't moved quickly enough to suit him.

Mickey was still very young when he realized he hated his father. It wasn't until he reached puberty that he knew he hated his mother even more. If he had had the vocabulary, he would have said "contempt" instead of hate. As a child, he felt sorry for her, but then one night he couldn't sleep and the noises from their room, the ones he used to try to shut out, came to him and he listened. And after that, things were never the same. He never felt sorry for his mother again. After that, he stayed awake and listened every night.

He joined in their nightly ritual until it reached a point where he couldn't sleep until he heard it. The silence of the house would be broken first by his father, whispering brusquely, so only the whole fucking world could hear him, "Suck my dick, bitch." The bedsprings would signal his mother's movement. Then the soft, wet, slurpy sounds of her lips on his father, followed by his father's throaty *uuuhhmming* and *aaahhhhing*. When the wet sounds stopped, his mother's voice: "Squeeze my nipples, baby. Now . . . Harder. Hurt me, Daddy." And moments later, soft moans from a full mouth. "Now put your cock inside me. Please. Oh, please. Put your cock inside me, Daddy." Then the noise would really begin. He knew his father was doing something to hurt his mother, but all he could hear were his father's muffled curses and his mother's suppressed moans. He hated himself for getting a raging hard-on at his mother's pain, but the images rocked his mind until he lost control. His hand worked furiously as he sought to time his orgasm with theirs. He'd gotten good at it. He imagined himself mounting a woman with his mother's body but never her face, her hands tied behind her, blindfolded, gagged. Her face was always contorted in ecstasy, her body wanting and needy. He listened, eyes closed, and came to know when it was time. It was easy. His father got very loud, the bed squeaked faster, and his mother, with something—panties, a stocking maybe—stuffed in her mouth, would be grunting like a sow. And when he heard it, when the bedsprings seemed to cry in tandem with his mother's choked screams, he would bury his face in his pillow, tissues wrapped around his cock, and he would come. After his spasms subsided, when the house was once again silent, when the shame of his thoughts lost the protection of his passion, he would sheepishly toss the evidence under the far side of the bed till morning. And then he would sleep.

■   ■   ■

Karen returned from the kitchen carrying two beers and a bag of potato chips. She handed him a beer, sat down beside him, took a handful of chips, and laid the bag in front of Mickey. "Help yourself," she said through a full mouth. Mickey sipped his beer, didn't touch the chips, and stared at the blank TV screen. Karen finished chewing, brushed her hands briskly together, and turned to Mickey.

"You're awfully quiet. Something wrong?"

"Nah, nothing's wrong."

Karen half-rose and swiped invisible crumbs from her skirt. When she sat again, she was much closer to Mickey, nearly touching him.

"You like music? I've got a pretty good collection."

"Yeah. I like music. Whatta ya got?"

"A little of everything. I collect records. What do you like? I'll tell you if I've got it."

"I don't know. Ya got any Chuck Berry? He's a coon, but I like the way he plays."

"Sure, I got his latest album. Want to hear it?"

"Okay."

Karen went to the stereo and lifted the lid. She opened the bottom doors and bent over to read the record labels, only she didn't bother to bend her knees and Mickey found himself looking up her miniskirt. She was wearing pink panties. And, of course, Karen knew exactly what she was doing.

The little bitch is asking for it, isn't she? he thought. But she did have a sweet body. Hell, these rich bitches were all the same . . . liked to tease. He should never have come over here. As soon as he made a move, she'd act shocked and maybe start crying like she hadn't shoved her ass in his face. Then he'd be really pissed. Better to just be cool. Let her beg for it. Sooner or later they all did. Just like his mother.

Mickey hadn't dared to test himself with a girl since his scrotum was sliced. At first he was self-conscious about the scar and shaved hair. But the hair had long since grown back and the scar could no longer be seen. Still, *he* was very much aware of it. He still lay in bed at night and listened to his parents, but he no longer took tissues with him. They weren't necessary. Mickey hadn't had an erection since "his accident," as he came to call it.

Karen took her time studying the records, shifting her weight from one foot to the other, her buttocks undulating, clenching and unclenching as she moved. Mickey watched, fascinated. They sure looked sweet. She had to know what she was doing, what he could see. She did want it. Fuck it, then. She wanted it that bad, he'd give it to her. No matter what she said. She'd asked for it and now she was going to get it.

Karen slid an album out from the stack, set it on the automatic spindle, and turned the machine on. She spun around, offered a bright, innocent smile, then came over and sprawled on the couch. Mickey felt a jolt when her bare thigh touched him. The record dropped and the clear sound of Chuck's guitar filled the room. Karen shifted, lifted her leg onto the couch, and turned her body so she faced Mickey. Mickey took another sip of his beer.

She touched his sleeve ever so lightly. "I hadn't figured you for the shy type."

"I ain't shy. Just thinkin'."

Karen reached up and traced the long scar on Mickey's cheek with her fingertips. He yielded to the gentle pressure and turned to face her. She leaned over and raised herself to kiss him on the mouth. Mickey kissed her back. She didn't protest when he cupped her breasts, so he began massaging and kneading them. He felt her squirm, heard her breath increase. She was plunging her tongue into his mouth now, moaning lightly in her throat. Mickey slid a hand around her and pulled the blouse out of her skirt. The clasp of her bra was undone almost as soon as he touched it. He lifted it above her breasts, grabbed the warm flesh and squeezed. Karen moaned louder. His other hand slid between her thighs and he was surprised to feel her legs opening to accommodate him. He felt the warm moistness of her groin through her panties and heard her gasp when his fingers pulled aside the flimsy material. God, she was wet. He'd never known a girl to be so wet. Her cunt was sticky and warm. No, *hot* was more like it. It felt like a goddamn furnace, he thought. She was moving her hips, trying to capture his fingers with her pussy, and he stuck one in. She sucked in a breath and moved closer.

"Yes, do it. Finger-fuck me, Mickey. Do it. Do it."

And then her hand was massaging and kneading his crotch. He pulled away violently. "Stop!"

Karen looked at him as if he'd slapped her. "What's wrong, Mickey?"

"Nothin'. I just don't want you touchin' me down there."

Karen's chest was heaving and she was confused. "Why? Did I hurt you? I'm sorry if I did. I'll be more careful." She moved to him again but he stiff-armed her shoulders.

"You *can't* hurt me."

"Then what is it? I want you, Mickey. Don't you want me?"

It was then that Mickey realized how wrong he'd been about her. She wasn't at all like he thought, the prim, proper rich girl. He'd been expecting *her* to pull away. It was the only reason he started, because he never thought it would really go this far. Now here she was telling him she *wanted it* and he didn't know if he could even get it up. He looked at her. Her eyes had a dreamy quality, glassy and far away. She was rubbing her thighs together as if she had an itch, and then her hand moved beneath her short skirt and she began to stroke herself through her panties. He'd never seen any girl do that! She looked deeply into his eyes. Mickey felt butterflies taking wing in his stomach.

"Mickey, I'll do anything you want. *Anything.* Come into my bedroom." She reached for him but kept her other hand beneath her skirt, rubbing, rubbing. Her touch jolted him but he allowed it and let himself be pulled from the couch. Walking backward, she slid her hand down inside the waistband of her panties and began a slow, seductive massage between her legs. Mickey was in a trance as she guided him past the kitchen to her room. She drew him in. An intoxicating mixture of feminine smells filled his nostrils. The room was all girl, pink and frills. The shade was drawn, casting diffused yellow light onto the single bed. Karen backed up to it and sat down, Mickey's crotch at eye level. She took his limp hands in hers, looked up for a moment, then bowed her head.

"I will do anything you tell me to," she said. "You can do anything you'd like to me."

Mickey looked at her lowered head. Her voice had changed. It was somehow different now, though he couldn't put his finger on just how. Had he been more eloquent, he'd have recognized it as the same voice he'd heard people use in church. It was the voice of a supplicant, a worshiper at the altar. He was stunned to feel his cock pushing against his jeans and it felt wonderful, delicious.

"Then suck my dick, bitch."

"Yes, Mickey. I'd love to suck your dick." Her hands moved to his belt and in moments his pants and underwear were at his ankles.

The warmth of her mouth was like a jolt of electricity and he moaned deeply, his legs almost giving out. Her mouth remained clamped around his cock as she helped him remove her blouse and bra. Her breasts were glorious, small and pert with long distended nipples. He leaned over, took one nipple in each hand and pinched lightly. She pressed her hands against his.

"Squeeze them harder, Mickey. . . . Harder . . . Hurt me, baby."

The instant she said it, he came. It felt as though his intestines were trying to squeeze through the tiny opening. A dam at the bottom of his soul burst and he nearly collapsed. His knees buckled; Karen reached out to steady him as he spurted a river into her mouth. He was shaking, wracked by spasm after spasm, still very hard in her mouth. She made no move to disengage herself. It was as if she was savoring it, sucking, working it until it actually became uncomfortable for him. He touched her head and she pulled back, his cock making a wet plopping sound. Then she swallowed deeply and looked at him. There was a small spot of cum on the corner of her mouth, and her tongue slithered out and licked it off. It was the most erotic thing he'd ever seen. Her eyes beckoned him as she lay slowly down on the bed. She reached over languidly, opened her nightstand drawer, pulled out a handful of silk scarves, and offered them to him.

Her words were more an appeal than a question. "Would you like to tie me up, Mickey?"

He moved to her, his soul soaring, feeling as if he'd met his maker. No. That wasn't quite right. Not his maker. He felt strong, invincible, immortal . . . like only God, or *a god* must feel. And in that moment, in that instant when the power surged through his very being, swirling through his mind like a tornado, the Sentry was born. And his first disciple was at his feet.

■　　　■　　　■

A short time after Mickey met Karen, Philly Stone was gunned down on the street after an aborted attempt to take over a Harlem numbers operation. Mickey decided then and there that he had no intention of following in his brother's footsteps or ending his life lying facedown in a puddle. He sat quietly on the edge of the bed in the room he used to share with his brother and began to think. Philly had been a fool. Mickey asked himself many questions and found that he had few answers. If anyone had asked him what he wanted from life, Mickey would not have been able to say. After much thought, the best he could come up with was ''More.'' That was it. He wanted More. More money. More class. More knowledge. More power. More possessions . . . *More.* The only people he knew who had the things he wanted were criminals, but they were thugs living on the edge, as likely to die as his brother had. No, the real money, the real power was elsewhere. He needed to find it, to tap into it. And he knew that he'd never get it if he continued down the road he was on. He decided to read.

Mickey Stone learned many things. He learned that money was power and power was more important than money. But you had to have one to have the other. He went back to school and started paying attention. He insisted that Karen do the same. After all, if he was going to make something of himself, he'd need an assistant.

The native intelligence that made him a natural leader among the tougher boys of the neighborhood began to work for him. He became a voracious reader and learned from the biographies of so-called great men, men who had gone on to become icons of respectability, who had, more often than not, made their fortunes by stomping on everything and everyone in their path. He began to channel his natural ruthlessness, realizing that simply being physically tough was not enough. After all, who had been tougher than his brother Philly? And he was dead. No, that was not the way.

He began to delight in his gift for manipulating people, getting them to behave in ways they would never have thought of on their own. He worked at it the way a craftsman would hone his skills with tools, or an artist might approach a clean canvas. He rarely let an opportunity pass that would allow him to write the script for the actions of those around him.

Karen helped. It wasn't long before Mickey realized that Karen's family was neither as rich nor as classy as he thought. But they started him down the right path. He made an effort to become acceptable to them and, in time, her mother, and especially her father, began to think of Mickey Stone as the best thing that had ever happened to their daughter. He dropped the leather look and took to wearing collegiate-style clothing; always brought Karen home at a respectable hour, held her chair out for her before dinner, opened doors for her, and treated her with the respect due all young ladies of character. The fact that their sex had become more and more violent, and Karen had ceased to be anything but Mickey's slave, wasn't known to her parents. Mickey was precise about inflicting her bruises below the neckline and above the hem.

His grades went up and he no longer spent his days brooding listlessly in the principal's office. The change in him was dramatic; when it was time to prepare his college-entrance applications, the school's guidance counselors bent over backward in their zeal to help the boy who had once made their working day a living hell. He applied to, and with the personal endorsement of his high school's principal was accepted at, City College, at the time arguably the finest free public educational institution in the country.

But there was much of Mickey that couldn't let go of the darker elements of his life. On weekends, dressed in leather, he would take Karen to prowl the more seedy clubs and bars. Together they discovered the underworld of New York's S&M scene. He began to get off on the duality of his life: the good student, good citizen, and helpful classmate on one side, and whips and chains on the other. Before long, it took almost no effort on his part. After one particularly explosive episode with his father, during which Mickey threatened to kill the old man, he and Karen took an apartment on Morningside Drive on the Upper West Side of Manhattan, close to the college.

Mickey Stone was in his junior year when he met Franklin Belzier, a sophomore one year behind in his credits, in one of his classes. Franklin was everything Mickey had aspired to be. He came from old money but had been ejected from every Ivy League school his father's considerable connections had been able to get him into. Franklin had a wild streak and Mickey recognized in him a kindred spirit. In spite of their vastly different backgrounds, each saw something in the other that would have been called "chemistry" were they of the opposite sex. Mickey convinced Franklin to change his major to Business Administration and take extra credits to make up for the year he'd fallen behind so they could graduate together. They talked about going into business together. Mickey saw them as a natural. With Franklin's class and connections and his savvy and smarts, Mickey couldn't see how they could fail.

Mickey was easily the stronger personality and it wasn't long before Franklin, too, fell under his influence. Mickey Stone perceived in his new friend the same repressed rage that had served to propel him, but understood instinctively that Franklin needed guidance and could be led.

They'd known each other two months when Mickey decided to share Karen with Franklin. He'd invited him to their apartment, and when they entered the living room, Franklin stared, wide-eyed, mesmerized. Karen, naked and glistening, stood on her tiptoes, legs spread wide, ankles secured to a pair of fold-down rings that had been installed on the floor. She was suspended from hooks in the ceiling connected to padded leather cuffs that encircled her wrists. Mickey explained nonchalantly that she was Franklin's to do to, or with, whatever he wished. Mickey watched Franklin carefully.

"Would you like to whip her, Franklin?"

A number of whips, riding crops, and clamps lay on the coffee table. Mickey selected a long cat-o'-nine. As Franklin stood feasting his unbelieving eyes on the stunning beauty hung before him, Mickey pressed the whip into his hands.

"Go ahead. She won't mind. Look at her. She wants you to."

And indeed, Karen was gazing at the whip, her look apprehensive but not at all frightened. Franklin took a long, deliberate appraisal of Karen's body. Her nipples were extraordinarily distended and jutted out seductively. And they had been pierced. A pair of small but sturdy-looking stainless-steel rings hung tantalizingly from firm, upturned breasts. A substantial gold chain encircled her narrow waist and was secured by a small gold padlock. The chain rested seductively on her hips to form a cusp below her belly button. The cheeks of her buttocks were perfect crescents which sat high on her hips and seemed exactly the right size. He could see from the indentations of the muscles on either side that her buttocks were clenched tightly together. He assumed it was caused by the strain of standing on her toes, till he walked casually around to look behind her and saw a thick, flesh-colored dildo poking out from between her cheeks.

Mickey said, "She is required to hold that in, regardless of what you do. If it slips out, she will be severely punished." He pointed. "Look between her legs."

Franklin walked around and bent down. Two matching rings dangled from her pierced labia, but what surprised him most was the sturdy, rubber-tipped clamp attached to her clitoris, connected to a two-inch chain at the end of which hung a small but substantial-looking brass bell. Her clitoris was noticeably stretched from the weight, and Franklin thought that if it wasn't extremely painful, it was surely very uncomfortable.

Without warning, Mickey landed a loud slap on her ass. Karen arched forward and Franklin heard a tinkling sound. My God, he thought, it *is* a bell. He met Mickey's smile and continued his slow appraisal. Her skin was smooth, and except for a few fading, yellow-brown marks dotting her body, it was the color and texture of polished ivory. And then he looked at her face. He had always admired her, but in her present position, damn, she was truly one of the most exquisite women Franklin had ever seen. He put a hand inside his waistband and adjusted his raging erection.

Mickey saw the beads of sweat form above Franklin's lip; watched as his friend moved tentatively closer; smiled as he reached out to touch Karen's breasts, hesitantly pulling at the nipple rings, kneading her nipples between his thumb and forefinger before grasping the rings and then, meekly at first, pulling more firmly. Karen moaned and he quickly released her. But as he watched her face, he saw that her moan was one of pleasure, not pain. She writhed seductively at the end of her ropes, squirming, a soft tinkling sound coming from between her legs. Her tits jiggled and her hips gyrated as if she was trying to squeeze her legs together to relieve an unreachable itch. At Mickey's urging, Franklin lay the whip on a small table and grew bolder, taking a nipple ring between the fingers of both hands. Karen shuddered. He squeezed and pulled the rings harder. She gasped, arched her body, and tried to follow in the direction he pulled, but she was tied tightly and her movement only served to make her appear even more seductive, more helpless. She writhed when he released the rings. He took hold of them again and looked directly into her eyes. Karen lowered her head demurely. He pulled and lifted, even more forcefully this time. She groaned, threw her head back, and whispered, her voice husky with desire, "Go ahead, Franklin. Do whatever you want to me. It's okay. Don't worry about hurting me. Please?"

She looks like a goddess, he thought as he searched her face. Karen was looking back at him, although not so boldly. But their eyes met as Franklin took a step back and picked up the whip. The cat-o'-nine hung at his side until he slowly and deliberately cocked his arm. Karen threw her head back, her tongue snaking seductively across her lips. The tips of the whip danced a little jig just above the carpet as his hand trembled and his face reflected a long moment of indecision. Then suddenly his arm was a blur of movement. As the separate thongs joined and coiled around her back, wrapping around her, the ends snapping loudly, raising a series of angry red welts on the soft flesh of her belly, Karen cried out, jerking violently, the bell tinkling madly. Franklin looked at her face and, to his utter astonishment, her eyes said, More.

After this first time, Mickey continued to share Karen with Franklin, frequently at first, but then less so. Increasingly, Mickey would withhold her sexual favors, making minor excuses for why Karen would not be available, until Franklin was almost mad with lust, totally obsessed with her.

Two months later, when Mickey casually remarked that perhaps Franklin would like his own slave, his friend was as eager as a puppy. Together, Mickey and Karen introduced him to the world of S&M. Mickey's ability to home in on human weakness, to feed on the frailties of others, would, years later, permit him to use the clubs and leather bars as recruitment depots. Most people in "the scene," as they called it, were plainly full of shit—weekend players in a rough sport. But sometimes, just sometimes, Mickey would come across that lone individual who wasn't playing at all, that special someone whose need to be dominated so overwhelmed every other aspect of his or her life that he or she would do anything for the person who fulfilled it. And it would be years later, when Mickey's power over people and his wealth began to expand beyond his wildest expectations, as his small circle of followers became ever larger, that he would use that wealth to buy, through intermediaries, a little girl kidnapped from a Brooklyn shopping mall. He would use it to buy Ellen Levy.

The world of S&M that they introduced Franklin Belzier to was not the world of clubs and dominants-for-hire advertised in the back of sex magazines. While they still occasionally cruised the leather bars and paddle clubs, Karen and Mickey had, for the most part, progressed beyond that. This new world was a deeper, much more hidden and mysterious place, one that even those who actively practiced the lifestyle rarely saw. This was a world of money, of exclusive private homes equipped with dungeons and chambers staffed by both male and female slaves trained to serve and obey every whim. Franklin was awestruck by the existence of such a world and once asked Mickey where the slaves came from. Mickey replied with one of his annoying laughs, "Like good old Mom used to say, 'There's a lid for every pot.'"

It wasn't long before Franklin came to depend on Mickey Stone for advice on all manner of things and rarely made a decision without first consulting him. Mickey was delighted to oblige. He convinced Franklin that it was a mistake not to take advantage of his father's money and power. Mickey waited until the time was right before allowing Franklin to introduce him to the Belzier family. Franklin's father couldn't have been more pleased with his son's amazing change of heart and attitude. And Mickey made sure that Franklin lay credit for his dramatic change squarely on the shoulders of Mickey Stone. Malcolm Belzier felt he owed Stone a great debt, and Mickey knew exactly how he'd want the debt paid.

When Mickey Stone and Franklin Belzier graduated in the top ten percentile of their class, it was a considerable accomplishment, since their competition was primarily the city's young Jewish and Asian population, known for their academic achievements. Malcolm asked them what they'd like for a graduation present. They informed him that they would like to go into the real-estate business together, and that seed money for their initial purchases would be necessary. Malcolm Belzier nearly burst with pride. Yes, Franklin said, a half-million-dollar interest-free loan would be more than sufficient to begin. Belzier-Stone Realty was incorporated a month later.

Their status as college students exempted them from the draft, and by the time they graduated in 1972, service was being determined by lottery. Franklin and Mickey celebrated the high numbers they drew with a night on the town and a weekend of power sex with Karen.

Mickey had been right. The combination of their talents and attributes made them a powerful force in the real-estate world. They began what was later to become their real-estate empire with the purchase of two six-story apartment buildings just off Broadway on 111th Street in Manhattan. The buildings were carefully chosen because they were close to home, and because Mickey correctly reasoned that with a finite supply of good housing stock in Manhattan, sooner or later, that part of town would see a dramatic rise in value. Many of the buildings in that section of Morningside Heights had been allowed to fall into disrepair and could be purchased at bargain-basement prices. The major obstacle to making money was the fact that they were subject to the city's archaic rent-control laws, which allowed tenants to pass the apartments down to other members of their families, even after death, like an heirloom. In some buildings there were families in which a grandparent had taken out the original lease, and as a result, a nine-room apartment, for example, virtually impossible to find almost anywhere in Manhattan, might be bringing in less than two hundred dollars in rent.

If Belzier-Stone was to make enough money to renovate the buildings, these tenants would have to go. Franklin thought that perhaps they should try to buy them out. Mickey smiled. "Leave that to me," he said. "I'll see that they move, and it won't cost us a dime."

Some years before, it had been impossible for landlords in the poorer, redlined sections of the city to obtain insurance at all. The federal government saw this as discrimination on the part of insurance companies, and passed what came to be known as The FAIR Act, whereby insurance companies were forced to create assigned risk pools and to offer insurance to any landlord willing to pay for it. Of course, like many high-minded programs of the federal government, it began nobly enough—why should a landlord in a poor neighborhood be unable to insure his investment?—but many ended up using it as a license to burn.

By 1973, entire sections of New York City had been leveled by fire. The havoc was primarily concentrated in the poorer sections of the city, especially the South Bronx, Harlem, and Bedford-Stuyvesant, and newspapers and magazines were filled with page after page of commentary on how landlords were managing to pull off the largest and most ruthless scam in city history. It revolved around their ability to jack up the value of a seemingly worthless piece of real estate through paper sales to relatives, friends, or associates, using thinly disguised corporate names and simply turning the property over a few times until reaching the point at which they'd reap the insurance profits by paying a junkie two hundred bucks to burn the building to the ground.

Mickey read everything he could get his hands on about the subject. If it could work in the slums, why not in a good neighborhood? By the time he went to work on the unsuspecting tenants of his two new buildings, ownership had passed four times to various shell corporations controlled by him and Franklin, and Belzier-Stone Realty was only one in a long line of landlords. Nobody would be able to put it together. Nobody.

Mickey Stone invented the tactics that years later, long after he'd stopped finding them necessary, were to become the standard operating procedure for landlords who wanted tenants out. Not that similar things hadn't been done before, but Mickey refined them to an art form. Later, much later, laws would be passed to prevent the reign of terror Mickey Stone inflicted on his unsuspecting tenants, but in 1973, no one, least of all the law, was prepared for the likes of Mickey Stone.

He went back to the old neighborhood and located two of his former cronies, young men who had dropped out and were living on tomorrow's dollar, men who would kill for lunch money. He planted a man in each building, anointed him superintendent, and gave very simple instructions: Make the tenants leave. They could do whatever was necessary short of getting arrested or revealing that Mickey was paying them for this purpose. He made it clear that if his name ever came up, they would not live to see another day. The Stone reputation in the old neighborhood had remained intact, and Mickey's new clothes and education did nothing to change it. Neither of the two Neanderthals doubted for a moment that Mickey's threats were anything but real. Besides, it was easy money.

The reign of terror lasted six months, during which time there were various changes in corporate ownership of the properties. It began with simple things: The tenants arrived home to find glue injected into their door locks. Two days later, the lobby intercom went out and a key had been broken off inside the outer-door cylinder. It took three weeks to get it fixed. The intercom never worked again. The elevator had suddenly become totally unreliable and was being used as a toilet. Some of the older tenants, unable to take the stairs, were stuck for hours between floors in elevators whose ventilation fans had ceased to work. No amount of disinfectant could remove the stench of urine that had permeated the linoleum. It became commonplace to find tenants walking the stairs carrying bundles of groceries; the elderly stopped venturing out altogether.

Young toughs appeared and used the front of the building as a hangout. The police, at first, chased them away, but they always came back and always had something to say to anyone entering or leaving the building. Fear became pervasive. Windows were mysteriously smashed. Tenants routinely waded through garbage rotting in the hallways.

Then the fires began.

At first, it was just a balled-up newspaper in front of a tenant's door; perhaps the doormat caught on fire. But then garbage cans filled with trash were strategically placed at the head of each landing and set on fire. When the tenants realized that they couldn't escape, panic raced through the building.

Some of the younger tenants complained to the police and fire marshals who responded to investigate the fires, but no one ever actually saw anyone start them. Small paper bags filled with human excrement were set on fire in front of the more vocal tenants' doors. The occupants, smelling smoke, would fling the door open to see the bag on fire and instinctively stomp on it. Someone was having fun.

Though people did start moving out, it was sporadic and not nearly as fast as Mickey had hoped. He gave his two goons specific instructions on a new tactic, and told them he wanted to be there when they used it.

It was a cold, blustery night, and the wind off the Hudson River, two short blocks from Broadway and 111th Street, was gusting southeasterly at fifteen to twenty miles per hour. The two buildings adjoined each other in the middle of the block, facing north onto 111th Street.

Twenty-three-year-old Mickey Stone sat comfortably in the window booth of a diner on the northeast corner of Broadway and 111th Street, his eyes fixed on the rooftops across the street. His seat provided an unobstructed view of the front of his buildings. He cradled a mug of coffee in his hands, elbows propped up on the table, and rotated his wrist to glance at his Rolex. His eyes were alert but impassive as he picked at a speck of lint on the sleeve of his new camel's hair coat, took a sip from the mug, and directed his attention back to the buildings. One A.M. Good.

On the roof of each building, a figure moved quietly across the asphalt and tar-pitch surfaces on sneakered feet. There were no lights on the roof but it is never fully dark in New York. Ambient light from the downtown skyscrapers and reflections from the streetlamps and storefronts below provided more than enough illumination. The men moved to their separate tasks, leaning heavily to one side due to the weight of five-gallon cans of gasoline. They carefully picked their way through haphazardly strewn wires and TV antennas. One man grinned crookedly. Knocking over the antennas had been his idea.

The buildings were of prewar construction and had been built with dumbwaiter shafts, which were designed to eliminate unsightly kitchen trash cans and save residents from having to carry garbage down to the street or basement. A dumbwaiter was basically a miniature, hand-operated elevator for trash, situated inside the kitchen or pantry.

The shaft's most inherent danger lay in the fact that it was like having a wood-lined chimney running through your apartment. Eventually they were made illegal, and those buildings that had them were required to permanently seal the doors and bulkhead on the roof that housed the pulleys. Modern-day firefighters still looked for them, and still feared them. A fire in a dumbwaiter shaft quickly became a blow-torch rocketing up through the building, threatening to spread horizontally through each apartment it passed.

The two thugs went about their work. They moved to each of the four bulkheads housing the pulleys and to the service access panels, strewn nearby where they had been tossed after their removal earlier that day. The men tipped the gasoline cans and poured an estimated one-quarter of the five-gallon cans into each shaft.

Over the years, and despite the best efforts of the buildings' maintenance crews, the shafts had been violated. As a result, the bottom of the shafts, from the basement to just below the first floor, were filled with old, extremely dry paper, wood, and trash. Open the top of the shaft and it differed little in form and function from a fireplace loaded with kindling and fuel.

The resulting fire went to a third alarm. Nobody died that night, but four people were seriously injured in the blaze, including a nine-month-old infant. It was no secret that the fire was arson, but the fire marshals who responded hit a brick wall trying to find witnesses, or *anyone* willing to speak to them. The case remained open and active for months afterward, but the marshals' efforts yielded nothing of substance. For all intents and purposes, the buildings were uninhabitable and the tenants long gone. Shortly thereafter, Belzier-Stone Realty bought the buildings from the dummy corporation that had owned them and began immediate renovations. They used the three hundred percent profit garnered from the insurance company to hire the best architect in the city. Mickey Stone's instructions were to gut and renovate the buildings and to spare no expense in the process. Security, a fire-detection and suppression system was installed, the lobby was tastefully furnished, and a doorman was hired. Rents were astronomical for the time, but the new tenants, culled from the Belzier family's friends, felt it was worth every penny. Everything in the buildings worked and the new superintendent and his crew had been trained to instantly fix anything that broke. That kind of service was a rare commodity in New York, and the new tenants found little to gripe about.

The buildings became cash cows; Mickey never again had to employ such crude tactics. From that moment on, Belzier-Stone was, if not wholly scrupulous, strictly legitimate.

Mickey discovered something about himself that night as he sat in the diner watching the flames lick the evening sky and listening to the thundering power of the fire engines pounding the streets, sirens and air horns blaring. He found himself drawn unexpectedly out of the diner, eyes glassy, heart pounding, and walked almost trancelike to the buildings. He stood on the corner as rig after rig pulled into the block, firemen scrambling with hose and tools toward the buildings; police diverting traffic; ambulances careening down Broadway to the scene of the fire. He watched as the victims were carried out, brought to the waiting ambulances, and loaded aboard to be transported to the nearest emergency room. Mickey Stone had never been prone to overstatement, but as he stood there, silently taking in the scene, chest heaving, palms sweating, he tried to separate his feelings from his thoughts, and he couldn't. The fact that he was the orchestrator of the massive power assembled on *his* street gave him a sense of omnipotence unlike anything he had felt before. He felt a kinship with the fire, and though he wouldn't be able to put it into words until much later, for the second time in his life, Mickey Stone felt like a god.

■   ■   ■

Stone quickly realized that not only would it be to his advantage, but he preferred to use Belzier as the front man for the business. His part in things would be nearly untraceable. Besides, it was Franklin and the Belzier name that could attract the better class of tenants, and that was what Mickey wanted. He knew that no matter how hard he tried, no matter how polished he became, he would always be "nouveau'' to the people of Belzier's world. As the years passed, few people even noticed that they had never met the elusive Mr. Stone of Belzier-Stone Realty. Some speculated that he didn't exist at all. While his name appeared on the corporation letterhead and business filings, if he existed, they reasoned, he must be the junior partner, and a very silent one at that. Franklin met all prospective clients, negotiated all real-estate purchases, and interviewed all new employees. But the company's strategies were conceived by Mickey and no deal went forward without his specific approval.

As the seventies yielded to the eighties, his real-estate empire grew, his wealth expanded exponentially, and his tastes became ever more bizarre. After a time, he thought of himself as, if not exactly a god, then at least godlike. If he believed in anything at all, it was the superiority of strength over weakness, cunning over naïveté, and power over reason. He equated goodness with stupidity. And while he searched for a central focus for those who followed him, it struck him, in a moment of total clarity, that if he had to honestly define himself, he was evil. If there was a God, then there was a Devil. And if there was a Devil, then surely he had his disciples. And Mickey would be no ordinary disciple. He would be *His* messenger, the guardian of *His* gate . . . *His* Sentry.

25

The rear door to the huge, nearly full-to-capacity underground garage gave easily. Matt Kincaid and Jake Morgan slipped in and quietly pressed themselves against the soot-covered wall, knowing that the slightest sound would reverberate off the cinder-block walls. They closed the door, turning the knob to prevent the latch from making noise. For several anxious moments, they stood listening. The stale smell of unventilated exhaust fumes filled their nostrils and the uneven ticking of cooling metal from a nearby car indicated a recent arrival. Overhead fluorescent lights, the bulbs coated with oily grime, did little more than cast dim, garish light. Their black clothes blended into the shadows and only their faces gleamed in the subdued light. At a nod from Matt, they unrolled black wool ski masks and pulled them on, becoming nearly invisible in the underground gloom.

Moving silently on rubber-soled shoes, they hugged the wall, using cars as cover, working their way toward the red exit sign above the door leading to the stairs. They stopped and listened for the whir of a motor from the elevators ten feet away. It was quiet. The tube of graphite lubricant they'd used on the outer door's hinges was applied to the stairway door as well, and it moved soundlessly as they opened it only wide enough to slip through. Matt pulled it closed behind them. Much of this part of their plan depended on the assumption that no one who paid the kind of rents the building charged would choose to use the stairs, especially at one-thirty in the morning. From the basement, it was sixteen flights to the fifteenth floor, and both men had the necessary experience to pace themselves for that kind of climb. They took the steps two at a time and stopped to rest between the eighth and ninth floors before continuing. It was hot in the closed stairway and the ski masks made it hotter still. They were out of breath when they reached the fifteenth floor.

Resting on the landing, Matt and Jake allowed their breathing and heart rates to return to normal while they used the time to slip on latex gloves and lubricate the hinges of the door leading to the hallway. Jake pulled it open, looked quickly around, and signaled the "all clear." Upon stepping into the hall, they moved to the light fixtures and unscrewed the bulbs, plunging their half of the hallway into darkness.

It took a few moments to adjust to the sudden absence of light, and they waited before moving to the door of the apartment. When they did, Matt put his ear to the door, as Jake watched and listened for movement down the hall.

Matt took a leather case containing a pick set from his back pocket and went to work on the door. Jake held a penlight on the cylinder and shot furtive looks down the hall.

The door had an upper and a lower lock set, which, considering the affluence of the tenants, were surprisingly inexpensive and offered almost no challenge. Matt turned the knob. The door opened soundlessly. They slipped in and Jake eased the door closed as both men drew their weapons.

They turned the corner from the foyer into the living room. A small stovetop light spilled out through the kitchen doorway, revealing a neat and tastefully furnished apartment. Nothing at all like they'd expected. From the description they'd gotten of its occupant, Matt had expected less elegant furnishings. Large sculptures stood at various places along the wall of the living room; paintings in gilt-edged wood frames lined the wall. The scent of the leather couch and chairs filled the room, and Oriental rugs accented the high-gloss oak floors.

Jake and Matt skirted the edges of the hallway, hoping to minimize the chance of a squeaking floorboard giving them away as they approached the bedroom. The door was ajar and they paused at the entrance. Enough moonlight shone through the open curtains to allow them to see dark outlines as they peered into the room. At Matt's signal, Jake moved to the far side of the bed.

Jeremy Patterson was sleeping on his stomach and they were on him in an instant, Matt pressing a heavy knee into the small of his back and Jake twisting his arms behind him. They'd cuffed so many men in their time that getting a guy while he slept was like child's play. He was cuffed, gagged, and immobile before he knew he was awake. They moved the pillows to either side of his head as Jake pressed his automatic into the base of Jeremy's skull.

Jake whispered, "Move and you die." Jeremy went limp. Matt thought he might have passed out. "You understand?"

He was relieved when the man nodded.

Matt spoke from the other side. "I'm going to ask you some questions. If you answer them, you will think you dreamed this in the morning. If you don't you won't see tomorrow. You will die a very slow and very painful death. Is that clear?"

Another nod. Jake lifted Jeremy's head by his hair and slipped a thin wire loop over it, drawing it firmly around his neck. He pulled it steadily closed and, when it was very tight, twisted it. Jeremy flopped like a fish but Jake held firm. When he finally released it, Matt put his mouth very close to the man's ear.

"The next time, my friend is not going to let go so soon," he said. "I'm going to remove your gag. Make any sound other than to answer my questions and you'll find the wire a relief from what happens next. Answer every question quickly and honestly. Got it?"

A murmur of acknowledgment made its hard way through Jeremy's tortured throat. Matt removed the handkerchief from Jeremy's mouth. He began to speak, but Jake jammed the barrel of his gun into the base of his skull and said, "Not till you're spoken to."

Matt sat on the bed. "We'll start with the easy ones. Do you know Eddie Cannell?"

Jeremy nodded and Matt asked, "Were you with him the night that the homeless man was burned?"

Jeremy coughed. "No. That was all bullshit. Cannell made it up."

"Why?"

"Because he's a fucking asshole. He gets off on setting those old geezers on fire. When you caught him, he didn't know what to do, so he gave you a name. My name . . . The little prick."

"Then you and Eddie didn't have a relationship."

"Fuck, no. The kid is weird, man."

"The kid is *dead,* man. Did you know that?"

Jeremy was silent, the news of Eddie's death obviously coming as a surprise. Matt nodded and Jake gave the garrote a small twist. "He asked you a question."

Jeremy choked and Jake let up. His whole demeanor had changed. He was rigid with fear, speaking only after Jake applied the garrote again, and then his answer was halting: "No. I didn't know he was dead."

Matt felt he had to be absolutely certain about his suppositions and asked, "Have you and I ever spoken on the telephone?"

"Hell, no."

"Are you the man they call the Sentry?"

Jeremy started to struggle at the mention of the name. Jake gave a warning tug on the wire.

"Fuck, no. Are you crazy or somethin'? Me, the Sentry?"

Even in his predicament he managed to punctuate his question with a derisive snort.

"Then answer this one and you get a prize. Where can I find him?"

Jeremy licked his lips, trying to get some moisture on his tongue. His voice came in a cracked whisper. "I don't know what you're talking about."

Jake gave the garrote a violent twist, then watched impassively as Jeremy fought for breath. Jake held it until Matt touched his arm. Jeremy coughed and gagged, wheezing through his aching windpipe. He was trying to move his head, get some air, but his face was pressed into the mattress. Even in the dark, his terror was thick and palpable. Matt felt cold and distant, oblivious to Jeremy's fears. If he felt anything at all, it was hate. He was certain that Jeremy Patterson was involved with what had gone down the past few days. And he was equally certain that he could lead them to the Sentry. Matt would see no more partners dead. No more little girls tortured. No more innocent victims burned. The bastard had to know that the rules had been suspended indefinitely.

They rolled him over onto his back. Matt pressed his knee into Jeremy's neck while Jake tied his legs, spread-eagled, to the corners of the bed. Jeremy's eyes bulged as Jake pulled a six-inch folding knife from his pocket and made a slow, deliberate show of opening it, then inching it closer and closer to Jeremy's chest. When the cold steel touched his skin, Jeremy bucked and wrestled with his restraints. Jake applied pressure and traced an unhurried line toward Jeremy's head. A thin red line followed the knife's path. He paused, lightened the pressure, and made small circles around his nipples before continuing up past his chin. When he ran the razor-shape edge around his lips, Jeremy froze in fear. And then Jake laid the knife crossways in Jeremy's mouth and pressed down.

Matt's face was only inches from Jeremy's, their eyes locked: Matt's cold, unfeeling, Jeremy's wide with terror. "I'm going to ask you one more time. If you say you don't know, my friend is going to slice your lying mouth open." Matt allowed his words and the edge of Jake's knife to achieve the maximum effect. "Now, where is the Sentry?" He leaned his weight into Jeremy's neck.

Jeremy tried to speak, his words mumbled, sounding like he had a dentist working in his mouth. "H-h-he will kill me anyway if I tell you." Jake lifted the knife, allowing it to hover just above Jeremy's lips.

Matt continued, "There is no reason he has to know. *We* aren't going to tell him. In any event, should you decide to protect him, your death here is certain. Whether he finds out is up to you. Now, where is he?" Jake pressed the cold steel to Jeremy's cheek.

"I-I only have a number to call. No one knows where he lives. He calls us when he wants *us*."

"What's the number?"

"Oh, God, he'll kill me if he finds out."

"Then don't let him find out. The number?"

"Five-five-five-nine-two-six-seven."

"Now, where do you meet him when he tells you to?"

"In an apartment on East Twelfth Street between Avenues B and C. Number six-three-oh, I think."

" 'I think' isn't good enough. Is that the address or not?" Jake nudged the knife.

"Yes, yes. That's the number. I'm sure. Six-three-oh."

"What apartment?"

"Third floor, west side of the building. It's an old tenement. Only two apartments per floor."

"Are you sure about the address?"

"Yes."

"And now, the sixty-four-dollar question. Who is he?"

Jeremy's eyes rolled. "My God, I don't know. I swear, I don't know. Nobody does."

"God? God? You don't have a God, you miserable piece of shit.

Don't you mention God to me, you fucking animal. Now, what the fuck is his name? Answer me before I decide to arrange a personal introduction to *my* God.''

Jake reached around out of sight and touched Matt's back. Matt responded with a short nod that let Jake know he understood. Yes, he told himself, Jake is right. Calm down.

"I'm telling the truth. Nobody knows his real name. Nobody. It doesn't work that way.''

"If you're lying about any of this, we'll be back. And you will die more horribly than any of his victims. Do you understand?''

Jeremy nodded quickly.

"Would you like to reconsider any of your answers?''

"No. I'm telling the truth.''

"Then none of this ever happened. You'll wake up in the morning and it'll all be a dream.''

Jake folded the knife, slipped it into his pocket, and removed a Ziploc plastic bag from his shirt. He opened it and removed a hand-kerchief soaked in ether. They covered their noses as Jake held it over Jeremy's face. When his body went limp, they untied his legs, removed the cuffs, and retraced their steps, relocking the door behind them as they left.

Safely in their car a block away, Jake turned to Matt. "Would you have done him, Matt?''

Matt Kincaid looked at his partner, then toward the building they'd just left, with hard, unblinking eyes. His voice was flat, the words slow and precise. "Yes, I would have done him. . . . Now let's get the fuck out of here.''

26

The streets were nearly deserted as Jake and Matt drove to lower Manhattan. They didn't go directly to the address Jeremy gave them; instead, feeling the need to wind down and allow the adrenaline to leave their systems, they'd bought coffee, found a dark street to park on, and sat wordlessly sipping. By the time they got going, it was 2:45 and Jake was still hyper, talking on and on as he drove about how they were going to nail this son of a bitch, make him pay, break the case. Matt wasn't listening and sat silently, deep within himself. His thoughts were on the things they had just done and he was feeling ashamed. He'd taken to it too easily, enjoyed the thrill of breaking into the apartment, the power trip when the man called Jeremy was at their mercy, the stealth with which it had all been accomplished. He tried to focus on the job at hand, shake off the bad vibes, but they nagged at him like a dull toothache. They were two blocks from the address when Matt finally emerged from the doldrums.

"Don't turn into the block. We don't know what his setup is, and as long as we're dressed for it, I think we should do the roofs. We can enter through the far corner building and walk across to 630."

Jake looked at him uneasily. "But that's a lot of ground, Matt. The more buildings we have to negotiate, the greater the risk of being seen. Wouldn't it be better if we entered from the next block, walked through the rear yards, and came in through the back of the building? Then we wouldn't have to worry about getting to the car in a hurry. We'd just have to cut through the backyard and boom, there we are."

Jake's idea made more sense than his own. Number 630 was in the middle of the block and that did mean traversing a lot of roofs.

"Okay, so let's swing into the block and see which one is 630. Don't drive too slow. We don't want to draw attention to ourselves. I'll count the buildings, you tell me which one it is.''

"You got it, m'man.'' Jake was acting chipper, almost too happy, and Matt didn't like it a bit. They were there on serious business and the Sentry was a dangerous man. His partner should at least be apprehensive. This wasn't a walk in the park and it called for caution, not bravado.

He put his hand on Jake's just as he reached for the shift lever. "What's with you, Jake?''

"What d'ya mean?''

"I mean, what are you so fucking happy about? You're acting like you think we're going to a party.''

Jake yanked his hand away. "Hey, lighten up. Is there some law against feelin' good?''

"No. But you don't seem to appreciate the gravity of the situation. This prick is a vicious and cold-blooded killer. I shouldn't have to remind you of that. We don't have a clue as to how many people he's done, and you don't seem the least bit concerned.''

Jake continued to smile. "I'm just trying to keep an upbeat attitude, is all. What's got up your ass?''

Matt shifted to fully face his partner. "Jake, I know this guy.''

"So you know him a little better than me. You're workin' on the case a few days longer, and that's supposed to make you an expert on this guy?''

"No. You don't understand. I mean, I *know* him. I know who he is. We grew up in the same neighborhood. This is personal. For him *and* for me.''

It took a moment for this new revelation to sink in. Morgan's relaxed attitude disappeared, and he became immediately angry. "What the fuck are you saying? You're telling me you know who this guy *really* is?'' He swiveled in his seat. "Why didn't you tell me before now? How long have you known?''

"I only found out yesterday during the hypnosis. I've been meaning to tell you.''

Jake's normally pleasant face grew dark. His thick eyebrows formed a sharp V as his eyes drilled into Matt and he erupted, "When? After we faced the fucking guy? How could you hold something like that out on me?'' He shook his head vigorously, stunned at both the news and the belief that his partner had misled him. "Who the fuck is he, then?"

Matt wiped away the spittle Jake had sprayed on his face in his excitement. "I just wanted to be sure before I said anything, that's all."

"And now you're suddenly sure? So who is he?"

Matt couldn't meet Jake's eyes. "Like he said on the phone, 'my worst nightmare.' "

"Hey, partner, you think you could stop talking in code long enough to be straight with me? Does he have a name?"

"Yeah, he's got a name. Mickey. Mickey Stone. At least that *was* his name when we were kids."

Jake regained some of his composure, his curiosity getting the better of him. "Okay, so his name is Mickey Stone. What's he got against you?"

"It's a long story. But he's getting even for something I did to him when we were kids growing up in the neighborhood."

"You mean to say you think this prick is killing people to get back at you for something that happened what, more than twenty-five years ago? You kidding me, or what?"

"No. I don't think he's killed people *because* of me. At least, I don't think it started out that way. But you don't know Mickey. Once he knew I was involved, I believe it's *become* his motivation. That's why he went after John's family. It's why my name keeps coming up. He's trying to spook me and make me look like a jerk. But if I know him, it's more serious than that. He wants me dead."

"What the hell could you have *done* to this guy?"

"I told you, it's a long story."

Jake leaned back, took a cigarette from his pocket, and put it to his mouth. "That's okay. Time's something I can spare."

Matt told the story in a flat, unaffected monotone. It took about twenty minutes to bring Jake up to the present. Afterward, they sat silently watching the sparse traffic passing by on the avenue up ahead as Jake absorbed the impact of the news.

When he finally spoke, Jake's demeanor was subdued, his voice hushed. "That's quite a fucking story, Matt. I ask you, who'da thunk it? I mean, *Je-sus H. Christ,* I always thought of you as one of the straightest guys I've ever known—Mr. John Q. Citizen—only to discover there's a dark side to you I never imagined. I guess I should have suspected it when you discussed this 'black bag' stuff. But I just figured you were desperate. Turns out you are one bad motherfucker.''

Jake was startled to see anger and suspicion flare on his partner's face. That guilt-laden image of himself was exactly the thing Matt had worked his entire adult life to change. He felt himself sinking.

His voice was a cold draft in the warm car. ''No, Jake. That *ain't* me. I am 'straight,' as you put it. I've spent years trying to atone for the wrongs I did as a young man. Trying to be the kind of person who could shave in the morning and not be ashamed of the guy looking back. Don't you tell me that suddenly all that has changed. Because it hasn't.''

Matt's rebuttal caught him off guard; Jake backed off, his tone conciliatory. ''Hey, man. That ain't what I meant. Don't be so damned sensitive. I was admiring your balls, that's all. I always knew you had 'em, it's just that I'm surprised as hell to discover that after all this time, I'm finding things out about you that I would have never imagined possible. Look, as far as I'm concerned, the son of a bitch got what he deserved. I wasn't knocking you. I'm with ya.''

Matt slumped back and leaned heavily against the door. It didn't matter anymore. A sense of resignation seeped into his bones and settled heavily in his heart. What's the use? he thought. After today, nothing would ever be the same. If he fought the Sentry on his own terms, no matter what the outcome, Mickey Stone would still win.

He pushed his thoughts aside. ''Still want to go through with this?''

''I told you, Matt, I'm with you one hundred percent.''

''Then let's do it.''

Jake started the car, eased onto the avenue, and turned left onto Twelfth Street. Matt counted the buildings aloud while Jake read numbers.

''That one, with the stone trim around the entrance,'' Matt said.

''Seven buildings off the avenue. Okay, let's get out of here.''

Jake made a right at the corner and another at the next. Many of the buildings had been abandoned by their landlords, but it was evident that people were still living in them. Flickering light sparkled through cracks in the boarded-up windows.

Although few people living outside of New York City had ever heard of Alphabet City, the area was high on every law-enforcement hit list. Even some native New Yorkers were unaware of its existence.

It was a target neighborhood for drugs, prostitution, homicides, and other violent crimes. It was where teenage runaways flocked to after arriving in the city, finding dangerous shelter in the many abandoned buildings. Because of the sharing of needles among intravenous drug users, its incidences of AIDS, hepatitis, tuberculosis, venereal disease, and infant death were comparable to the worst of Third World countries. Harlem seemed like Shangri-la in comparison. The strangest mixture of people in the city—whites, blacks, Hispanics, Asians, Arabs—all shared the same few blocks. The New York chapter of the Hells Angels had their headquarters there. It was the city's most homogenized neighborhood. And possibly its most dangerous.

It was also one of the few places in Manhattan where finding a parking space was no trouble. Few of its residents could afford the cost of insuring even a beat-up heap to park on these mean streets, and even if they could, it wouldn't have lasted a week.

It was 3:15 when Jake eased into a spot close to a hydrant. They'd have no trouble pulling out fast if they had to. He switched off the lights and motor and scanned the street for movement. Their luck was holding. The street was deserted. Except for the muted sound of music and voices coming from the buildings, all was quiet. Matt pulled the bulb from the dome light before they got out and eased the doors closed.

Garbage was piled two feet high in the alley. The stench of rotting fruit, food, and discarded baby diapers nearly overwhelmed them. Their vision was severely limited; Matt cringed at scurrying sounds beneath the mounds of trash. Yet as gross as the place was, others had beaten a trail of sorts leading to the rear yard.

The target loomed ahead. A three-quarter moon was on its descent, casting eerie stripes of shadow through the slats of the fire escape onto the ocher-colored brick. Matt counted up three floors on the west side of the building. Moonlight glinted off glass, but otherwise, the apartment was black. Maybe no one was there. Or maybe the windows were covered from the inside. Jeremy had said they used it as a meeting place and only when the Sentry called.

They picked a careful path across the concrete remnants of a rear yard, broken up into large uneven chunks. Grateful that the rusted drop ladder of the fire escape was down, Matt grabbed it, trying to silently test its strength. He whispered to Jake, "We'll go one at a time. I don't think it can take both of us at once."

Jake nodded. Matt gripped the rails, remembering one of a firefighter's cardinal rules: Never grab the rungs of a ladder; use the rails and place your feet near the welds.

It seemed to Matt as if he'd spent his entire adult life on rickety fire escapes. As he neared the top, the ladder shifted and he pulled himself into it and froze. A long moment passed. It held, and he continued to the garbage-strewn first landing. When he looked down, Jake was already halfway up. He offered an assist, but Jake stepped catlike over the railing and landed soundlessly on the platform.

There were more gaps than steps on the stairway leading to the second and third floors. No picnic in the dark. But that wasn't what concerned them. If they had to make a hasty retreat, the combination of missing steps, rusting metal, and near-total darkness could spell disaster. Getting down was never as easy as going up, even under the best conditions. Fire escape stairs were sharply angled. The laws had been lax when these tenements were built and little consideration was given to the stairs' actual use in an emergency. Firefighters went up *and* down facing the stairs; if they lost their balance, they'd fall inward. Civilians used the stairs in a normal manner, and a misstep pitched them helplessly outward into space.

They drew their guns as they neared the third floor, and when they got there, Matt took one side of the window, Jake the other. They squatted, pressing their ears to the glass. A heavy drape blocked their view of the interior, but a thin sliver of light twinkled through a narrow slit at one edge. Jake's expression, as their eyes met, said, Now what? It struck Matt with sudden clarity that they hadn't spent enough time putting this part of the plan together. If Mickey or his crew were inside, how could they enter through the window without catching a bullet or a crowbar in the head? The decayed window, if it opened at all, was sure to give them away. They listened quietly, thinking, and hearing no sound from the apartment, wondered what to do next.

Matt craned to see the windows of the apartment above. Gaping black rectangles stared out at the night sky. There was no glass or, for that matter, frames in the windows, and no light or sound spilled out into the night. He pointed upward with the muzzle of his gun. Jake nodded. Matt offered a silent prayer to the god of fire escapes and idiots as they began their ascent.

The stairs held, and they took positions on either side of the pitch-black cavity. With the frame gone, the window was more like a doorway, and Matt cautiously turned on his penlight and played the narrow beam around the room.

It looked like a thousand other rooms in a thousand other vacant apartments: Garbage, fast-food wrappers, bottles, candle stubs, and ragged, urine-stained mattresses revealed it as a place where people flopped for the night. Jake peeked in and directed his small light to the opposite side of the room. More of the same. Jake covered Matt, who switched off his light and quickly stepped in. He pressed his back against the wall, gun at his side, and thought about how to best proceed. He remembered his first partner, the grizzled veteran Simon Rosenthal, and the many vacant buildings they'd searched together, and the many lessons he'd learned.

In the movies, cops held their weapons straight out, aiming down the barrel. But a gunfight inside a building occurs, almost by definition, at close range, mitigating the need to sight your target. Walking into a room gun first was an invitation for an assailant to disarm you. Instead, you held it at your hip and used your other hand to ward off attackers or train your light, giving you time to recover and fire.

Jake slid into the inky blackness behind him. Even with flashlights, moving across an old wooden floor was going to be dangerous. Doing it silently was going to be a miracle. Many times holes in the floor were covered by cardboard or some other flimsy material.

Now that they were there, it seemed a lousy alternative. Matt was angry at himself. There seemed little chance that their presence wouldn't be detected. Everything was against them—the quiet, the condition of the building, the darkness. Every man who had ever tried, knew how impossible it was to be silent when trying to creep in quietly after a late night out. Under ideal conditions, and in familiar surroundings, he'd bump or trip over every object in the room. In a strange, rubble-strewn building, they'd sound like stampeding elephants.

They nearly leaped out of the window as the yelling began.

"Bitch! You took the last of my stash? You fucking bitch! I'll kill your fat white ass."

"No, Tyrone. It wasn't me. I didn't take your shit. Robby was by. He must'a took it."

"You lie, you stupid cunt."

Slapping sounds, tumbling furniture, screams of protest and pain, curses, and then occupants of other apartments shouting, "Shut-the-fuck-up! People-are-trying-to-sleep!'' And Tyrone yelling back, ''You don't shut up yourself, I'll come down there and kick *your* fuckin' ass.''

The building was pandemonium. Because they were able to use the commotion as cover, Matt and Jake took only seconds to traverse the small apartment. The front door, hanging from its top hinge, was wedged in a half-open position. The racket was getting louder and Matt chanced a look. Nobody was stepping out into the hall. It was all bluster and bravado, destined to come to nothing. No one wanted to really get into it, or die over someone *else's* stash getting stolen. Big John would have said they were ''just sellin' woof tickets.''

The clamor increased as Tyrone worked himself into a frenzy of abuse. It was going to be a long night for him without his junk and someone, apparently the woman he lived with, was going to pay.

''Don't you lie to me, you slimy bitch. I can see it in your fuckin' eyes. You already high. And on *my* shit! What am I supposed to do now?'' Slap. Crash. Cries of protest.

They stole out of the apartment to the head of the stairs. Interior stairs in these buildings could be more treacherous than the fire escape. Sometimes there'd be nothing but air between floors.

Cupping the beams of their lights in the palms of their hands allowed enough light to reveal that, sure enough, the entire section of stairs was gone between the landings. Two long, wooden planks stolen from police sawhorse barriers had been erected to bridge the gap. The outcries were dying down and time was running out. Keeping a hand on the wall for balance, they tightrope-walked down the planks, across the words POLICE LINES: DO NOT CROSS, and jumped the remaining three-step gap. They switched off their lights and tiptoed to the apartment.

A dim, flickering light winked erratically beneath the door. They took positions on either side. Matt slowly turned the knob as Jake raised his automatic. The door yielded; a thin beam of light spilled into the hall, widening like a sunrise.

Matt flung the door open and it banged loudly as they threw themselves in, crouching low, guns poised.

The room was still. A dozen candles flickered lazily inside tall glass containers at various points around the room. Slow-motion shadows of the sparse furnishings danced lethargically on the floors and walls.

But something was very wrong. Who would leave candles burning in an empty apartment? Were they expected? Was someone still here or about to return? What the hell was going on?

Matt glanced at Jake, who looked as worried and confused as he felt. Matt signaled to him to close the door and turn the deadbolt. They didn't need any unpleasant surprises.

At the far side of the room near the windows, a group of helium-filled balloons anchored to a brick by a one-inch piece of string bobbed and swayed eerily in a draft. They approached cautiously, Jake covering their backs. Each of the balloons wore a crudely drawn Have a Nice Day smile-face that watched their approach. Each face had only one eye.

Jake, gripped by a sudden wave of nausea, turned away, choking back the rising bile in his throat. Matt just stared. There was a pool of blood on the floor beneath the table. Set in the middle of a group of seven balloons was Jeremy Patterson's head, his mouth sliced from ear to ear in a grotesque parody of a smile-face. One eye was taped shut and the other was opened wide, staring in surprised shock at the two fire marshals. A stick-on bow was attached mockingly to the side of his head. His tongue was hanging out and a note lay on top of it. Matt lifted it off.

> ARE WE HAVING FUN YET? JEREMY COULDN'T MAKE THE PARTY, SO HE SENT THIS ON A HEAD. SINCE YOU SEEMED SO INTENT ON KNOWING WHAT WAS INSIDE OF IT, I THOUGHT YOU DESERVED TO SEE FOR YOURSELF. HE SAID NOT TO BOTHER WAITING, START WITHOUT HIM.

Matt was incredulous. How could Mickey have known? Nobody saw us. I *know* nobody saw us.

But as a result of the janitor's phone call following Matt and Greg's first visit to the building, Jeremy's apartment had been bugged, and Matt and Jake's interrogation of him only hours before had been overheard. Jeremy was still unconscious when they left him. Two men entered the building using the same route Jake and Matt had taken. Except they didn't have to pick the lock. The janitor had given them a spare key snitched from the superintendent's office. The rest was easy. While Matt was relating his youthful experience with Mickey to Jake Morgan, Jeremy Patterson was dying.

There was another element they were unaware of. . . .

They whirled quickly at the scraping sound coming from somewhere down a long dark foyer. Matt signed to Jake to take the far wall. It was going to be a difficult search. The hallway offered no cover, and any shot, even one fired blindly, was almost certain to find its mark. Without flashlights they could see nothing, and if they used them, they'd be sitting ducks.

Matt motioned that he was moving up. Jake knelt, braced his gun on the archway, and aimed into the blackness. Matt pressed against the opposite wall, out of the line of fire, and sidestepped slowly, feeling for doors.

He stopped when his fingers brushed a door frame. Matt waved Jake forward and indicated that he would go in and wanted Jake to provide cover. He laid his small flashlight on the floor, turned it on, and rolled it into the entrance, whereupon the room exploded instantly with staccato bursts of gunshots and strobelike light.

27

Greg Townsend paced like a hungry cat. Where the fuck were they? Matt promised he'd check in every couple of hours and he hadn't heard from him since he and Jake left at seven P.M. He checked his watch for the hundredth time. Three thirty-five A.M., eight and a half hours since they left. He looked around the empty squad room and cursed the walls. Goddammit, why did he ever agree to let fire marshals work with them? They were used to much more latitude and probably felt no obligation to report to a boss in another department. If they're not already dead, I'm gonna kill them, he thought. This is bullshit. The world is at home in bed and I'm sitting here waiting for these guys to give me the courtesy of a phone call. Did they say they'd be going home without coming back? Maybe he missed that. He couldn't remember anymore. No. He told them to call, to check in every two hours. He remembered that distinctly.

Greg had the PD radio scanning citywide, listening for any sign that they were in trouble. Three reports of gunshots and two gut-wrenching, immediate-assistance signal 10-13's, and he was hovering over the radio like a rookie.

He flopped down at his desk and tried reading through the day's reports, but his mind wouldn't absorb what he read. He tossed them aside, reached into the bottom drawer, and took out a bottle of scotch he'd had since he was promoted to detective sergeant. He poured a healthy dose into his coffee and stared at it a long time before he sipped. His face screwed up in distaste. I *hate* scotch, he thought. It's no better than cough medicine. Why the hell do I keep it in my desk? Because that's what everyone else drinks. It was also one of those times when life imitated art. Cops weren't immune to the images portrayed on TV or in the movies, and he'd formed the impression it was an integral part of being a detective sergeant to keep a bottle handy in his bottom drawer. What bullshit, he thought. I probably haven't given out two drinks in five years, and then it was with friends who'd stopped by. He poured the foul-tasting concoction down the drain of the water fountain.

Radio traffic was unusually heavy, and even after years of deciphering cryptic messages through often-heavy static, he was having trouble separating the bullshit from the significant. But the instant he heard this call, he knew it was them.

"Nine David Kilo, respond to a report of shots fired in a building in the six hundred block of East Twelfth Street. Nine David Alpha, you take their backs."

Acknowledgments came in from the sector cars. Nine David Kilo asked for further information or callbacks. The "Nine" meant the 9th precinct, David/Kilo were sector and unit designations.

The dispatcher responded, "We're now getting multiple reports of shots fired. Reported to be a building in the middle of the block, East Twelfth Street, between Avenues A and B, north side of the street. Nine David Bravo and Nine David Charlie, respond as further backup for Nine David Kilo and Alpha."

Nine David Bravo and Charlie acknowledged instantly. Greg was only inches from the radio. Nine David Kilo came on to say they had just rolled into the block and that they had heard no shots, but tenants of a derelict building were pouring out into the street.

It was another long minute before all four cars acknowledged their arrival at the scene. Nine David Kilo relayed the information that the tenants had heard numerous shots being fired on the third floor. Kilo said they were going in to investigate with Alpha and Bravo. Nine David Charlie would cover the rear.

"This is Nine Sergeant, Central. Ask all units to maintain position until my arrival. Repeat . . . Maintain their positions. Do not move in. My ETA is two minutes."

"Ten-four, Nine Sergeant. All units on the scene of the shots fired, six hundred block of East Twelfth Street, hold your positions by order of Nine Sergeant. Repeat . . . Hold your positions. He requests you await his arrival. ETA: two minutes. Acknowledge all units."

The first jabs of a punishing headache hit Greg with the unremitting pressure of a vise closing steadily on his temples. He heard his own heartbeat as he awaited news of the sergeant's arrival, hoping the sergeant would bring a semblance of order to the search. He thought a moment, picked up the telephone, and dialed.

"Dispatcher, this is Sergeant Townsend of Special Operations. Please advise all units in the vicinity of the shots fired that there is the possibility of a two-man team of fire marshals operating in the area. They are in plain clothes and have no PD communications."

Before he could hang up, the voice of the central dispatcher passed the information to the sergeant, who, while acknowledging the message, told the dispatcher he was now on the scene and in charge.

The sergeant began organizing the search. Greg heard him say that he was proceeding with the Kilo and Alpha units up the stairs. He reaffirmed that the Charlie car was covering the rear and ordered Bravo to follow and stay one flight below as backup.

The dispatcher continued to transmit other alarms, his voice reverting to its flat, droning quality. Acknowledgments were lackadaisical and subdued. Other cops were waiting to see what was going to happen at the "shots fired" call.

Greg envisioned the men cautiously picking their way up the stairs. The cops were probably very young. Everyone on the job these days was young. He tried to guess their thoughts and put himself in their place. It seemed like a million years since he'd been on the street in uniform, and like all people who'd been there, he felt a tugging nostalgia for those days.

The radio crackled to life. "Central, this is Nine Sergeant. We have four male whites down. Two are DOA, and two are wounded and unconscious. Have EMS, the duty commander, and the shooting team respond. Two of the victims have been ID'd as fire marshals."

Greg picked up the radio with shaking hands. He depressed the transmit button. "Nine Sergeant, this is the Sergeant, Special Ops. The fire marshals are working out of this office. Are they alive?"

"Wait one, Special Ops."

Greg's headache erupted full-blown and the pressure behind his eyes caused the room to spin.

28

Jake struggled to free himself from the crushing weight of his partner. When all hell broke loose, they dove to the side and Matt landed on top of him. Then Matt rolled over, freeing Jake, stuck his automatic into the doorway, and returned fire. He blasted away, spraying the room haphazardly with bullets, trying to force whoever was shooting at them to take cover. Jake, beside him, emptied a magazine from his Walther PPK into the room.

Matt's Glock held seventeen rounds but he'd forgotten to count his shots. He'd been too excited. But he was certain the shots fired at them from the room were from two different caliber weapons—one, a larger caliber, most likely a .38 Magnum; the other, a .25 or .22. He was carrying two extra magazines for the Glock and a six-shot Colt Python on his hip. Unless they were loaded for bear, he and Jake had them badly outgunned.

Two shots blew through the wall, showering them with plaster. Matt ducked and tried to bury himself in a crack in the floor. He quickly fired six more rounds while Jake changed magazines in the PPK. The shots boomed in the bare hall and he flashed on an image of the battling couple upstairs, running out of the building as fast as their feet could carry them.

His heart hammered wildly and he wiped his forehead with his sleeve. How the fuck were they going to get into the room? They'd decided against bringing a radio because it made so much damn noise. He wished he had it now.

His flashlight sat in the doorway casting a narrow yellow beam along the floor. He chanced a quick peek into the room. A fusillade of shots splintered the wood frame just as he pulled back. He wished they'd taken a better look at the layout of the apartment upstairs. The brief glance inside revealed the outline of a large room, a stack of mattresses, two stuffed chairs, and a couch. The bastards could be anywhere.

Well, maybe they didn't have to go in at all. There was no way out except through the door, and sooner or later someone would hear the shots and call the cops. They just had to keep the fuckers inside until the cavalry arrived. Doing nothing might be the best tactic of all. The PD had a lot more experience in situations like this and could bring as many men as necessary onto the scene. Hell, he didn't know what to do. . . . Just wait. That's it—just wait.

"Hey, assholes! There's no place to go. You can't get by us, and in a couple of minutes this place will be swarming with cops. Throw out your guns. Now!"

A very high-speed weapon, either a Mac 10 or an Uzi, opened up a zipper on the wall, splattering plaster everywhere. They scrambled in opposite directions, away from the door, down the hall. The firing stopped. Matt heard furniture crashing and heavy footsteps approaching the entrance. He braced himself for the onslaught, knowing any second someone would come through the door spraying automatic-weapon fire at them. He tried to make himself small and felt huge, aiming at the door, straining to see Jake in the dark. Be careful, he told himself, don't fire unless you have a target. He couldn't take the chance of hitting Jake.

"Jake, they're coming out!"

No answer. Was he hit or laying low?

Jake dove blindly into the blackness to escape the bullets drilling through the wall and ended up colliding headfirst with the corner of a bureau lying on its side a few feet away. He was unconscious before he felt the pain. Blood gushed from the wound on his forehead and he lay motionless, deaf to his partner's warning.

Matt got scared. Really scared. In moments the hallway would be filled with flying bullets and he had no idea why Jake wasn't answering. Was he wounded? Dead? Fuck!

"Jake! For God's sake, answer me! Jake? Are you okay?" The malignant silence filled him with dread.

The blackness erupted in brilliant strobes of lightning and thunder. Matt rolled and fired, his finger jerking instinctively on the trigger again and again, aiming at the flashes, praying he killed the sons of bitches.

"Fuck you! Fuck you! FUCK YOU!" he screamed, punctuating each word with a bullet, muzzle flashes nourishing his anger, his worry, his fear. But his thoughts were on a higher plane. "Please, God, get me out of this. Let me and Jake live. Please. I'll do anything."

He felt naked in the confining space. Plaster and dust and needle-like splinters of wood pelted him, stabbing his cheeks and hands. He continued firing blindly toward the door, thanking God he'd reloaded just before the shit hit the fan. But he was badly outgunned now, and no answering fire came from Jake's end of the hall. The shots raced closer and his balls drew up inside his groin, anticipating the bullet that would tear his belly open. And then it stopped. Dead silence . . . The metallic clank of a magazine hit the floor. The shooter was reloading. It might be his only chance. Did he have any bullets left? It didn't matter. He scrambled to his feet and rushed the door. Get there before he can reload and fire again. He screamed and charged through the blackness. Above the animal wail of his own voice, he heard the lethal snap of a magazine, and as the bolt slid home, he fired into the sound. A grunt, just in front of him. He fired twice more. A sliding sound and a thump as a body hit the floor.

But where was the other one?

He moved forward and his toe touched the soft, yielding flesh in the doorway. One down. Should he chance a reload? He couldn't. There was no way to predict if, or when, the other gunman would rush him. He leaned heavily against the wall, trying to regroup, catch his breath. A scraping sound and a minute vibration through the plaster placed the gunman directly opposite him. His mind's eye drew a sil-houette on the wall and he pushed off, twirled, and fired his last three shots at the spot. He froze. His weapon was empty and he fumbled with his shoulder holster, trying to get his last magazine out of its pouch, his fully loaded Python forgotten in the confusion. His fingers felt like thick sausages, clumsy and numb. Finally, the snap yielded and he grabbed the magazine, dumped the empty, and inserted the fresh one. He found the slide release with his thumb and a round slammed home.

A voice, cracked with agony, said, "You motherfucker. Come and get me."

He crept to the doorway, pressure tight on the trigger, ready to fire with the merest twitch. The door frame loomed before him as both protection now and ominous barrier if he had to cross it. Wounded, perhaps more dangerous than ever, the gunman lay in wait on the other side. He had to take him out, one way or another. He inched closer, face twitching, heart pumping full throttle. He braced himself and lunged wildly into the room, whipping his gun toward the voice.

Matt saw the flash of the small automatic as it fired at him, but heard no sound as something bit him hard near the temple. His finger snapped reflexively on the trigger, and that final round entered the gunman's heart, killing him instantly. Matt crumbled to the floor, his mind imagining the barking laugh of a jackal coming nearer, growing louder, resounding hollowly inside him until it filled his head, blocking his thoughts and taking him down, down.

29

A pungent, ammonialike smell assaulted his senses. His lungs rebelled and Matt tried to turn away; he jerked fitfully and coughed. He was disoriented, unsure of his surroundings. His eyes fluttered open and bright overhead light stabbed his pupils. He squinted through one eye. A tom-tom thumped ceaselessly in his temples. He awakened slowly to the sound of voices talking over him and tried to focus on the words, but they came through a thick gloom, dissipating as they reached his brain. He shook his head, tried to look around, but was punished by a bolt of pain and black dots bursting behind his eyes. He moaned. Sleep beckoned like a pretty girl and he felt his eyes succumb, close again; he felt himself wanting to sink back into sweet oblivion. What did he remember? The gunfight! Two men. Flashes of light. Jake. Oh, my God, Jake! Is he okay?

"I think he's coming to, Sergeant." The voice was unfamiliar, hollow.

He tried to slap at fingers prying his eye open but his arms were pinned down. A bright beam of light played across an eyeball and a salvo of needles pelted his brain.

"He's got a mild concussion. Probably should get an X ray as soon as possible."

He tried to clear his mind, speak, but his throat was dry, constricted, his tongue like sandpaper.

"Jake . . . Where's Jake?"

"What'd he say?"

"I don't know."

"Matt, this is Greg. Can you hear me? Matt, wake up. . . . It's Greg. Wake up."

Matt licked his lips, willed them to move. "Where's Jake? Is he okay?"

"Yeah, Jake's fine. He's right here next to you. He's fine. You're both gonna be okay."

"Good . . . Wanna sleep . . . Go away."

A different voice answered, "Sorry, buddy. No can do. You've got to wake up. You've got a mild concussion and we can't let you sleep."

Matt moved his head trying to find the source. "Fuck you. I'm sleeping."

"'Fraid not." He felt rough hands shaking his shoulders, then lightly slapping his face. He hated having his face slapped. And each tap resounded like a thunderclap inside his head. What kind of way was this to treat a head injury?

His head began to clear. "Hey, fuckface, you don't quit that, I'm gonna kick your ass."

"Sure. Go ahead. Kick my ass." The slapping stopped. "He'll be okay, Sergeant. You can talk to him now."

"Matt? . . . Matt!"

The over-bright interior of the ambulance felt like a klieg light in his face. Greg Townsend was leaning over him. "What?" Matt asked.

"What happened in there?"

"In where? Where's Jake?"

Greg pointed to the gurney on the other side of the ambulance. Jake was holding a clear, plastic bag filled with ice to his forehead. He met Matt's eyes, smiled wanly, and lifted the bag. A large, angry-looking, bluish bump was forming just above his right eye, and he looked like he was still dazed. Jake managed to convey through an almost imperceptible shake of his head that he hadn't said anything yet. Good. They'd prepared a story in case anything went wrong. And the story they'd made up wasn't so far from the truth that what really happened couldn't be weaved in. Now to find out exactly what everyone *thought* happened.

"Matt, I gotta know what went on if I'm gonna help you," Greg said. "You've got to trust me."

Matt tried to roll over but a strap had been placed around his chest and waist, pinning his arms to his sides.

"Get these straps offa me."

"Does he need those anymore?"

"No."

"Then take them off."

The EMS paramedic released the straps used to keep him in place on the ride to the hospital. Matt, no longer restricted, rubbed his face and felt the edge of an oversized padded bandage near his temple.

Greg turned to the paramedic. "Can you excuse us for a few minutes? I have to talk to these men about a confidential investigation." The paramedic glanced around, felt the tension, and realized he was being ordered out of his own ambulance. He was about to protest, tell them this was his turf, but none of them looked like they were in the mood to take any shit, so he left and closed the door loudly behind him. Greg waited a moment and looked from one man to the other.

"So?"

Matt shielded his eyes. "What do you want to know?"

"What do I want to know? *What do I want to know?*" Tinged heavily with exasperation, his voice rose and his words spilled rapidly out. "Are you shittin' me, or what? I want to know everything. I want to know what the fuck happened here. Why you were here in the first place. Who those dead men are. Why you're wearing fuckin' Ninja costumes. And"—he slowed the tempo of the questions, swiveling from one to the other, jabbed the air and glared at Matt—"I want to know whose fucking head is sitting on a table full of balloons!

"And that's just for starters." He held up his hand to keep Matt from speaking. "Now, don't bullshit me, Matt. I don't have the time for it. You guys have been freelancing, and unless we"—he made a circle in the air that encompassed the three of them—"can come up with a plausible explanation, what little is left of our careers can be kissed good-bye. 'Cause if you think Captain McDonnell is going to go to bat for you guys, you'd better think again. It just ain't gonna happen."

Matt felt sorry for Greg. He was on the outside and, through no fault of his own, in as deep a pile of shit as they were. As a boss, Greg had to ask for the truth. But what he wanted, what he really *needed,* was something believable and probable enough to explain their actions. The "truth," if it were told, would sink them all.

"Hey, Greg, calm down, okay? It's not as bad as it seems. Me and Jake visited that guy Jeremy. He decided to open up to us, tell us what he knew about the Sentry. Told us about this place . . . that it was where they held their meetings. Except that Jake and I didn't come here right away, and it appears that Jeremy's place was wired. Somebody got to him just after we left and did him. That's *Jeremy's* head on the table. We must have arrived before those two guys could finish their artwork and get out of the apartment. Next thing we knew, shots were flying." Matt looked at his sleeve. "As for the clothes, we stopped to put these on after we passed the building and saw what kind of shape it was in. We didn't want to stand out like sore thumbs or climb fire escapes in suits and ties." Matt toyed with his mustache, his pale eyes staring intently at Greg, wondering if he bought it.

Greg wasn't stupid and he sure as hell wasn't fully satisfied, but they could see he was calming down, digesting the story, checking it for flaws, wondering if it was something that could be believed by *his* bosses. Matt watched him carefully, saw his expression soften, his body assume a less aggressive posture. He was gonna bite.

"But why would this Patterson guy tell you anything? And why would the Sentry wire his apartment?"

"Hey, Greg, I really don't know. Maybe Jeremy had a score to settle. Maybe he was scared. As far as bugging the apartment goes, when you think about it, it was a logical move. The Sentry had to know we'd visit Jeremy sooner or later. Hell, maybe he knew you and I talked to the doormen. By the way, we should send a crew over there. Maybe we can still find out what happened after we left."

Greg squinted suspiciously. "Did anyone see the two of you go into the building?"

"I don't think so. We entered from the garage." Matt looked over at his partner. "Anyone see us, Jake?"

"Nah, the garage was empty. We just lucked out. Someone forgot to lock the door and we were able to get in."

30

It looked as though the proverbial bull had been let loose in the room. Broken furniture and glass carpeted the floor, holes gaped like open wounds in the walls, metal folding chairs lay twisted and bent, debris was scattered everywhere.

The Sentry stood bare-chested in the middle of the devastation panting noisily, his thin, wiry body heaving as the adrenaline flow he'd subjected it to subsided. The handle of a fireman's pike ax, its heavy head resting on the floor, lay limp in his hand. Sweat dripped freely off him to the floor and his dark eyes still held a hint of madness as he scanned the room. Mickey Stone (although he rarely thought of himself as such anymore) had changed much over the years. The handsome face that girls once flocked to had come somehow to reflect the inner workings of his mind. It was lean, cadaverous, and devoid of the healthy glow that had marked his youth. The five-inch scar on his cheek was flushed a deep purple against his parchment-colored skin. He wore the jet-black hair that used to be a great source of pride, in the easy way it fell into place, cropped short, chopped unevenly, like in the famous self-portrait of Van Gogh, and like Matt's, it held the first onset of gray at the temples.

Almost nothing survived intact. An hour of unabated fury had passed since he'd thrown the first chair, and his rage had grown, sucked into a vortex of loathing. He was exhausted. But at least *now* he was at peace. *Now* he could *think*.

While he felt nothing for them, the loss of two of his best men, key players in his drama, left him to confront a situation much like a director whose stars are hit by a truck on opening night. He'd entrusted them with eliminating the traitor, Jeremy, and delivering his message to Kincaid and his new partner. It was apparently more than they were up to, and he was left to wrack his brain for substitutes to carry out his final plan.

Calm down, he told himself, you have plenty of options. But those men were your best. The crème de la crème. He realized now how heavily he'd depended on them. He'd made a tactical error and wasted valuable assets. But no plan should depend on select individuals. There were plenty of others to choose from, two in particular he'd had his eye on. And the plan wasn't so much complicated as it was bold. The more he thought about it, the more certain he became that nothing would have to change except personnel. And they were expendable.

He sensed another presence in the room and turned. A lithe young woman stood framed in the entrance. She was naked, head bowed, and her body was covered with soft-edged, bluish bruises that looked as if they'd been airbrushed on. Her pert nipples were pierced and small gold rings hung from them, glinting in the light of the only lamp that had survived his wrath.

"What do you want?" he asked.

She fell to her knees, pressed her forehead to the floor, and spread her arms. "I'd like to do something for you, Master. Ease your anger . . . Please let me help."

He felt a stirring in his groin. "Come here."

The woman rose, never taking her eyes from the floor, and stopped just in front of him. She knelt again and prostrated herself at his feet.

"So, my beautiful little slut, you'd like to ease my anger?"

"Yes, Master. Anything to help you."

"Then ease it."

She rose to her knees, her face level with his crotch. Her hands joined at the clasp of his leather pants while her lips pressed against his fly, kissing the leather and the lump beneath it. A moment later, his cock was in her hands and she stroked it, kissed it, licked it, teased it until she felt his hand on the back of her head. She took the semi-swollen cock into her mouth and was gratified when she felt him begin to relax. She concentrated on pleasing him, eyes closed, plunging him deeper and deeper into her mouth. The ax handle hit the ground and startled her. He grew large quickly and she slowed her movements, knowing he liked it that way. Her tongue circled and tickled the tip between long, agonizingly slow strokes into her mouth. His hand pressing harder on the back of her head was his signal to speed up, go faster, deeper. And then his cock was plunging like a dagger into the back of her throat. He stooped over and cupped her tits, massaged her nipples. He grasped the small gold rings and pulled. She gasped, then moaned. It was time. She said the words she'd been taught a long time ago.

"Hurt my nipples, Master. Harder. Hurt me, Daddy."

He shivered, his knees buckling, and she grabbed his buttocks to steady him. The geyser of warm, salty sperm hit the back of her throat, filling her mouth quickly, and she fought the urge to gag. She believed she had done well. The change in him was already noticeable. Much of the tension had left his body. He had needed this and she was happy as she held him in her mouth awaiting his signal.

And then she became very frightened. Because . . . he laughed. And his laugh was the only thing about him that *truly* frightened her. Because he never laughed when he was happy. Because the only time she'd ever heard him laugh was when he was cold and about to be particularly cruel. And she was alone with him.

"That was nice for a start, slut. Now we're going to have some real fun. Turn around."

She whimpered, her fear tangible. But she turned on her knees like an obedient dog, faced away from him, and put her forearms on the floor, her buttocks high, accessible. He sensed her fear, heard it, smelled it, tasted it, loved it. He moved to her and the room filled with the terrifying sound of his laugh.

31

The Sentry lay sated and lethargic on the king-sized bed. In a room devoid of any real furnishings or character, the bed stood out, lush and full. The woman lay curled at his feet, her body crossed with angry red lines tinged with bluish bruises. They would soon turn a much darker shade. He would have to keep her fully clothed when they went out. But she was of no consequence. She was nothing. He felt better, almost good, and that was what was important. The woman stifled a sob, a hiccup really, much as a child did when the pain of an injury was abating. He allowed it. It's what the bitch was born for. Soon she would stop her sniveling and crawl up to him, craving his touch, his approval. And he would give it to her, as he often did when his emotional storms had blown themselves out. He knew no matter how severe he was, no matter how frightened she was, he could never satisfy her need for degradation or pain. She had no self-esteem and found her worth in his need for her; proved her value by being a whipping post, a vent for his anger and needs. It was all very symbiotic: a lid for every pot. He smiled at how everyone came away happy and satisfied.

It was time to go forward with his plans. He'd wasted two good men in order to prolong the pleasure of watching his enemy squirm. Changes would have to be made, but they would be minor. He hated dwelling on his mistakes, and a steely determination was steadily replacing his initial anger. Except now he would take care of it personally. He needed to see Kincaid's face when final justice was served, with no-fucking-mercy-at-all.

He pictured in his mind's eye the agony his enemy would know. He saw the anguish in Matt's face as the pain struck him like a hammer blow, the surprise of it all. No one could have any idea of the scope of his revenge, the carnage he had planned for them. When it was over, when all the bodies were buried, he would find his way to the stone that marked the place his enemy lay. And he would stand near the headstone, over him, alone. He would take out his cock and piss on his grave. Just as he'd promised himself many years ago when he lay in his hospital bed. Like he'd dreamed so many nights since.

He luxuriated in his soon-to-be-reality fantasy and smiled at the ceiling. Through his reverie, he heard the soft moan of the woman at his feet and felt the bed shift as she crawled up his body. He watched as she straddled him and bent to offer him her breasts. Two thin lines of blood crisscrossed one breast and he raised his head to lick a still-wet drop. She shifted and moaned again as his lips touched the tender wound, and he tasted the salt of her blood and sweat and he felt his sex revive. The woman moved down, kissing his chest, his belly, and then took him in her mouth. And soon, under her expert ministration, his cock awoke and grew hard again. He took her hair in his fist and pulled her to him. Her hand moved to put him inside her. She gasped, as she always did, when the object of her worship entered her. When he pulled her down and pressed her to him, he was, in his way, gentle and compassionate. She moved in the long, slow strokes he liked so much, and although he had spent himself only moments ago, he felt himself nearing orgasm. His mind filled with the image of his enemy, hastening the moment when he'd lose control, feel the cum shoot from him. He focused on it and his urge became stronger, unbearable, almost painful. As he spilled inside the woman, his thoughts were not on sex, not on pleasure, not even on the blackness that usually surrounds that moment, when all thoughts are blocked. No, the image he saw in vivid detail was Matt Kincaid, standing alone, arms outstretched, pleading . . . Matt's mouth open wide, frozen in a silent scream, his eyes bulging in fear. And . . . the flames.

32

Horace Fieldstone was in a dither. The mayor's aide, charged with organizing all his social functions and appearances, was having a very bad day. Nothing was going as planned. From the moment he got out of bed and stepped in the vomit his temperamental dachshund had deposited in his slippers, he knew he was in trouble. A late starter, Horace hated getting up early, anyway. Cleaning up dog puke before he'd had his morning coffee was a decidedly inauspicious way to start a day in which he knew that all of his various talents would be sorely tested. His very expensive Persian rug needed cleaning, and he now realized that the morning's events had been mere omens, and he should never have left the house.

But of course he had to. Horace was the absolute monarch of his small domain. A "benevolent despot" is the way he thought of himself, ruling the legions of people and services required to pull off one of these events. And even if he said so himself, he did it with a flair unmatched in city history.

The job required him to stay in the background, lest he upstage his boss. When everything went well, the mayor grabbed the credit and accepted the compliments, as if it was *his* organizational genius that had brought it about. But when things went badly, as they seemed to be right now, it was Horace who would find himself standing uncomfortably before "The Man."

He'd arrived forty-five minutes late at the grand ballroom of the Prince Henry Hotel and the place was in chaos. Nothing had been done and they were still cleaning up after the previous night's festivities. He'd begun by taking a huge verbal chunk out of the catering manager's ass, which went only a short way toward relieving his anger. It was a poor substitute for kicking the dog, which he knew would have made him feel *a lot* better. And if the little bastard hadn't stayed hidden under his bed, growling and snapping each time he reached for him, he'd have seen to it that the mutt was the surprise hors d'oeuvres for this evening's affair.

It had taken two hours to set things properly in motion. He surveyed the room; his trained eye picked out the yet-to-be-attended-to details that had to be done before he could even think of relaxing and catching a bite to eat. He made a mental note to find out why the florist had not yet delivered the table arrangements he'd ordered weeks ago and why the dais was set at such a poor angle. Movement near the side service entrance caught his eye. Two workmen in gray coveralls were wheeling a dolly loaded with large stainless-steel fire extinguishers into the room. He scurried over and blocked their path.

"*What* are those?" he asked, his voice near screeching, his finger pointing in appalled distaste at the shiny canisters.

The taller of the two answered, his tone nasal New York, surly as only city workers with tenure could be. He produced an invoice from his jumpsuit pocket, traced a dirty finger across the page, and pronounced each word as deliberately as if he were reading to a slow child.

"These are the ten two-and-one-half gallon pressurized water extinguishers that were ordered delivered to the grand ballroom of the Prince Henry, four of them, newly charged, to replace the ones already here, and six extra to be spread around the room."

"Well, *I* didn't order them and you are not bringing those . . ." he waved his hand imperiously toward the cart, "*grotesque* things into this room."

The workman folded the invoice and tucked it back in his pocket. "Hey, suit yourself, pal. My boss told me to deliver them by one P.M. That's all I know. He said they were ordered by the mayor's security people. You don't want 'em, that's okay with me. I get paid whether you take 'em or not." He flipped a thumb over his shoulder and spoke to his partner. "Let's get out of here, Charlie."

Horace pondered the consequences. Those fucking security people were always, and he meant *always,* fucking up his arrangements. Some last-minute *little thing* that they'd forgotten to tell him about. Some self-important detective who felt that security and *not* appearance came first. How was he supposed to work these squat, ugly little monsters into the carefully arranged and studied elegance of the goddamn *grand ballroom?* But Horace knew better than to ignore the security force's request. If something went wrong, they would need a scapegoat, and he had spent too much time in city government to become one now.

"Well, fine, then," Horace said. "But *I* will tell you where to put them."

"That's okay with me, pal. You can throw them away for all I care."

He led the men around the room, strategically placing the extinguishers where they'd be as unobtrusive as possible, clucking his tongue each time he looked back, offended by their ability to draw attention to themselves no matter where he put them. It took thirty precious minutes to move the offensive containers from one location to the next, as he constantly changed his mind and had them moved again, sometimes just inches from the previous location. He was like a bride deciding where, *exactly,* the new couch should go. Finally, when Horace Fieldstone was as satisfied as Horace Fieldstone could ever be, he signed the receipt and stiffed the workmen, deliberately withholding the tip. Fuck the disrespectful sons-a-bitches, he thought. Then, that problem behind him, he turned his considerable talents to making the evening's gala the best that it could be.

33

The entourage weaved its way through a sea of mostly black, smiling faces, the white security people sprinkled among them as obvious as grains of salt in a pepper shaker. The mayor worked the crowd, oblivious to the heightened security. He snaked left and right, grinning, taking his time, shaking hands with anyone within reach, saying a few words to those he recognized and pretending to recognize those he did not. Glad-handing was a Jeffrey Wilkins forte. He ate it up. It was at these moments that he knew, absolutely knew, that this was what he was born to do. Unfortunately for Mayor Wilkins, there were fewer and fewer of these moments.

No one was more surprised than Jeff Wilkins to receive the phone call informing him that he'd been voted Man of the Year by the National Black Urban Caucus. The city he governed was in a new fiscal crisis; the respite following the mild economic recovery in the early nineties had been brief. He had been elected on a platform of social-services expansion, but instead was presiding over the most massive downsizing the city had ever seen. Unemployment was setting record highs, twenty-five thousand homeless roamed the streets, crack addicts owned the neighborhoods, and crime of every description was running roughshod over the largest city in America. Jeff Wilkins couldn't understand why everything was turning to shit in his hands. It all seemed so *overwhelming.* He longed for the days when he was simply borough president. Now, *that* was a job. He could sit back and criticize the decisions of the mayor while taking no responsibility himself. All in all, a very pleasant existence. He cursed the bastards who'd convinced him to give it up and run for mayor. Jeff Wilkins liked being liked, and it was some time since anyone had liked him. The press was pillorying him, calling him the least effective mayor the city had ever elected. His main constituency, the black and Latino community, was withdrawing their support. As far as they were concerned, he had abandoned them just when they needed him most.

His friends—that is, those who still admitted being his friends—couldn't bring themselves to tell him that he'd been chosen to receive the award for the very reasons baffling him. He was, after all, only the second black mayor in New York City's history. The fact that he *was* so embattled was the very reason the National Black Urban Caucus Board of Trustees had felt the need to "rally round" and show support. Had he been doing merely a mediocre job instead of a terrible one, his chances of getting the award would have been nil. Jeff Wilkins was perhaps the most surprised Man of the Year the National Black Urban Caucus had ever chosen.

Matt stood with Jake Morgan and Greg Townsend near an emergency exit in the Prince Henry ballroom. They'd taken a spot with a good view of the main area and the dais. Greg was trying to locate the rest of his contingent. The crowd had risen to their feet when the mayor entered and it was difficult seeing over their heads. A few of his people were easily identified by the color of their skin; most of the others were blocked from view. The noise was very loud and Greg had trouble hearing what was said over his Handie-Talkie as various team members checked in with situation reports. So far, nothing unusual had been reported.

Five days had passed since the shootout in the building on East Twelfth Street, and both men had insisted on an immediate return to full duty. The swelling on Jake's forehead had diminished to where it was only slightly discolored and barely noticeable. Matt's wound was hidden by a small adhesive bandage at his temple. There had been no further threats or communication of any kind from the Sentry and they used the five-day lull to run down all leads that stood even a remote chance of bearing fruit.

They began with Eddie Cannell's parents, who, while cooperative, were able to shed little light on whom their son associated with or where he spent his time. They gave Matt and Jake permission to look through Eddie's room, but the search turned up nothing of value; not so much as an address book.

Ellen Levy's parents were another matter. Matt confirmed Tracy Gold's initial assessment; the Levys were, indeed, a couple of odd ducks. They seemed reluctant to cooperate, but neither Matt nor Jake were able to uncover any evidence that would indicate that they were anything but what they said they were, which was concerned parents.

Matt and Jake visited Ellen Levy on several occasions, hoping that she might turn out to be their ace in the hole. Any expectations they had envisioned for an imminent solution vanished when both Tracy Gold and the psychiatrist assigned to Ellen's case insisted that she was too fragile, emotionally and physically, to be pressed for information. Her caretakers, understandably, were reluctant to jeopardize the small gains they'd made and any questioning would have to wait until she was considerably stronger.

When they returned to the burn center to reinterview Victor Hildaldo, the receptionist referred them to the staff psychiatrist who informed them that Mr. Hildaldo was delusional and probably had been for many years. Diagnosed as a paranoid schizophrenic, he was going to be transferred to Bellevue for further evaluation as soon as he recovered from his burns.

While it was obvious that Victor had been right about the existence of the Sentry, no one was certain how he came by that knowledge. Jake theorized that perhaps he'd heard it on the street, or that Eddie Cannell may have said something to him during the attack, that he no longer remembered. Either way, the doctor refused to allow an interview, and Victor's value as a witness dropped to zero.

They tracked down the most insignificant leads, pursuing anything that could set them on a path to the Sentry. They interviewed the officers and men of the fire companies who responded to the Twenty-third Street fire and spoke to the paramedics who took Victor Hildaldo to the hospital. Nothing. Working with a dozen detectives from Greg's unit, they canvassed the neighborhood for two square blocks on the off chance that Eddie had not acted alone and someone might have seen an accomplice. They extended the search to include every fleet and independent cab company in New York City, looking for records of a pickup and drop-off at the locations Eddie specified, hoping to come up with another name or face. The bartenders at the Centurion, the leather bar Cannell mentioned, said that they could not remember anyone fitting Eddie's description and had never heard of the Sentry. Conversations with runners, dog walkers, and anybody who came near the pool building in Flushing Meadow Park drew nothing but blanks.

Interviews with bus drivers and sanitation men who worked the Twenty-third Street route were another dead end. They were grasping at straws when, one week to the day following the Hildaldo incident, Jake, Matt, and another team of detectives spent the entire night parked at either end of Twenty-third Street between Fifth and Sixth Avenues, hoping to find someone who might use that route to return from a night shift job. When Greg requested that they work the Prince Henry detail, it actually came as a welcome relief from the daily grind.

Jake and Matt had little experience with security work. They were at this function because Greg Townsend wanted them included and because they were another set of eyes and ears in case of trouble. Because of the Sentry's threat to the mayor his security detail was there in full force, all regular time off having been canceled. Greg and his people supplemented the already beefed-up security.

Matt had inspected the huge ballroom prior to anyone's arrival, checking on those items that fell within his area of expertise. He noted the location and number of fire exits, and checked the "panic bars" on the doors, ensuring that they could be opened easily from the inside, while offering full security from the outside. He was pleased to see the large number of two-and-a-half-gallon pressurized water extinguishers in the room, mentioned it to Greg, and was told that Wilkins's security people had probably ordered them. Matt concluded that whoever headed the detail was unusually far-sighted; fire safety was not usually a major concern of those charged with the mayor's personal protection. Still, he wondered why they thought they needed so many. Civil service overkill, he supposed. If five were good, then ten were twice as good. He was impressed with the apparent thoroughness of Wilkins's people. Every contingency had been anticipated, and he could suggest nothing to make the place more fire-safe.

As the mayor's contingent reached the dais and took their seats, the master of ceremonies stepped to the microphone. The room quieted as the audience settled in. Matt watched the security people peel away and drift to their posts near the doors and around the periphery of the room, relief written visibly on their faces, the tension of watching their charge move through a standing crowd temporarily over. At least now, any extraordinary movement coming from the seated group would be easily noticed.

The MC was obviously comfortable in his role, beginning his introductions by poking fun at the distinguished people assembled on the dais. He started with some inside humor that Matt didn't entirely grasp and moved on to anecdotes about the current state of race relations. After a humorous review of the history of the organization, he turned the subject to the reason for the gathering. He introduced the president of the caucus, then shook his hand and took his seat.

■   ■   ■

Construction of an effective incendiary device is exceedingly simple, requiring only two common household chemicals placed at opposite ends of a folded envelope. An arsonist need only unfold it and shake it to mix the ingredients, in order to produce an extremely violent, self-combusting flame. No metal detector would detect them, and the chemicals were far too ordinary to alert even the best-trained dog. Many envelopes could be carried unobtrusively in the pocket of a jacket or purse with no one the wiser.

Two men wearing white busboy jackets entered the large ballroom carrying empty trays, and without so much as a sideward glance at the dais, went efficiently about the business of removing empty fruit cups from the tables.

■   ■   ■

Had he cared, Horace Fieldstone might have recognized the men backing through the swinging doors of the kitchen as the ''workmen'' who delivered the fire extinguishers earlier. The men placed the trays of soiled dinnerware on a long line of stainless-steel rollers leading to the dishwasher. Thick clouds of steam rose and roiled at ceiling level, filling that section of the kitchen with an unpleasant brew of food waste, perspiration, and soap.

One man removed a small stack of sharply folded business-size envelopes from inside his jacket and the other quickly followed suit. Each man took one envelope, slid the rest up his sleeve, and covered his arm with a folded towel. They felt for the grainy powder at one end, unfolded the envelopes, and tapped them against their legs. The powder fell to the bottom and mixed with the gel-like substance there. They stepped to the linen closet and laid both envelopes side by side on top of the lowest pile of napkins. One man took a napkin and placed it tentlike over the envelopes. They closed the closet door and moved in tandem through the kitchen, into the main ballroom.

As the pair weaved unhurriedly through the main room, around the tables filled with laughing people, a violent chemical reaction was taking place inside the envelopes. While the crowd's attention was focused on the speaker at the dais, white smoke began puffing from the corners of the envelopes. Thirty-five seconds after the powder mixed with the gel, there was a distinct browning of the paper. At fifty seconds, they burst into white-hot columns of flame.

The men split up and took opposing paths to the main entrance, walking with deliberate nonchalance. The procedure was repeated as, one by one, they dropped the envelopes under drapes, on top of trays, and beneath tables. The security people never saw a thing.

Detectives were posted at every entrance, confident that anyone attempting to enter would be intercepted. Once the mayor was seated, the team's concerns naturally focused on the seated crowd. All bases were covered. But, as with Horace Fieldstone, to the security detail, the waiters and busboys quickly became as much a part of the room as the tables and chairs.

When the first whiff of smoke drifted through the kitchen, the arsonists were two-thirds of the way to the front doors. The mixture of chemicals had been carefully measured to assure them the confusion of fires at timed intervals. While attempting to deal with one fire, another would break out.

And one other little surprise had been added to the ingredients in the envelopes: powdered magnesium. Rather than suppress the flames, water reacted with the magnesium as a violent catalyst, creating an even hotter, more volatile flame.

The kitchen had been chosen as the ideal place for the first fire. There are no smoke detectors in commercial kitchens, as the ovens and stoves would constantly set them off. Instead, fire-suppression equipment is aimed at the appliances and operated manually, by pulling a pin and pressing a button. While the closet quickly filled with smoke, the fire attacked first the linen and then the beautiful old oak shelves. As the staff went efficiently about their business, the smoke seeped through the space in the upper part of the door. It was disguised for a time by the steam of the dishwasher and the heat and odors of cooking food.

(Smoke is not in the triangle of fire, which is formed by heat, fuel, and oxygen; in a fully efficient fire, there is no smoke. Hence, the smokeless nature of a natural gas stove. Smoke is simply unburned particles of fuel. Should oxygen be introduced suddenly to an enclosed space already containing the heat and fuel to support combustion, the minute particles of fuel—smoke—will spontaneously ignite, creating the condition known as a backdraft. Oxygen is sucked into the space by the starved flame and millions of particles of unburned fuel, already hot enough for combustion, ignite instantaneously. Heat expands the oxygen at an exponential rate, exploding outward toward the path of least resistance.)

A waiter about to leave the kitchen thought he smelled something burning and traced the odor to the walk-in closet. The fire, having consumed most of the contents and air in the small space, was smoldering. When he opened the door, the fire sucked in a huge breath of air, held it for a split second, then blew it out, roasting the waiter standing in its way.

Moments after the first fire was unleashed, another licked hungrily at the floor-to-ceiling drape hanging just outside the kitchen. The drapes were treated with a fire-retardant chemical, and while they would not support flame, the chemical used to arrest it gave off copious amounts of poisonous smoke. A third and fourth flare-up broke out moments later, one behind the opposite drape, the other beneath the nearest table. Fire attacked the trouser leg of a tuxedo, just as the man wearing it noticed the blaze at the base of the drapes. When he stood to shout a warning, a searing-hot pain shot from his ankle to his thigh and he beat wildly at his leg. His companions looked on in gape-mouthed silence.

Another guest recovered sufficiently enough to look frantically around for something to put the fire out. The glint of stainless steel caught his eye and he ran to the fire extinguisher, his chair crashing to the floor. Other guests jumped to their feet, picking up glasses of water, trying desperately to hit the moving target on fire. In their excitement they missed him, but sprayed the small pillar of fire emanating from the envelope beneath the table. As the water made contact, it joined in an unlikely marriage. The flakes of magnesium sucked at the hydrogen and oxygen in the water like a hungry infant gorging itself. It flared, delighted at the feast, then burst like a Roman candle beneath the table. White-hot sparks spread rapidly along the bottom, biting at the edges of the table and linen. People started yelling, "Fire!"

Hands shaking, fumbling desperately with the handle and nozzle, the guest who'd retrieved the extinguisher aimed it at the burning, screaming man, squeezing the handle over and over. It didn't budge. He looked at it for what seemed an interminable time, baffled, feeling betrayed. He squeezed harder, pumping the handle, as if by milking it, he could make it work. Another guest yelled for him to "pull-the-pin, pull-the-fucking-blocking-pin." It took a moment to compute, to realize the safety pin prevented him from depressing the handle. Fires broke out all over the room. Terrorized guests screamed and scrambled for the nearest exits. The arsonists, already near the main exit, allowed themselves to be pushed along and swept out in the first wave of the panicked crowd.

The mayor's security team moved in to surround him, fighting, pushing, punching their way to his side. Jake grabbed the nearest fire extinguisher while Matt searched his memory for where he'd seen the house hose line. Short seconds later, the exits were blocked by a mass of humanity fighting to get out. A woman fell and was crushed. Two others tripped over her and disappeared.

The guest wielding the extinguisher, by now nearly unable to function, finally found the blocking pin, pulled it, and aimed the hose at the burning man. The stream, propelled by more than one hundred pounds of pressure, barely arced as it leaped from the nozzle. His sigh of relief caught mid-throat as the liquid contacted the already-burning man, ignited in a growling *whoosh,* and engulfed him in flame. The fire raced back to the nozzle and suddenly, the once-benign fire extinguisher was a blazing flame-thrower. The guest released the handle but it flopped, limp and ineffectual. He whipped the nozzle to the side, trying desperately to point it away from the human torch, and instead sprayed three of the people nearest him. Cruel, unrelenting sheets of flame shot across the floor in front of him. A desperate confusion wrapped itself around his brain as the last man ignited, now a whirling pillar of fire, ran to him in an apocalyptic bid to get him to stop. As he reached his would-be savior, he enveloped him in the last embrace either man would ever know. The fire joined and consumed them. As the well-intentioned guest battled to disengage himself, his last confused thought on earth was that the man clutching him so desperately reeked of gasoline.

No one could have imagined that the benign-looking extinguishers, placed around the ballroom with such attention to detail that afternoon by Horace Fieldstone, had been filled with gasoline. The springs had been removed from the handles, and once the handles were squeezed, letting go had no effect. Each incident of an extinguisher producing more fire was remote enough that it was impossible to see the connection.

The center of the room became a cyclone of flame, swirling to the massive ceiling as gasoline fed its fury. Amid the roar and screams and choked pleas for help, those remaining calm enough to try to put the fire out saw their efforts punished by the horror of a still greater holocaust. Six of the ten extinguishers were eventually used, adding fifteen gallons of gasoline to the inferno.

The beast fed itself, devouring everything in its path, snapping up every tidbit offered. The temperature rose in progressive increments and the room's contents reached ignition temperature. First, the lighter, thinner items, then the heavier, solid ones. Paper, tablecloths, drapery, and clothing were followed quickly by tables and woodwork. The delicate glass bulbs and crystal of the chandeliers turned to molten liquid, raining fiery droplets on the screaming crowd.

Fire's partner in death, smoke, banked down inexorably from the high-domed ceiling, replacing what air remained with its poisonous breath, sealing the fate of the terrified crowd.

Exit doors, never meant to accommodate such masses of people, were choked with fallen bodies. The crushed, broken forms of the trampled formed a bottleneck of death.

Courage and common sense were the fire's initial victims and they fled the room with the first wave of escaping guests. Nothing in their lives had prepared the men and women in that room for the *fear*. The overwhelming, all-consuming, I-don't-want-to-die-like-this fear. The I-would-do-anything, sacrifice-anyone, kill-whoever-gets-in-my-way fear. Men beat their way past women, women scratched and clawed past smaller women, shoving, kicking, punching, gouging their way to the nearest exit, only to discover it blocked by bodies unresponsive to their violence.

Jake found an extinguisher near the front entrance. Trying to escape the onslaught of the crowd, he crouched low and pulled the extinguisher behind him. He knew it would be like pissing on a volcano, but he hoped he might find a use for it.

Wires melted and the lights went out, presaging an even more fierce and determined assault on the exits. Firelight pranced mockingly on fear-ravaged faces as hurricanelike sheets of heat drove the crowd to sanity's precipice.

Jake fought the urge to escape, to run, knowing his only hope of staying alive, of surviving, would be to keep his wits about him, stay calm. He moved further into the room to an area vacated by the fleeing crowd. Dragging the extinguisher, he probed blindly along the floor for bodies.

With everything happening at once, neither Matt nor Jake had seen the extinguishers turn into flame throwers. As firefighters, or marshals, they'd always arrived *after* the fire started, never *as* it started. The unconstrained violence, the suddenness, the quick fury of this one took them totally by surprise. They knew something was terribly wrong. Something was driving it, propelling it beyond normal limits. They knew an accelerant had been introduced to the fire—nothing else could make it behave this way. But in the absolute bedlam of the room, knowing how and where would have done them little good.

Matt remembered where he'd seen the standpipe and hose line and crawled along the wall until he came upon the glass case. The door came open easily. The cheap cotton-jacketed hoses were unreliable, and optimally, two people were needed to operate them—one to stretch the hose and aim the nozzle, and another to turn the water on. He grabbed the sleeve of a man running for his life. As he gasped instructions for help, he was punched viciously on the forearm as the guy wrenched loose and continued his headlong flight. Matt grabbed the nozzle and pulled it from the case. He'd have to stretch the hose, get back and turn the valve to start the water while the nozzle whipped wildly about, then crawl up the thrashing line and hope for the best. He had no help, and no other choices.

The hose peeled away easily and Matt was thankful. He was gasping for air, exhausting himself, praying the line would hold. Water was life, and any good it did would be welcome. A helping hand tugged at the hose, and through the dense smoke and tears, Jake Morgan, grim as the Reaper, appeared.

Matt shouted above the crowd. "I got the line, buddy! You get the valve."

Jake followed the hose. It was an old firefighter's trick: "Follow the line and find the door." Except that this time the line led to the valve. The heat was one hundred degrees higher five feet off the floor. He grabbed the wheel and a searing pain shot through his fingers and palms. The valve was hot as a coal. He grabbed the extinguisher, aimed it at the valve, and prayed the water wouldn't crack the hot brass of the wheel. He put his finger over the plastic nozzle to form a spray the way he'd done ever since he was a probationary firefighter. Surprisingly large amounts of fire could be put out by two and a half gallons of water if used properly. He pulled the pin and pressed the handle.

A cone of flame spewed from the tip of Jake's finger. Though stunned, he released the handle, but not before the fire wrapped around his hand. By the time it struck him that releasing the handle had no effect on the flow, he was holding a blowtorch. He howled and thrust his hand under his arm to smother the flames. The sensitive skin rubbed against the cloth of his jacket, and he used his good hand to point the nozzle toward the fire, watching in horror and fascination as it bellowed and grew. By the time the extinguisher spent itself, waves of heat drove him backward. He almost tossed it aside but thought better of it. There was still some fluid in the can; they never fully emptied. If they ever got out of here, they'd need evidence. Matt appeared at his side.

"What's wrong? Why haven't you turned the water on?"

Jake pointed to the flaming hose case as the last strand of it detached itself and fell to the floor. He shouted above the roar of the fire: "The extinguishers have been filled with gasoline and the springs have been removed from the handles. That's what's been making the fire take off. We've got to try to get out of here. Nothing is going to put this fire out. The building is a total."

A quick glance around served as sickening confirmation. Jake started for the main exit but Matt grabbed his arm. Years of habitually checking rooms for fire exits was about to pay dividends.

"This way, Jake. . . . The kitchen."

Jake understood immediately. There was always a service entrance through the kitchen for food deliveries and garbage removal. Matt had actually rattled the door when he checked the room earlier. It was just past the ovens. Since the first fire broke out in the kitchen, no one, except for the kitchen staff, had used that route of escape. Chances were excellent that it wasn't blocked.

Matt and Jake dropped to their bellies to escape the searing heat, with Matt leading the way as they crawled and pulled themselves along the floor, dodging burning debris, overturned tables and chairs, and fiery pieces of ceiling falling to the ground.

"Here it is."

The kitchen had almost burned itself out, but the heat reflecting off the stainless-steel and ceramic-tiled surfaces was still incredible. The two men snaked their way along the floor, which was slick from burst containers of oil, food, and overturned pots, past the stoves and then to the exit door. Matt found the release bar and pushed. Hot metal scorched his flesh. He searched for something to wrap around his hands. Finding nothing but hot slime, he knelt on one knee, rammed his shoulder into the panic bar, and bounced off of it.

"Jake, give me a hand. The metal is swollen from the heat. Don't touch it. On the count of three, push with your shoulder." He looked at his partner and saw the fire extinguisher. "What the hell are you doing with that?"

"If we ever catch this cocksucker, we'll need physical evidence. I don't think much is going to survive this fire."

"Fuck it, Jake. We can't be draggin' that can around with us."

Jake coughed. "I ain't leavin' it behind."

Matt wasn't going to argue. He shrugged and motioned for help with the door.

"One. Two. Three." They threw their weight into the bar and tumbled into a cool corridor. The lights were on but were dimmed by the smoke haze hanging at ceiling level. Compared to what they'd just left, the air was fresh as a mountain meadow. Jake slammed the door shut and collapsed beside Matt. They lay limp as seaweed against the wall, wheezing and coughing. Their faces were nearly coal-black, as if they'd been made up for a minstrel show, and the whites of their eyes, while badly bloodshot, appeared startlingly bright. Soot-filled mucus flowed freely from their noses, clinging to Matt's mustache and Jake's chin. Their hair was filthy and pasted flat to their heads. Charcoal crust caked the corners of their mouths and nostrils.

Matt tried to get his bearings. He made the assumption that the corridor led to an alley or the rear of the hotel where the garbage was put out. "I think the street is that way," he said, pointing.

"Sounds right. Let's get out of here; try to get to the front of the building, where we can do some good." Jake was thinking about the people in the ballroom, many probably dead, the rest certainly in bad shape.

Matt wondered what had happened to the mayor, Greg, and the security detail. Had anyone made it out? It was a certainty that the fire had spread to the upper floors of the hotel, and there was no way to know how many people had been trapped or killed. It was also a certainty that this fire would rank among the worst disasters in city history. And there was no doubt as to who was responsible. This was what the Sentry had been planning. The words "the fires of hell" rang in their ears and took on a new, hideous meaning. No one could have imagined he'd planned anything as horrible as this, as evil as this, as deadly. Filling the fire extinguishers with gasoline was an unthinkable abomination.

Their lungs were scorched, and unsteady legs carried them down the dimly lit corridor, the screams and chaos a dim clamor behind them. Sirens wailing in the distance served as reassurance that help was on the way and they were heading toward the street. The air was fresher and cooler with every step, and soon they drew deeper breaths, coughing spasmodically, trying to clear their lungs.

░   ░   ░

Jeff Wilkins was reduced to hysteria. He was coughing, crying, and shaking in alternating fits of fear. Even in the confusion, the security team found time to loathe the man they were trying to save. Those unable to muster enough energy to hate him were merely ashamed for him.

This was the man who had closed firehouses, reduced manning on fire trucks, and cut the number of fire marshals by one-third. The bean counters at City Hall had convinced him that only "X" number of people would die as a result of a few minutes' delay in response time. The city could easily cover the liability of a lawsuit for less money than it took to keep the firehouses open. It all came down to money. The firehouse that had originally served as the first-due company to the Prince Henry had been one of the first to go. Statistically, it shouldn't have made a difference. But it did.

Jeff Wilkins wasn't helping efforts to save him. Petrified, he fought every attempt to move him. Finally, when it became clear that he was going to get them all killed, the lieutenant in charge of the detail pulled a leather sap from his hip pocket and deftly clocked Mayor Wilkins behind the ear. Wilkins slumped to the ground unconscious, giving the detail its first moment's peace. Grim and silent, they dragged the mayor by his hands and feet to the exit.

* * *

Greg Townsend, burned and blind, crawled on his belly, inch by inch, along the wall. One of the first to react when the fire broke out, he'd run to the nearest extinguisher and tried to use it on a fire under a table. His efforts were defeated, as were those of all the others who'd tried to help, except, in his attempt to divert the stream of flame, he'd sprayed himself. Several people had rushed to smother the fire that consumed him, but left him a smoldering heap on the floor as the inferno grew and their own lives became foremost in their minds. Trampled in the midst of the stampede to the exits, he'd been unconscious for a time. He awoke to find his face burned and his eyes fused shut. Disoriented, he had no idea where the exits were. Screams and shouts came from his left, which he guessed to be the front of the ballroom. He decided to go right. The crowd would surely kill him in his condition. There were other exits along the wall; he'd checked them himself, but he had no idea if they were blocked or already engulfed in flame. Every fiber of him screamed in agony, and it struck him as peculiar to feel chilled in the rising heat of the room. He shook his head and fought the urge to succumb. Just move, he told himself. Keep moving.

The further he slid along the wall, the more distant the sounds of terror became. And the more distant the sounds, the more intense the heat. He guessed he was moving toward the middle of the long wall and remembered the exit door not far from the dais. He hoped he was close. Fatigue and pain and anger and fear battled for control. A powerful desire to stop and rest, to give in and give up, took hold. He tried to fight it, but it was strong and he was weak. A coughing spasm ripped through his seared and tender lungs, doubling him over. He used his last ounce of strength and willpower to pull himself up and lean against the wall. Tired, so very tired, he slumped, tucked his face between his knees, and wrapped his arms around his legs. And then, in his quiet way, with the soft-edged dignity he'd possessed throughout his life, Greg Townsend closed his eyes, went to sleep, and died.

■   ▓   ▓

Horace Fieldstone tried to save no one. He was on his way into the kitchen, about to warn the chef for the third time that he wanted the main course served while it was still hot, when the waiter opened the linen-closet door and was roasted. The man hadn't hit the ground before Horace reacted as Horace would. He whipped the swinging door shut and ran, past the table where a guest was on fire and another was trying to get one of those damned fire extinguishers to work; past dozens of horrified people, to the front of the room and out into the lobby. And in that time, Horace never uttered a word of warning, never yelled, "Fire," never told anyone to get out, never did a thing except save the most important person in Horace Fieldstone's life—himself.

▓   ▓   ▓

The upper floors of the forty-five-story hotel were filling rapidly with smoke. Air ducts spewed the lethal brew into every room and hallway. The multimillion-dollar computerized air-conditioning and heating system was supposed to shut down instantly at the first detection of smoke, but because it had been installed while the hotel still operated, and testing it while the building was occupied would have inconvenienced the high-paying, high-profile guests it catered to, the hotel's owners felt it easier on everyone concerned to simply falsify the test records rather than conduct a real test. They were assured by the contractors that, in any event, it was fail-safe. They were wrong.

Guests poured into the halls in every state of dress. In the early stages, many just poked their heads out, assuring one another that it was probably nothing—the hotel was, after all, fireproof. Then suddenly fire alarms were shrieking and even the bravest among them decided that discretion was the better part of valor. Forty-five stories full of people, all trying to exit the building at once, some with luggage in hand, crowded the narrow corridors. Those on the upper floors who wouldn't, or couldn't for medical reasons, conceive of attempting a walk down forty-five flights of stairs waited nervously in quickly banking smoke for elevators that would never come.

As soon as the first smoke detector sounded an alarm, the computer automatically returned all elevators to the lobby. Elevators and elevator shafts were death traps in a fire, but firefighters used them anyway.

The alternative was to walk up forty-five flights of stairs in heavy boots, carrying seventy-five pounds of gear, and exhaust yourself before you even began fighting the fire itself.

An unmoving mass of people lined the stairs trying to get to the lobby. Initially, because there were no air vents in the stairwells, they remained relatively clear of smoke. But that soon changed. The anxious crowds waiting to enter held the doors open, and smoke from the hallways began entering the stairwells. The crowds jamming them reacted with a surge of claustrophobic panic. And then things got worse.

When the first guests reached the lobby and opened the door, the beast raced out of the ballroom and blew its black-orange dragon's breath into the open stairwell door. The nearest guests were fried instantly, their bodies piled like cordwood at the foot of the stairs. Those not immediately killed tried to claw their way back up the solid wall of humanity blocking their way. A chain reaction of fear stampeded up the stairwell in a ripple effect to the highest floor. The stairs became a huge chimney for the heat and smoke. Not knowing what was going on, those waiting to enter the stairs, attempting to flee the danger of the now smoke-filled halls, faced a Hobson's choice and refused to move. Others ran back to their rooms in a futile attempt to break the Lexan windows and get some fresh air. Later, much later, the fire department would count a combined 322 dead in the ballroom and stairs, and another 247 dead in the halls and rooms. Most had been untouched by fire but had suffocated by toxic smoke.

■　　　　■　　　　■

As Jake and Matt staggered down the hall, voices from behind a recessed doorway caught their attention. Could anyone *not* know about the fire? Would they linger in the building? They exchanged confused looks. The sign on the door said, ELECTRICAL SERVICE ROOM, and below: KEEP OUT. NO UNAUTHORIZED ENTRY.

Matt pressed an ear to the door. He had difficulty focusing; horribly intrusive images of screaming men and women bursting into flame played in his mind like an old-time silent movie. An angry voice vibrated through the metal door. He forced himself to listen.

"Are you both crazy? Ten?! You filled all ten extinguishers with gasoline? I told you to fill three or four at the most."

"But, Master, we thought, what if they picked up the wrong ones?"

"That was the idea, you idiot. I expected that only one would ever get used, maybe two. But all ten? Are you both insane? It was supposed to be controllable within limits, not a fucking holocaust! This will bring every law-enforcement agency in the country down on our asses. How long do you think it'll be before they find us now? I wanted it to stay local."

Matt's mind was reeling. It took a moment for the words to register. Jake looked at him expectantly.

Matt backed up and drew his weapon, his voice an incredulous hoarse whisper. "They're in there. . . . *He's* in there."

"What? Who's in there?"

"*He is,* goddammit! The Sentry. Mickey Stone. He's in that fucking room!"

Jake set the extinguisher down and slid the PPK from its holster. Matt grasped the doorknob and slowly, carefully, turned. Nothing. The solid-wood, metal-sheathed door was locked. No way they could get in without tools. But there'd be no other exit from an electrical service room. When they came out, Matt and Jake would be waiting.

Matt listened again. The voice said, "We'll discuss this later. Right now, we have to get out of this area."

Approaching footsteps. They took positions on opposite sides of the door. Matt felt a thrill of anticipation mixed with fear when he heard the latch turn. At last, he thought, face to face with my enemy. What would he look like after all these years? What will he do? How will he react?

The knob turned and the door slid open on silent hinges. Matt and Jake drew back and pressed harder into the wall.

The low whirring and clicking of electrical meters and motors drifted out as the gap in the door widened. One of them would be sure to sneak a look before stepping into the hall, Matt thought. Sure enough, a face appeared and Matt saw the barrel of a gun come up toward him. Matt squeezed off three quick rounds; at least one of the hollow-point bullets did its job, expanding on target, driving the assailant backward with the force of a Marciano right hand.

Jake reached past Matt and stuck his gun into the doorway a blink too late. Electric pain raced up his arm as something heavy struck his hand. He snatched it back and an immediate tingling numbness set in as he bellowed loudly and cursed his own stupidity. The door began to close and Matt lunged, grabbed the dead man's leg, and pulled it into the open space. The door slammed hard; the leg jerked wildly as it was kicked and pushed from the other side. A fusillade of bullets shot through the door, splintering the wood and punching jagged holes in the sheet metal. Matt jumped to the side and stuck his gun in the opening, firing wildly and repeatedly. The door swung free. Matt didn't know if he'd hit anyone or they'd let go and retreated.

"You okay, Jake?" Matt turned and gasped.

Jake leaned heavily against the opposite wall, his shirtfront soaked in an ever-widening red stain. His eyes were wide with surprise and his hands clutched his chest. Matt rushed to his friend, helped him to the floor, and propped him up against the wall. Jake's breathing was shallow and ragged.

"You're gonna be all right, buddy. I'm gonna get help." Matt took a handkerchief from his pocket and pressed it to the wound, placing Jake's hands over it. "Just lie still. Don't move." He started to get up.

"Matt? Don't go."

"I've got to, man. You're hurt. You need help."

"It doesn't matter. They'll come out when you're gone and finish me off. You've got to go in and get them now." Jake's eyes fluttered closed and he slumped sideways to the floor.

No. Not again. Not another dead partner. Not another dead friend. You fuck. You rotten-fucking-scumbag. Fury, fed by an all-consuming hatred, swirled like a cyclone inside him. I'm gonna kill you now, Mickey. I'm gonna rip your fucking throat out and make you pay, you cocksucker. Matt Kincaid picked up his Glock, rushed the door, rammed it with his shoulder, and rolled in.

Two shots ricocheted off an overhead pipe. Matt darted behind a fifty-five-gallon drum of lubricating oil. The room was much larger than he'd imagined. Then he remembered how vast the hotel was and realized the electrical service requirements would have to be comparably large.

Row after row of panels of circuit breakers and phone connections filled the room. The soft hum of electrical motors combined with the clickety-clack of circuits opening and closing. A smoky haze hung from the ceiling, diffusing the fluorescent lighting into a cold vaporous glow.

Matt felt light-headed; a sense of certainty, rightness, filled him. One way or another, this was the end.

"Mickey?" His voice rebounded off the hard surfaces. "Mickey? Talk to me, you cocksucker."

The room noises faded into the background as he waited for a response, then: "So you finally figured it out, huh, Matt?"

"Yeah, I figured it out. And now it's over. You're meat, asshole. It's time to pay the tab."

A voice, edged with gravel and dripping sarcasm, taunted him. "Ooohhh, Matt. Please don't scare me." And then the laugh assailed him, careening like a misplaced shot off the concrete walls and metal pipes, driving Matt to an almost blind rage, a rage that swirled up inside him like a prairie storm, sudden, violent, primal. Mickey Stone would not have the last laugh.

"First, I'm gonna put your friend out of his misery, Mickey. Then I'm coming for you. Remember what I did to your balls? Did you ever get it up after that? This time, you're gonna be awake when I cut 'em off. Then I'm gonna let you die."

Matt struck a nerve. Mickey wasn't laughing anymore. He was remembering the greatest humiliation of his life.

His voice hissed from the shadows. "You're right, Matt. Only one of us will walk away from this. But it won't be you. In a very real way, you're the reason for all that's happened. Think about *that,* my friend."

A shuffling sound came from his right. Matt spun and aimed. The sound stopped. He had a vague notion where Mickey was. But where was the other guy?

There! The sound again. Matt, crouching, moved deeper into the room. His left knee throbbed and threatened to give out. He touched it. It was tender and sticky with blood. He tried to remember how he hurt it but couldn't.

The room offered at least a dozen places large enough to conceal a man. Matt got on his hands and knees and peered under the panels. He saw nothing.

He inched closer, feeling more exposed, more vulnerable with each step. Crossing through the center of the room was probably the least prudent approach. They could attack him from any direction. But he wanted this over as quickly as possible. Prudence wasn't going to make that happen. Exhausted, his body was beginning to betray him. His muscles were drained, rubbery. Twitches in his biceps and thighs were signaling a fatigue no amount of willpower could overcome. The inferno in the ballroom had drained most of his reserves and he was operating on instinct and anger alone. Years of firefighting had taught him that you could only tap the well for so long. He needed this to be over soon; caution would have to suffer.

A large metal junction box loomed before him. He hated to be near high voltage. There were dozens of blown circuits and shorts caused by the fire, and it all passed to and from this room. He shivered. Where are you, you son of a bitch?

The bullet slammed into his back, hurtling him into the panel. He fell, arched backward, and craned to reach the source of the pain, writhing on the floor like a dog with an itch. The pain radiated along his shoulder blade into his neck and arm. They'd close in now, he was sure. He heard a voice, not Mickey's, cry out triumphantly, "I got him! I got him!"

Matt's survival instincts took over. This was it. Get your wits about you. Worry about the pain later. Survive. Live. Win.

■   ■   ■

Jake Morgan stirred, then came groggily awake. He pushed himself off the floor and sat upright. He was light-headed and couldn't figure out whether the pain he felt radiated from his chest to his arm or the other way around. It came to him that he'd been shot, adding to the growing list of injuries he'd already suffered. I'd like to see what my fucking biorhythm chart has to say about today, he thought.

He reached tentatively to the wound in his chest, probing carefully with his fingers to assess the damage. Goddamn, I can feel the fucking bullet just under the skin; it hadn't pierced the sternum, for Christ's sake. He looked across the hallway to the thick metal door. The son of a bitch absorbed the impact, probably saved my ass. Jake gritted his teeth, pinched the bullet, and after several tries, managed to pry it out. Exhausted, panting from the effort, he held it up, looked at it dumbly for a time, and just as he lost consciousness, thought, Thank God for metal doors.

■   ■   ■

That scuffling sound again. This time very close. It took Matt's last ounce of reserves to rise to a sitting position and prop himself against the metal panel. His left side was useless, his arm hanging limp and lifeless at his side. He gathered his knees with his good arm, dragged them up, and using them to steady his automatic, took aim.

The sound was almost on top of him but he had trouble focusing.

He waved his gun aimlessly back and forth, straining to see through the dizziness and nausea. And then, from around the next panel, he saw a gun's malignant black eye aimed dead-center on his chest. His ass puckered and he knew that he had lost. He was dead and there was nothing he could do to stop it. He fired, but his shots ricocheted harmlessly off the walls and metal panels. The black eye never flinched. It was unafraid of him and he felt ashamed at his impotence, his inability to instill fear and some modicum of respect in this, his final moment. He was going to die with the evidence of their contempt staring at him and it pissed him off. He held his breath as he waited for death.

And then a shot nearly deafened him. His body jerked involuntarily but he felt no pain. Maybe everyone had it all wrong, you *do* hear the one that kills you, you just don't *feel it,* he thought. My God, I heard the fucking shot! It wasn't his gun *or* the one pointing at him. He'd seen no muzzle flash.

The somber black eye, so steadfast seconds ago, wavered and pulled back. Then a form lurched forward holding his throat, staggering, giving Matt a clear, beautiful silhouette in the aisle. He fired and fired again. And someone else was shooting beside him. The figure, too close to miss, jerked with the impact of each bullet entering his body, until he fell to the floor like a sack and lay still.

Jake was at his side and fell to his knees. He was breathing heavily. "I leave ya alone for a second and look what happens," he said.

Matt was still trying to adjust to the fact that it wasn't him lying dead on the floor. It took some time to respond. "I thought you were dead, for Christ's sake."

"Well, don't sound so fucking disappointed."

"Are you okay?"

Jake rubbed his chest, balled his fist several times, and wiggled his fingers, testing his hands. "Well, I'm hurting, but that door saved my life. I'll live. What about you?"

"I'm shot in the shoulder blade. I can't seem to make my arm work."

Jake swiveled around to get a better look. "It's a big fucking hole, all right, Matt. Let's get the fuck outta here."

Matt looked at the nearby body. "Which one is he?"

Jake grabbed the dead man and strained to turn the body over. "I don't know what he's supposed to look like, Matt. This one is young, though. Twenty-five or -six, I'd say. Can't be our man."

"Then he's still in the room, Jake. Don't let him get out."

"It's too late, Matt. He's already gone. I heard the door open and close after this guy went down."

"Then go after him. We can't let him get away now. We're too close. And who knows what he'll do after this. You've got to go after him."

"No way, Matt. I'm shot. Literally and figuratively. We both need to get to a hospital. We blew it this time, but there'll be other chances to get the bastard."

Matt, feeling like a knife was sticking in his back, squirmed in pain and agitation. "No, goddammit! Next time? When? After he sets fire to a fuckin' orphanage? How many people will he kill next time? If you still got something left in you, Jake, then get him now! Do it, Jake. Get him now!"

Jake was tired, hurt, and unsure of his ability to go on. But he knew Matt was right. It had to be now. "I'll be back for you."

"Don't worry about me. Go! Go!"

Jake Morgan stood, steadied himself on a column, and with a look of finality, said, "If I get killed, I'll never forgive you, you son of a bitch."

"Then don't get killed." He pushed Jake feebly toward the door. "And make sure you let him know I sent you."

"Don't worry, partner, he'll know." Then Jake was gone and Matt slumped down, his mind in a battle with his body, struggling against the urge to just give in and free-fall into the void to escape the pain.

34

Mickey Stone heard the shots, followed by his disciple's triumphant shout. Kincaid was hit. Mickey moved in for the kill, a gleaming stiletto his weapon of choice. No gun for him. Like they said on TV, "up close and personal." He had some long-overdue surgery to perform. And the razor-sharp blade would do the job very nicely, thank you. Yes, Matthew, you will taste your balls and blood before this day is out. A series of shots interrupted his thoughts and he paused mid-step, listening.

The shots registered as something not quite right, but too vague to pinpoint. Something about the shots. Wrong direction? Too many? What? He learned long ago to trust his instincts, and they were telling him that his enemy was not yet out of action. He'd seen Kincaid enter the room alone. Had his partner returned? That had to be it. Mickey had wondered where he was.

He assumed that, with two of them pitted against him, his disciple was dead or wounded. Muffled voices, coming from the other side of the room, confirmed this for him, and then it struck him with a jolt of pleasure that he was between the voices and the door. He moved silently toward it.

Reduced to being a doorstop, the first of his men to go down lay where he'd fallen, leg poking out of the room, the corridor lights glinting off his lifeless eyes. Mickey dragged the body in, dropped it, and heard the dull thunk as its skull made contact with the concrete. He started to leave again, but changed his mind. No, he thought. We end it now. Once and for all. The door closed with a satisfying clack as he retreated to a nearby panel and waited.

■　　　■　　　■

Jake moved quickly to the door, feeling certain that the danger from within was gone, unaware that he was being watched.

The Sentry held his breath as Jake passed.

Jake hesitated at the entrance before opening the door. He aimed his weapon and grasped the doorknob. Mickey thought it comical to watch him prepare for the danger on the other side when here he was, right behind him, a short leap away.

Jake jerked the door open. The corridor was clear and he stepped out. It struck him as strange that the Sentry had taken the time to move his accomplice's body from the doorway before fleeing. Why would he do that? He concluded that Stone probably didn't want anyone discovering the body until he was well away. Jake shrugged, depressed the unlock button on the face of the door, and allowed it to close behind him. The Sentry smiled and listened as Jake's footsteps faded into the distance. And then, with the stealth of a cat, his smile departing along with Jake, he turned and maneuvered toward the object of his loathing.

＊　　　＊　　　＊

When the door closed, Matt settled in for the wait. He was tired but was kept alert by sharp stabs of pain and the tumult roiling in his mind. He had no idea how Jake was going to go about finding the Sentry; the lead time was probably insurmountable, and Jake was wounded himself. If Mickey had walked directly down the corridor to the street, he'd be long gone. Their only chance was that he'd do the unlikely and linger to see his handiwork. Although it was fairly common for those who set fires to stay at the scene, fascinated by their ability to destroy, the Sentry did not appear to be a man who made many mistakes. The teenager Matt once knew did, though. *That* Mickey Stone would have stayed to watch. He hoped there was still much of the boy in the man.

Matt was alone and in no immediate danger, but his body kept reminding him how badly he was hurt. His shoulder was a throbbing kettledrum of pain, and when he tried to wiggle his fingers, they were numb and unresponsive. His arm lay like a rag in his lap. He poked at his forearm, testing it, the sudden fear of paralysis gripping him. What if I never get any feeling back? What if I lose the arm? Shut up, he told himself. You'll be okay. Nobody dies from shoulder wounds, and there's almost nothing they can't fix in that area anymore. His inner voice was unconvincing and he silenced it, deciding it was counterproductive to maintain that line of thought. He rearranged his legs, trying for a modicum of comfort, then picked up his gun and laid it reassuringly alongside the useless arm in his lap. His attention turned to the room and his surroundings, and he strained to hear sounds of people outside the door. But only silence answered his prayers for help.

Mickey Stone couldn't see all of Matt, just a bloody shoulder and legs poking out beyond a column no more than twelve feet away. But it was Kincaid, all right. A flutter of excitement stirred in his belly as he prepared for his final assault.

The hair on the back of Matt's neck stood up and he shuddered. Something was wrong. He's here! He didn't know how he knew it, but every instinct shrieked, warning him that Mickey Stone was somewhere in the room.

The sounds of the machinery faded into background noise and his hearing became acute, able to focus through it. His pain had vanished along with his sense of safety. Suddenly he was tense and wary. His good hand caressed the gun.

■   ■   ■

A narrow aisle led to Mickey's next victim and he reckoned how to best traverse it. He was certain that Kincaid was still armed, less so about his ability to defend himself. Matt hadn't moved since he'd come upon him. Maybe he was unconscious. Maybe dead. That would be a tragedy. No matter, though. They'd find the mutilated body. But he'd feel cheated if he could not deliver the coup de grâce.

A stack of four-foot-long metal reinforcing rods leaned against a nearby panel and he plucked one from the pile with the deftness of a child playing Pic-Up-Stix.

And then he swiftly closed the distance. Matt sensed the movement and tried awkwardly to bring the gun to a firing position with his left hand, but Mickey was on him, swinging hard, and the sickening sound of cracking bone mixed with the dull clang of metal as the rod smashed down on his hand and gun. Matt bellowed, the gun clattering to the ground. Mickey kicked it away and it skidded across the painted concrete, stopping at the far wall. He was quick and efficient, the razor tip of his stiletto grazing Matt's neck, drawing blood, as he towered above him.

Mickey Stone was a study in fury, rekindled hatred contorting his corpselike face. The wound that Matt had inflicted years ago had become a deep, ugly scar reaching from the corner of Mickey's ear across his cheek to the tip of his chin. It seemed to pulse. A gold eyetooth caught the dim light. It struck Matt that Mickey no more resembled the boy he once knew than a tadpole resembled a frog.

The point of the blade moved in concert with Mickey's heaving body. Matt tried to draw back but the knife bit deeper, planted under his chin.

"Did you know that I dream about you, you fuck?" Mickey asked.

Matt was weak, exhausted. He almost wished it was over. But God, how he hated this motherfucker. The death he's caused, the suffering . . . He regretted only that he would not see Mickey die. He closed his eyes and allowed a sense of resignation to set in.

"Oh, no you don't, Matt. It's not gonna be as simple as that. You don't get to die with your eyes closed or with your mind dull. Give me your belt."

Matt's chin rested heavily on his chest and his voice was barely audible. "Fuck you, Mickey."

The point of the knife traced a deep path up his cheek to his eye. Matt tried to draw back but Mickey held him by the hair. The cut felt warm, then hot, as blood oozed from the wound.

He prodded the knife into the flesh at the corner of Matt's eye. "Give me the belt or I'll cut your eye out."

With one nearly lifeless arm, the fingers of his other hand broken and useless, he tried to unbuckle his belt. The last of his strength abandoned him and he slumped back, exhausted from the effort. "Do what you want. I can't get it off."

Mickey grabbed the buckle and dug his foot into Matt's bleeding shoulder for leverage, pushing with his foot and pulling with his hand. Matt almost blacked out from the pain. The belt gave and slid from his waist. Matt groaned, and a thin smile compressed Mickey's lips.

Mickey looped the belt around Matt's neck and the narrow metal column supporting the panel. He threaded it through the buckle and pulled hard. Matt gagged as the leather cut into his throat. Then Mickey grabbed Matt's arms and twisted them back behind the pole. It felt as if a branding iron was pressed to his shoulder. He cried out and Mickey roughly shoved an oily rag into his mouth. He used electrical wire to tie Matt's hands tightly behind him, digging deep grooves into his wrists. When he was through, Mickey Stone whipped the back of his hand brutally across Matt's face and stood, just beyond Matt's legs.

If he moves just a step closer, I might be able to kick him in the knees or nuts, Matt thought. But what would that accomplish? It would only piss him off and prolong the inevitable. Listen to me—I'm worried about making him angry. Like if I *don't* piss him off, I might be able to placate him. Look at his eyes. The guy's playin' poker with a pinochle deck.

Mickey brandished the stiletto, the metal picking up the harsh fluorescent light as it twisted in his hand. He took the metal rod, tied lengths of wire to each end, and knelt at Matt's feet. "If you try to kick me," he said, "I will smash your kneecaps. Understand?"

Matt's eyes bulged as he slowly nodded his assent. Mickey attached the wire and rod to one ankle, then grabbed the other and jerked roughly. A muscle tore in Matt's groin. He could barely move, barely breathe, as his legs were splayed helplessly before him. Just another victim, he thought. As vulnerable as Ellen or Eddie must have felt. Shit, the son of a bitch was humming. Mickey finished and rose to admire his handiwork.

Matt's pain was astonishing. He flashed back to an old Dick Van Dyke episode where Rob Petrie comes back from a ski trip in a total body cast and Laura asks him if he's okay. Rob points to a single spot at the corner of his lip and says, "See that spot? See that *one* spot? *That* doesn't hurt." And, because it hurt so much, because he never cried, because he didn't know what else to do, a low chuckle started in his throat. The chuckle grew to a laugh and the laugh to hysteria. The incongruity of the situation, his helplessness, his agony, his thoughts of Dick Van Dyke at the moment before his death, struck him as so funny, he began to choke. The belt cut deeper into his neck and spasms of pain radiated to his hand, his arm, his groin. And he laughed. And Mickey, incredulous, grew angry. This was not at all what he wanted. He'd dreamed too long, fantasized this moment for too many years, and it never went anything like this. Kincaid was ruining it. The son of a bitch was ruining everything.

The Sentry lashed out, the first blow catching Matt flush on the mouth. He punched furiously, rhythmically, alternating fists, Matt's skull bouncing off the metal stanchion as his head flew from side to side with the pounding, blood pouring from his nose and mouth. But he had finally stopped laughing. He almost stopped breathing.

Mickey stood above him, winded. "Not so funny anymore, is it, Matt?" He looked around the floor, searching for something. "Let's see if you find your death as funny." He didn't find what he wanted and moved toward the entrance to the room.

He turned at the end of the row of panels, and in the millisecond before the gun barrel smashed into his forehead, he saw Jake Morgan grimace. Mickey slumped to his knees. Jake drew back and again whipped the gun down viciously behind Mickey's ear, shattering the delicate bone. Mickey Stone's face hit the floor with a sickening splat and he lay very still.

Jake tucked the automatic into his waistband, looked down, and said dispassionately, "That's for John. You haven't paid for the others yet."

Grabbing Mickey's ankles, he dragged him to Matt. Kneeling, concern etched on his face, he surveyed his partner's condition and undid the belt and freed his hands.

"Looks like you got yourself in quite a situation here, partner."

Matt's grateful eyes gazed up at him. He moaned as his wrists were freed. Jake helped him gingerly bring his wounded arm around. He removed the gag and untied his feet. The sudden turn of events left Matt speechless, weakened and faint. The room spun out of control. Jake caught him before he could collapse to the floor.

"Whoa, Matt. Not yet. You've got to stay awake a little longer. You're too fucking heavy to carry." Jake propped Matt up against the column, then turned to the Sentry. Matt wondered idly why Jake was using wire to tie Mickey's hands instead of handcuffing him. But he was still too weak to talk and too out of it to care. His face felt cold and drained. Jake dragged the Sentry to a column opposite Matt.

Matt tried to speak but words came hard through his damaged throat. He managed a raspy "What are you doing?"

Jake turned. "What?"

Matt swallowed and repeated the question.

Jake continued securing Mickey to the column. "I'm doing what should be done. I'm seeing to it that this maniac pays. That he never gets a chance to hurt anyone again."

He glanced at his hand and remembered the last time he was burned, the months of rehabilitation in the burn center, the skin grafts, the pain . . . the incredible fucking pain. He thought of the innocents in the ballroom, the dead and the dying, and the millions of nerve endings begging for the blessed relief that only death could bring. And then he thought of the cause. This animal, this subhuman piece of shit. He tied the last knot and turned to Matt. "Let's get you out of here. You think you can walk if I help you?"

Matt managed a small shrug that said he didn't know. He looked at his old friend and whispered, "Are you sure?"

"Yes, Matt. I'm sure. It's the only way I'll be able to live with myself."

"Then do it, Jake. Do it."

Jake allowed a small, grim smile. "I knew you'd be with me, partner."

He hoisted Matt up by his armpits and draped an arm over his shoulder. "Help me, Matt. I'm tired. You've got to help me. Move your legs."

Matt drew a deep breath and summoned the last of his strength. He put one foot in front of the other as Jake struggled to pull him along. They reached the door and made it to the corridor. Jake helped his friend slide to the floor and leaned him against the wall. He wanted very badly to drop down beside him, but he pushed himself to his feet, paused at the door, and leaned down to pick up the almost-empty fire extinguisher. It felt light after dragging Matt. He opened the door and walked back in to the electrical service room.

※   ※   ※

Mickey Stone awoke to the feel of cool liquid cascading over his head and down his face. For a brief moment, he was a young boy under a small waterfall in the Catskill Mountains. The sun was shining and the lovely water felt deliciously cool on his warm skin. His brother and parents stood watching on the banks of the stream and he was happy. The air was clean and fresh and a sense of unbridled innocence filled his soul.

And then his nostrils filled with the stench of gasoline and he was confused. He opened his eyelids and screamed, whipping his head violently side to side as the gasoline attacked the soft membranes of his eyes. He blinked repeatedly, but saw only the dim outline of a figure backlit by a bright light. And then it struck him. Oh, no. Oh, my God (the word hung, foreign to his thoughts). It's a bluff, he thought. They don't have the nerve. They're trying to scare me. But he was drenched in gasoline and the room was alive with high voltage. The slightest spark would blow him to hell. Mickey Stone couldn't remember ever truly being afraid, and were his circumstances not so dire, he might have enjoyed the novelty of the experience.

His words were swollen with bravado as he spit out, "You don't have the fucking balls."

He cocked his head, blinking spasmodically as the end came to him first as sound, and then as light, as the match hissed and flared to life through his filmy vision.

The voice speaking to him was cold, brittle. "I've got just four words for you, asshole: 'Payback is a motherfucker.'"

Through the hazy blur, the arc of a glowing flame rose lazily, before descending slowly toward him, seeming to float of its own accord. A throaty, whooshing sound was accompanied instantaneously by an all-encompassing pain. Fire engulfed him and his body bowed and stiffened in agony and he screamed and the flames sucked his breath away. And he wished for death but it did not come. He lived for a time past the moment when he looked dead. His mind lived on, much beyond the point when he ceased to move and his mouth froze in a grotesque, silent scream—beyond even the time when his body looked like a bizarre parody of a mannequin. He suffered, and his last conscious thought was, "So this is what it feels like."

Jake lit the match, tossed it, turned on his heel, and walked away. He knew Mickey's screams would haunt him for eternity, but they would be muted by the grateful smiles of his many victims. He could live with that. He reached the door, his hand on the knob, listened a moment, then walked resolutely out, pulling it firmly closed behind him.

Matt was as he left him, but his eyes were alert, bright. He looked expectantly at his partner. Jake shrugged. "It's over," he said.

Author's Note

There is a lot of crime in New York City. And a lot of cops to fight it. Excluding federal and state law-enforcement agencies and counting only local (NYPD, Transit, Housing Police, and various others), you begin approaching the number forty thousand. It's a gargantuan figure when one considers that only a few countries on earth have *armies* that are larger.

In stark contrast to this overwhelming number are the 226 New York City fire marshals charged with combating arson within the five boroughs. And no place on the planet has more intentionally set fires than New York City.

Arson is a cowardly crime, usually committed in the dead of night, when people are asleep and most vulnerable. It kills indiscriminately, destroying homes, buildings, jobs, and neighborhoods, eating at the very fabric of life.

It is hard to imagine a death more horrible than one by fire. Fear of it is why people jump from the twentieth floor of a burning building; why a mother flees in panic, leaving her children behind to burn and die. It is a fear as old as man, embedded deeply in the most ancient part of our collective memories, written in our genetic code. It is no accident that fire transcends cultural barriers as the almost universally accepted description of hell.

All fire marshals in NYC are experienced former firefighters who became detectives for the fire department by passing a civil service promotional exam. A difficult transition period exists for those who choose to make the move from firefighter to fire marshal. For someone who's spent years, in most cases fifteen or more, being viewed by the public as a heroic figure, it can be a formidable task to go from *saving* life to taking away people's freedom. Everyone loves firemen. Few people like cops.

Many marshals are unable to cope with the new image and responsibilities, and voluntary demotions back to firefighting and a return to the camaraderie of the firehouse are commonplace. Those who stay bring a unique perspective to police work. Unhardened by dealing with street crime as uniformed policemen, they are "do-gooders" swimming in a sea of sharks. The zeal for helping people, ingrained from their first days as firefighters, remains with them throughout their careers. Because they've been made wise by what they've seen and felt—death, destruction, mutilation, tears, and pathos—who better than they know the ravages of fire? Knowing their brothers will suffer if they fail—what better motivation could exist?

Except for their partners, there are no backups for marshals when trouble strikes. This knowledge sharpens their skills as negotiators and arbiters, making their technique routinely nonconfrontational. Entering areas and buildings regarded by regular cops as too dangerous to approach without a large force of men—Harlem, Bedford-Stuyvesant, the South Bronx, Alphabet City, Brownsville, South Jamaica, and East New York—they go where brave men fear to tread. Caution and stealth are their hallmarks. They operate in law enforcement's twilight zone. As police officers, they work under the yoke of not being part of the "brotherhood in blue." As former firefighters, they're no longer accepted as one of the "guys on the line." They live in a never-never land in which there is no set place for them. They investigate more fires in a year than most fire departments respond to in twenty. And they are absolutely the best at what they do.

Fire marshals are acknowledged by this nation's courts to be "expert witnesses" in the cause and origin of fires, which means that, unlike ordinary detectives, they are allowed to offer their *opinions* in court. The skills necessary to perform their duties require that they be part chemist, physicist, electrical engineer, building construction expert, investigator, psychologist, weapons expert, legal expert, and have a working knowledge of pathology and forensics, along with a myriad of other, no less necessary skills that enable them to do their job.

Within city government, however, there is a relentless movement to do away with fire marshals. City Hall, reeling from massive budget deficits, sees the elimination of this small force as an easy money saver. The police brass see fire marshals as a threat to their power, outside their control; the fire brass see them as a nuisance and a drain on resources. There is no one to fight for them. When those in power within the fire department are ordered to make cuts, they inevitably choose to do so from within the Bureau of Fire Investigation (BFI); few people even know it exists. Close a firehouse and face the wrath of the media and public. Do away with a hundred fire marshals and who would know?

Unlike fire departments throughout the rest of the world, which spend most of their time, money, and manpower on fire *prevention,* within the U.S., and especially within our major cities, fire departments concentrate on fire *suppression.* It is an ass-backwards approach to the problem. The chiefs—"white hats," as they are known to fire marshals—are not entirely at fault. Their background, education, and experience is in fire suppression. The accent has always been on one's ability to put *out* a fire. No one gets a medal for preventing one.

When New York City, and the Bronx in particular, was burning to the ground in the late sixties and on through the seventies, when landlords found enormous and risk-free profits in burning their buildings, there were approximately sixty fire marshals working citywide. And the scourge of fire destroyed more than just the tens of billions of dollars' worth of usable housing, in many ways it destroyed the city itself. Trace the flight to the suburbs by the middle class and you will find it coincides with this phenomenon.

Then, in 1980 Charles "Joe" Hynes was appointed Fire Commissioner. Mr. Hynes, a former prosecutor, recognized that he had within his department the means to stop the city from burning. The fire marshals, of their own accord and initiative, had begun an experimental program called "Red Cap," to reduce arson. Joe Hynes knew a good thing when he saw it. He embraced the idea and raised the number of marshals to 320. In each area they were deployed, arson plummeted, along with every *other* category of crime. The results were dramatic enough that any community board with an arson problem clamored to have a Red Cap Task Force operate within its district. In fact, there may never again be a time where 320 men, in a city of seven and a half million, are able to have such an impact. They fanned out within targeted high-arson areas and put the word out: If you start a fire, you are going to be caught, arrested, and prosecuted. It was a success story without parallel within New York, but the program died an agonizingly slow death after Mr. Hynes's departure in 1986 to become Special State Prosecutor (later he would become Brooklyn District Attorney).

The awful truth is, fire, like crime for the police department, represents job security. Success at reducing fires, particularly arson, gives the city an excuse to decimate the fire department budget. The resulting firehouse closings, reduced manpower, and widespread budgetary cuts have sent a message to those in fire suppression: Fire marshals, the first line of defense in any war on arson, are a threat, not a cure. The more successful they are, the less money comes to the department. While the number of arson-related fires was falling, crime in general was rising. Result: expanded police budget, decreased fire budget. The message was simple and clear: If you're efficient and successful, you'll face the budgetary axe.

These men (and women now) have offices in buildings otherwise condemned for use by firefighters—firehouses too old and ill-equipped to meet Occupational Safety and Health Administration standards. As of this writing, the Brooklyn fire marshals' base is above a wholesale meat market; the Bronx base is in a firehouse formerly abandoned by the FD as unfit for firefighting units; the Queens base, opened, closed, then opened again, is a former GI movie theater converted for use by the fire marshals at Fort Totten. The Manhattan base described in this book, located in a converted warehouse, was closed for two years due to lack of money, and has only just reopened. No one knows if it, or any others, will be around come the next budget crunch.

Fire marshals are refused a normal rotation of new cars and, instead, drive battered and beaten wrecks that the department no longer has any use for. Equipment considered essential to fire investigation in every other jurisdiction in the world is withheld. Cameras, film, flashlights, batteries, shovels, typewriters, tape recorders, forensic equipment—anything that would aid in their duties—is often paid for out of the fire marshals' own pockets; sometimes they pool their money to buy a high-priced item, like a camera.

Fire marshals' work hours are changed often and capriciously. It has long been recognized in the police services that steady hours promote better work, increased productivity, stable family relationships, reduced fatigue, less emotional and physical stress, and a generally more efficient force. Even the NYPD, years behind the nation's more progressive police forces, has finally adopted a policy that grants its officers steady hours and unchanged tours. A fire marshal work chart, in contrast, begins with a day tour from nine A.M. to six P.M. The next day brings the marshal in at ten P.M. and he works until eight A.M. the following morning. That same day he returns to work at six P.M. and works through the night to nine-thirty A.M. the next morning. A seventy-two-hour break follows before the cycle begins again, and it takes more than half that time simply to get the body's systems working properly again.

Though marshals are promoted through a competitive examination, the fire department refuses to recognize them as fire officers. Their supervisors and chiefs have no official standing within the normal chain of command and are denied "line officer" status.

The city's latest folly has these highly motivated and skilled *investigators* acting as security guards for social club inspections, formerly a PD function. The city forced the bureau to take on the additional responsibility in exchange for a promise of more manpower at some unnamed future date. Using experts in fire cause and origin to do this, instead of investigate, has resulted in a minimum 46 percent reduction in fire investigations. Thousands of fires are not being investigated in New York City, yet fire marshals prevail. They succeed *despite* those in charge. This story is for them.